GETTING *LUCKY*

DC BROD

TYRUS
BOOKS

a division of F+W Crime

Published by
TYRUS BOOKS
an imprint of F+W Media, Inc.
4700 East Galbraith Road
Cincinnati, Ohio 45236
www.tyrusbooks.com

ISBN 10: 1-4405-3198-6 (Hardcover)
ISBN 13: 978-1-4405-3198-9 (Hardcover)
ISBN 10: 1-4405-3195-1 (Paperback)
ISBN 13: 978-1-4405-3195-8 (Paperback)
eISBN 10: 1-4405-3196-X
eISBN 13: 978-1-4405-3196-5

Printed in the United States of America.

10 9 8 7 6 5 4 3 2 1

Library of Congress Cataloging-in-Publication Data
is available from the publisher.

This book is available at quantity discounts for bulk purchases.
For information, please call 1-800-289-0963.

Dedication

For Joan O'Leary,
friend and book lover
(and thanks for the ride)

Acknowledgments

Many thanks to writing friends and others for offering generous dollops of wisdom and support: Susan Anderson, Terra Ayres, Miriam Baily, Mary Brown, Brian Davis, Susan DeLay, Gail Eckl, Carol Haggas, Mary Lou Kelly, Joan O'Leary, Rachael Tecza, and Laura Vasilion. And, of course, Don Brod.

And to Alison Janssen, my editor, and Ben LeRoy, publisher.

Chapter 1

Weekly coffee sessions with my mother at the Twisted Lizard had become a ritual. I say "ritual" because it wasn't always pleasant—although it could be—but it was necessary. For her, it was getting out among the "normal" folk and away from the "decrepits" at Dryden Manor. For me, it was a relatively easy hour spent with my not-always-easy mother.

We both liked the Lizard. It boasted tasty coffee and an abundance of breakfast pastries to tempt us. And if our conversation lagged, there were usually fellow patrons for us to deconstruct.

We had just finished conjecturing on the profession of a pretty young woman with tattoos up one arm and down the other. I had decided she was an art student, while my mother wasn't nearly so generous. "Probably a drug addict," she opined.

Before I could come to the woman's defense, my mother said, "Robyn, I've been thinking . . ." she dabbed a tiny wedge of butter onto her croissant, "about our . . . my . . . inheritance."

It took a gulp of coffee to wash down the lump of bagel that had gone dry in my mouth. This could go in any direction, none of which were good.

Placing her knife across her plate, she peered around the small, wooden table, pushing aside the napkin holder. "Is there any of that . . . oh," she fisted her hand and rapped on the table, "that slow, golden stuff . . ." She gave me a sharp look. "You know—"

"Honey?"

1

"Yes, honey."

"One second." I went to the utensil bar and plucked a small tub from one of the bins.

"Thank you, dear," she said when I returned and presented it to her with the foil cover pulled back.

I settled into my chair and sipped my coffee while she dripped several pea-sized globs of honey onto her croissant. Outside, cars hissed by on the wet pavement of downtown Fowler, Illinois.

She licked a smear of honey off the tip of her thumb and said, "Do you know what I'd like to do with that money?"

I peered at her over the rim of the mug. "What's that, Mom?"

She cocked her chin, examining the work she'd done on the pastry, and said, "I'd like to buy a house." Biting off the corner of the croissant, she nodded to herself while chewing. "Nothing fancy, of course. Just room enough for the two of us." After a moment she added, with a small frown, "And, I suppose, that silly dog of yours."

Overlooking the insult to Bix, I said, "A house?"

"You heard me." Her pale blue eyes began to ice up as they often did when she sensed resistance.

Of course I'd heard her. I'd been expecting this. Dreading it, actually. And in the two months since that inheritance, I should have been able to come up with a better response than, "Hmm." But what with the abrupt spike in my blood pressure, it was the best I could manage.

"Is that all you can say?"

I looked around at today's group of coffee drinkers. Not one of them seemed inclined to help me out. Nor did a noteworthy hairdo or skimpy outfit provide distraction fodder. I took a deep breath and told myself this was probably a whim, a whim that would fall prey to her short-term memory loss.

Fingers crossed, I turned to my mother and said, "I thought you liked Dryden Manor." It was the nicest assisted-living facility in the area. And now that she could actually afford it, she was looking elsewhere. Were we Guthrie women ever satisfied?

"Oh, it's all right. I suppose. If you don't care about privacy or decent food."

"I thought you liked the food."

"It's fine." She twisted her mouth. "If you like institutional dreck."

"Aw, come on." I smiled. "I thought you loved institutional dreck."

She gave me a sour look. There was no stopping her now. "I think you need a house, Robyn. Somewhere to live other than that dismal apartment."

I set my mug down. "It's not so bad."

"I just don't understand why you wouldn't want to buy a house with me."

Where to begin?

She leaned toward me. "Are you and Mick getting serious?"

"No, Mom, we're not," I replied, a bit too quickly. Now was not the time to tell her we actually had talked about moving in together. Although it would have been a perfect way out of this situation, it was also the kind of thing she might bring up the next time she saw Mick. And I didn't want her nosing around in that part of my life.

Relaxing, she nodded. "Just as well. Your children would have been short."

"I'm a little old for the children thing." Truth was, I'd punched my biological snooze alarm so many times, the silly thing had broken.

"You're in your forties. Aren't you?"

I nodded. We'd been here before.

"I just saw something on that morning show." She tapped her forehead with a knuckle, and her face scrunched up. "What is it? The one with the weatherman who used to be fat."

"*Today Show?*"

"Yes, that's it. Women in their fifties are having children."

"Yeah, well, maybe I'll think about it when I'm in my fifties."

She sighed. "Oh, that's all right. I suppose I've long ago given up the dream of being a grandmother."

Wait for it, I told myself.

Settling into the chair, she said, "Can we talk about this house?"

Lizzie Guthrie had never lost her touch with timing.

"How much is the rent at Dryden?" she persisted.

"A lot."

"How much?"

I was pretty sure she remembered, just like she knew my age, so there was no point in doctoring either figure.

When I told her, her eyes widened. "My Lord. For that hellhole?"

"It's hardly a hellhole, Mother."

"Think of how much I . . . we . . . would save."

Financially speaking, there were a lot of good reasons to buy a house. Dryden was expensive. A house would be an investment. We would save money. It was a buyer's market. But for every good financial reason, there was at least one mental health reason that made it the worst idea since *Waterworld*. It would not happen.

Just then, the "Mission Impossible" theme song erupted from my handbag. My mother watched, eyebrows bunched together, as I pulled out my cell phone. She hates any handheld electronic device. Especially when it interrupts her. Me, I could have kissed it.

When I saw it was Nita Stamos, friend and editor at the *Fowler News and Record*, I thought how perfect it was that I could delay this housing conversation with an assignment.

"Hey, Nita."

"Robyn—" Nita's voice broke off.

"What's wrong?" I looked up at my mother, who was now busy scribbling something on a square paper napkin.

"You didn't hear?"

"Hear what?"

"It's Clair." She drew in a ragged breath. "She's dead."

"Clair?" As though I hadn't heard her.

"It's—" she couldn't finish.

"What happened?"

"Hit by a car. Last night. She was out walking Scoop."

Not Clair. I'd just seen her two or three days ago when we ran into each other at The Fig Tree. "Are you at the office?"

"Yeah. We're all here."

"I'm on my way." I disconnected the call and stared at the blank screen where Nita's name and number had just faded.

"What is it, Robyn?"

I looked up at my mother and was a little startled by the concern I read in her eyes.

"This young reporter at the paper is dead. Hit by a car."

She put her hand to her mouth. "Oh, that's terrible."

"I need to go there."

"Of course you do." She folded the napkin and thrust it into a pocket on the side of her purse. "We'll talk about this later."

In the car, my mother asked me about Clair.

"She's been with the paper for a couple of years," I told her. "Good reporter. Smart. Everyone loves her." I realized I was speaking in present tense, but there was no other way to talk about Clair. "She has great instincts, you know. About stories. People."

"Were you good friends?"

I considered that for a moment or two. "Not really. But we were friendly. We used to talk about our dogs—" What had happened to Scoop? In the scheme of things, Scoop's fate should have been minor. But it wasn't. Clair loved that dog—a gangly yellow mutt. If Scoop had died too, then that much more of Clair was gone.

"I'm sorry," my mother said after a time.

"Thank you."

I couldn't imagine what the office would be like. How they'd have to keep working to get the newspaper to bed tomorrow. How someone would have to cover Clair's stories.

As I stopped for a red light, I turned the wipers up a notch and squeezed my eyes shut against the rain hammering against the windshield. The rain had started last night, and the weather guy had predicted it would be with us, off and on, over the weekend.

"Robyn?"

I slowly opened my eyes again and saw my mother watching me. "What?"

"Does that newspaper have real estate listings?"

I turned on her. "Is that all you can think about?"

"Well," she looked down and began blinking. "I—I just—"

Behind me a car honked.

"Will you shut up!" Not that the woman behind me could hear. I popped the clutch and we stalled. "Shit!"

"Robyn—"

"Not. Now. Mother."

She folded her hands and tightened her mouth.

I didn't speak again until I dropped her off at Dryden. I walked around to the passenger side to give her benefit of the umbrella for the short distance from the car to the porch. The October wind had picked up and the umbrella wasn't much protection from the rain gusting at us from the side. But I managed to get both of us to the entrance mostly dry, and as I held the door open for my mother she made no move to walk past me. Finally, because there was nothing left to do, I said, "I'll call you later today."

Her smile was small and timid, as though she feared my unchecked rage. "Will you think about the house?"

I sighed. "Yes, Mom." I didn't say what I would think about it. Probably not very much.

Chapter 2

I drove straight to the newspaper, on the other end of town. The *News and Record* was a good weekly paper with a hard-working staff. I'd been stringing for them since I'd moved to Fowler a couple of years ago, which was maybe a month after they hired Clair. I make a living as a freelance writer, and my news stringing is a fairly small part of my income, but I found I liked the connection the newspaper gave me to the town. And I especially liked the people. They were a tight-knit group. Nita was the oldest member—around my age, mid forties—and considered herself a mother to them all.

Although I wasn't a member of the staff per se, they included me in most of their social events, and recently I'd begun spending some Thursday evenings with them up at Fingal's Tap.

Nita greeted me at the door with a long, powerful hug, which I'd braced for. I'm not what you'd call a hugger, but I do understand that some people are. Nita engulfed me and held on. For such a tiny woman, she had a lot of strength. Both kinds.

When she finally released me, she took a step back. Her eyes were red-rimmed and swollen. She wiped her face and pushed her hands through her short, dark hair. "God, Robyn, why? Why?"

I had no answers. So I asked, "How did it happen?"

She pulled me into her paper-cluttered office. The cream-colored sweater over a pair of snug jeans indicated she must have learned of Clair's death before she came in. Normally, she wore a suit or a dress to the office.

Instead of sitting behind her desk, she fell into one of the faux leather chairs intended for guests. I sat in the identical chair next to hers. She looked down at her folded hands and began to chip away at the red polish on her thumbnail. "She was walking Scoop by the side of the road—Keffling, near Regent."

I nodded and she glanced at me before continuing, "The police are still investigating, but from the tire tracks they think the driver swerved into her."

"They *think*? Was it hit and run?"

She looked up, as though surprised. "I didn't tell you that?"

I shook my head, slumping deeper into the chair. Getting hit and killed by a car was one thing. Being left there in the rain to die was another. She was still watching me as I asked, "Do they think it was intentional?"

"No. Probably got distracted. Either that or the driver was drunk. There's a couple of bars out that way. It was ten thirty, eleven." She swallowed. "They'll find him. Or her."

"Yeah, they will," I said, and had to ask, "Scoop? What about Scoop?"

"He's okay." She almost smiled. "Tough mutt. They found him sitting next to Clair. Some driver saw him and then saw Clair."

"Where's Scoop now?"

"Amy took him for a walk, but she can't keep him." Nita was watching me. "Do you know anyone who could take him? For a while. Clair's folks are coming up from Bloomington. Maybe they'll want to bring him home with them."

I could foster Scoop—I wanted to—but I knew that Bix couldn't handle it. A roomie would put him in the doggie bin. But I did have an idea. "Let me call Mick. He knows a lot of people. One's gotta be a soft touch." I thought of the goofy way Scoop cocked his head with one ear up and the other just hanging there. "No, on second thought, I'll just take Scoop to his office."

Responding to Nita's puzzled look, I said, "He'll melt when he sees that face. Maybe he'll adopt him on the spot."

"Hasn't he got a—what is it?"

"Ferret. Yeah," I conceded. "That probably won't work. But I'll bet he can help." I sure hoped he could. I couldn't leave this sad dog here to remind everyone of their loss.

Nodding, she glanced out the window to the inner office. "Thanks, Robyn."

"Anything else I can do?"

She raised her hand in a helpless gesture. "I don't know."

We sat in silence for a minute or two, and then Nita said, "The police were here. They wanted to know what she was working on."

"Did you tell them?"

"Sure. I mean, maybe there's something there." She sighed. "But I think they were just going through the motions."

"Did they ask for her notes?"

"Of course."

"Did you give them up?"

She glanced my way with a little smile. "Of course not." With a shrug she added, "Actually, I don't know where they are. She must have had them at her apartment."

"What else did they want?"

"They wanted to know if anyone had a problem with her."

I almost laughed. "She was a reporter. Of course people had problems with her."

I thought of the story she'd written on how an aldermen had arranged to have the road leading to a new bridge across the Crystal River take a precipitous turn so it didn't send traffic down his street. He had railed against Clair and the *Record* until he'd been voted out of office in the next election.

Beside me, Nita tilted back her head so it touched the wall behind her and pulled in a deep breath, releasing it slowly as one hand worked the remnants of a pink tissue into a misshapen ball. I didn't know what else to say, so I glanced around the room for something to focus on, finally settling on the floor. Just as my vision began to blur, a long, narrow shadow split the beige and black tiles. When I looked up, a tall man stood in the open doorway. I felt my shoulder and neck muscles contract. Later I would think how strange it was that my subconscious recognized him before I did.

He took a step into the office. Nita had opened her eyes and now she stared at him for a moment before saying, "Can I help you?"

"You're the editor?"

"I am. Who are you?"

He glanced my way, and that was when it clicked. I remembered the eyes. They were narrow and heavy-lidded and darted back and forth as though constantly evaluating his environment.

"My name is Kurt Vrana."

He was probably around forty and wore a three-quarter-length brown canvas jacket over jeans and a slate-colored shirt. Water drops beaded on the shoulders of his jacket.

"What can I do for you, Mr. Vrana?" There was an edge to Nita's question, which suggested that this man had best step carefully.

"I'm here about the reporter you lost."

"Clair?" She sat up. "Do you know something?"

Instead of answering, he asked, "What happened?"

Nita eased back in her chair. "Who are you?"

"I'm an investigator," was all he said.

"If you're an investigator, you probably know just about as much as we do."

"What was she working on?"

Instead of answering him, Nita asked, "Who are you working for?"

"Freelance."

"You knew Clair?"

His gaze shifted from Nita to me and back to Nita. I could feel the hairs on the nape of my neck start to rise.

"Yeah, I did."

"How?"

He shook his head.

"Well then, I can't tell you anything either."

Vrana lifted one corner of his mouth in an approximation of a grin. "I didn't realize her assignments were a secret."

"They're not. I just don't like not knowing who I'm giving information to." She crossed her arms over her chest. "How about you tell me what story you're interested in. Then maybe—"

We were interrupted by a soft rapping at the door. One of the reporters, Amy, stepped around Vrana and came into the office. "Sorry, Nita," she began. "I brought Scoop back from our walk, and now he's curled up under Clair's desk." The girl's eyes were red. "This is just ripping us up. I don't think he can stay here."

Nita looked to me.

I stood. "Don't worry."

"Are you sure?" Nita asked.

"No, but if Mick can't help, I'll figure something out." I'd have to. Scoop wasn't going to a shelter.

Vrana watched me as I left, but I couldn't read his expression. I wasn't at all sure about leaving Nita with this guy, but as an opinionated editorial writer, she'd gone up against worse. I was just glad to get out of there, and I was a little ashamed of myself for that. While I wanted to know what came of his request for information, I found any room that contained this guy was uncomfortable for me. We had a brief history. I promised Nita I'd call her and went to collect Scoop.

I'd seen Scoop only a couple of times before and then, as now, he reminded me of Old Yeller—a yellow mixture of several hound and terrier breeds. I reached out, and after he sniffed my hand I clipped the leash to his red collar. It took both Amy and me to coax him out from under Clair's desk.

The rain had eased up to a light drizzle, and off in the west the clouds had lightened. Scoop plodded through the puddles I sidestepped. Once I got him into the back of my Matrix, I dug one of Bix's toys out of the glove box—a sock puppet—and gave it to Scoop along with Bix's blanket. He ignored the toy, nuzzled the blanket, and curled up on the bare deck. Chin resting on his paws, he looked up at me, sighed, and closed his eyes.

My eyes streaming, I pulled out onto Main Street and headed toward Mick's office. Once Mick saw the dog, he'd think of someone. Mick knew more people than I'll meet in a lifetime. Blinking and wiping away tears so I could see well enough to drive, I tried to refocus my emotions and found I only had to look as far as Kurt Vrana. Our paths had crossed once before at a bar called Swanee's, where I'd been a few months earlier celebrating a friend's divorce.

I hadn't known Monica well. We'd met at the health club during my brief foray into the world of social fitness about six months ago. I didn't take to it, but had gotten to know Monica because we were in the same Yoga class. I'd heard all the gory details of her divorce—more than I wanted to know, actually—and so when it became final I'd offered to take her out for dinner and a few drinks, figuring I'd assume the role of designated driver. If nothing else, it was a good excuse to get out of my apartment. And I was happy to provide the wheels. Not that I don't drink—I do—but I'm more inclined to drink too much when I'm home alone. Sad, I know.

That night I had my usual one Scotch on the rocks and then switched to Club Soda with lime. Monica was drinking fluffy martinis. Then she started chasing the martinis with shots of something pink. Before long, she excused herself and teetered off to the women's room. I drained my glass and got another free refill. When almost ten minutes passed and Monica hadn't returned, I decided I'd better make sure the recently liberated one hadn't fallen into the toilet.

When I rounded the corner to the restrooms, I saw Monica flattened against the wall by a tall, broad-shouldered man, the slice of his nose inches from her. He had a hand braced against the wall on either side, creating an effective cage. Although he wasn't touching her, his proximity threatened, and Monica was looking at him, eyes wide and mouth agape, as though she wanted to bolt, but was afraid he'd squash her against the wall if she tried.

Then she saw me. "Robyn." It was a plea.

I hate bullies and this guy seemed to be enjoying the squirming woman he had up against the wall. So, without thinking, I lunged, grabbed her arm and yanked her out from under the man's shadow. The man retreated, hands raised—the universal sign for "I'm not armed." His glare settled on me, and I got my first look at those creepy eyes as he watched me, his jaw set. He looked like he was about to detonate.

As I hustled Monica down the narrow hall, he called after her, "You think about it."

I shoved her ahead of me, into the bar. Once we merged with the crowd, I thought I could feel his eyes boring into my back, but I didn't look so that might have been my imagination. As I steered Monica past our table, she grabbed her drink, which I snatched from her, leaving it on the bar as we walked out the door.

"Who was that guy?" I'd asked, figuring it was her ex husband. But she mumbled something about him being a friend of her ex's, and from there she became less coherent.

We made it home without further incident, and the next afternoon when I talked to Monica—who'd spent most of the day waiting for her bedroom to stop spinning—I didn't learn much more about the guy, except that his name was Kurt Vrana and, for unspecified reasons, he was a jerk. That much I had already figured. Monica left Fowler a week later. It seemed sudden, but she claimed the divorce had made her crave a new setting, and she had always wanted to live in Virginia. I understood the desire to start over. We'd e-mailed for a while, but eventually that petered out. I hoped she'd found whatever it was she was looking for out east.

Now I knew a little bit more about Vrana. I still believed he was a creepy bastard, but he was also an investigator—if he was telling the truth. For who or what I did not know.

As I pulled into the parking lot of the Arthur Floyd Tart building where Mick worked, it occurred to me that Vrana might not have recognized me in Nita's office. He'd made such an impression on me that I figured I must have done the same to him. But maybe Monica wasn't the only one drunk that night. Or, maybe Vrana intimidated women all the time, so the faces kind of blurred together for him.

It was also possible that I'm just not that memorable.

Chapter 3

Mick had a new receptionist—not at all unusual. He went through them faster than I went through lip balm. Once I'd asked what he did to make them move on so fast, and he just told me they got better offers. They were all young and attractive. Frequently blond, always curvaceous, which made me wonder what he saw in me. I hadn't met this new one; she'd started only a week ago. According to the nameplate on her desk (no matter how short their tenure, these women always had nameplates) she was Gretchen Peterson, and she looked up as Scoop and I walked into the office. On the desk in front of her was a newspaper folded to a half-finished crossword puzzle.

I smiled. These women were not known for their warmth, but it never hurt to try. "Hi, Gretchen. Would you let Mick know that Robyn is here."

She had shoulder-length mussed blond hair and flawless skin. Expressionless, she looked from me to Scoop and, as she picked up the phone, said, "Which one of you is Robyn?"

I felt the color rising from my chest. "The tall one."

I thought I saw a trace of a smile, but it may have been a smirk.

"Robyn's here." . . . "Sure." A little giggle. When she hung up, she said, "Can you wait a minute?"

"Sure." Beggars couldn't afford to get huffy. I settled into one of the nubby beige chairs and pulled Scoop next to me.

"What's your dog's name?" Gretchen asked.

"Scoop." I decided not to explain that Scoop wasn't actually my dog and how I hoped to find a home for him before I left Mick's office.

"Does it need some water?"

"No. Thanks. I think he's okay." I couldn't help but soften a bit. Nonplused, Gretchen returned to her crossword.

I leaned over to pet Scoop who had seated himself, legs splayed, beside my chair. After about four minutes, Gretchen got a call from Mick letting her know I could enter his domain. This was my first clue that I'd be navigating choppy waters today. Normally, Mick would either step out of the office to greet me or at least open the door. I wondered if he might be having a bad leg day. Mick had been a fairly successful jockey until a horse fell on his leg, crushing it. After numerous surgeries, he still walked with a slight limp. Some days were worse than others.

Although he smiled when I walked in, the lines spraying out from his eyes deepened and he had that tight look as though he were fighting some pain. I glanced around, sensing that something was out of place, but seeing nothing unusual. Mick's memorabilia lined the walls. In addition to degrees and certificates, he had photos from his racing years, beer coasters, and there was a cluster of photos featuring his newest acquisition, a high-strung thoroughbred Mick called Loco and his companion goat, Sassy. But all the paraphernalia was pretty superficial, because, like an iceberg, most of who Mick Hughes was went way below the surface.

"Hey." He tapped his keyboard and pushed it away.

He wore his hair on the long side and today it looked like he'd been running his hand through it—a habit that surfaced when he was tense. The color was what lots of women would pay lots of money for in a salon—a warm, toasty brown shot with streaks of gold.

I'd seen him last just a few days ago, and we'd done a lot of talking. We'd been dating (or whatever it's called at this stage in life) for a couple of months and our relationship was at a point where we needed to either agree that it was serious or agree to step back. I was never quite sure where Mick stood, and I'd come to see our relationship as a sort of dance with neither of us sure who was leading. But when we had that talk, we both seemed to be heading in the same direction. And then there was the possibility of my moving in with him. I'd left his house the next morning with a good feeling about us.

"Who's the dog?"

"This is Scoop."

I expected him to continue. He's good at keeping the conversation going. Then it occurred to me that he wasn't the one who had arrived unexpected with a strange animal. Problem was, I hadn't rehearsed where I was going with this.

I plunged in. "Do you remember Clair Powell? From the *News and Record.*"

His brow puckered and he shook his head. "Should I?"

"I'm not sure you ever met her."

Beside me, Scoop had begun to pant and kept bumping up against my leg, almost as though he sensed the way this was going.

"I thought you had."

He shrugged.

"Are you okay?" I asked.

That half smile. "Just busy."

I wasn't sure I believed him.

"Okay, well I'd better get to the point."

He started to lean forward, dipping his head, but I plunged onward. "Clair died in a hit and run accident last night."

Mick's eyes narrowed as he looked into mine, as though trying to read me. As if I'd be joking about this.

"She was a nice kid," I said. "A good reporter. They're devastated at the paper."

"I'm sorry to hear that."

I had his interest now, but it was clear he had no idea where I was heading.

"Scoop," I bent slightly and gave his smooth head a pat, "was her dog." I swallowed. "He was with her when she died."

"So, there's a witness."

It was flip, but I knew it was also Mick's way of telling me to get to the point.

"He's got nowhere to go right now. Clair's parents are coming up from Bloomington, so they may take him, but in the meantime, Scoop really needs a place to stay. Where he can feel safe."

Mick sighed and bowed his head. After a moment, he began shaking it.

"Not you," I said, and added, "unless you want to . . ." I hurried on. "But you know a lot of people, and I thought one of those people might be looking for a little four-legged companionship."

He swiped his hand across his mouth and rested his chin on his fist. "Who did you have in mind?"

"I don't know. They're your friends." I threw out a name. "How about Rudy?"

"Rudy has four cats."

For some reason that didn't surprise me. I pressed, "Isn't there anyone?"

After a moment he shook his head. "I'd have to give it some thought."

"Would you do that?" I looked down at Scoop. "He's such a nice dog, but I don't think Bix could handle the competition."

And then, feeling reckless, I guess, I went where I hadn't planned to go. "Have you ever thought about a dog?"

"Fredo—" he began, invoking the name of his ferret.

"Fredo lives in a cage."

"Not all the time. If he were in a cage all the time, he'd go nuts. Why do you think I've got screens over all the vents and any other hole he can fit in?"

"I thought you were filtering the air." I hurried on, knowing that was lame. "You're okay with Bix."

"Bix is *your* dog."

Before I had a chance to appreciate the sacrifice this implied, he went on. "Besides, Bix is kind of an odd dog."

This was true. Despite the fact that Bix was mostly a rat terrier, I was pretty sure that a writhing rodent would probably terrify the poor beast.

He nodded toward Scoop. "Most dogs—that one included— would probably go after Fredo."

I looked down at Scoop, who was watching Mick. "You wouldn't do that." His tail began to wag.

"Robyn . . ."

Of course he was right. I should have known better.

"Okay," I conceded. "Bad idea. Just let me know if you think of anyone." I turned to leave, hoping he'd stop me before I twisted the doorknob. But I was halfway out the room before he said, "I'm sorry, Robyn."

At that point it was too late for me to do anything but nod and close the door behind me.

"He's in a bad mood today," Gretchen said as I led Scoop toward the door. I turned. "But you probably noticed that."

I almost laughed. "Yeah, well, I tried to foist a dog off on him, so I guess I can't blame him."

With her pen, she pointed toward Scoop. "That little sweetie?"

"Well, he has a point. Scoop would probably go after his ferret."

Gretchen looked at Mick's door as though this factoid edged him toward the "bosses to be wary of" category. "He's got a ferret?"

Pleased that she didn't know Mick well enough to be privy to Fredo, I began to warm up to her. "Yeah, Fredo's a cute little guy. If you like squirmy."

She set down her pen. "So, what's the dog's story?"

"Last night his owner was hit by a car. She died—"

Her eyes widened. "You mean that hit and run?"

"That's right."

Pushing her chair away from the desk, she rose to her full height, which must have been close to six feet. The short skirt and striped leggings she wore accentuated her long legs. Made her look coltish.

Crouching in front of Scoop, she reached out to him, running her hand across the dog's back. Scoop sniffed, seemed to find her all right, and began to enjoy the attention.

"He's a nice dog," I said, though Scoop had already made the point.

Gretchen looked up at me. "Why can't you take him?"

"I guess I'll have to, but it can't be permanent. I've got a neurotic dog."

She nodded as though no further explanation were required. "Is it just for a while?"

"I'm not sure." I sighed. "Clair's folks are coming into town from downstate, but to be honest, I don't know whether they'll want him."

She nodded again as she stood. "I'll take him."

I didn't say anything. It was really too much to ask. I wanted this woman to be Scoop's—and my—savior, but . . .

"I live with my sister," Gretchen said. "She's a nurse. She's got a yard."

"Won't she mind?"

"Nah. I know her."

The problem was, I didn't know Gretchen at all. How could I hand Scoop over to a stranger?

She must have sensed my inner jousting, because she smiled a little and said, "Ask Mick. He'll vouch for me."

I knew that was true. Whatever this young woman was, she was not an animal abuser.

"That won't be necessary." I hesitated. "I don't know how long this will be. It might—"

"That's okay. Really. I'm thinking about getting a dog. Scoop will be a good practice pup. And maybe," she slipped her hand under his collar and rubbed his neck, "maybe this is the dog."

Chapter 4

The morning of Clair's memorial I stopped by Dryden to bring my mother clean laundry and a couple of magazines that I tucked into a shelf on her oak veneer nightstand.

Five days had passed since Clair's death. Her parents had taken their daughter home, and the funeral had been on Friday. Now it was Sunday, and they were back in Fowler to move things out of her apartment. They seemed to appreciate the fact that the paper had delayed Clair's memorial until they could be there. Nita and one of the reporters who'd been close to Clair had attended the funeral, while the other five staff members and a couple of stringers, including me, were getting the paper out. Now her parents wanted to meet all these people who had been such a large part of their daughter's life.

When I walked into my mother's room, the TV was tuned to some western starring Glenn Ford. He was one of her favorites, so I figured she'd be caught up in the trail dust, and I'd be able to make my exit before we had a chance to talk about homes. I'd had a busy week, and so I'd seen her only once, a quick lunch in the Dryden dining room. She'd mentioned her house-buying then, but I'd managed to distract her with the chocolate éclair I'd smuggled in. After that, in our phone conversations, she hadn't brought it up, and I'd begun to hope that it had fallen prey to the beast devouring her memory. I wasn't proud of this wishful thinking, but there it was. I'd have been wise to remind myself that her best defense against memory loss was sheer stubbornness. And her mule-headed attitude was just fine, thank you.

As I culled a few older magazines out of her pile, the TV cut to a commercial.

"Did you remember my Chablis?"

I sagged. *Damn.* "No. Sorry. I'll bring some by this afternoon."

"I'm out."

"You'll last until tonight."

"Easy for you to say," she muttered, and with her next breath, she said, "Have you given any more thought to that house we should buy?"

Damn.

You'd have to know my mother to appreciate that transition.

Of course I'd given it some thought. I'd thought how this would doom any chance I had with Mick. What better way to show a guy that you were interested in a future with him than moving in with your mother?

"I have." I picked up the basket of clean clothes and walked across the room to her dresser.

"What kind of house would you like?"

Part of me—a large part—wanted to end it right here and now. This wouldn't happen and it was best to dash her hopes before she started choosing color schemes. But I'd need a script to follow. I didn't want to hurt her. So for the time being, I'd play along.

"I've always liked prairie style."

From the way she nodded—with no enthusiasm—I could tell she didn't see us ending up in anything Frank Lloyd Wright had inspired.

"You don't?" I prompted.

"Well," she picked a piece of lint from the arm of her chair. "I just don't know if I'll be able to manage the stairs."

"Good point." I should have thought of that.

"A ranch house. Yes, that would be nice." Like she hadn't been leading me there all along. "You'll be glad for a ranch house when you develop arthritis."

I had my back to her as I placed a pile of knit tops in her dresser drawer, so she didn't see my grimace, which was as involuntary as a knee jerk.

When I didn't respond, she said, "You don't think this is a good idea, do you?"

I drew in a deep breath and released it, which allowed me to suppress my gut response, which was *God, no.* Instead, I turned toward her and said, "I don't know, Mom."

The TV was blasting a commercial for insurance for the uninsurable. Before I could return to the dresser, my mother said, "I'd like to ask Robbie."

I stared at her. Again, I was trying to think of something to say other than *He's dead, Mom.* Of course, I knew that didn't matter to her. For the past two months my mother had a standing appointment every other week with Erika Starwise, psychic extraordinaire, who, my mother believed, could communicate with my late father.

"I don't know, Mom," I repeated. It was all I could come up with on short notice. I honestly didn't mind her thinking she could connect with him, talk with him. Whether it actually happened or Erika was simply inventing this dialogue didn't matter so much because it made my mother happy. But if she was going to start asking this ghost—I didn't care if he was my father—for advice, well, I'd have to have a word with him on my own. And I didn't relish the idea of telling a ghost to butt out.

My thoughts were reeling, and so it was a moment before I realized that my mother had spoken again, asking me something.

"What?"

"What is today?" she said, pronouncing each word slowly, as though English were my second language.

"Sunday."

"Don't I have my next appointment with Erika on Wednesday?" She began digging through papers on the little walnut veneer end table, looking for the scrap of paper she'd written it on.

"Yes, Wednesday."

She stopped rummaging. "Will you come with me?"

"Last time I came with you he didn't show up."

"Yes, I know." She gave me a sharp look. "Can you blame him? Your cynical nature is not very welcoming."

"Erika told you that, didn't she?"

"She didn't have to."

I shook my head. "I'm sorry, Mom. I can't fake it." Actually, I'm pretty good at faking it. And getting better every day.

As she sighed, her shoulders slumped. "All right. I suppose I'll have to ask him myself. Through Erika."

When she leaned over, pulled the knob on the end table drawer, and dug out a pack of Juicy Fruit gum, appearing to have given up the fight, I knew I'd lost. There was no way I could let that conversation occur without being present, and my mother knew it.

I did not like the idea of her consulting Robbie on our living arrangements. Not that I had anything against him, but we'd never known each other, and so how did the mere fact of his being dead suddenly make him an expert on who I should live with? But I couldn't stop my mother. "I'll be there," I said.

By now she was focused on peeling the silver foil off of a stick of gum. I began to wonder if she'd heard me. But then, after folding the gum over twice, popping it into her mouth and giving it a few good chews, she said, "That's good, Robyn. He's been asking about you."

I closed my eyes so they could roll in private.

Chapter 5

Clair's memorial was held at Fingal's Tap. I got there almost twenty minutes late—not that anyone would be keeping track, but it mattered to me. I tend to be lax in many areas, but punctuality isn't one of them.

I'd picked up that liter of Chablis and dropped it off at Dryden Manor. While I was there, my mother made a point of introducing me to Azalea, whom I had met on numerous occasions, but who didn't seem to remember any of them.

Fingal's Tap was only about a block and a half from my apartment. Yet another in the long, long list of reasons not to get a home with my mother. I would miss being able to walk to coffee shops and bars. Not necessarily in that order. Of course, I'd also miss that if I were to move in with Mick, but if I were living with Mick I probably wouldn't need as many distractions.

The pub hadn't been reserved for the newspaper crew and Clair's friends, but they'd taken over a good two-thirds of the place—three large tables and a couple of smaller ones in the northwest corner, under the Pabst Blue Ribbon sign.

As soon as Nita saw me, she pulled me aside. "Two things," she said.

"As long as one of them is what happened last week with Vrana." With things being as crazy as they were, I hadn't had the chance to ask her.

She made a face. "Not much to tell. He wouldn't say what story he was interested in, and so I wouldn't say what she was working on. Guess you'd call that a stalemate." After a pause, she added, "It is curious though."

"What do you mean?"

"Just that I really wanted to know why he wanted to know."

"Yeah. Well, he's a creepy guy. I don't like him."

She shrugged. "He's not the warm cuddly type, I'll give you that." But then she smiled a little, and before I could ask what that was about, she changed the subject. "Speaking of Clair's stories, there's a feature she was working on that I'd like you to handle. We can talk about it tomorrow."

"What story?"

"Cedar Ridge."

"Oh."

"You sound disappointed."

I was. What I was hoping for was the brothel-in-the-midst-of-Fowler story. "Later," I said. "What else?"

"That's it for now. Amy and Scott are covering the city council and schools. I need you for this feature."

There was more. I waited.

"Okay." She steered me toward the rear of the room. "I need your help." I could hear the click of a fussball machine in the small, adjoining game room. "You see that woman sitting by herself at the end of the bar near the kitchen?"

I looked and saw an attractive, middle-aged woman with chin-length blond hair and a patrician profile. Her hand covered the base of the wine glass sitting in front of her as she stared toward the mirrored wall behind the bar.

"I see her."

"That's Clair's mother," Nita said.

"Yeah, Clair looks like her, doesn't she?"

"Please go talk to her."

"Well, sure, I was going to tell her how sorry I am." It occurred to me that Nita was asking for more than this. I looked down at her.

"But what am I supposed to say after that?" My plan had been to express my condolences to her parents, have a drink and be home before the nine o'clock news.

Instead of answering, Nita said, "You're more empathetic than I am."

"No, I'm not." I looked around. "Why is she alone? Where's Clair's father?"

Nita gestured toward the large round table in the corner. Sitting with four newspaper employees and talking to Ike, the *Record's* photographer, was a pleasant looking, middle-aged man with thinning hair and an animated way about him. Since he was the only one at the table I didn't recognize, I figured he was Clair's father.

"Maybe she wants to be alone," I said to Nita, who gave me a sour look.

"Well, her daughter just died. Everyone is drinking. Maybe she's doing all she can to hold it together."

"Just try," Nita urged.

I sighed. Further discussion was pointless.

Nita patted my shoulder as I headed toward the end of the bar.

"Mind if I sit here?" I asked the woman, whose name I just realized I didn't know.

She turned to me with sad, tired eyes and a look that implied she knew who sent me here.

I tried again. "Nita can't stand to see anyone on the outside. Even if they choose to be there." I slid onto the barstool. "I'm Robyn Guthrie. I'm a stringer for the *Record*."

She studied me for a moment. Close up, her features weren't quite as severe. Mainly, I think it was her eyes that softened her.

Finally, she said, "I'm Mara."

"Nice to meet you." I hastened to add, "Although I wish the circumstances had been different."

She just nodded.

I glanced over toward the table where her husband was still chatting with Ike. "Is that Clair's father?"

She followed my gaze. "Yes, that's Jack." A tight smile. "He has the gift of gab. And he's not even Irish." She blinked a couple of times. "He loves people, feels comfortable around them. That's where he needs to be right now."

Tommy, the bartender, came over. "Hey, Robyn, the usual?"

"Sure," I said and Mara raised her eyebrows. I smiled. "It's good to be consistent." I nodded at her almost-empty glass. "Can I get you another?"

When she hesitated, I said to Tommy. "Both of us."

After he left neither of us spoke.

I was thinking I'd get my drink and leave her to her thoughts, seeing as that seemed to be what she wanted, when she drained her glass, set it down and said, "I really don't need any more of these."

"I know. Their wine isn't the best."

She smiled. "No, I mean this is my second glass. I don't usually imbibe."

"Sometimes it's nice to imbibe." That sounded lame, and I gave myself a mental thunking for uttering it.

"There's a real temptation to drink and forget, but I'll know I'll wake up tomorrow and it'll be the same."

"Only you'll also have a hangover."

Artless of me but, to my relief, she chuckled, then glanced over her shoulder at her husband who was gesturing with his hands, like he was estimating the size of a fish.

"They're probably comparing their lens lengths," I said.

At first she didn't seem to hear me, but she smiled a little, watching her husband as though collecting a memory. "We argued over the 'e.'"

"The 'e'?"

"We both liked the name Clair, but he thought there ought to be an 'e' at the end. He said that was the way to spell a girl's name. It was prettier."

I waited.

Her voice tightened. "But I wanted her name to be like the song—'Clair de Lune.' That means twilight." She turned toward me. "My favorite time of day."

"Mine too," I said, before I could stop myself.

She gave me a dubious look, which I deserved.

"No, it is. It's the purple time of day. My favorite color."

Tommy delivered our drinks. I took a sip off the top of my Scotch and realized I hadn't said what I'd come here to say. "I'm so sorry about Clair."

"Thank you."

"I can't begin to know what it's like. I don't have children."

She looked at me, canting her chin. "By choice?"

I gave it a minute. "And circumstance."

She drank and licked the moisture from her upper lip. "Clair was our only child. I think I realized that if I had another, he or she would not be as easy as Clair was." She shook her head. "No child is perfect, but Clair . . . she was sweet, thoughtful . . . and I don't know why." She laughed. "I'm none of those things."

I laughed too, figuring she was being hard on herself.

"No," she added, "really. Another child might have been . . . normal. What would I have done then?"

"Clair was an amazing young woman," I said. "I didn't know her all that well, but she seemed very self-assured. And not in a pushy way. She knew who she was." Then I added, "Some people spend their whole lives trying to figure that out."

"You're right. She was."

With her thumb, she wiped some moisture from under her right eye. "I just can't believe . . ."

I waited.

She struggled with the words. "That someone would . . . do that and . . . just leave her."

"I can't either," I said. "But the police are working on it, Mara."

"Forgive me if I'm not optimistic." She dug into her purse and produced a tissue. "I wasn't terribly impressed with Fowler's police department."

"Who did you talk to?"

She wiped her nose. "We talked to the officer who took the call. Her name was Danvers." She swallowed. "She said they didn't have anything yet, but they are interviewing people." She looked at me. "Who is there to interview?" She asked as though she expected an answer.

"I don't know."

"We're thinking of offering a reward."

I nodded, and Mara continued, "We have money we were going to give to Clair." She lifted one hand in a little wave. "For whatever. A wedding. Travel. A house. And now . . ." She looked over at me, "Do you think they do any good? Rewards?"

"I think sometimes they can. Everyone has a price. If there's a reluctant witness . . . money can be very convincing."

"I don't know how much. What do you think?"

How could I put a price on a mother's peace of mind? "Talk to the police. They can give you an idea."

She nodded as though that made sense.

That was when I felt someone coming up behind us, and I was a little ashamed by my relief.

"Mara, hon."

It was Mara's husband, Jack. He put his arm around his wife and gave her a peck on her cheek. "Someone you need to meet."

We both turned and there was Gretchen, Mick's secretary, with Scoop at the end of a new red leash. I wondered how she'd learned of the memorial, not that it was a secret or anything, then figured it must have been Mick who told her.

I left them to get acquainted with their daughter's dog, murmuring a thanks to Gretchen as I passed her. I had the feeling that Scoop would be in good hands.

For the next half hour, I kept an eye on Mara. Jack had joined her at the bar and people were drifting over there in groups of two or three, so they weren't alone. Thinking it was time for me to make an exit, I was working my way out of the room when, once again, Nita intervened, waving me over to one of the small, round tables adjacent to a row of mullioned windows facing the street. She was sitting with a dark-haired man wearing jeans and a forest green sweater. When I headed their way, Nita leaned over and grabbed an empty chair from the next table and dragged it into the space between them, patting the seat, swaying a little as she braced with her hand. When I sat, she leaned across me to touch the man's forearm. "I want you to meet Mr. Patchen. Glenn Patchen. Glenn, this is Robyn Guthrie."

We shook hands and I settled into the chair. She moved her hand to my arm. "Robyn, what are you drinking? Scotch? Beer?" Before I could answer, she was flagging down the waitress. Glenn and I exchanged looks. He was pleasant looking with intelligent eyes behind a pair of rimless glasses and a wide mouth that turned into a nice smile. I guessed he was in mid- to late thirties. Like a lot of people at Fingal's that evening, he was a little sad around the edges.

Nita ordered me a beer and herself another glass of merlot. Glenn shook his head when she instructed him to give the waitress his order and indicated the half full glass of beer in front of him.

"I wanted you two to meet," Nita said, crossing her arms and leaning on the table. Then she picked up a discarded plastic straw and began twisting it. I figured what she really wanted was a cigarette—a craving that tended to elevate along with her alcohol consumption.

Glenn and I exchanged another look. His smile was waning a bit.

Nita finally continued, "Glenn is the architect for the Cedar Ridge development."

Cedar Ridge was Fowler's foray into green technology. The fight for zoning approval for the project had been hard-won. David de Coriolis, our district's congressman, had had his eye on the area as a prime location for an outlet mall. Despite his best efforts and his clout, the environmentalists had won. The fact that sales at Cedar Ridge were unimpressive, to say the least, may have proven his instincts correct, but no one—especially our district's representative—was doing any gloating. Fowler needed every break it could get. "Clair had been working closely with him on the story."

I looked at him again. He was watching Nita as he sipped the beer and settled it onto the coaster. He had large hands and long, slender fingers. A gold band embraced the ring finger of his left hand.

"He planned the whole thing."

"Well—" Glenn spoke for the first time, "—it wasn't entirely my—"

"Oh, stop," Nita raised a hand, "do not be modest, young man, I—"

Just then our drinks arrived, diverting Nita's attention as she made sure that we each got what we'd ordered.

I took advantage of Nita's distraction and turned to Glenn. "I'm a stringer for the paper."

"She's a great stringer, and the only reporter I trust with this story." Nita could refocus faster than anyone I knew. She poured the remaining quarter inch of wine from her old glass into the new one and swallowed it off the top.

Again, I wasn't thrilled about the Cedar Ridge story. Nita always asked before assigning, and I liked that she appreciated the fact that I was freelance and didn't work for her. But Clair's death had everyone acting a little weird. No matter, it was work and I needed it. Still, I made a mental note for a request in return.

"Clair had interviewed you?" I asked him.

"Yeah. And I guess you could call me one of her sources. She was real interested in the whole environmental housing movement. And seeing as how sales haven't been what we'd hoped, she thought this story might generate some interest in the unsold lots." He nodded, as if to himself. "She cared."

"That's right," Nita said.

"How much of the development is completed?"

"We've got two duplexes ready for occupancy and a third under construction."

"Are there other places you've designed like Cedar Ridge?" I asked.

"One in the northeast. Suburb of Concord."

"Is that where you're from?"

"No. Chicago."

Just as I was marveling over what a helpful source this man would be, it struck me—I can be slow—that the subject of one of Clair's stories had taken the time to come to her memorial. Fowler was fifty miles from Chicago. Glenn Patchen was either a charitable man or Clair had made quite an impression on him. Then I scolded myself. Why did my thoughts always sink to the dregs? As I grappled with the grim realization that I was becoming more like my mother with each waking day, Nita was singing my praises to Glenn who smiled and nodded as she spoke. The gestures seemed more mechanical than sincere. I started to feel a little sorry for him. It's not easy being trapped with Nita when she's feeling garrulous.

I glanced around the room, searching for an escape and noticed Clair's parents had left their table and were saying emotional good-byes as they headed toward the exit. I leaned toward Nita. "The Powells are leaving."

Nita broke off in mid-sentence, told me to save her seat, grabbed her glass and wobbled off toward the couple. I felt kind of bad about siccing her on Mara and Jack, but someone else from the paper would see that she didn't overwhelm them.

When I turned toward Glenn, he was smiling. "She's a force, isn't she?"

"An absolute force."

In a typical Nita maneuver, she had left me, a woman with zero small-talk skills, marooned with a stranger who may be at least as conversationally impaired. I gave Patchen a stiff smile and drew a gulp off my beer, grateful that I had something to do with my hands. Patchen concentrated on finding the appropriate spot for his Bell's Stout on the coaster. Centering it just right.

"Is that an architect thing?" I asked.

He looked up.

"Coaster positioning?" I nodded toward his beer. "A spatial thing."

The lines in his forehead deepened. "Sorry?"

I shook my head. I didn't want him to be sorry. "No, really, architects have to have good spatial skills don't they?"

When he continued to regard me with trepidation, I blundered on. "I'm really bad with spatial stuff." I glanced toward the ceiling. "For example, I live above a woodworking store. They specialize in handmade picture frames. And even though I'd been in the store several times, I had no idea my bedroom was right above the sanding room until I was awakened one morning . . . and the noise. It sounded like someone was being skinned alive." I stopped. That was an unpleasant analogy.

But Patchen's brow relaxed and he smiled a little as he nodded, as though my bizarre statement had popped into context. "Yeah, I guess I've got to have an idea of where and how everything goes together." He finally brought his eyes to focus on mine. They narrowed as he studied me. "But you're a writer. So, you've got to have some abilities in that area. Spatial concepts aren't just visual."

I must have looked confused, because he hurried on. "No, you just used one. You said the sanding sounded like someone being skinned alive. Right?"

"I was half asleep," I reminded him.

"But it's still a metaphor." He added a thoughtful shrug. "Kind of a gruesome metaphor, but a metaphor. And what is a metaphor but a spatial relationship—linking the known with the unknown? It's an abstract relationship, but it's still spatial. As a writer, you've got the job of making me see something with words. Engage my imagination. Move it from one place to another and make the connection. By comparing the sound of sanding to a scream, well, you've nailed it."

I was still dubious, but he was on a roll, so I nodded and smiled. "I feel better about my disability." Not wanting him to slip away, I grabbed the first question that occurred to me. "Are metaphors used in architecture?"

Without hesitation, he said, "Absolutely," and proceeded to deliver an example involving Antonio Gaudi's work, invoking mythology, beehives and flights of fancy.

He talked for some time without any prompting from me and, although the premise was interesting and his enthusiasm contagious, I came to realize that I'd have to steer him toward the dock if I wanted to be out of here before last call. At the same time I didn't want him to think he was boring me—he wasn't—so I waited for him to pause and fed him a new question. "Okay, now that makes me wonder. When you design a place do you use metaphor? If I look at a drawing of Cedar Ridge, what will I see? A colony of bees?"

"Not bees, specifically." He smiled. "What I hope you'll see is an organism." He held his empty glass up for the waitress to see, and I shook my head when he gestured toward mine. "If we think of architecture as an organism rather than a machine, we're compelled to make it sustainable. A machine supposedly acts independently of its environment . . ." Almost as though talking to himself, he added, "But of course it doesn't."

He stared at the now-empty coaster and seemed to drift off. I thought I'd lost him again, so I prompted, "But an organism would interact with its environment."

That seemed to wake him, because he picked up again as though there'd been no distraction. "Right. It's a mindset. A mindset that's naturally going to affect how we build. We're going to look carefully at the materials we use, the design, its impact."

"Going back to our roots?"

He cocked his chin.

I tried to clarify. "I guess I'm talking very old roots. But buildings, homes, used to be made out of whatever was available in the surrounding environment. Adobe. Mud."

"Exactly." He was really excited now, handing the waitress a ten dollar bill when she brought his beer and waving off the change. "And there's incredible progress being made here. One day homes will be designed that not only use no energy at all, but give back to the environment. Places that collect and treat water. Not just save energy, but create it. Cedar Ridge is a step in that direction."

He continued talking about the future and Cedar Ridge and how it fit into this large scheme. I listened, glad that I'd found a sure-fire way to get the guy to talk. At the same time, my story-generating brain cells kicked into overdrive. This piece could have appeal outside of Fowler in publications other than a weekly newspaper.

He was halfway through his beer and had veered off the subject of Cedar Ridge and was telling me about a Bronze Age settlement in the Shetland Islands when he paused for breath.

"Are you a teacher?" I asked.

He shrank back into his chair, as though he realized he'd been lecturing. So I added, "No, really. You're so passionate about this. If you're not, you should be."

He studied me, as though trying to determine if I was being genuine. I was, and he must have decided that because he leaned forward again and nodded. "I am. I'm adjunct faculty at Northwestern."

"I figured something like that."

He smiled and sighed, then focused on the glass in front of him. After several seconds, he looked up and said, "Clair also had a curious intellect."

I nodded and waited.

"She would ask me the kind of questions that I wish my students would ask." His mouth tightened into a thin line and he squeezed his eyes shut. When he opened them again, they glistened. "She could have brought so much to this world." He swallowed.

"You're right."

We sat in silence for a minute. I was trying to figure a way, other than the obvious, to explain his emotional attachment to Clair. One of the reasons I'd so admired Clair was her integrity. I believed she was the kind of young woman who wouldn't make some really, really bad choices, like I had, at her age. Sleeping with a source would qualify as one of those.

"Did you know she was a photographer?"

I looked up, blinking. "No, I didn't."

"She was. Had a wonderful eye for imagery and . . ." he paused, searching ". . . the right detail. You know what I mean?"

"I think so."

As I was about to ask him how he knew this, Nita returned to the table, effusive as ever. "Robyn, I see you've got a jump start on your research."

"I have," I said, taking a moment to recall the subject of the piece. "And I think I've got an idea for a couple of sidebars for the series."

Her enthusiasm flagged. Nita wasn't in love with sidebars, thought they belonged more in magazines than newspapers. But they'd be good for the paper's website.

I seized another angle and kept going. "I could interview Glenn about the future of sustainable housing." I nodded at Glenn, who was working on his beer.

It may have been the booze, but Nita puckered her eyebrows and pondered my suggestion. "Okay. Good idea. Make it happen." And she walked away.

Now Glenn was smiling. He set his glass on the coaster. "Sorry I went on like that. Get me started and—"

"Don't apologize. Really." I snatched my handbag from the floor beside my chair. "Why don't I schedule some time with you in the next couple of days?"

We agreed on Tuesday morning at Cedar Ridge, where Patchen worked out of a trailer. I stood, and said in all honesty, "I'm really looking forward to this."

"Me too," he said, sounding a little surprised.

As I walked past him toward the door, he called after me, "And thanks for that metaphor."

"It's what I do," I told him. Although, technically, it had been a simile.

Chapter 6

I stopped by the newspaper the next morning and Nita and I spent some time discussing Clair's assignments. Cedar Ridge was mine, but I was still hoping I'd also get the Stella Burke trial. She'd been arrested for running a call girl ring out of her lovely Victorian home right in downtown Fowler. (The fact that the home had been featured in last year's House Walk was a source of supreme embarrassment to the Fowler Historical Society.) There was some negotiating going on between Burke and the state's attorney regarding a rather impressive list of clients, and apparently her solemn vow of discretion wasn't holding up well under the threat of prison time. It would have been interesting.

But I let go of that one because I was about to ask for something in exchange. "Okay, I'll do Cedar Ridge. I'd also like to do Clair's story."

Nita looked at me, puzzled. "Amy did a nice piece on her. I don't—"

"No, I want to follow the investigation."

"Why?" she asked and with a quick shake of her head added, "I mean, unless they find who did it, there's not going to be much more to report on."

"I'd just like to be the one to keep reminding them."

"Her mother got to you, didn't she?"

"Sort of."

In the end, Nita acquiesced and agreed I could cover anything the investigation turned up.

The Cedar Ridge story would be a multi-part feature to appear in the *News and Record* over the course of a month. The news peg was that the first families would be moving into their homes within the month. And although it would take some work chasing down families and sources—aside from the architect—it was a feel-good piece without the time pressure involved in Clair's other stories. In fact, it was such a feel-good piece, it didn't seem like a story Clair would care for. That was more Amy's bent.

"How did Clair wind up with the story? Seems she's . . . was . . . always going after the stories that were more controversial. She liked that potential for danger."

"Yeah, she did. But this one I gave her because Glenn Patchen—you know the architect you were talking to?"

I nodded.

"Patchen requested her."

"Really? Why?"

"He liked the writing she'd done on the piece about Brandon School's construction." With a shrug, she added, "And then she wanted to do it."

Again, it didn't seem like a story Clair would pursue, but Nita hurried on before I could voice that.

"In addition to Patchen, you'll also want to talk to Joe and Katherine Kendrick." She paused, tapping the end of her pencil against her chin. "You know who might be interesting to interview?"

I waited.

"David de Coriolis." She nodded to herself. "He's never been a fan." She paused, reflecting. "But now that it's a reality, he's got every reason for it to succeed." She gave me a wink. "Catch him on one of his magnanimous days and you never know what he'll say."

Smiling, I jotted his name down. Nita liked nothing better than goading de Coriolis, and made frequent use of the *Record*'s editorial space to criticize him. "I'm sure he'll be delighted to chat with me."

I had gone over some of Clair's notes—her parents had found them when cleaning out her apartment—and read the downloads from her computer, which included more notes and research. I hadn't tackled her handwritten notes yet. Her writing was better than mine, which wasn't saying much, but, like a lot of reporters, she had her own form of shorthand. I figured I'd have to put on my cryptology hat and sit down with a Scotch before I could make any real headway. But I would, because that was probably where she kept her personal opinions and observations.

Chapter 7

Clair had scheduled a meeting with Joseph Kendrick, who was behind the Cedar Ridge concept, but she hadn't lived to do the interview. When I called Kendrick he said he'd heard about Clair's death and said what a shame it was. He offered to meet me at a nearby country club at eleven thirty. Of course, he had every reason to be accommodating. This would be good publicity for him. Still, it was my experience that some of these mogul-types like to appear elusive, often at their own expense. I'd hoped to talk with his wife at the same time, but Katherine Kendrick wasn't due in Fowler until the next day.

The closest Fowler came to a country club was a par three golf course that consisted of nine rather scruffy holes. Or so I've been told. The golf bug missed me by a triple bogey. So, I had to drive about ten miles east to the Douglas Grove Country Club. I'd never been there before, but it had been the location of several golf tournaments, mostly hosted by local celebrities. Such as they were. It was hard to miss, just a half mile off the main road, and looked like an antebellum mansion—white pillars, wrought iron rails and balconies. It seemed out of place in northeastern Illinois, and I decided whoever designed it had an unnatural appreciation of the South. But, in all fairness, I love leaping to baseless conclusions. If there's ever a Mental Olympics, I'll be on the pole-vaulting team.

I found my way to the dining room where I was supposed to meet Kendrick. The hostess, a blond, tanned woman who wore a

44

black sleeveless dress and four-inch heels, steered me into the bar and to a table next to a window overlooking a patio and some hole on the golf course. I sat by the window and set my messenger bag on the chair beside me.

As she handed me a single-page, one-sided menu, she said, "Mr. Kendrick is finishing up his round. He'll be with you shortly," punctuating with a smile. "He said I should get you a drink."

I didn't often meet sources in bars or restaurants and figured I couldn't let him pay for a meal, not that I wanted one, but it might be all right to let him pop for an iced tea. At what point did it cross the ethics line? A Scotch was too much, especially a name brand, but was iced tea okay? The hostess's smile trembled from the effort. Clearly, my ethical dilemma was of no interest to her. "I'll just have some water," I said.

"I'll let the waitress know."

After she left, I looked around, checking out the waterfall bubbling into a pond beneath the vaulted ceiling. It felt slightly humid, probably because of the waterfall. Most of the tables were empty, it being a Monday, but there were a couple of small groups at the mahogany bar that stretched the length of the room. Outside, the October weather had turned cool, so the patio tables were empty and their umbrellas lowered. Beyond the patio, a golf cart made its way toward the clubhouse. I hoped it carried Joseph Kendrick. I didn't mind waiting when there was good reason—car troubles or an emergency appendectomy. But a golf game?

My water came and I thanked the waitress—an older, cheerful woman who seemed so concerned when I said I didn't need anything else that I ordered a pilsner and paid for it when she brought it. I never used to drink beer. Not until Mick entered my life with his home brewing hobby. At first, I think I enjoyed his creations because drinking them seemed just a little like indulging in contraband, even though I know that it's perfectly legal. I remember one night sitting in his family room, closing my eyes as I sipped from his latest batch, and imagining myself in a smoky, basement speakeasy. Mick teased me, called me Gladys, and one thing led to another. . . . Theatrics aside, the beer he brewed was tasty, and I began to appreciate the brew itself. I'd developed an enthusiastic amateur's nose for the varieties and nuances. It wasn't Scotch, but it had my respect.

I decided to try my hand at cracking Clair's handwriting code while I waited.

Although her drafts and extensive notes were on her computer, she did a lot of her scribbling in a spiral reporter's notebook, and used both sides of the paper. Questions to ask, observations. Some of it was in shorthand, and some of this was easy to interpret: "CR" was "Cedar Ridge," "GH" was "Green Haven Foundation," Joseph and Katherine Kendrick's creation that counted among its good deeds helping renters become homeowners. This was their first venture into green building. Clair used initials for the story's sources. JEK and KK were the Kendricks. GP was probably Glenn Patchen. RW would be the builder. DD was David de Coriolis? Who was CW? I couldn't recall these initials from the computer notes, where I'd found portions of the first article—an overview of the homes— partially completed. I hadn't run across a CW there. Contractors? I jotted down the letters in my own notebook for further digging.

The initials were one thing, but on one page she had what looked like an index: each set of initials listed, each followed by a few shorthand squiggles. I wanted to crack those squiggles. I was scanning her notes for recurrent marks when someone pulled out the chair across from me.

"Robyn Guthrie?"

I looked up to see a nice-looking man with gray-streaked hair and deep squint lines.

"That's right." I stood. "You're Joseph Kendrick?"

"That I am. Sorry to make you wait. We had a meandering four-some ahead of us."

We shook hands, and I found myself saying, "That's okay," even though I'd intended to just nod and let him know that it really wasn't.

Although middle-aged spread had begun to claim his waistline and his face was a bit jowly, Kendrick gave the impression of being the image of health. His smile was warm and energetic, and when he shook my hand I felt as though he meant it. He was one of those shakers who moved in with his other hand and grasped my elbow as he pumped. Nothing unseemly about it, but I'm one of those people who appreciates the concept of personal space.

"You put that on my bill, didn't you?" He pointed at my beer.

I waved him off.

For a second he looked confused, but then he grinned and sat in the chair across from me. "Do you golf?"

"No."

"Never?"

"Once."

Again, he waved his hand. "Oh, that's not enough. You've gotta give it another chance."

"No, thanks." I wanted to say: It's kind of like marriage. Sometimes once really is enough. But that's not the sort of thing you say to a person you met thirty seconds ago.

He whisked the menu from the table and perused it as he settled into the chair. In less than five seconds, he'd tossed it on the table and flagged the waitress over, placing an order for a BLT, requesting wheat toast and crisp bacon and lettuce, and a draft beer.

"Sure you won't have anything?"

"No. Thanks."

He told the waitress, "Get her another beer when that one gets low."

"No. Really. One will be enough. I've got to drive back to Fowler."

"I don't like to drink alone," he said, pouting a little.

"I'll drink slowly."

He shrugged and dismissed the waitress with a nod.

Settling his elbows on the table, he leaned toward me and folded his hands. He wore a thick wedding band centered with a large diamond.

"So, ask me questions," he said.

"Okay. For starters, tell me about Green Haven."

"Katherine—Kat—and I started it up about ten years ago. You know, a way of giving back. We both earn a comfortable living. Before Kat was a partner with a law firm in L.A. she'd worked for Habitat for Humanity. I made some money in Silicon Valley. Computer chips. Our main focus now is the environment and sustainability." He went on to describe some of the projects they'd developed, which included new models for community-based natural resource management.

"It's a 'for-profit' business, right?"

"That's right. We don't have a board to answer to. Kat and I work better on our own. But also, we're trying to show that there is money in the green movement." He leaned toward me. "A lot of money."

"Tell me about Cedar Ridge," I prompted.

"Right. At Cedar Ridge, we're developing a community of affordable green homes and offering low-interest loans to help people buy those homes."

"Why this area?"

"Well, we looked at a number of potential sites in the country. Most are a lot like Fowler—once prosperous manufacturing towns that have fallen on hard times. But Fowler stood out as a community with real potential. Your city council is actively working to bring business here, like the deal with Artemis. That's huge. And it's just the start."

Artemis was a sports clothing and equipment company geared toward women that was considering Fowler as a location.

"Have you seen the property yet?" Kendrick asked me.

I told him I hadn't.

"It's lovely. Not far from the river. Actually, Stratford International is looking at that riverfront property as a potential casino site."

This was news to me. "That's Stratford as in Stratford hotels and resorts?"

"The same."

"So Cedar Ridge might wind up next to a casino?"

"Not without a buffer." With a shake of his head, he added, "I know. It's an odd juxtaposition, isn't it?"

"Seems to be."

"But I think what really sold us on Fowler is that my wife, Kat, is from the Chicago area."

"What part?"

"LaGrange."

I stopped writing. "Really? That's where I grew up."

"No kidding."

"Do you know where she went to high school?"

"Sure do. She dragged me to her twenty-fifth reunion a few years ago. Lyons Township."

Oh, Jeez. I had missed my twenty-fifth reunion. In fact, I hadn't given much thought to high school since I'd left.

"We might have been in the same class," I said, thinking an inside source on this story might be a good thing.

"You remember Katherine Jamison?"

I took another drink, not because I was thirsty or wanted a sip, but to keep my jaw from dropping. Swallowing, I set my glass down and pushed it away. "Kitty."

"It's Kat now," he reminded me.

Of course. "Yes, I think I do remember her." Isn't it great the way life loves to bite you on the butt every now and then? How the mere mention of a name evokes all that high school angst, reminding you that we never, ever, really get over it. Your face may clear up and you may be earning enough to put a roof over your head, but a high school moment still has the power to flatten you.

I realized he wasn't talking anymore, and was, in fact, watching me. Compelled to give him something, I just said, "It'll be fun to see her." Why I said that and not something honest like, "Keep that bitch away from me," I'll never know. A meeting with Katherine Kendrick, nee Jamison, seemed about as joyful as a flat tire. In a blizzard. At two A.M.

But I needed to move past this, at least for now, so I asked him to elaborate on the concept of Cedar Ridge and took notes as he talked about the number of units—duplexes—and the whole environmental idea behind it.

"Sales haven't been what you'd hoped for, have they?"

"No, but they are what we anticipated. We knew this would be slow getting off the ground, and we've budgeted for that. But we've got two duplexes built and another started—those two are under agreement."

The waitress brought Kendrick his plate—the normal-sized sandwich was dwarfed by a huge mound of cottage fries.

When Kendrick gestured toward my half-empty beer, I shook my head, said, "No thanks," and returned to my questions.

"How many families?"

"Three will be moving in shortly." He bit off the end of a fry and finished chewing before he said, "The fourth unit we're using as a model right now." He went on about how, despite the slow sales, they were on schedule. "Wait'll you see the place next summer when we've got the landscaping in and the playground established."

As I asked questions and recorded responses, I began to give up the hope of finding something other than a housing development to report on here. The environmental aspect was interesting, but beyond that there wasn't much to chew on. I wondered if Clair had found a more interesting angle or if she'd resigned herself to writing a promotional piece for Cedar Ridge.

While scribbling, I happened to glance up and noticed a man watching our table. He seemed to be focusing on Kendrick rather than me, so I was able to observe him with impunity as he stood by the bar waiting for his drink. He was in the company of a girl, about ten, who was watching some talk show on the TV behind the bar. I assumed she was his daughter. I say this not only because they had the same dark good looks, but also because they wore coordinating tennis outfits—the girl in a white tennis dress with navy blue trim and the man in white shorts and a shirt with the same trim. They were an attractive pair, so they almost pulled it off. The whole dress-alike concept is just a bit too cloying for me. As I watched, the man handed his daughter a soft drink, took a sip from his hard drink and started walking toward our table.

He had almost reached us when Kendrick looked up and saw him approaching, stopping his sentence in mid-word. He leaned back, his eyes narrowed and hard.

"Hey, Joe," the other man said, his hand on his daughter's shoulder. "How's the game?"

Kendrick nodded without a trace of emotion. "Ed."

Ed was average height and weight with thick, dark hair and eyes rimmed by rather long lashes. "How's the game?" he repeated.

"Okay," Kendrick kept nodding.

My interest piqued. Whatever was going on here was poten-tially more compelling than low-income housing. Even if it was environmental.

"I didn't know you came here." Thick, dark brows drew together. "Who do you know who belongs?"

If Kendrick considered the question out of line, he didn't let on. All he said was, "I know several members."

"Do you now?" At this point, Ed was eyeing me. Kendrick must have noticed because he introduced us.

"Robyn Guthrie, this is Ed Leoni. Robyn is doing a feature on Cedar Ridge for the *Record*."

"That's a familiar name," Leoni said. "You a regular at the *Record*?"

"Stringer."

"Who else you write for?"

Where to begin? "The Sunday *Trib*, online newsletters, magazines—"

"Any I read?"

"I'm guessing you're not a *More* reader, but I've written for real estate magazines, *Chicago*—"

"Dad." The girl next to him whined as she cocked her hip.

Leoni gave her an indulgent smile, as though she'd just done something remarkable rather than rude. "My daughter, Mercedes." Mercedes sighed and her mouth thinned into a lifeless smile.

"Mind if we join you?" Leoni pulled out the chair next to mine and waited for me to move my messenger bag before gesturing for his daughter to sit. She did, setting her drink on the table without looking at me.

"Um, excuse me," I said, leaning on the table. Leoni looked at me like I'd spoken out of turn. "I'd like to finish this interview."

"That's okay." He waved me off. "You keep talking."

"Ed," Kendrick said, "can't this wait?"

"What? Can't what wait? I just thought we'd catch up on a few things. Haven't seen you since the sale." He sat next to Kendrick, who had started to turn an unhealthy shade of red.

"Like I said," I folded my hands over my notes, "I'd like to finish this interview. I'm on deadline." I wasn't, but what did he know?

He ignored me and nodded at his daughter. "Mercedes, why don't you tell . . . uh . . . Robyn about your tennis camp." He smiled. "Mercedes was number three seed."

I looked down at Mercedes, who wore a smug little smile. "Number three?" I said and added, "Oh," like that was too bad.

The smile faded and she turned on me the coldest eyes I've ever seen on a kid. It was disconcerting. But I held on, determined not to let her get to me.

Then her father was flagging over the waitress, ordering a hamburger for Mercedes and a ham on rye for himself.

Turning back to Kendrick, he asked how far Cedar Ridge had progressed. He never gave Kendrick much of a chance to respond, because he kept changing the subject. Talking about environmental homes one minute, then the country club and the golf course, saying how they needed a course like this in Fowler.

As Leoni waxed on, Kendrick, who had begun to perspire, mainly nodded and produced monosyllabic responses. Apparently that was all he had to do, because Leoni seemed capable of long chats with himself. I also noticed he didn't quite focus on Kendrick, looking past him, toward the patio, as though something there distracted him. Diverted him. Almost like he was admiring something. When I followed his gaze, I couldn't figure out who was out there. The tables were empty and no one was strolling across the patio. And that's when I realized what it was—he was flirting with his own reflection. When it hit me, I tried not to laugh. He must have realized he'd been busted when he glanced my way and saw me struggling to contain myself. He abruptly broke off his fixation and turned toward Kendrick.

At this point I felt the toe of a tennis shoe smack me in the shin. With a small gasp, I looked down at Mercedes, who continued to smile at her father. But she'd crossed one leg over the other and was swinging her foot, so I braced for another smack, which came.

"Mercedes," I said, "that's not the table you're kicking."

"Sorry," she said, but added that little smirk.

Her father was talking about how he'd let the land go at a steal, just so needy "green" people would have housing.

I interrupted. "You sold them the land?"

Leoni had been so into his monologue that he went on for another few sentences before he realized someone had asked him a question.

"Yeah," he finally said. Smiling a little, he nodded toward Kendrick and added, "Joe here knows how to get to me." He laughed and patted Kendrick on the shoulder.

Kendrick managed a weak smile but didn't look at Leoni. He seemed to have forgotten about his sandwich. Actually, he looked like he'd like nothing better than for Scotty to beam him out of here.

Leoni bounced back to the subject of golf, "You got somebody to play with tomorrow?"

"I can't tomorrow. Katherine will be in town."

Leoni brightened. "Hey, how is Kat?"

"Fine."

The waitress delivered the sandwiches and Leoni popped a French fry into his mouth and chewed as he watched his daughter pour ketchup onto her burger. "Hey, Mercedes, Robyn's not eating anything. Why don't you give her half that?"

Mercedes looked up, eyes wide, looking like her dad had just whacked her cat. She set the ketchup on the table and sat up straight so she could look down her nose at the burger.

"That's okay," I said.

Leoni nodded at my beer. "Can't drink on an empty stomach."

Before I could tell him that, in fact, I could, he flagged the waitress down again and told her to get him another plate.

"Mercedes, cut that in half." He reached across the table and handed his daughter her own knife.

"I don't want it," I said.

Leoni nodded at Mercedes to start cutting.

I swallowed. "I don't eat red meat."

Now Mercedes looked at me. "Why not?"

There were many things I could have said. "It's personal."

"It's a cow."

I looked down into her hard little eyes. "And it deserves a better fate than lying on a bun on your plate."

She held my gaze for several seconds then burst into laughter, covering her mouth in an attempt to contain her convulsions. Across the table, her father was chuckling and even Kendrick looked amused.

"Ed."

The laughter stopped. I looked up and saw we'd been joined by a dark-haired woman wearing crisp jeans and a red jacket.

"I thought we were meeting out front. My father is expecting us at one thirty." She seemed more hurt than angry.

Leoni looked at Kendrick. "We got hungry. I saw my old friend here." Kendrick flinched as Leoni patted his shoulder. "Tabitha, this is Joe Kendrick. Joe, this is my wife."

The woman reached across the table to shake his hand and then turned toward me with an expectant look. I assumed that Leoni had either forgotten my name or never bothered committing it to memory, so I shook her hand and introduced myself. When I told Tabitha I was with the *Record*, she turned toward her husband.

"You shouldn't be bothering these people, Ed. They've got work to do."

"Joe is a friend," Leoni said, leaning toward his wife and speaking each word with ominous precision. Tabitha backed off and looked away, as though trying to collect herself. Her gaze fell on her daughter, who had spent the exchange staring at her plate. The muscles around her mouth seemed to be working hard to suppress that delightful smirk of hers.

"How'd your game go, honey?" Tabitha asked, although the question seemed forced.

"Okay," Mercedes said, sounding bored. She looked up at her father and was rewarded with a smile, which Mercedes returned.

This touching family scene was interrupted when a series of chimes went off, and Tabitha dug through her purse, a bit frantic, until she came up with her phone. When she checked the number on the screen, her shoulders unclenched and she almost smiled.

"Hi, Dad," she said. She listened for a minute, and turned away from us as she said, "It's okay. We'll be th—" She sighed. "Sure, Dad." She handed the phone to Leoni. "He wants to talk to you." With that she lifted her chin an inch.

Leoni took the phone with, it seemed, some reluctance. "Yeah . . . sure . . . yeah . . . I understand." A long pause and then, "Yeah, Chris, I appreciate that. . . . Yeah, thanks." He tossed Tabitha her phone as he pushed away from the table.

"Well, I'm afraid we're going to have to leave you." He patted Kendrick on the shoulder again, and, waving a hand over his barely eaten sandwich, said, "You'll take care of this, okay?"

Kendrick looked away with a mixture of disgust and resignation.

Beside me, Mercedes stood, turned, and, in a contrived gesture, smacked the ketchup bottle, which hit the table, releasing a blob of thick, red muck that landed on my lap.

Before I could react, Tabitha swooped in, grabbing her daughter by the arm, jerking her around so they faced each other. Still, Mercedes wouldn't meet her mother's anger. "What do you think you're doing?" She increased pressure on her daughter's arm.

"It was an accident," Mercedes said, looking past her mother and toward Leoni, who hadn't entered the fray. She tried to twist her arm out of her mother's grip and uttered a whiny little "Ow."

Between Tabitha's glare and Mercedes' determination to recruit her father into the fray, I'd seen more of this family's dysfunction than I cared to see. I just wanted this to be over. "It's okay—"

"Thank you, Robyn," Tabitha said to me, "but it's not okay." She released her daughter, who wasted no time fleeing to her father. He put his arm around her. Mercedes let her head fall against his shoulder and kept up her "whipped puppy" expression.

Tabitha handed me a business card, Tabitha's Designs, an interior decorator service. "That stain may not come out. Please get yourself another pair of slacks—Hauser's has a nice selection—and send me the bill."

Although she was probably right about the stain not coming out, I didn't want this poor woman paying for it. But when I started to object, Tabitha put her hand on my shoulder. "Really. I want you to do this."

"Okay," I finally said. "Thanks."

With that she left, walking past her husband and daughter as though they weren't there, which was what she was probably wishing. Leoni nodded at Kendrik and then he and his demon seed followed Tabitha.

As I mopped up the spill—maybe there was hope for these slacks—I pondered why it is that ketchup takes forever to leave the bottle when poised over a pile of fries, but aim it a pair of light gray pants and *woosh*.

When I went to dip the napkin's corner in a glass of water, I noticed Kendrick was staring out the window, apparently oblivious to my small disaster.

"Tabitha seems nice," I said, squeezing the excess water from the white cloth.

He turned, regarding me for several moments without speaking. I wasn't even sure he was seeing me.

"Mercedes, on the other hand, could be featured in birth control ads," I said, thinking a little jest would snap him out of it.

Instead of a chuckle, or even a wry smile, his expression darkened. He wiped a hand across his mouth, pulling at his lower lip. Distracted, he shook his head as though trying to clear it and glanced at his watch.

"Oh, Jesus," he said. "I've got a meeting I need to get to. Can we continue this another time?" He removed several bills from his wallet and tucked them under his plate.

"As I said, Kat will be here tomorrow. Give her a call. She'll fill in any of the blanks."

Great. I thanked him for his time and he just nodded.

I watched as he left the bar, walking with his shoulders hunched, his head lowered and his cell phone to his ear. I knew it wasn't my questions that weighed him down. Leoni had quite an effect on Kendrick. And while I figured their relationship was probably a more interesting story than a green community, it wasn't the one I'd been hired to write, so I tried to put it out of my mind.

I decided to give my pants a few minutes to dry before I left, so I took my time finishing my beer and watched as the bar began to fill with people. It was going on twelve thirty and I figure this place must be a popular watering hole for the local professionals looking for a lunch-time pick-me-up.

As I sat there killing time, I updated my notes and started a fresh page with a few questions to ask David de Coriolis. Then I gathered up my handbag, brushing at the dark stain on my thigh, which, although it had dried a bit, hadn't been helped much my by ministering. These weren't my favorite pants—the fact that they weren't jeans was one big strike against them—but they'd been a serviceable pair for occasions when a little dressing up was in order. My anger flared for a second. I imagined all kinds of unpleasant fates for Mercedes, most of which I'd engineered.

Fortunately, I'd scheduled my interview with Glenn Patchen for the next morning, so I could head straight home and tend to the blob on my pants. Besides, Bix hadn't seen me for—what?—almost four hours and would be getting antsy by now. He was a great little dog, and it was nice to be the most important person in some creature's world, though at times the responsibility seemed daunting. Kind of like with my mother, only I suspected if she'd had another daughter, a more caring (i.e., submissive) one—or better yet, an adoring son—I would be the daughter she spoke of in hushed tones. But there was no one else. I was it the number one person by default.

Bix, on the other hand, had chosen me at the animal shelter. The two-year-old rat terrier mix had not taken his eyes off me during the time I surveyed the cages of dogs up for adoption. And while other dogs had either gone wild with enthusiasm or ignored me, Bix sat there calm and collected, staring. Just staring. Until the attendant took a sheltie out of her cage for me to meet. Then he went nuts, barking and throwing himself at the cage door. When the sheltie wouldn't make eye contact with me, we moved on to the little rat terrier. He stopped barking and stepped out of his cage like he knew where he was going. And he never stopped staring at me. To this day I'll often look up and see Bix's dark little eyes fixed on me. I wasn't sure whether he was the dog of my dreams or a reincarnated stalker. I'm still not.

As I left the country club, I was surprised to see Kendrick, standing at the foot of the steps engaged in an animated discussion with the valet.

"How long is it going to take *someone* to get here?"

The valet, in his early twenties with curly blond hair and a soft mustache, was trying to tell him how sorry he was about the flat tire and that he'd called someone who would be here shortly. Kendrick didn't seem at all moved by the gesture as he sputtered, "I hand my keys over to you and now my car is undriveable. Why didn't I leave the damned thing in the middle of the road with its keys in the ignition?"

"I'm sorry, sir," the valet said again. "Would you like to speak to management?" I suspect he hoped Kendrick would agree to that. Clearly, he wasn't being paid enough to put up with this abuse.

"I don't give a damn about management. I have to be in Schaumburg in twenty minutes. Can you get that tire fixed in time? I don't think so."

He looked like his head was about to explode.

The valet tried again, "I can call you a cab—"

"I don't have time to wait for a cab."

The valet winced and raised his hand, palms skyward. "I don't know what else I can do. I swear—"

I stepped forward. "Mr. Kendrick," I began, not believing I was hearing myself say this. "I can drive you to Schaumburg."

* * *

We'd been on the road for at least ten minutes before the color of Kendrick's face returned to normal. But it wasn't until I heard him breathe a deep sigh that I attempted to initiate conversation.

"Must be an important meeting," I said.

As I glanced his way, I saw him nod. He sighed again and looked my way, his features softening slightly. "Thank you."

A little surprised, I just shrugged. "Hey. I know how cars can turn on you."

He chuckled, then fell silent again.

After a minute or two, he said, "I would've waited for a cab, but this meeting is, well, it's with someone who doesn't like to be kept waiting."

I nodded, wondering who that might be. I supposed that Kendrick didn't like waiting either, but it was a food chain kind of thing. There's always someone bigger and meaner than you are.

Then, out of the blue, he asked, "How did you and Kat know each other?"

When I didn't answer right away, he said, "I know you said it was high school, but were you in classes together?"

"I don't remember exactly how we met." My first lie to this man. (Second, if you counted my "It'll be great to see Kat again" line.) "High schools—even ours—are really small communities. Probably a class." Glancing his way, I added, "We weren't close or anything."

"Really?"

"Kitty—Kat and I weren't in the same circle." I adjusted my grip on the steering wheel. "You know how that is. High school is kind of a caste system."

A moment or two later, he chuckled. "Let me guess. Kat was a Brahmin."

So, she hadn't changed. "Yeah, I wasn't an Untouchable, but . . . well, not usually." I glanced his way as I stopped for a red light. "I think most of us had those moments."

He was nodding, staring ahead. I tried to imagine Joe Kendrick as a teenager. He'd turned into a nice-looking man—his skin was a little puffy, but he had compelling eyes and good hair. But he might have been one of those people who had improved with age. My mother once told me that I'd been an "odd-looking" child—she said I reminded her of a squirrel—and it wasn't until I got to college and slowly turned the corner into adulthood that she stopped doubting I was her daughter. (I don't know how she explained the whole giving-birth-to-me thing.) From the way Kendrick had fallen silent, I sensed he hadn't been one of the charmed ones either. "Yeah," he finally said. "High school isn't for the weak, is it?"

"Where did you grow up?"

"Boulder, Colorado."

"A pretty area."

"The mountains are nice."

Something about his clipped delivery made me suspect that, to Kendrick, there wasn't much else to say about the area.

Intrigued, I tried to keep him talking. "Let me guess. You were on the football team."

He barked a laugh, "Just one year. I didn't actually grow until I was a senior."

The light changed to green and I accelerated, taking my place in the stream of cars heading east on Golf Road.

"Theater," I said. "I think Kat and I knew each other through theater." Theater was the great equalizer. You didn't have to be popular; you just needed some talent. And I wasn't a bad little actress. In fact, I was good enough to beat Kitty out for the role of Laura in *The Glass Menagerie*. I remembered how she told everyone it was only because she was too attractive to play Laura. Squirreliness has its rewards.

"I was on the debate team."

"And yet you didn't turn into a lawyer." I said. So many of them did.

"That's right. I went the business route." He sighed. "Kat is the lawyer."

"But she got her training in theater class." Without thinking, I added, "If you can't bury them with the facts, then wow them with histrionics."

After a few seconds, he said, "Kat wouldn't have given me the time of day in high school."

I glanced at him. "Good thing we don't carry those labels for life."

"Amen to that."

"I think it would be difficult to be a huge success in high school and then land in the real world with a mediocre job and life—which most of us have." I stopped. Didn't want to wax philosophical in the left lane on my way to Schaumburg.

"Kat wouldn't have settled for mediocre. No way."

The way he said that—with a hint of both resignation and pride—I had to laugh.

I could feel him watching me. "You weren't particularly fond of Kat, were you?"

What could I say?

Recalling the look in Kitty Jamison's spite-filled gray eyes as she confronted me that day in the hall between World History and English lit, I had to smile a little. Especially with the perspective that almost thirty years had given me. "I was a nobody dating a football player. Their prized kicker. It was unheard of." I glanced at Kendrick. "In the off-season he dabbled in the arts."

"I imagine Kat wouldn't hear of that."

"True. Basically, Kitty informed me that I was dating up, and if I didn't break up with Brad, they'd have to do an intervention on him."

As we passed a forest preserve on my left, the trees blurred into each other. To this day I've never been able to put myself into a Kitty Jamison mindset. I'd looked at it from all angles. Was I that much of a threat to her little clique? Or did she just enjoy stepping on people? I'd probably never know. I could feel Kendrick watching me. "So, what happened?"

"He stopped calling and started dating Kitty's best friend."

"Ouch."

"Yeah, well, at the time it was the worst thing in the world." I laughed. "Don't I wish."

"How much worse can it get?"

"War. Climate change. Leaf blowers."

When that got no response out of him, I looked his way and saw that he was watching me, smiling a little.

As I was wondering if it was just me or if this conversation had taken a weird turn, he asked, "Did you ever want to get back at her?" It wasn't me.

I was turning into our destination—an office building near O'Hare—when he asked, and I pulled up to the curb and put the car into park before I answered. "I know they say that revenge is a dish best served cold—"

"*Wrath of Kahn*," he interjected.

I acknowledged with a nod.

"Sorry, I interrupted."

After a moment, I said, "I guess I don't care much for leftovers. Warm or cold."

He studied me for a moment before saying, "Point taken." But then he winked at me as he opened the passenger-side door. "Thank you for the ride, Robyn. I'll be in touch."

I didn't ask how he was getting home.

Chapter 8

By the time I got home it was after three. Not enough time to be chasing down more interviews, but plenty of time for a quick phone call, which I placed to Fowler's police department. I asked to speak to the detective in charge of Clair's death investigation and was pleased to find myself talking to Rick Hedges. I knew him from a past encounter, and he'd been a reasonable man, even when I had been a bit evasive.

When I asked if he had some time to talk about Clair, he said, "I thought they had someone else covering this."

"They did. But I'm continuing with the coverage."

The pause on the other end of the line extended. "How come?"

"I don't know," I admitted. "I guess when I met Clair's mother, the woman kind of got to me."

When that didn't prompt a comment, I said, "She told me they might put up a reward."

"They did. Ten thousand."

"Is that the going rate for snitches?"

"Depends on their greed-to-fear factor."

"Yeah, I guess."

"I don't think I've got anything new to tell you."

"What do you have so far?"

"No one saw anything. We've interviewed the owner and bartender at The Roadside and some of the people who were there. Got the names of a few people who were overserved. Followed up with them, but we came up empty. We've got a tip line set up and we're looking at each one."

"Have you had a lot of calls?"

"Enough to keep us busy."

"Did you find skid marks? Tire tracks?"

"No skid marks. We got partial tire treads, but it's a common tire." He added, "Probably an SUV or a van."

Knowing what kind of vehicle it had been compelled me to visualize the accident. Clair and Scoop and a big van that I imagined as white. "Would there have been damage to the vehicle?"

"Yeah, but we've got to find it first."

I checked my notes for my next question. "Who made the nine-one-one call?"

"A guy driving by the next morning."

That stopped me. "They didn't find her until morning?"

"Yeah. Early. Around five thirty. He was on his way to work."

I took a moment to let that sink in. For some reason I'd thought that she'd been found before then. The idea of her lying there all night in the rain, with Scoop sitting next to her, was beyond sad. Had she died on impact?

"Is there anything that makes you think it might have been something other than an accident? Drunk driving? Or . . ."

"Or?"

"Well, she was a reporter. I imagine there are people out there not real happy with some of the stories she'd written."

"We're looking into that as well."

Now he sounded a bit guarded.

"Can you give me anything?"

"Not so far."

Just because Hedges was a kind, reasonable man, didn't mean he was going to be overly accommodating. But then he asked, "Were you two friends?"

"I guess you'd call us friendly acquaintances. I liked her."

I heard his sigh on the other end of the line. "Well, we're not giving up. These kind of cases can take some time, but eventually someone talks to someone. And then they'll talk to us. That ten thousand dollar reward may help."

"One more question."

"Shoot."

"Do you know an investigator named Kurt Vrana?"

"Vrana? Never heard of him. Why?"

I decided to be honest. Maybe he'd give me a little something in return. "He was at the *Record* asking about what she was working on."

"Huh."

That was helpful.

"Listen," he said, "I've gotta go."

"Sure. And thanks, Detective. I'll check back in a couple of days."

"I'll be here." Then he added, "And if you hear anything, you'll let me know."

I assured him I would and before he could hang up, I said, "Wait. I'd like to take a look at the place. I know it was on Keffling Road, but where exactly?"

"About a half mile east of Regent. On the north side. You can't miss it."

* * *

When I got there, I understood what he'd meant. There was a cross surrounded by flowers. I pulled off the road and got out to examine the scene closer. In addition to the multitude of flowers, which, with the exception of a single, long-stemmed rose, were mostly grocery-store bundles, there were also a few stuffed animals that hadn't weathered the continual rains very well. I understood the urge to place flowers at the site and was annoyed with myself for not thinking of bringing some, but I've never understood the stuffed animal thing. Wet, soggy stuffed rabbits and bears are just plain sad. That single rose was also sad, and I had to wonder who had placed it. As far as I knew, Clair wasn't seeing anyone romantically. If she had been, surely he'd have been at the memorial.

The crime scene investigation had concluded, so I knew there wouldn't be much to see. I looked up and down the road, a straight piece of two-lane highway for at least a quarter mile in either direction. No lights, no sidewalks. Just a rough shoulder and a ditch. Clair's apartment was about a half mile to the east, so she and Scoop had gone for quite a long walk that night. I wondered if she'd walked Scoop at the same time every night. Had they always taken the same route? And the choice of a route seemed odd. Why walk in the dark when neighborhood streets are so well-illuminated? Especially in the rain. Of course, maybe this had happened before the rain started.

I tended to be in a bit of a rut when it came to walking Bix, mainly because Bix insisted. If I was home at nine thirty P.M., and I usually was, he'd be there with his imploring look and his little tapping terrier feet. Impossible to resist. We had about three different routes we took, depending on how much time and energy we had. It wasn't always easy to plan my life around our walks, but that's what you did when you had a dog. Otherwise, you'd settle for cats.

But there were times when it just wasn't possible. So a lot of dog owners had backup walkers. Some neighbor they trusted with their key who would take the dog out in a pinch. I didn't know anyone well enough, but maybe Clair, with her erratic reporter schedule, did have such a person.

As I got into my car, I noticed a car parked about a quarter of a mile east. I didn't think it had been there when I'd arrived. I couldn't tell the make of car—that's not something I'm good at from far away—only that it was small and dark. And it was too far away for me to make out the person sitting in it. My plan was to drive the route that Clair had probably taken that night, but now I decided that a brief detour was in order. I did a U-turn and headed back east on Keffling, half expecting the mystery car to do the same. But it just sat there, and when I slowed as I came alongside of it, the occupant made no effort to hide himself. In fact, he turned my way, and I found myself staring into Kurt Vrana's dark eyes. He started to roll down his window and I, certain I was about to be staring down the business end of a gun, slammed my foot on the gas. The Matrix leaped forward and stalled. (It's important to remember to select a gear at a time like this.) My foot trembled as I depressed the clutch, and when I thrust the gear into first, something made me glance toward Vrana. He was not pointing a gun at me, but was watching my antics with what I would later recognize as a bemused expression. At the time, I couldn't get away fast enough.

I left him sitting there in his little car and drove directly to the The Roadside, a bar about a mile east, where I pulled into the parking lot and turned off my engine. I sat there for several minutes trying to make sense of what had just happened. Vrana must have followed me. Why? And, instead of wanting to shoot me, maybe he'd just wanted to talk. Again, why? Or, maybe it wasn't all about me. Maybe he was also investigating the crime. As I pictured him sitting there in his car, I stopped imagining dire scenarios long enough to think about the car he was driving. I'd only gotten the briefest of looks, but I thought it was a Mini Cooper. How out of character.

Vrana was a scary guy—to me, at least—and I expected to find him driving a Darth Vader car. Maybe a black Hummer—not a Mini Cooper. Although, it was black. I told myself that the fact that he didn't drive a threatening car did not mean that he wasn't a threat.

I was curious now. Well, if he wanted to talk with me, apparently he knew how to find me.

When I ventured west again, his car was gone. I was, at once, relieved and disappointed.

I drove the route that Clair had probably taken that night. East to Gunderson, north a few blocks to Avery and then headed east a half block to her apartment building. Again, I wondered at her choice of a route. There were lots of residential sidewalks, and I'd even passed a small park. Why walk on the shoulder of a road when you had better options?

Clair's building was connected to an identical building by a two-story entrance. It wasn't the kind of place where I expected to find her—cookie cutter brick blocks of apartments. But then I remembered her telling me she'd had a hard time finding a place that allowed pets, so I guess she'd sacrificed personality. I'd been lucky to find a place that would take Bix, and had gotten an apartment with plenty of personality. No closet space, but tons of personality.

I parked on the street and when I got out of my car, I looked up and down the block for a dark little car. Seeing nothing suspicious, I told myself that Vrana had decided I was too skittish to bother with.

The apartments were secure buildings, but I had no problem slipping in behind a guy carrying a large box. I helped him as he struggled with the door. Once on the elevator, I held the "open door" button until he and his burden were safely on board and once again when he got off on the third floor. I didn't get so much as a "thank you," but I took some satisfaction in knowing that he'd helped me breach his own building.

It was late afternoon on a weekday, and I didn't expect to find many people home. I was right. Of the two neighbors who did answer their doors, one didn't know who Clair was, and another, an elderly woman who walked with the aid of a cane, said how sorry she was and what a sweet girl Clair had been, and then invited me in for tea, but I declined, thanking her. At the next door, I had some success. Although no one human was home, I heard a dog barking—a small one, judging from the rather high-pitched yap. I wrote down the apartment number. It made sense that Clair would partner up with another dog owner. Perfect sense.

When I left the building, I found the name "Newman" on the mailbox for 604. I hoped that he or she had a listed phone number.

Chapter 9

When I got home, I called Mick on his cell phone. Even though it was after five, he was probably still at work, and when I got his voice mail I didn't think much of it. Just left a message for him to call me. I knew the story I was being paid to write was the one about Cedar Ridge. But I was curious about Kendrick's reaction to Leoni, not to mention Leoni's rather aggressive behavior toward Kendrick. Some strange chemistry there. And Mick Hughes knew a lot of people. Depending on what circle he ran in, Edward Leoni might be one of them.

I also had a message from my mother informing me that she'd just learned that her friend Azalea's daughter—whose name she could not recall—was a realtor. "Isn't that a wonderful coincidence?" she said, adding, "We'll have to arrange for you to meet her." While Bix danced at my feet, claws clicking on the tile floor as he did the rat terrier shuffle, I deleted the message.

The thing was, since my mother suggested buying a home, the idea had taken hold in my mind. Kind of like a song you're not crazy about, but after you hear it enough you find yourself humming it. I'd thought about buying a condo, but all the ones I'd seen looked like apartments. Boxy apartments. Like the place where Clair had lived. What was the point? The place I was in now at least had a little character. The slanted ceilings, tiny bedroom and dearth of closet space weren't necessarily selling points, but I found I liked living above a store, on a busy street. I felt connected to the town.

And there was no lawn to mow, no snow to shovel. There was, of course, the snow I had to scrape off my car, and winter was just a couple months away. A garage would sure be nice.

But while the house idea had plenty of appeal, there was no getting around the fact that I'd be living with my mother and wouldn't be doing it because it was the right thing to do. I'd be doing it because she came with the house. Although, I was fairly certain my mother harbored similar ambivalence. She'd rather live on her own, but knew her mental faculties made that impossible. Short of hiring a live-in companion, I was her only option. So, there we were. Maybe we deserved each other.

I clipped Bix's leash onto his collar and we descended the wooden stairs that took us from my kitchen door to a patch of scraggly back yard and the parking lot my car shared with the patrons of Framed and the beauty salon next door.

The night was chilly, and I wondered if I should have grabbed a jacket instead of a sweater. But it was good walking weather, and so I took Bix on the long route—first to Brigham Park and then into town, walking up the north side of Main Street. We stopped at the seafood market where I bought a piece of black cod for dinner and Barry gave me a few salmon scraps for Bix, who has odd tastes for a dog. We continued another three blocks before crossing the street and heading back west. A number of the storefronts we passed were empty, but I knew there was a real push to bring in new businesses and a few new places had opened—a top and jeans shop and a rug merchant. Fowler wasn't the most scenic town on the Crystal River, but it was the cheapest in the area for setting up a business or buying a home. And we were about the farthest west suburb from Chicago, so people were finding they'd rather have a nice, comfortable home than a shorter commute. I stood in front of an art supply store that sold local crafts—pottery, painting, jewelry—bending over to point out a purple ceramic dog dish with little white bones circling it. "What do you think, Bix? Your style?" In typical dog fashion, he was more intrigued with my finger than what it was pointing at. We moved on, past the newspaper office and a deli. The Crystal Dragon was next, Mick's favorite Chinese restaurant. As Bix and I walked past the big window with the white dragon painted on it, Bix stopped to investigate a piece of gum stuck to the sidewalk. While he pawed at it, I looked up and saw my reflection, a little surprised to find myself looking so glum. Must have been a premonition, because then I looked past myself and saw Mick sitting at a table near the rear of the small restaurant. I started to wave, thinking this was a nice coincidence and if it wasn't for Bix I'd go in and say hi. But I stopped myself. Seated across from him at the table for two was a young woman. I moved fast, turning away and heading back up the street, dragging a startled Bix along. I didn't think Mick had seen me. But I'd gotten a good enough glimpse to see the woman; she was dark and pretty, and probably twenty years younger than me. And Mick.

It was almost a full block before I slowed my pace, and for that Bix seemed grateful. I kept telling myself that there were probably a hundred explanations for their being together. Maybe she was interviewing for a job as his next receptionist. But I'd spotted wineglasses on the table. This bimbo was too young to appreciate the subtleties of beer, so Mick had gone with wine.

I opened the door to let Bix into our apartment. He followed me to the kitchen where I unwrapped his salmon scraps and nuked them in the microwave for a few seconds.

There were a lot of explanations, but the obvious one kept floating to the surface.

What I didn't understand was how I could have misread our evening together just over a week ago so badly. We'd been up most of the night talking. About places we wanted to see, books that made us think, all that. I hadn't had that good a conversation with a man since . . . well . . . never. Maybe I was more angry with myself for caring this much than I was hurt. But I thought about that and decided, no, I was hurt. Really hurt.

"Would you like red or white with that?" I asked Bix as I scraped the salmon into his dish and watched him bury his snout in it. I turned to the cod I'd brought home for myself. My appetite had left me, and I couldn't help but be a little annoyed with myself for splurging on the pricey stuff. I must have been feeling buoyant. *Pop.*

I put the fish in the fridge, thinking maybe my appetite would improve tomorrow—it never strayed for long—and threw together a turkey sandwich along with a small bag of chips. After feasting, I poured some Famous Grouse into a glass, tossed in a few ice cubes and a drizzle of water. In order to get my mind off Mick, I decided it was as good a time as any to see if I could find Clair's dog-owning neighbor.

I lucked out on a White Pages search for someone named Newman at the same address as Clair's building. I wrote out a few questions to ask and called.

A woman answered. Fairly young from the sound of her voice. I asked if Miss Newman was there.

"This is Heidi Newman," she said, her voice thick with wariness, which is how I sound until I'm sure the person on the other end of the line isn't trying to get money out of me.

I introduced myself and said I was with the *Fowler News and Record.* "I wanted to ask you a couple of questions about Clair Powell."

"Oh, Clair." She sounded both sad and relieved. "What do you want to know?"

"Did you ever walk Scoop for her?"

"Yeah, I did," she said as though that were an odd question. "How did you know?"

"Lucky guess. I was there this afternoon, trying to find some neighbors who knew Clair. Most weren't home. But you've got a vocal little watchdog, so I thought maybe you and Clair might have helped each other with the walking." I quickly added, "I've got a dog, Bix, and I know it's not always possible to work your schedule around their habits."

"Well, yeah, you're right. I did walk Scoop sometimes. And Clair did the same for Rufus." With her next breath she asked, "How's Scoop doing?"

"He's okay. I think we found him a good home with a young woman in town."

"That's good to hear. He's a nice dog."

"What kind of dog is Rufus?"

"A Shih-Tzu."

We chatted for a minute, comparing rat terriers and shih-tzus. Then I swung the conversation back to Clair.

"How often did you walk Scoop?"

"Oh, not often. Maybe once every couple of weeks. Sometimes more."

"Did you ever walk Scoop along Keffling Road?"

She paused. "You know, I didn't. And when I heard where it happened, I wondered why Clair would go that way."

"Me too. There are lots of sidewalks and open areas near your building."

"Exactly." Another pause. "It seemed odd, but then I don't think I ever asked Clair where she walked Scoop."

I mulled that over.

"Do you think it matters?" Heidi prompted.

"I don't know. But I'm going to mention it to the police. Detective Hedges is the officer in charge. He may call you to follow up."

"Sure. Anything I can do to help." I heard her sigh. "It's just so sad. We weren't close or anything, but she was really thoughtful. Nice." She laughed softly. "Last Christmas she made dog cookies. Brought some over for Rufus."

I thanked her for her time and for talking with me and gave her my cell phone number in case she came up with anything else that might be useful.

Next I did a search on Kurt Vrana. Nothing much. I did learn that "Vrana" meant "crow" in Slovenian. Although it wasn't all that unusual a last name, I wondered if it was his real name. Shady people often assumed names.

It was too late to call Hedges. I didn't have anything other than his office number, and leaving a message about a suspicious name seemed, well, paranoid, so I pushed it from my mind and spent the next hour going over my notes and piecing together the first of the three articles on Cedar Ridge. Whenever my mind wandered in Mick's direction—which was often—I tried to concentrate on my job, without much success. Twice I almost called him, but fear of finding him in the middle of some assignation deterred me. What would I say to that? The obvious—who was that woman and who is she to you?—was too hard. I needed to retreat from the emotional brink before we talked. Weird the way you're never sure you want something until you think you've lost it.

"Work, Robyn."

When I flipped the page in my notebook to KittyKat Kendrick's phone number, thoughts of Mick took a break. I needed to call her. I've found that it's sometimes possible to replace one unpleasant thought with another. Talking to KittyKat fit that bill.

I steeled myself with a sip of Scotch and placed the call. Of course, KK was too busy to answer her phone, so I left a message. I wondered what she'd think when she heard my name. It also occurred to me that it would be funny—and not in a humorous way—if she didn't remember me at all.

Around nine o'clock, I made myself a cup of tea—a mix of green with toasted rice—and took it out on my tiny rear porch, which has stairs leading to the parking lot. There wasn't room for much other than a couple of small lawn chairs and an old TV tray. Bix joined me, curling up on his folded green blanket I'd placed in one corner. I wore a heavy sweater and propped my feet on the middle wrung of the railing. Pushing aside thoughts of Mick again, I tried to imagine how my life would change if my mother and I were to buy a house. It wouldn't all be bad. A yard would be nice. Maybe a patio. I wouldn't miss these stairs. In the winter they iced up and could make the trip down to my car a challenge. I'd have to hire someone to stay with my mother when I couldn't be there. While I supposed that there were people who did that sort of thing, I didn't know how to find them. But there were the times when it would be just the two of us. And what about her smoking? Her habit was easy enough to regulate when I kept her cigarettes here. But if we lived in the same house, it'd be tough. I had an image of her sneaking around in the middle of the night looking for a ciggie stash. And this was the point in my interior argument where my rational side piped in with "What are you thinking, girl?"

I was so lost in my rambling thoughts that I didn't notice that Bix had perked up, his skinny tail doing a slow wag. I didn't realize that I was no longer alone until someone said, "Hey."

Fortunately, I had a pretty good grip on my tea mug. But I did bang my ankle on the railing as I swung my feet down so I could turn to see who had joined me. Of course, it was Mick. I knew his voice and there weren't many people Bix got up off his furry butt to greet.

The bare, forty-watt porch bulb threw light on the right side of his face, the side where the little scar bisected his eyebrow. Where he'd fallen on a piece of glass as a kid.

"Mind if I join you?" He wore a denim jacket with his hands shoved in his jeans' pockets.

I shook my head.

He sat in the chair on the other side of the tray and Bix wagged his way over to him. Mick leaned forward, rubbing Bix's head, hitting the spot behind his right ear that turned him into doggie mush. Still rubbing, Mick said, "Saw you at the Dragon."

"Yeah," I nodded. "I need to work on my discreet exits."

He was watching me but didn't say anything.

I tried to read his expression, with no success. "Want some tea?" I asked. "A beer?"

"Beer would be good." As I started to rise, he stopped me with, "I'll get it."

Bix trailed him into the kitchen where I heard the fridge open and close, followed by the spurt of carbonation as Mick wielded the bottle opener. I also heard him dig in the drawer next to the dishwasher for a doggie treat.

When they returned, Bix, still chewing, settled onto his blanket and Mick leaned against the wooden railing so he faced me. He took a swig of the India Pale Ale and set the bottle on the broad top rail.

East of us a freight train echoed in the night as it made its way toward the Argyle Street crossing.

"It was about that talk we had the other night," he finally said.

Puzzled, I tried to recall what I might have missed. "I thought it was a good talk."

"It was." He smiled a little. "It really was."

"There must have been something you didn't like hearing."

He fell silent again, staring out toward the parking lot next door. Turning back to me, he said, "You don't want kids."

I laughed. "No, really."

When he didn't respond, I realized he was serious. "And you do?"

He sighed and crossed his arms over his chest. "I don't know. I guess I'm not ready to say no to the possibility." He shifted. "I mean, it's not like I want to go out and have one right now or anything." He focused on me. "I guess I don't know how you can be so certain."

I pushed up on the arms of the chair to sit up straight. "At some point it's physically impossible."

"I know, I know." He paused, eyeing me. "But it's not too late now. Is it?"

"Well, technically, no." I cocked my chin. "What are you asking?"

"No, no. No." He breathed a frustrated sigh. "I just don't know. That's all."

"Do you want kids?"

"I don't know."

Although I'd visualized and rejected myself as a mother on many occasions, now I took a moment to add Mick to that picture. I was a little ashamed that, despite my feelings for him, the results were still the same. "That would be a deal breaker." I sighed and looked into my mug, thinking the green tea seemed inadequate. "So, what? Right after our talk you ran out and found a young, fecund thing?"

He smiled a little. "Fecund. That's a nasty-sounding word, isn't it?"

"You're changing the subject." I paused. "But, yeah, you're right. It does sound a little obscene."

My cell phone vibrated against my butt. I glanced at the screen and saw that KK Kendrick was returning my call. Great timing, KK.

I silenced the phone. "So, tell me about her."

"That was Kelly. She teaches kindergarten." He reclaimed his beer.

"How did you meet a kindergarten teacher?"

"She's also a client."

I nodded. That was how we met. "So, that's how you respond to this . . . ambiguity of yours. You hook up with the first young thing that crosses your path?"

"That's not true. It wasn't even a date. Not really. She was my last client of the day . . . it was late . . . and she suggested talking over dinner."

"So, it wasn't a date."

He shifted. "Not exactly."

I looked his way and saw he was avoiding me. "You went home with her?"

"No."

"You told her you'd call her?"

He took a gulp of beer, swallowed, and said, "Yeah, I did."

I needed to digest that. Technically, we weren't sworn to each other. There'd been no promises or declarations of love. Still, we'd been a steady item for two months. At least I had. But maybe I'd never passed by the Crystal Dragon at the right moment. It was all about timing. No, I thought. Mick was many things, and they didn't add up to a Boy Scout, but he'd always been honest with me. I sipped my tea, which had turned lukewarm. When I looked up at Mick, I saw that he was waiting for me.

Someone had to say it. "Okay, let me make sure we're both on the same page. You want kids. I don't. Therefore, this isn't going to work out."

"No. Not exactly. Like I said, I'm not sure. But I feel like I'd be leading you on if I said it didn't matter. When I don't know if it matters. But . . ."

"But?"

"I like you. A lot."

"There's that L word again."

"Can you quit being a smart-ass for just a minute?"

"What do you want me to be? What's there to talk about? I don't want children. I have nothing against them. Some of my closest friends have them. Believe it or not, I used to be a child."

He watched me, his head tilted to one side, without speaking for several moments. Then he said. "I'll bet you were an old child."

I did a quick flashback to the childhood of Robyn Guthrie and landed on an image of me watching my mother getting dressed to go out with my stepfather. She was trying various belts over her deep blue shirtwaist as she told me there was Coke in the fridge, and I'd find a partial bag of chips in the pantry. I was twelve and had been babysitting myself for three years at the point. I gave Mick a wan smile. "I was not anticipated. And, yes, I guess you could say I was self-raised." I tipped my head back and looked up into the sky, focusing on some constellation I couldn't name. Maybe Perseus. "I need you to tell me what you want to do." I dropped my head so I could see him. "This is your decision." I wanted to keep talking. To rant until dawn so he wouldn't have to say anything. But I felt my eyes misting up and knew my voice would break, so I swallowed and kept my mouth shut.

"I think," he finally said, "we need to let things cool for a while."

My eyes filled. I swallowed again. "'Let things cool.'" I knew what he meant. He knew I knew what he meant, but I had expected a gutsier response from him.

"At least until we can figure this out."

"We?"

"You have it figured out?"

"I don't know." I blinked a couple of times and looked up at him. "I wonder. If we hadn't had that great talk the other night, would we have blithely gone on until my uterus had shrunk to the size of a raisin and all your brawny, robust sperm had been depleted?"

"I don't think so."

I stood. "Okay, you let me know when you've decided what immortality track you've chosen."

"Robyn—"

I stuffed my cell phone into my jeans' pocket. "I really don't feel like talking anymore right now."

I opened the door to my kitchen. "Come on, Bix."

The warmth in the little galley kitchen felt like a cottony shroud. I dumped the remains of my tea into the sink, rinsed the mug and left it there. It wasn't until I turned to switch off the light that I realized that Bix had chosen to stay on the porch with Mick.

Men.

I stood in the kitchen with only the sound of the electric clock plugging along. After what seemed like a long time, but was probably less than a minute, I heard Mick descending the steps. Not long after that came the scratch on the door. Bix knows who keeps him in kibble. But he walked into the room with an expression that made obvious the origin of the term "hang dog," and so I couldn't help myself but to scoop him up and gave him a hug. Besides, I knew how he felt. He's not a cuddly dog, but he put up with it for a minute before he started squirming. I dug a treat out of the cupboard and gave it to him without requiring a cheesy trick in return. He dropped to the floor and began crunching.

* * *

It was almost ten, later than I normally phone people, but Kitty Kat had waited until nine thirty before she tried to get hold of me, so I figured she'd be up. Besides, she was easier for me to deal with if I considered her a distraction. And sure enough, she answered on the second ring. "Kat Kendrick."

"Hi, uh, Ki-Kat. It's Robyn Guthrie."

"Robyn!" You'd have thought we shared more than a few nasty exchanges between classes. "How are you?"

"Okay. Doing okay."

"I couldn't believe it when Joe told me you were doing this story. Is it a small world or what?"

"Sure is." *A small, stupid world.*

"It's a shame about that poor girl—what was her name?—"

"Clair," I said. "Clair Powell."

"Yeah, that was so sad to hear. Were you friends?"

"I knew her. We were friendly." I stopped there, doubting Kitty Kat cared one way or the other.

When she didn't continue, I asked, "Do you have some time to talk?"

"Over the phone?"

"Well, I know you're busy." *And I have no desire to see you.*

"Why don't we get together? We can do some catching up. I'll be in Fowler tomorrow morning. How about lunch?"

As luck would have it, I was taking my mother to the dentist in the late morning and had promised her lunch at our favorite Mexican restaurant afterwards. The promise of a margarita would mellow her. The dentist would thank me. "Oh," I hoped my delivery conveyed disappointment rather than relief, "I'm taking my mom to lunch tomorrow."

After a pause, she said, "Lizzie? She's still . . . in the area?"

I figured what she almost said was "still alive," but gave her credit for the save. "Yeah, she lives at Dryden Manor. Assisted living."

"I remember your mom."

Most people from that place and time did not actually remember my mother. What they did remember were the circumstances surrounding my stepfather's untimely (not to mention unseemly) demise. He'd been trysting with the church organist when the big one hit, leaving the diminutive musician trapped beneath a rather large, very dead, bank vice president. The organist's cries brought help, but the woman never lived down the humiliation and moved to California later that year, where, I suspect, she abstained, at least from the missionary position.

Before I could suggest another time or place to meet—figuring coffee would be the most expeditious venue—KK said, "Why don't I join you? I'd love to see your mother."

"I don't know. She can be—"

"I love old people." She went on as though she didn't recognize how stupid that sounded. "Besides, if we don't do it tomorrow, I won't be able to make time until next week."

What was it about people who said they loved "old people," as if all old people were the same? It was sort of like saying "I love purple" when what they really love is soft lilac hues and can't handle the harshness of eggplant. But all I said was, "I don't really have that many questions. Your husband—"

"Don't be silly. We'll deal with the questions and then we'll visit. It'll be fun. Like I said, we'll catch up."

With an inward sigh, and only because I really hadn't gotten much information from Joe Kendrick and knew this might take some time, I told her where and when we were eating and said I'd see her at one.

"Great. I'll see you tomorrow. Can't wait," she said and hung up before I had to respond.

Chapter 10

After a restless night, I got up at six the next morning and spent the duration of my shower thinking about Mick. If I hadn't walked past that window when I did, what would have happened? Mick wasn't the kind to sneak around, but how would he have broached the whole thing? By the time I stepped out and tugged the towel off its hook, I'd decided that, for now, there was nothing I could do. He had the choice to make. I'd give him some time with it, but if he expected me to hang around for months while he pondered the pros and cons of fatherhood, he didn't know me all that well. Over the years, I'd learned that my patience and understanding in difficult situations had limits. Funny. When I first met Mick more than two years ago, I never dreamed we'd become a couple. And once we were, I never imagined it would last. And now, here I was feeling like I stood to lose—not only a lover, but a good friend. Maybe my best friend.

I had my interview with architect Glenn Patchen to concentrate on, which was scheduled for ten. I had a little research I wanted to do first. But before I did that, I placed a call to Detective Hedges. Maybe they'd already considered the odd dog-walking route. Or, maybe none of the investigators had dogs, and so it hadn't occurred to them. Hedges was out of the office, and so I left a non-emergency message. If she didn't usually walk Scoop along Keffling, why was she there the night she was killed? Aside from a weird whim, the only reason I could come up with was that she was meeting someone. But why on foot and with her dog?

I started the coffee brewing and made myself an egg white omelet, which I consumed while searching online for information about Patchen.

Per our conversation at Fingal's, I knew this wasn't his first venture into green housing. My Internet search confirmed that he'd made quite a reputation for himself on the east coast before moving to Chicago twelve years ago. I could find no reason for the move other than his marriage to Joanna West, who owned a public relations firm in Chicago. It was really amazing what the Internet will cough up about a person. Private lives were so twentieth century.

Patchen had won a number of awards and just last month he'd spoken at the National Green Building Conference in Raleigh.

After jotting down a few questions, I returned to Clair's notes. Among all the green stuff, there was a reference to Town and Country Residences that had me puzzled. As far as I could tell, it was a nursing home and had nothing to do with Cedar Ridge. I made a note to ask Nita if she knew what that was about. I supposed it was possible that Town and Country was a green nursing home, but I had the feeling that a nursing home wasn't a place to explore environmental innovations. My mother squawked when the temperature in her room dipped below seventy-five.

I dropped that tangent and returned to the notes regarding the design of Cedar Ridge, which were fairly easy to interpret. Like her writing, Clair had a quiet, self-possessed way about her that I really admired.

I remembered one day last spring we had lunch together. Amy, one of the other reporters, had been with us. Amy was your basic fun person. She had an infectious laugh and a way of bringing people out. In the midst of lunch, she'd gotten a call from a source she'd been trying to connect with and had to run over to city hall. That left Clair and me to finish lunch together. It wasn't that I didn't like her. I did. But Amy had been our connection. She'd kept the conversation going. I've never been good at small talk and always been nervous about prolonged silences.

I sat there playing with the bits of shrimp on my salad and tried to think of what to talk about while Clair dropped a few oyster crackers into her Manhattan clam chowder. She was one of those young women who had eschewed long hair, opting for a short, layered crop. She had the features to pull it off—slightly turned up nose sprayed lightly with freckles, deep blue eyes that were so well defined they didn't need eyeliner or mascara. I was studying her, trying to figure out if she actually did have a really thin layer of liner on her upper lid—maybe a tattoo?—when she lifted a spoonful of soup out of the bowl and I noticed for the first time she did have a tattoo on the inside of her right wrist—several curved, squiggly lines.

"That's an interesting tattoo," I said.

She turned her palm up so I could get a better look at it. "It's an Om symbol."

"Oh," I said. "That's Buddhist, right?"

"Yes, it means 'the breath of life.'"

"Are you Buddhist?"

Smiling, she dipped into the chowder again and lifted one shoulder in a shrug. "Kind of, I guess." She began to blend the crackers into the chowder. "I'm not any one religion. I guess I think most faiths have something to teach."

I wasn't sure what to say. Mainly, I was kind of ashamed of myself for being totally bereft of spiritual inclinations. But I was also curious. I was impressed by Clair's composure—she was only twenty-five—and now I wondered if it was a Zen thing.

"Do you meditate?"

"I do. Twice a day." She smiled. "A guy I dated in college was really into it. I took it up so we'd have that in common. Turned out it was the only thing we had in common."

"Been there." I nodded. "Is that when you got the tattoo?"

She'd just taken another mouthful of chowder and had to put her hand to her lips when she started to laugh. After an audible swallow, she said, "You guessed it."

We chuckled over that for a minute, and because I was afraid to wade too deeply into the spirituality quagmire, I asked her where she went to college.

"Mizzou."

"How did you end up at the *Record*?"

"I wanted to work on a weekly. The *Record* was the first place I applied."

"Why a weekly?"

"I want to be connected to a community. Make a difference there." She ate another spoonful of the chowder, chewing thoughtfully before swallowing. "Someday I'm going to own a weekly."

Just like that. And, for some reason, I didn't doubt her.

I remember sitting there, wondering if I'd ever been that sure of myself. When I thought about it, I was certain that I never was. At twenty-five, with my life still ahead of me, it was as though I looked into a crystal ball and saw my future clouded with failure and stupid choices. And like some character in a Kafka novel, I'd spent a lot of years yoked to that future.

Clair had impressed me so much that day that I tried meditation. It didn't take.

Chapter 11

Glenn Patchen sat behind a scarred wooden desk, a mug of steaming coffee cradled between his hands. The chair was also wooden and old, and it creaked when he moved. He had a habit of rocking, so it was as though a loud, persistent cricket had joined us.

I'd met him at the Cedar Ridge development. His office was in a small trailer parked on the perimeter of the site. Trucks labeled "Hurley Construction" rumbled along dirt roads, and a man wearing a yellow hard hat with a set of blueprints tucked under his arm nodded at me as I drove by. The Cedar Ridge area had recently been annexed by Fowler and now constituted its northern boundary. I crossed Riker Road, which was rapidly becoming a string of strip malls and box stores, and drove another couple of miles to a wooded area filled with poplars, ashes and pines, which created Cedar Ridge's southern border. These trees were splashed in shades of red, gold and green. (Interesting to note that not one of these trees resembled a cedar.) The Crystal River was about a half mile farther south.

Two of the duplexes had been completed, and according to my research, there were another twenty-two planned. I'd taken a moment to drive past them.

The first thing I noticed was the solar panels affixed to the steep roofs. I counted fifteen on the side facing me. Beneath the panels was an attractive duplex. The first story of the eastern-most home was painted green and the other side a deep tan. Their second stories shared a white exterior. The building beside it was half two-story and half ranch, all the same shade of pale green. The yards were still dirt, and I assumed that planting would wait until spring.

When Glenn ushered me into his office I was impressed. I didn't expect much of a temporary office set up in an unremarkable trailer. And it wasn't the way it was decorated, which was minimalist, but rather the instant impression of organization that struck me. Metal shelving held neatly stacked books, folders, and a few personal items—a photograph of three young children, a boy and two girls—and a pile of CDs beside a small radio/CD player. The top CD was U2's *The Unforgettable Fire*. Aside from the family desk photos, there were three on the wall, all black and whites capturing images of trees and mountains. I paused at a photo of a tall, pyramid-shaped tree. "Let me guess. A cedar?"

"That's right." He paused. "Clair took that photo. Had it framed for me."

I turned to look at him. Without taking his eyes from the photo, he continued, "Clair took a couple of photography classes from my wife."

Wife? "Really?"

He nodded. "In the city. Joanna is a good teacher, but Clair had some natural abilities."

"I can see that," I said, relieved to learn that Patchen's connection to Clair was through his wife.

I moved on to a large, framed, drawing of Cedar Ridge.

"This will be the finished product?" I asked as he filled a mug of coffee for me. I shook off his offer of cream and sugar.

"That's it," he said with obvious pride.

All the homes were duplexes and most two-stories, but, like the one I'd driven past, three of the units were a combination two-story and ranch.

When I asked about them, Glenn said, "Those have been designed for the disabled."

For a bizarre moment, I wondered what my mother would think of one of these places. Then I executed a virtual head-thunk. Wasn't going to happen. Besides, she wasn't disabled. Not by a long shot. Her short-term memory was seriously impaired, but she could move like a whippet when motivated. Move on, I told myself.

"How many units have been sold?"

Patchen canted his head. "Not as many as we'd hoped by now."

"Why's that?"

"The economy, partly. Also," he pushed his hands into the pockets of his jeans and sighed, "these places are different. They're not luxury by any means. So if you're looking for gourmet kitchens and separate suites for the kids, that's not gonna happen. But now that we've finished the first two, we've got more people looking at the places. I think this is going to be a situation where they sell slowly at the outset, but once potential buyers see that this is not only a responsible life style, it's also a comfortable, affordable one, then I think there'll be a waiting list." He added, "The Kendricks are anticipating that, by the way. They've got their eyes on another piece of property north of here to develop a second community after this one hits ."

I jotted this down beneath Clair's notes that I'd transcribed into my own notebook.

"I'm sorry we've got to go over this again," I said, although he'd given me no indication that he didn't have the time for me. "Clair used shorthand in her notes, and though I can make some of it out, I want to make sure I've got the facts and figures and terms straight."

"Shoot."

"I should have looked this one up, but what is fly-ash concrete?"

"That's a powder-like substance mixed with concrete that improves its performance. We use it in the foundations."

I fired off a number of terms, which he promptly explained. The same with the initials Clair had used.

"JS is Josh Sterns, the Hurley foreman, RD is Rhonda Denholm, the landscape architect," and he went on, explaining what each person did.

I flipped through the notes again. "Speaking of who does what, I found something in Clair's notes about permits, along with the initials CW."

He didn't answer right away. Then he frowned and said, "CW?"

"Right."

Shaking his head, he sighed. "Don't know who that is."

"I can't find the initials anywhere else in her notes. Now I'm really curious."

He flipped his hand in a dismissive gesture. "They're notes. Maybe it doesn't mean anything."

"No. It means something. Just not sure what."

He nodded, but seemed to drift a bit before he said, "That memorial party they had for her. That was a nice thing to do."

"Yeah, it was." I glanced down at her words, rewritten in my hand. "It's the kind of thing they do whenever someone leaves the paper. This time it was a lot sadder."

His cell phone rang and, after checking the number, he pushed a button on the phone and returned it to his pocket.

"Hey, why stand here and look at this drawing when the real thing is fifty feet from here?"

"Let's go." I shoved my notes in my bag and tossed it over my shoulder.

Indian summer had gone and taken with it the warm gusts of air coming up from the south. The sun barely filtered through a crack in the overcast sky. The chill reminded me that we were slipping over into the winter edges of fall. I would have to trade my lightweight jacket in for something warmer soon.

"I drove past these homes before I stopped at your office. They're nice-looking, although I admit the first thing I noticed was the solar panels."

"Yeah, but I think one day we'll be used to them, and they'll be what roofs look like."

As we headed toward the homes, I had to walk fast to keep up with him; both his legs and his stride were long. He swept his arm toward the east. "We're leaving a wide berth between Cedar Ridge and Riker Road, although the property comes right up against the western boundary of all those stores along Riker. We're making the area a park with a walking path. Maybe some picnic tables. The trees stay. I don't know what they've got planned for the riverfront." He gazed off toward the south. "But if they decide to put up one of those casinos, we want to make sure we've got a buffer."

"Is that the plan?"

"There are rumors."

From his tone, I gathered this wasn't a happy thought for Glenn. I couldn't blame him. The idea of a green community rubbing up against a gambling haven seemed an unpleasant juxtaposition.

As we approached the homes, Glenn said, "These are all situated to take advantage of the southern exposure for both passive and active solar energy. Either the back or the front of each home faces south. The windows on the south side all have high efficiency windows. Double pane. On the east, north and west sides where you need more efficiency, we're using triple pane.

"And over here," he gestured toward land east of the homes, "this will be the community area. A community garden, a barbecue, and a playground covered in TotTurf." He looked down at me. "Uses recycled rubber tires instead of mulch."

I tried to visualize this and did pretty well imagining families, dogs and the smell of burgers—organic, of course—on the grill.

He'd slowed his pace now, taking in the surroundings. "We're hoping to build a true community, not just a place where people live."

"When does the landscaping happen?"

"In the spring." He stopped and looked around at his work in progress. "We need to manage the new growth carefully. Rhonda is handling all that. There have to be maximum mature heights for all plantings so they don't interfere with solar access."

"Was this area in use before Green Haven bought it?"

He paused, shaking his head. "Not to my knowledge. But the Kendricks would know better."

"How do you like working with them?"

"Mostly I deal with Kat. She's a bright woman." He grinned. "Of course, she hired me, so I would say that, wouldn't I?"

We continued toward the buildings. "These units have from two to four bedrooms. All of them have a small footprint—fourteen hundred square feet—and an open floor plan." We walked a few more steps. "These homeowners can expect to save about twenty-five hundred dollars annually in energy costs."

"Impressive."

"It is." Then he said, "Let's take a look at one."

As we headed toward the first duplex, the one with the green and tan exterior, a small hatchback came up behind us, a woman behind the wheel. Glenn waved to her as she drove past and pulled into a driveway.

"That's Mary Alice Tucker. You'll want to talk to her. She and her two sons will be the first family to move in. This weekend, in fact. But she's been bringing stuff over." He smiled, "She says they're planning to move everything themselves—everything that doesn't take a burly man to lift."

Mary Alice climbed out of her car and reached under the dashboard for her purse. The passenger doors opened and two boys—

probably around ten and twelve, although I'm not the best judge when it comes to kids' ages—spilled out. The older one had the same wavy red hair as his mother and was already an inch or two taller. The younger boy had dark, straight hair and was a bit stockier than his brother.

Mary Alice approached us, smiling. She was trim and petite with clear, gray-green eyes. "Hey, Glenn, you come to lend a hand or are you just showing off?"

Glenn returned the smile. "You might be able to talk us into making a trip or two, provided you give us the grand tour."

"It's a deal." She stopped in front of us and the boys came up behind her.

When Glenn introduced us, Mary Alice said to me, "God, I was so sad to hear about Clair."

"Thanks. We all were." After we shook hands, I asked if she'd known Clair.

"Yeah, she interviewed me as the first homeowner." She laughed a little. "Called me a 'pioneer.' She was so nice." Mary Alice gave me the once over, and I felt as though I were being sized up, with Clair Powell representing the ideal. But then she introduced me to her sons. The older boy's name was Alex and he sort of grunted a greeting. I guessed he was at an age where he wasn't sure what to do with his growth spurt yet, and he slouched a bit. Although the younger boy, Bobby, said it was nice to meet me, I sensed this was a scripted line and, judging from the way he was bouncing around, he wanted to get moving.

With a warm smile, Mary Alice said to me, "I'll bet you weren't counting on heavy lifting today."

"It's okay. I was looking for an excuse to skip my weight training."

"Let's get some moving done," Glenn said.

The rear of the car was crammed with boxes, bags and a large, wicker basket piled with yarn.

Glenn and I grabbed whatever Mary Alice told us to grab and headed for the house. She ran ahead and unlocked the door. "Just put everything in the living room. We'll sort it all out."

It took us each about three trips, but eventually the contents of her car joined the pile of boxes already there.

"Thanks so much," she said with a sigh when we'd deposited the last box. "I can't believe one two-bedroom apartment held all that crap. Even though we did get rid of a lot of stuff."

"That may be the best reason to move. Crap trimming."

"Isn't that the truth?"

The boys had each selected a box with their name on it and were headed up the stairs to the second floor.

"You start putting that stuff away now and there'll be less to do when we're all moved in," Mary Alice called after them.

"Sure, Mom," Bobby said. Alex just kept climbing.

Mary Alice turned her attention back to us. "I'd offer you something to drink, but we haven't got anything in the refrigerator yet. Anyone like a glass of water?"

"No, thanks," I said. "I'd just like to see the rest of the place."

With a flourish of her hand, Mary Alice turned the tour over to Glenn. "I'm going to unpack some things in the kitchen."

Glenn looked down at the wooden floor and tapped it with his foot. "Okay. Starting here. The flooring throughout the house, except for the kitchen, entryway, and bathroom which are linoleum, is bamboo. Sustainable."

The living room was a decent size with a closet tucked into an alcove off the entrance. The room opened to a dining room and a galley kitchen. Adjacent to the stairs was a half bath.

"But what really sets these places apart is something you can't see here. I'll have to show you in one of the places under construction." He walked up to the east wall and put his hand against it and patted. "There are double walls. There's twelve inches between the inner and outer wall and that twelve inches is filled with cellulose insulation."

"What's that?" I asked as I jotted in my notebook.

"You'll like this." He smiled. "It's made from recycled newspapers."

I nodded. "I do like that." And who said we don't need the print media anymore?

He pointed toward the ceiling. "Those panels you saw on the roof convert solar radiation into direct current radiation for electricity and hot water."

As he explained how this happened, I had the feeling he'd delivered this speech many times before. But, he could still work up some excitement. And when he said, "These homes are zero-net-energy. They produce almost as much energy as they use," he was nearly giddy. It was nice to see someone so outwardly proud of what he'd put together.

Glenn's phone rang again and, after checking the number, he scowled briefly before answering the call. As he listened, his expression darkened. "What the hell—" He stopped as he looked at me, lowered the phone and after taking a deep breath said, "Excuse me for a second, Robyn. I've got to take this." Without waiting for my response, he walked away, and with his long stride was halfway out the door before returning to the call. He slammed the door behind him with such force that the house shook.

Mary Alice stuck her head out of the kitchen. "What was that about?"

"I think he was just testing the structure." I added, "It seems quite sound."

"Well, I guess there's a lot of pressure in that job he's got." She ducked into the kitchen.

I took the time to check my notes to see if there was anything I was forgetting to ask. When Glenn returned a scant minute later, he looked like he'd dragged one of the low-hanging clouds in with him. "Sorry about that," he said, seeming embarrassed by his outburst.

"Anything wrong?" I asked.

He shook his head. "No . . . well, yeah. A problem with a supplier." He focused over my shoulder. "This stuff happens."

"What's—"

"I'm sorry, but we're going to have to continue this some other time."

"No problem. Can I come by later this week?"

He shook his head again. "I don't know. I'll call you."

"Yeah. Okay, sure."

"Look, I'm sorry. Really." He stuffed his hands into his pockets. "I've got to get this taken care of or we're off schedule by a month."

"Sure, I understand. But I am on deadline. This is due next week." I wasn't and it wasn't, but I didn't care for the way he was running off on me.

"I'll call you," he said again as he inched his way toward the door. Mary Alice was watching from the kitchen. "I'll show her around."

He thanked her and ducked out.

I watched him walk down the street, his head bowed and his shoulders stiff. If this kind of stuff happened with regularity, Glenn Patchen probably needed a masseuse in his life.

"Glenn's a really good guy," Mary Alice said after hoisting a box onto the kitchen counter. She opened one of the cupboards, which had already been lined with shelf paper.

"He is," I had to agree. "If I were moving into a home, I'd sure like to have the architect helping me move boxes."

I glanced around the room, noting a few empty boxes and plenty of full ones. "I see you've already been busy."

She patted the shelf. "My mother was a stickler about shelf paper. She wouldn't put a paper cup on a shelf that wasn't lined."

"Our mothers," I said.

"Yeah."

Mary Alice used a small knife to slice open the box, which was filled with items wrapped in newspapers.

"Let me help you with that," I said.

"Oh, thanks. You've already done plenty." She stopped. "Wait. I was going to show you around wasn't I?" She shook her head. "I swear, I need a prompter."

"Don't worry about that now. Why don't I help you with this first? I'd like to keep up the direction Clair was going with this article, and getting to know you will help. You talk and I'll listen and try to be helpful."

"Okay. Thanks. You unwrap these glasses and I'll find homes for them."

"How did you learn about Cedar Ridge?" I asked as I uncovered a blue tumbler.

"A friend of mine works for an architect who knows Glenn. This friend knew I was looking to find a reasonably priced place for me and my boys. I loved the idea of the development. I'm trying make the boys more aware of their impact on this planet. It's hard. We were in an apartment that wasn't doing recycling, so I started taking bottles and papers to the facility myself. Got the boys involved. You know, I'm not any fanatic, but I do know there are ways to change how you live just a little bit and maybe make a difference. I mean, you can't look at all the waste a small family like mine produces and not feel a little queasy about it."

"I know what you mean." I handed her a pair of wine glasses. Actually, I didn't do much beyond recycling, and I wondered if it weren't picked up by the city, would I bother to take it to the center?

"And the boys, God, they're excited. They've always shared a room. They're pretty good about it, but they're boys, you know?"

I just nodded and plucked out a water glass.

"And they're excited about the neighborhood. Can't wait till there's more families and kids moved in. This winter will be kind of tough for them, I think, but once the homes get built and filled up, it'll be good.

"And, you know, I've got to admit that I'm as excited as they are. I'm thirty-six years old and, since I've been an adult I've never lived in a place I haven't rented."

That sounded familiar. I just gave her a sympathetic nod.

She moved one glass from the bottom to the middle shelf and pushed it back a ways. Then she looked at me as I held out another piece of glassware on its way to its new home. "God, I am going on, aren't I?"

"You're excited and I don't blame you. This is going to be a real community. That's got to be kind of hard to find in an apartment."

I looked out the window at the lot across the street. "Does it bother you that not many of the units have sold?"

"Yeah, it does. But I think once they start showing off the model, they'll start selling. I hope."

Just then the sound of a small person pounding his way down the stairs interrupted us. Bobby, the younger boy, burst into the kitchen.

"Okay if I go check the place out?" His eyes were bright as he bounced up and down on his toes in his excitement.

Mary Alice glanced at her watch. "Okay, but we're leaving in thirty minutes, so don't be long."

"I won't."

He had turned and was about to launch himself out the door when his mother stopped him. "Bobby, say good-bye to Miss Guthrie."

Slamming on the brakes, he looked up at me and said, "Good-bye, Ma'am." As an afterthought, he added, "It was nice to meet you."

"Thanks, Bobby. Nice meeting you too." Even though I hated being called "Ma'am."

"What's your brother doing?" Mary Alice asked him.

"I don't know. Looking out the window, I think."

"Okay, go. Have fun. But not too much."

His feet banged across the wood floors and the door slammed shut behind him. Watching after him, Mary Alice smiled and said, "I love that sound. At the apartment, the boys have to walk around the place with their shoes off so the couple downstairs doesn't bitch."

"You said Clair called you a pioneer. Do you feel like one?"

"A little bit. I think once spring comes there will lots more places filling up. I know I took a chance on this, but I know a good thing, and this is a good thing."

"You're not worried about being out here by yourself and one or two other families?"

"No. Not at all." She laughed. "Besides, I'm used to being alone. Bobby and Alex's dad split five years ago."

"Sorry," I said.

"Most days I'm not."

"So, you're officially moving in this weekend?"

"Saturday. Can't wait. I guess the Sanduskys are moving in next week."

"Your neighbors?"

"Yeah, seem like a nice couple. Have a set of twins. There's another couple with one kid, I think. Not sure when they're moving into the other unit."

Mary Alice folded the flaps in on the now empty cardboard box, set it aside and leaned against the counter, sighing as she crossed her arms over her chest. "I hope we like it." It was then, when she wasn't animated, that I noticed how stress had etched itself into her face. She was a pretty woman, but she was also a tired woman and had probably had way too much on her mind for a long time. "This is it, you know," she said quietly. "I'm putting everything I've got into the place. Money and energy." She looked at me. "What is it about the American dream that says we all should want this? I don't know, but it sure is ingrained, isn't it?"

After a few seconds, I nodded and said, "Yeah, I guess it is."

"Well, you've probably got a lot to do. I don't mean to keep you and put you to work."

"That's okay. I enjoyed it." I nodded. "I'm happy for you."

"Thanks."

I lifted my purse off the counter. "Can I take a peek at the upstairs before I go?"

"Of course." She hesitated. "I need to make a quick phone call. Bobby's teacher. Can you just go on up? Alex is there. He'll show you around."

"No problem."

I climbed the stairs, which were next to the kitchen, and emerged into a small hallway with a bedroom door entrance to the right. The bedroom was empty except for a few boxes marked "Mom." There was one full bathroom and two more bedrooms, one of which had boxes marked "Bobby." In the third bedroom Alex was sprawled on the floor, using the mottled afternoon light to illuminate the pages in a book. When I saw he was reading, I decided not to disturb him, but as I backed away, he looked up, startled.

"Sorry," I said. "I just wanted to see the upstairs."

Self-conscious, he got to his feet, finger combing a thick lock of hair off his forehead. "S'okay."

"What're you reading?"

He held up a paperback edition of *The Two Towers*. I nodded. "I love those books."

His shoulders jerked a little in what might have been a laugh or just a sign of agreement. "Me too."

I looked around this room with boxes marked "Alex." "How do you like your room?"

"It's awesome." He almost smiled.

"Can you show me around?"

"Uh, sure." He folded the corner of the page on his book and tucked it under his arm. "Um, this is my room. I got to pick. I'm oldest."

"Seems fair." I glanced around. "Why this one? It's not the biggest, is it?"

"No, but it's got this cool thing in the closet." He showed me how the closet had a built-in shelf in one corner, which held a few books and computer games.

"That is cool," I agreed.

"And I like looking out the window."

I took in the view of the north where park and walking path would be located. "Really," I said, "there's not a bad view here, is there?"

"Guess not."

He showed me the rest of the second floor, explaining how they were used to one bathroom and had worked their schedules so no one suffered.

"And that," he pointed at an exhaust in the ceiling, "circulates the outside air through the house."

"Quiet, isn't it?"

"Yeah, my mom likes that."

I thanked Alex for his tour of the upstairs and told him I hoped he enjoyed his new home.

Back in the kitchen, I found Mary Alice sitting on the floor with her back against a cabinet drinking a glass of water. "Chairs," she said. "I keep forgetting to bring a chair or two."

When she started to push herself up off the floor, I stopped her. "Don't get up. Just sit. Relax. I should be going. But I would like to talk with you again when you're moved in. Maybe get a few photos."

"Sure." She looked past me, as though distracted by some thought.

As I turned to leave, she said, "Do you think they'll find who killed Clair?"

"I don't know," I said truthfully. "I hope so."

"She wanted to see the place after we moved in."

I nodded.

"I called her that day. That night, actually. She'd wanted to talk to me about something. Not sure what. But we were having trouble connecting." She shook her head. "Strange thinking I might have left a message for someone who wasn't alive anymore."

* * *

On the way home, my cell phone went off. I pulled over and took the call, which was from Hedges. After I explained my dog-walking theory, he said, "I've got a dog. We walk wherever he wants to go."

Figured.

But he continued, "You have any ideas who—if anyone—she might have been meeting?"

I admitted that I didn't. "But Clair was smart. She wouldn't have been meeting just anyone at that hour. What time do they think it was? Ten or eleven?"

"That's the estimate."

"It would have to be someone she knew. And trusted."

"If she was smart—and I'm not arguing that—why would she be meeting someone on a dark road?" he asked.

"Maybe he or she didn't want to be seen talking to a reporter."

He sighed deeply, but, before he hung up, he said he'd look into it.

I was pretty sure I'd be the only one pursuing the dog-walking-route theory. But it didn't hurt to set someone else to thinking about it.

I tried de Coriolis again. I'd called him yesterday and asked one of his minions to have him get back to me. He didn't. This time I talked to a female minion but was no more optimistic that my call would be returned.

Next, I called Nita. I wanted to see if she knew about Clair's interest in photography.

"Come to think of it," she said after I asked, "I did see her schlepping around a serious-looking camera on occasion."

"Do you know what happened to it?"

"I think Ike gave it to her father at the memorial."

"Speaking of the memorial, did you know that Clair was taking a photography class from Glenn Patchen's wife?"

"What's that got to do with the memorial?"

"Nothing. Just reminded me."

"Her photography teacher?"

"That's what I said."

"Really."

"That's what Glenn told me." I didn't think Nita would care for my next question, but I had to ask it. "If you'd known that, would you have given Clair the story?"

A pause. A long one. "I don't know. Maybe not." Then she added, "Although this is hardly an exposé."

That wasn't the point and she knew it—a conflict of interest either was or it wasn't. This was. "So, Clair's parents have her camera."

"Right. B-but what's the camera got to do with anything?" I could tell I was starting to exasperate her.

"I'm not sure, Nita. But it seems as though Clair processed a lot of things visually—"

"Again, what's that got to do with a story on Cedar Ridge?"

"Maybe nothing. Probably nothing. It's just something I want to follow through on. I mean, she might have taken some photos she meant to use."

"That's what we've got Ike for."

"Humor me, Nita."

I heard her sigh. "Robyn, I know we're all handling this in different ways. She was hit by a car. It's sad and tragic and really ugly that no one came forward, but it happens. I just . . . don't want you making more out of this than what it is."

"What if there is more to it?"

She didn't respond, but I could hear her breathing.

"Are her folks still in town?"

Finally, she said, "Yeah. They're staying at her apartment."

"If there is more to this, you'd want to know, wouldn't you?"

I could picture her, glasses off, pressing the bridge of her nose between her thumb and forefinger. "Just don't be upsetting them, Robyn."

"They already are upset, Nita."

Chapter 12

Any meeting I had with Mara would have to wait until after my mother's dentist appointment, followed by a late lunch with my mother and KittyKat. I had a little time. So I went home and took Bix for a short walk before heading over to Dryden to collect my mother.

The dentist appointment went fairly well. These places usually made my mother anxious, but she was proud of the fact that she hadn't lost any teeth, so she endured. I'd managed to find a dentist who was used to working with older people and, unless there were shots involved, my mother did all right. Today was just a cleaning, and I hadn't been called out of the waiting room, so her agitation factor must have been low. As the hygienist escorted her back to the waiting room, I could hear my mother asking her what kind of margarita she preferred.

Mom and I arrived at Ernesto's about ten minutes before I told Kat—I had to remember to drop the "Kitty"—we'd be there. I wanted to get my mother settled, her drink ordered and the menu discussed.

"Mrs. Guthrie," Janine, the waitress, greeted her. "It's good to see you."

"And you too, dear," my mother's smile wavered—a sure sign that she had no idea who this young woman was.

"Hey, Janine," I said. "My mother will have her usual," I looked at her for confirmation, "Strawberry margarita?"

"*S'il vous plait*," she said with exaggerated graciousness. My mother had taken two years of French in college and although she may forget my name at times, she almost never fails to dredge up a French phrase—sometimes badly mangled—when she wants to flaunt her charm.

When Janine went to fill our drink orders, I said to my mother, "You remember I told you that Katherine—Kat—Jamison will be here today."

"Of course I remember." She buried her nose in the menu. I suspected she'd been bruised by the lapse with the waitress and was trying to regroup. She got frustrated with herself when her memory failed, as it was doing more often lately. I knew there might come a time when she wouldn't remember that she'd forgotten, and I wondered if that would be preferable.

"Robyn!"

I looked up and there she was—Katherine "Kitty" Jamison—looking even better than she had in high school. Whenever I bemoan the world's lack of justice, I wonder if it's a karma-related thing. Everyone who gets dumped on in this life had it coming from a previous existence. If so, I hope I enjoyed being an awful person.

Her dark hair had lightened to a soft shade of red and she wore it long with the edges curling over her shoulders. Her fitted green jacket was open to reveal a low-cut white sweater that showed some cleavage. She bottomed out the outfit with a pair of skinny jeans. She looked tan and fit. When I thought about it, she'd always been one of the first to tan, but her face today showed hardly a line. Where was the justice?

I stood to greet her and she embraced me like I was her long lost sister. "It's so good to see you, Robyn." She placed me at arm's length for a good look. "I love your hair," she said.

"Um, thanks," I said, not sure if I should obsess over what she said or what she didn't say. *Later*. I gestured toward my mother who had placed a finger on a menu item while she watched the exchange.

"This is my mother, Lizzie Guthrie."

"Of course it is." Kat grabbed my mother's hands, pressing them between her own bejeweled fingers. I folded my own fingers against my palms when I noticed her French manicure. Kat seemed oblivious to my mother's moment of panic. She'd lost her place on the menu and might never remember what she'd decided to order. But I was proud of her because she recovered quickly and when Kat said, "Do you remember me, I used to be Katherine Jamison," Mom barely batted an eye before saying, "Of course I do."

By the time we'd settled into our chairs, Kat had flagged over Janine and ordered a margarita. My mother beamed. Kat patted her hand before releasing it and opening her menu.

"So, tell me what you've been up to all these years, Robyn." She looked up from her menu with that huge smile of hers as she cocked her chin.

How to sum up an undistinguished life so it didn't sound pathetic? But I'd anticipated the question, so I'd prepared a pat response. "Oh, the usual ups and downs. Been making a living at writing. Ghosted a few books." In truth I'd ghosted only one book, but that was the beauty of ghosting. How would she know if I'd embellished? "What about you? And I want to hear about the foundation."

She glanced up at the molded tin ceiling with a sigh. "Oh, where to start?"

My mother focused on Kat as she related her life's adventures since high school. First there'd been college—University of Illinois and Georgetown for law school. Work at a prestigious (I'd have to take her word on that) law firm in Los Angeles. Meeting Joe Kendrick while on a trip to Tibet. Marrying him six months later in an outdoor wedding at the foot of the Himalayas. "Our sherpa was best man!" They'd both worked for a number of years before having a family. "Russell, our son, is on an internship in the Amazon."

Good Lord, I thought as she paused to give Janine her order, I was living the Christmas letter from hell.

My mother's crooked finger hovered over a couple of items in the menu. She seemed to be wavering, so I leaned over. "You usually like the chicken fajitas." Just as she nodded and opened her mouth, Kat jumped in, "Have you ever tried a quesadilla, Lizzie? They're wonderfully cheesy and not real spicy." My mother brightened and said to Janine, "I think I'll try one of those."

Janine had left our drinks and I wrapped my hand around my Scotch. Usually, if I drink at lunch, it's only wine or beer, but today called for something stronger.

Kat raised her eyebrows as she watched me take a sip. Perhaps she'd have commented on it, but that might have changed the subject, so she quickly got back on track. "Joe and I have always loved travel." She broke of the corner off a nacho chip and dipped it into the salsa. "Do you travel much, Robyn?"

"Not as much as I'd like to," I said. *Right this second I wish I were in an alternate universe.*

"You know," she paused, reflecting, "it's difficult to be closed-minded if you travel a lot. Joe and I have seen so much of the world. We developed great respect for other cultures, people. And great respect for this amazing planet. Its diversity. It's a living organism."

I nodded, thinking I didn't need to write this down; somehow I was sure I'd remember the gist here.

"And we recognized the fragility of the ecosystem and how man's presence has compromised it. We wanted to do something about it. So, about eight years ago we started Green Haven Foundation. Our purpose is to fund projects and causes that work to protect the environment." She leaned across the table to make her point. "Someone has to do this. This needs to be done."

Without warning, she snatched her purse, which was slung from the back of her chair. "Excuse me for just a moment."

As she headed toward the women's room, I sat there wondering how I could find someone whose beliefs were probably quite similar to mine so thoroughly sanctimonious.

I glanced my mother's way to see how she'd reacted to Kat's life of introspection and dedication, and was a little surprised to find her studying me.

Slipping into defensive mode, I said, "What?"

"Have you ever thought of showing some cleavage?"

She dabbed her finger at the crusted salt rimming her glass and licked it.

When Kat returned to the table, I noticed she'd reapplied her lipstick. Who did that right before eating? And with that margarita, she'll have salt sticking to her lips.

I told myself to chill. High school had been more than twenty-five years ago. Kat had obviously moved on. Maybe it was time for me to do the same.

Over lunch Kat did most of the talking and my mother listened, apparently enraptured by my classmate's wisdom and worldliness. We heard how she and Joe got into green housing—a combination of foresight and concern for the environment. They lived in Minneapolis. She talked more about their son, Russell, who was spending his Amazonian internship searching for the cure for cancer and, at the same time, attempting to save the rain forests. I took notes, but I'd also brought a recorder so I didn't miss anything. It seemed to me that she enjoyed talking about herself and her son more than Cedar Ridge, but my take may have been just a tad skewed.

* * *

My mother wobbled a bit when I returned her to Dryden—probably those two margaritas. I knew the second wasn't a good idea, but it's hard to deny a woman a drink when she has the rest of the afternoon to nap. She'd indulged in the strawberry-laden variety, and I could appreciate how much she enjoyed them. And now

I wanted to make sure she got to her room and her bed without incident, so I dropped her at the door with orders to wait for me on one of the porch benches while I parked the car.

There must have been some kind of guest activity going on because there was a dearth of parking spaces in the lot. I wound up pulling into a space beside a lamp pole in the farthest row. As I strolled toward the entrance, enjoying the brisk weather, I got to thinking about Mick and how I probably owed him a phone call. But I wasn't sure if I was ready to make it yet. Putting myself in Mick's place that night we had the "really good" talk, I could see how the whole "I don't want kids" thing might have set him back on his heels. I guess I'd never mentioned it before because I didn't think it needed saying. I mean, wasn't it obvious that I was not the nurturing type? Maybe Mick didn't see it that way.

Anyway, he'd said he needed some time to work things out, and maybe I needed to tell him that that was okay. I wouldn't promise to wait for him—I mean, who knew what (or who) might come along while he was out there dating the nubility? But maybe I did need to be more understanding. I have a tendency to cling to my gut reaction—and I felt betrayed seeing him at the restaurant with someone else—riding it like an out-of-control horse that sometimes took me along with it over a cliff.

I was musing over my propensity for self destruction when I looked up and saw two women sitting on the cedar bench across from my mother and I stopped. Of course, there was nothing to do but keep going, but I really did consider doing an about-face and scurrying back to my car. Since she wasn't alone, surely one of these women would see that she found her way to her room. But not even I was capable of such behavior. Although it meant that I would have to confront my mother's friend, Azalea and, I assumed, her realtor daughter. She had the same thick hair and widow's peak as her mother and the same way of tightly crossing one leg over her other. Already my mother was waving at me as though she were flagging a cab in a hailstorm. I sighed and kept moving.

"Robyn, dear, what perfect timing." She glowed. "This is Azalea and her daughter—the one I was telling you about."

"I'm Sharon," the woman said, smiling as she stood to offer me her hand.

"Nice to meet you," I lied, noting that her firm grip went along with her tall, athletic build.

I said hello to Azalea who looked as though she were about to nod off and settled on the bench next to my mother. She must have still been feeling those margaritas because she patted my leg, an unusual gesture for a Guthrie. Then she leaned forward and said to Sharon, "Dear, would you tell my daughter what you were saying about the housing market?" She spoke in a loud whisper, as though she were afraid someone might overhear some nugget about the market that only realtors were privy to.

Sharon pushed a lock of dark hair behind her right ear and, giving my mother a smile and wink, said to me, "It really is the perfect time to be buying, Robyn. Especially here in Fowler. You can get a lot of home for your money."

Beside her, Azalea's eyes drooped as she said, "I think I need to go to my room, dear."

Before Sharon could respond, my mother clasped her slender hands together and looked up at me, almost as though she were directing a prayer my way. "Do you hear that, Robyn? We could get a nice place. A large place." Sharon was nodding, as though encouraging my mother to keep going. She should have known it wasn't necessary. "Robyn, I know your place is too small." A little snort. "Why, it's barely large enough for you." Addressing Sharon, she continued, "She's got one bedroom, a wretched little living area and a kitchen you can barely turn around in."

"It's not about the kitchen," I said. "It's about the cook."

Sharon turned her wide, toothy smile on me. "Isn't that the truth?"

I nodded, not wanting to encourage the housing discussion with a verbal reply. I unhooked my mother's cane from the bench's arm and put my hand under her elbow to help her up.

As I did, my mother's smile melted. "Aren't you going to talk to her about the house?"

"It's not a good time, Mom. I've got to be somewhere in—"

"You never have time for me," she started. "Why you—"

"Lizzie," Sharon interrupted, "this really isn't a good time. I don't have listings with me. I have nothing to show you or Robyn. And," she patted her mother's shoulder, "I need to get Mom to her room."

Azalea was having a hard time keeping her head upright.

"Oh." My mother teetered beside me.

"Maybe we could set up an appointment," Sharon suggested, her smile wavering.

"Good idea," I said, and before I could steer my mother into the building, Sharon had whipped out a business card and was handing it to me. I took it.

"Can you come by tomorrow? Around ten?"

When I hesitated, she added, "No pressure, Robyn. We can talk." She glanced at my mother when she said that, and I had the feeling she sensed the dynamic.

I found myself liking her despite the havoc she had the potential to wreak on my life, and so I agreed to be there around ten. She seemed a reasonable person, and once I explained my ambivalence—or should I say aversion—to living with my mother, Sharon would understand. Surely, she would understand.

Chapter 13

It was late afternoon before I got to Clair's. Mara opened the door. She looked more tired than she had at the memorial. She wore a pair of red-rimmed glasses, which seemed to only accentuate the dark circles under her eyes. But she smiled when she saw me and stepped back so I could walk past her and into the room. It was filled with boxes, and there was little trace of Clair's personality in the bare walls and the few pieces of furniture left. I'd never been in Clair's apartment, but I imagined the rooms would have been profoundly Clair.

"How are you doing?" I asked Mara.

She sighed. "Moving along. I think it helps that there's things to be done. Once we get home, I think it'll be harder."

"What are you doing with her things?"

"Donating them. Mostly. There are a few items we'll take home. Some of her paintings. A few knick-knacks. Part of me wants to box everything up and take it home. But there are people who can use her clothing."

I smiled, thinking of Clair's quirky style. "Interesting people."

She nodded.

I glanced around. "Is your husband here?"

"Jack took some boxes to Goodwill."

I gestured toward the window facing the street. "I've got a hatchback. Why don't you let me take a load when I leave?"

"Thank you. That would help."

She moved into the kitchen. "Would you like some wine?"

"Sure," I said, not at all sure I should be joining her.

"White okay?"

"Fine."

She opened the white refrigerator door and pulled a three-quarters full bottle of sauvignon blanc from a wine holder, yanked the cork out and poured generous portions into two juice glasses. As she took a sip from her own, she handed me a glass with lemon wedges printed on it. Then, with the heel of her hand she jammed the cork into the bottle, and after a moment's hesitation, returned it to the fridge.

We took the wine into the living room where there was only a magenta futon to sit on. We drank in silence for a minute. The wine had a sour aftertaste.

Just as I was thinking the silence had gone on too long and was searching for something to say, Mara said, "I really don't know if I want to go home. I know Clair hasn't lived with us, well, really, since college, but she's always been a real presence. We'd tease her about converting her bedroom to a workout room, but we never would have. I always wanted her to have a place to come home to."

I set the wine on a box beside the couch. "There's no hurry to do anything with her room at home."

Swallowing, she nodded.

"I thought we'd have grandchildren. I would have enjoyed that."

"The rest of your life is going to be different. But that doesn't mean it can't be good."

The way she looked at me, I thought she was going to tell me I had no idea what the rest of her life would be like, but instead, she gave me a weak smile and said, "You didn't come here to listen to me."

"I'm a pretty good listener." For some reason, the purpose of my visit seemed to have diminished in importance. And the last thing I wanted to do was cause Clair's mother any more pain.

"Thank you," she said, and returned to her wine.

I was thinking of something to say when Mara surprised me with: "The landlord said the police had been here."

"Really?"

Turning toward me, she nodded. "That bothered me too."

"It was probably part of their investigation. Standard procedure."

"I suppose."

Now I was back on track. While it might have been standard procedure, it also indicated they thought they might find something.

"Did Clair have a camera?"

"Yes, she did. That photographer at the newspaper gave it to Jack the night of Clair's memorial."

I remembered Ike talking with Jack at the table.

"Would it be okay if I took a look at the photos?"

"Why?" She turned toward me, folding one leg under her other as she shifted on the couch. "Did you learn something?"

"I don't know, Mara. Probably not. I just don't want to miss anything."

After studying me for a long moment, she set her glass down and pushed herself up from the couch. "I put it in my bag. Looked at some of the photos. There's a lot there. Mostly it seemed to be friends. And her dog."

She retrieved a Nikon SLR with a serious-looking zoom lens from her bag on the kitchen counter.

When she handed it to me she said, "What are you looking for?"

"I'm not sure." I shook my head. "I'm probably looking for something that doesn't exist."

"Would you like some more wine?"

"Sure. Thanks." I hadn't made much of a dent in my wine, but she'd already gone for the bottle.

Most of the three hundred photos didn't require much examination. There were the usual shots of her friends. Many of Scoop. And, yes, Patchen had been right. Some of the photos were quite good. She had a talent for choosing the right detail. A pink blossom growing out of a stone wall. A close up of a young wood duck so vivid you could practically feel the texture in its pin feathers. I showed a few of them to Mara.

Then I came to a group of about ten photos without much in the way of artistic merit. It looked as though they'd been taken from a car—in one I could see the top of the door. The subject was another car—a blue Acura—and I couldn't see more than silhouettes inside. The car had pulled next to a Mercedes in a parking lot. There were two photos of the Acura, another of someone emerging from the passenger side. The car blocked the camera's view. There were also a couple shots of the Acura pulling away and another shot of its rear, with the license plate visible, although blurred, and then the camera returned to the former passenger opening the door of the Mercedes. And lo and behold . . .

I stopped.

"What?" Mara must have read my expression.

"I'm not sure. Is it okay if I copy some of these to my computer?"

"If you tell me why."

Fair enough. "Look at these photos." I flipped through the series I'd been examining. "These aren't photos of friends or nature shots. It looks like she's photographing some kind of meeting. I want to know why."

"Who is that man?"

"I'm not sure," I lied. I didn't want her getting involved. "But I promise I'll tell you if I learn something." That I could do.

After downloading the photos onto my computer, I tried not to rush through my wine, although I was anxious to get out of there. And when Jack returned about fifteen minutes later I grabbed the chance to leave, but not before I helped him load several boxes into my Matrix.

On my way to Goodwill, I considered my next move and decided, against my better judgment, that it would involve Mick.

I hated going to him right now about something work related. But we worked well together, so maybe that was a good way to get us communicating again. Besides, I didn't know who else could help me. I suppose it might have been coincidence that the guy in this photo—Ed Leoni—had entered my life at the same time this Cedar Ridge story and Kendrick had, but I doubted it.

Chapter 14

I pulled into Mick's driveway around eight P.M., an hour after I'd called him. I hadn't mentioned the reason for my visit, just said I wanted to stop by, but figured he would assume I was coming to talk about the elephant that had entered our room. And while I was sure the subject would come up, the purpose of my visit at this time had everything to do with the man in Clair's photo and only partly reflected my desire for Mick to make a decision. Maybe because I knew if I pressed him, it would be "Bye bye Robyn." I'd come to learn that Mick Hughes did not like being pressured. We were alike that way. As I rang the bell, it occurred to me that even though my mother had known me considerably longer than Mick, she had yet to figure that out.

And as I stood there waiting for him to answer, it occurred to me that the prospect of losing him as a friend was worse than the idea of losing him as a lover. I wanted him in my life, and I'd put up with this long enough to see where it led. If it went south, I would try to bail before I made a fool of myself. It wasn't his fault that he hadn't worked through the whole parenting thing like I had. He didn't have to. He was a man. If our situations had been reversed, I had no doubt I'd need time to think. I just didn't know what I'd do with myself until he made up his mind.

He answered the door wearing a pale blue sweater that I've always liked on him.

As I walked past him and into the foyer, I tried to shake off the premonition that this would be the last time I'd come to his house. If this let's-be-friends thing didn't work out, I'd sure miss being able to pick up the phone and call him. And now I wondered how long it would have been before he called me. Looking at him, he seemed so calm. Like his insides hadn't been knotted for twenty-four hours, and he hadn't spent a sleepless night wondering if he'd just lost the best thing he had going for him. I swallowed a lump in my throat.

"Good to see you," he said, breaking the silence.

"You too."

He nodded toward the rear of the house. "I made you a drink."

This guy was so thoughtful.

I followed him through his living room and into the kitchen/family room where most of his living went on. Before he switched off the TV, I saw that he'd been watching the cooking network.

We clinked glasses—he had a beer going—and I settled onto the end of the brown leather couch. A sip confirmed that no one—other than me—knew exactly how much water to dribble into my Scotch. Mick had taken the "command" chair, with the herd of remotes clustered on an end table beside it.

"You want some pistachios?" he asked.

"No thanks."

He sat there, waiting, and I found myself going where I hadn't planned to go. Not yet anyway. "I wanted to apologize."

He shook his head. "Not necessary."

"Actually, it is. I got real pissy. It must have come out of the blue for you." Then I pointed out, "Although, when you're dating a forty-something woman who isn't dropping hints about her biological clock, it's something you should consider. Just for the future."

"Point taken."

"Look," I said, figuring since I was already poking around in awkward places, I might as well go deep, "if you want to see other people, I understand. I just don't want to lose you as a friend." This sounded so corny, so lame, but I didn't know how else to say it.

"Thanks."

I was expecting more. "Maybe a pistachio or two would be nice."

He left his beer on the table and walked a few feet to the kitchen where he had a small pewter bowl filled with the little beige morsels. He offered the bowl to me and I took a small handful; then he set it on the coffee table.

"So," I tried to sound casual, "are you seeing anyone?"

He gave me a crooked smile. "It's only been a day." He took a sip of his beer. "You're not the only one who's doing some thinking, you know."

"Of course not." I leaned back, taking my glass with me and feeling its familiar chill against my palm.

He wagged his head the way he did when he had a difficult proclamation to make. But it still hurt when it came out. "I am going to give that woman a call."

I nodded. Quickly. I didn't want him to think that I was the least bit surprised by this when, in fact, I was. Maybe I'd been thinking that he'd had enough time to realize that he wanted me, no matter what the price.

"The thing is, Robyn. I still don't know." He leaned toward me, grasping the bottle around its neck and resting his elbows on his knees. "I always kind of liked the idea of having a kid or two. You know?" Looking up at me again, he continued, "But I don't know whether it was the idea I liked or the actual doing."

"Yeah," I nodded, "there is a difference." He was waiting for more, and so I dug a bit deeper and said, "But I'm not sure that's something that everyone figures out. Sure, some people—both men and women—are born to have kids. Others not so much. But that doesn't make them any less good at being parents. Maybe the lower expectations actually help."

He smiled. "So you have given this some thought."

"Of course I have." I returned the smile. "I just had that particular discussion with myself a long time ago."

He nodded and swallowed a gulp of beer. I was afraid that this was where he'd cut me loose for good, and I didn't think I could finish what I'd come here to do if that happened.

So I snapped open a pistachio shell and said, "There's actually something else I need to talk about." The nut tasted dry, but I forced myself to chew and swallow.

He looked a little confused, as though he couldn't decide whether to be disappointed or relieved, but he waited while I brushed the nut dust from my fingers and pulled my laptop from my bag. "There's something I need you to look at."

Before I could get my laptop open, his cell phone rang and when he glanced at the number, his eyes narrowed. "Hold that thought," he said. "Gotta take this."

I picked up a copy of *Brewer's Times* and pretended to lose myself in the table of contents while grumbling to myself. This was probably "her." And he'd interrupted a moment with me to take the call. But I began to doubt my own analysis when his manner changed. And then he said, "Hold on, Gretch. Take it easy. Take a breath . . . Count to three. Okay, what happened?"

He was standing with his back to me now, facing the fireplace. "Are you sure?" He held up a hand as though fending off some protest. "All I'm saying is you're not a doctor. You're sure?"

He sighed real deep and blew a shot of air up toward his forehead. "Okay, stay put. I'm on my way."

As he slipped the phone into his pocket, he said, "Sorry, Robyn. It's Gretchen. She's in a . . . bind."

"Can I help?"

He hesitated, then shook his head. "Better not."

"You said something about a doctor. Is she all right?"

"*She* is."

"Who isn't?"

Another hesitation. "Her john."

Her john. Gretchen? I had no idea.

"She thinks he's dead."

By now I had my laptop in its bag. "I'm coming with you."

"She didn't—"

"Is she hysterical?"

"Sort of."

"You'll need me."

Our eyes locked and for a second I thought he was going to kiss me, but he just nodded and said, "Let's go."

On the way there, Mick told me what he knew. "She thinks he had a heart attack."

Oh, God. Why did this keep happening in my orbit?

"Where is she?"

"At home."

"She entertains clients at home?" For some odd reason I wondered how this behavior might affect Scoop. Strange, I know.

"She's getting out of the business. That's what I'm trying to help her with. But I guess this guy is an old client."

"Doesn't she live with her sister?"

"Yeah, but she's a nurse. Works nights."

"What are you going to do?"

He shook his head. "Guess I'll start by making sure he's dead."

* * *

Gretchen and her sister lived on the west end of Fowler in a small brick ranch with a trimmed lawn and a white shutters. Gretchen had left the light on for us and before Mick could ring the bell, she was at the door with her hair wrapped in a towel and her body wrapped in a silky flowered robe. She nearly sagged when she saw Mick, but when her eyes found me, she froze.

"What's she doing here?"

"Just helping out."

"How can she possibly help out? I've got a—"

She'd raised her voice and Mick gently pushed her into the foyer before she could finish the sentence. He shut the door behind us and turned to face Gretchen, who had pulled the edges of her robe together and tightened its sash. A triangle of a white T-shirt peeked out from the robe's v-neck. "It's going to be okay, Gretch."

Her mouth had firmed into a tight, thin line as she pulled in a couple of deep breaths. Exhaling, she said, "This has never happened before, Mick. I swear."

"I believe you. C'mon, let's sit down for a second."

"Aren't you going to—"

"In a minute."

He was talking to her the way he talked to high-strung horses, his voice low and soothing as he led her to an overstuffed floral couch against a yellow wall.

"Where do you keep your liquor?" he asked.

"Kitchen," she said. "Cupboard next to the sink."

With a nod, he gestured for me to see about that. I assumed he meant for her, but at this point I was thinking a spot of something might work wonders on my own fraying nerves. There were mostly sweet liquors in the cupboard, but I managed to find a bottle of

Crown Royal and poured an inch into a juice glass. After taking a sip off the top, I brought it into the living room. Mick was sitting on one side of Gretchen and Scoop had planted himself on the other side. Gretchen had her arm around the yellow dog and was holding onto him for dear life.

"Thanks, Robyn," she said as she took the drink from me. "Sorry, I just wasn't expecting—"

I shook my head. "It's okay."

"Stay with her," Mick said to me. "I'll be right back."

"He's in the room at the end of the hall," Gretchen said. "I gave him CPR. I tried." She added, "My sister taught me how to do that."

As Mick left the room, I pulled up a footstool and sat near Gretchen. She kept running her hand over Scoop's softy, shiny head. When she spoke, her voice was thick. "I don't think I could have done anything." She swallowed. "But maybe I should have."

To be honest, I was wondering that myself. Why had she called Mick and not 9-1-1?

She kept talking and so I listened. "I was in the shower when it happened. He was weird that way. He—" She stopped and we both looked up to see that Mick had returned. He'd barely been gone a minute. Certainly not long enough to administer CPR. He just shook his head and returned to the couch.

Gretchen continued with her broken delivery. "I was telling Robyn, he's weird. He liked me to shower before. And I guess I was in there a while. He wanted me to wash my hair." She swallowed again. "He really liked the smell of my shampoo. When I got out of the shower I—found him." She shook her head. "He was a nice guy. I'd been, uh, seeing him for a couple of months, when he's in town."

"I think we need to call the police," Mick said.

She released Scoop and grabbed Mick's arm. "You can't, Mick. Kelly can't know about this. Can't we move him somewhere?"

He shook his head and looked as though he were about to say something, but Gretchen kept talking.

"If my sister finds out I'm still doing this, I'm out on the street. She was real clear on that. I need this place. At least until I get my degree."

So she was working for Mick, going to school and hooking on the side. And the thing was, if her sister threw her out, that meant that Scoop didn't have a home either. Not that it was all about the dog. I really needed to evaluate my priorities.

I looked at Mick. "Whatever we do, we'd better do it before rigor mortis sets in."

Mick gave me a look that implied I wasn't helping matters at all and said, "Give us a minute."

I nodded and got up from the stool. I figured since we were going to be occupied for a while, one way or another, and I needed to relieve myself, now was a good time. I excused myself and went in search of the bathroom, which I found at the end of the hall on the right. After using it, I was returning to the living room when my peripheral vision picked up the end of a bed behind the partially closed door and the corpse's brown leather shoes and the edge of his jeans. This stopped me. He was dressed. I'd figured there was a naked corpse on the other side of the door. At the same time, something else struck me. For some reason, I did not expect a call girl's client to be wearing jeans. A suit with creased slacks, yes, faded denims no. And then I had to see what the rest of him looked like. I reached out, hesitated, and then pushed the door open, revealing the top of the bed and the rest of the body. When I saw his face, I froze.

"Holy shit," I said.

I must have spoken louder than I'd thought, because the next thing I knew, Mick was at my side.

"Robyn? You okay?"

"Holy shit," I said again.

"Yeah, I know." Mick put his hand on my shoulder and tried to steer me out of there. But I wasn't budging. He looked from me to the dead man and back again. "You know him?"

"That's Joseph Kendrick." I could not process what this meant.

"He said his name was Michael Stout." It was Gretchen, joining us and still clutching at the edges of her robe. "Of course, I figured that wasn't his real name."

"I interviewed him yesterday about the Cedar Ridge development. He owns Green Haven, the company behind it."

Mick's eyes widened as the big picture began to take form.

"I had lunch with his wife today."

None of us spoke for several seconds and then finally Gretchen said, "We've got to get him out of here, Mick. If my sister finds out, I'm out of a place to live."

Mick gave her a harsh look that I interpreted as, *You should have thought of that before you invited him over here.* From the way Gretchen shrank back, I gathered she'd translated it the same way. But Mick shook it off and refocused on the dead man.

I was thinking of Kat, my old nemesis. It didn't matter what she'd done to me in high school; no one deserved this. Even after all these years, when I think of the woman my stepfather had been with when the big one hit, I sometimes wish she had thought to stage a more proper death for him. My mother would have been spared the humiliation and would have received the respect due a widow. Instead, she became the wife of guy who died while doing the nasty with the church organist. I imagine she felt that every time she walked into a room and the conversation stopped. She was determined that I would finish high school at Lyons Township, but the ink wasn't dry on my diploma before we moved. I was sure the experience toughened her. But there were better, easier ways to become tough.

"Maybe she's right, Mick," I said.

Now his annoyance was apparent as he looked from Gretchen to me. "Well, I don't know what you two think I can do. Believe it or not, I'm not in the corpse-moving business."

"But you must know someone who is." I was rewarded with a withering look.

I focused on the body. There was a blue tinge to Kendrick, and I recalled how he'd turned an unhealthy shade of red when he'd been confronted by Leoni at the country club.

None of us spoke for a few seconds. I had to think. Mick was not in agreement with Gretchen and me, and Gretchen was still in shock. "Okay, okay," I said. "What if we put him in his car and drive him somewhere?"

Joe Kendrick wasn't a huge man. The three of us could get him out to the car. Fortunately, he was still dressed, so we wouldn't have to do that for him.

I kept thinking. "What if we make it look like he'd been trying to get to a hospital? You know, he felt it coming on."

Mick turned and walked into the hall, pushing his hand through his hair with one hand while the other was buried in his pocket. Gretchen and I exchanged looks.

Finally, after a long minute or two, Mick nodded and said, "Maybe it'll work. Griffith Park is on the north side of Kirkville and that's on the way to North Central Hospital. There are a couple small parking lots just off the street. We park the car in there and it'll look like he pulled off."

A phone warbled some rock song I didn't recognize. The sound came from the nightstand. Mick snatched a tissue from the table and used it to pick up the phone. He read the screen and glanced at me. "You know a Katherine?"

I closed my eyes and nodded. I didn't know what kind of marriage she had with Joe. They traveled to exotic places. A sherpa married them. But all the odd little details she'd mentioned at lunch hadn't given me much insight into their relationship. Whatever their relationship was, it must not have been working on at least one level. But she was a woman waiting for her husband to come home. And he never would.

"His wife."

Mick set the phone down. "Okay, let's do this."

Lucky for us, Gretchen's sister had an attached garage and Kendrick's silver Lexus was parked in it, next to Gretchen's Fiesta. After we all donned plastic cleaning gloves, Mick relieved Kendrick of his car keys, and the three of us managed to maneuver Joe through the galley kitchen and into the garage. The hard part was getting him into the passenger side of his car and belted in place. He needed to look like a guy sleeping one off and not one in a permanent state of slumber.

I backed Mick's Porsche out of the driveway and parked it in front of the house. Mick said he'd drive the Lexus, with Gretchen and me following in her Fiesta. It was only about three miles to the park, but we all recognized it would be a very long three miles. If Mick got pulled over, we were all toast.

Chapter 15

The next morning someone knocked at my door at nine fifteen. Even if I'd been asleep, I'd have heard it. The kind of sharp, staccato rap the police use, designed to wake the dead. So to speak. I patted Bix's rump. His ears had perked and his eyes opened, but he didn't move his head from my lap until the next series of knocks.

I waited. And when I didn't hear a voice booming, "Police! open up!" I overcame my initial urge to jump out the bedroom window—with Bix tucked under one arm. I extricated myself from my dog and got up from the couch, brushing Cheeto crumbs from my chest. I made my way to the kitchen door. But I couldn't bring myself to twist the knob until I heard the voice on the other side.

"Robyn?"

Mick. I slumped against the door.

"It's Mick."

I swallowed against the dry lump in my throat and opened the door.

Forgetting that we'd broken up, I threw myself into his arms. Holding me, he pushed me into the kitchen and shut the door behind him.

"I thought you were the cops," I mumbled into his chest.

"Sorry. I just wanted to make sure you're okay." He took my shoulders and put me at arm's length. "Are you?"

I glanced down at my rumpled gray sweats and *Serenity* T-shirt. "I'm better than I look. Although not by much."

"You get any sleep?"

"None."

He grabbed me again and held on. He smelled so good—like sweaty grass. I took one more deep breath, pushed away, turned and padded into the living room.

"Coffee?" he called after me.

"Yeah. Sure." After last night's drama, I should not have been thinking about our relationship issues. But I was. There was nothing I would have liked more right now than to take Mick Hughes by the hand and lead him into my bedroom. But that wound had barely a membrane over it and I knew better. At least at this moment I did. I couldn't account for a minute or a half hour from now.

After greeting Bix, Mick began to assemble the coffee maker.

"I was on my way to the gym," he said.

Never mind that my apartment isn't on his way to the gym.

"Sure you're okay?" he asked again, a heaping scoop of coffee poised above the coffeemaker.

"Yeah, still okay. How about you?"

He just nodded.

I patted the couch and Bix returned to his spot beside my thigh. "I mean, we didn't do anything terrible, did we?"

"No. Maybe illegal."

I thought for a minute. I'd been there before. "I'm okay with that." But not entirely. "It's just the getting caught part that worries me."

"You're not going to get caught." He took a couple of mugs from the cupboard above the counter.

"You keep telling me that."

I asked about Gretchen. Last night we'd all returned to her sister's after "dropping off" Kendrick, swore fidelity and gone our separate ways.

"Last I talked to her—must have been around one—she sounded okay. Her sister's home. She's planning on coming into work today. I told her to take the morning off."

"You're a nice boss," I said, wondering if he'd realize that was also the understatement of the year. I glanced at the clock. "Speaking of work, shouldn't you be there?"

"Haven't got any appointments this morning."

He was a busy guy, and I wondered if that were true. Either way, I was glad he was here.

He came into the living room, tossed his jacket on the table and sat in my purple recliner. It's the chair I usually occupy, although it fit him pretty well. We were close to the same size. I've got a couple of inches on him, but he's solid with muscle, something I never fail to notice when he's wearing a T-shirt, as he was now.

"Has there been anything on the news yet?"

"I haven't been watching."

I picked up the remote and punched the On button. I'd been tempted to do it all night, but kept chickening out. Thought I'd freak out if news of Kendrick's death broke. I still might have a bad moment, but at least Mick would be here to keep me from imploding. He was good at that.

I switched on the Chicago news station, figuring if they'd already reported it, the news would be looping and they'd be repeating themselves before long.

"What are you doing today?" Mick asked.

I muted the volume. "I've got work to do. That'll be good. Need to follow up on a couple of interviews. Go with my mother to see Erika." I didn't mention my appointment with Sharon, which I was already thinking about canceling. I just wasn't in the mood.

"Erika? What for?"

"She has an appointment twice a month. Wants to ask Robbie if we should get a house together."

Mick's eyebrows rose. "You're shitting me."

"I wish."

"You're going to—"

"No. I'm not. It's just going to take some convincing my mother." When he didn't respond, I added, "Don't worry. It's not going to happen."

He kept watching me. Clearly he wanted to console me somehow, but was at a loss for words. "Don't worry about it," I said. "I'll think of something."

"Maybe Robbie will think it's a bad idea."

"It would be nice if he finally came through for me."

I saw an image of my mother and me wrapped in our robes and watching the shopping network all night. *Shoot me now.*

"Let's talk about something else." Then I remembered the photo I'd wanted to show him last night. "That's right. I wanted you to look at this."

I retrieved my computer from the coffee table and brought up the photos I'd copied from Clair's camera yesterday, clicking on one to enlarge it.

Turning the screen toward Mick, I said, "Do you know this guy?"

He set his coffee on the table beside the computer and leaned forward. After studying the photo for no more than a second, he turned toward me. "Where'd you get this?" His expression had turned harsh and his tone sounded accusatory, which I didn't need.

"I copied it from Clair Powell's camera."

He looked back at the photo.

"You know him," I said.

"Yeah, I do. That's Ed Leoni." Then, as though talking to himself, he added, "Lucky Leoni."

"Lucky?"

He nodded, still staring at the photo.

"Lucky," I repeated.

Mick turned toward me again. "What's this guy got to do with anything?"

"I'm not sure. But the day before yesterday I interviewed Joe Kendrick about Cedar Ridge. While I was talking to him at Douglas Grove Country Club, Leoni came up to the table. Made Kendrick real uncomfortable. Then I found these photos on Clair's camera. Wondered if I was missing the real story."

Mick slumped into the chair, setting his coffee mug on its wide arm.

I could tell he was working something out in his head, so I gave him some time. But when I couldn't stand it any longer, I said, "Okay. What's with this guy? Is he the next Batman villain?"

No response.

"And where'd he get that nickname? Lucky. Sounds kind of hokey."

I finally detected a trace of a grin. "Had it all his life," he said. "Literally. He was one of a set of triplets. On the way home from the hospital his dad was driving drunk. Hit a train. His two brothers died."

I stared. "That's terrible."

"Well," Mick said, taking a sip of coffee, "look at it this way. There could be three of him."

Okay, that was a little funny. "So, people call him Lucky?"

"Some."

"You know him," I pressed.

Instead of answering me, he asked, "Lucky knew Kendrick?"

"I told you. He and his daughter barged in on the interview I was doing with Kendrick."

Mick sighed and shook his head. "You ever hear of the Grecco family?"

"Um, yes, I think so. Is that as in organized crime family Grecco?"

"The same." He paused. "Lucky is married to Chris Grecco's daughter."

I didn't think I cared for the strange direction this story was taking, but I did need to follow it. "What can you tell me about, um, Lucky?"

Mick sighed, probably out of resignation. "He's an unpredictable guy with a real high opinion of himself. Pain in the ass. He'd be small potatoes if it weren't for Tabitha."

"His wife." I nodded. "I met her."

"When?"

"She showed up at the restaurant." After a moment, I added, "Have you met the daughter?"

"Mercedes?" Mick laughed. "Oh, yeah. The apple of her daddy's eye and a chip off the old block."

I was glad I wasn't the only one to have such a harsh response to a ten-year-old.

"Tabitha seemed to be the best of the lot," I said.

"Yeah. She is."

"You know her?"

Instead of answering me, he leaned toward the computer and tapped on the cursor pad, flipping through the other photos.

"Got any of the guy in the car?"

"No, but there's a blurred license plate."

He squinted into the photo. "We might be able to make that out."

"I need to know. If Clair was following this pair, it was for a good reason."

"Steer clear of this guy. You don't want to mess with anyone in the Grecco family."

"I just want to ask a few discrete questions."

"There are no discrete questions when it comes to these people."

I shot back at him: "Since when are you an expert?" But I stopped myself before I could go further. "Never mind." Actually, Mick was sort of an expert.

"You don't have to be an expert, you just need some common sense."

"I have common sense. Don't be—"

Suddenly Mick grabbed the remote from my hand and punched the volume button.

On TV, a pert, dark-haired anchor was speaking, ". . . was found early this morning by police in the far west suburb of Fowler. The victim's name has not been released pending notice of next of kin. Cause of death has not been released and the police say they are not ruling out foul play."

I gripped the mug tighter. "What?"

Mick shook his head. "They have to say that. Until there's an autopsy."

"Do you think Kat doesn't know yet?"

"Kat?"

"Katherine. Kendrick's wife. I knew her back in high school." I'd been thinking about her off and on all night, feeling weighted down by the knowledge of her husband's death, and wondering how long it would be before she got that phone call. Or would the police come to her door? Did she know anyone—other than me—in Fowler? She must have been alone when she found out. Was she still alone?

I thought I had my answer to the latter question when my phone rang. I picked it up from the table next to the couch half expecting to see "K Kendrick" on the screen. Instead, I saw "Dryden Manor."

I gestured for Mick to wait and answered the phone.

"Robyn?"

"Yeah, Mom."

"Robyn?"

This wasn't good. From the sound of her voice, she was disoriented. "It's me, Mom."

"Wh—where are you?"

"I'm home, Mom."

She didn't answer. "Mom, you're in your room at Dryden."

"Where's my breakfast?"

"You go downstairs for your breakfast."

"Wh—why that's ridiculous. Now don't be like that."

She'd started to whine. Tears would follow. "Mom, look around your room. Look at the photos on the window ledge."

"What photos?"

"Behind the curtain." I'd always found it weird that she liked putting them on the wide ledge, which a curtain covered at night, rather than on her dresser. Almost like she didn't want our old dachshund and me staring at her while she slept.

"Just a minute." I heard a gentle thump as she set the phone down, probably on her nightstand.

"She okay?" It was Mick, sitting forward in the chair, hands clasped. I nodded and said, "Just confused. I think." He didn't know my mother well, but he'd developed an understanding of our relationship. In a weird way I think he respected me for it. But I had to wonder how he'd feel if the three of us ever became a household. Not that that was going to happen.

"Robyn?" She sounded shaky.

"Yeah, Mom."

"I don't know what's wrong with me."

"Nothing's wrong," I lied. "Did you just wake up?"

"I . . . I think so."

"You're just a little disoriented."

DC Brod

"I'm not disoriented," she snapped, switching from confused to indignant so fast it was like she'd skipped a page in her script. "I'm hungry."

"I know you are. You go downstairs for your meals."

No response.

"Mom, you sit tight for a minute. I'll get someone to help you."

"Are you coming?" She perked up so fast I began to wonder if this had been her goal all along. And then I was ashamed of myself. She never faked the kind of confusion I was hearing now.

"Not right now. But I'll be there later."

"Robyn—" she started to whine.

I covered the mouthpiece. "Can you talk to her for a minute?" I whispered to Mick.

He didn't look pleased, but he took the phone. "Hey, Lizzie . . ."

I dug my cell phone from my bag and punched in the number at Dryden, asking for the second floor nurse's station.

While I waited, I heard my former boyfriend—or whatever he was—"It's Mick. You know, Robyn's . . . friend."

To my relief, whatever she said made him smile.

Then Vera, the nurse, picked up the line.

"It's Robyn Guthrie, Vera," I began and explained the situation. It was early and a busy time for the staff at Dryden, but Vera didn't rush me. I knew that my mother—for reasons I'll never begin to understand—was a favorite of Vera's, although I also knew that had nothing to do with the nurse's quick response. She was just that good at what she did.

"I'll go right down there now, Robyn." She hung up without waiting for my response.

I held my hand out to Mick, offering to take the phone, but he raised a finger, indicating that he needed to wait for my mother to

140

finish. He was half smiling, and when he got the chance to respond, he said, "But, you know, houses can be a lot of trouble."

I rolled my eyes heavenward and slumped into the couch. I should know better than to ever be surprised by my mother.

Mick handed me the phone. "Someone else is there."

I put it to my ear and could hear Vera talking to my mother.

"Aren't you going to breakfast, honey?"

"Oh, I'm bored with breakfast."

"Don't lie to me, girl. Pancakes? I know you love your pancakes."

It went from there. And once I heard by mother begrudgingly agree to go downstairs, Vera quietly hung up the phone. I pushed the disconnect button, sighed, then reached out and touched Mick's hand. "Thank you."

He smiled. "No problem." And I knew it wasn't.

I glanced at my watch. "I'm supposed to be at a realtor's office in twenty minutes."

"You're not going, are you?"

"No. Guess I need to call her."

"That would be the polite thing to do."

For some reason that struck me as funny. I mean, here we were moving bodies in middle of the night. How polite was that? But, I figured you did what you could with what you had.

Mick's phone rang next. He glanced at the screen before taking the call. "Hey, Gretchen."

His eyes widened. "Take it easy."

Not again.

"You're sure it's his?"

He listened for another ten seconds. "Okay. Sit tight. I'll call you right back."

"What?" I asked when, after disconnecting the call, he just stared off into space.

He brought his eyes to focus on me. "Kendrick's phone. It's still at Gretchen's."

"Shit."

Mick shook his head. "Not sure it's that big a problem. I mean, he could've lost it anywhere."

"True, but anything that looks unusual may arouse suspicion. You know that."

"Not necessarily. And when you think about it, it backs up the heart-attack-on-the-way-to-the-hospital scenario. Why drive yourself when you can call a paramedic?"

"True."

With a sigh that was almost a groan, he said, "But now we need to figure out a plausible place for him to have left it. Where do you lose a phone?"

"In my purse. If it's a big purse," I added. "Or leave it somewhere."

"We don't know where he'd been."

After considering that for a minute, I said, "He and Kat are staying at the Grenada Suites."

He was watching me now, nodding slowly.

I kept going. "At Gretchen's he had it on the nightstand. Maybe it fell behind the one in his hotel room."

"No. It'd be better if it were someplace he could have lost it without realizing he lost it."

"Okay . . ." I drank more coffee, hoping the caffeine would activate a few brain cells.

Mick said, "Health club. Or what about that country club?"

"No, he had it with him when he left. In his pocket." I patted the cushion beside me. "I've had mine swallowed up by the couch."

Mick nodded for me to keep going.

"Set it to vibrate and slip it between cushions. Could have fallen out of his pocket."

"You sure they have a couch in the room?"

"Kat said they were staying at Grenada Suites. I'm guessing there's a couch involved. And, knowing Kat, they've got the biggest room."

"Okay. How do you suggest we get it there?" He was smiling now because he damned well knew I was the only one who could do it.

I sighed. "I'll pick up the phone from Gretchen." Recognizing my bargaining potential, I added, "If you'll check out that license plate in the photo."

He gave me a reluctant nod. "I will."

I thought it through. I could wait until I heard something on the news and then show up at Kat's to offer my condolences. But maybe I didn't have to wait. "I could call Kat with some follow up questions." I thought about it and was a little relieved to find that it troubled me some. "Not a nice thing to do. Pretend to be doing my job just so I can pull off a deception."

After a few seconds, Mick said, "Would you rather she knew where the phone was?"

"No," I sighed.

Mick punched in a number on his phone. "When should I tell Gretchen to expect you?"

"As soon as I get my act together." I drew in a deep breath and released it with a sigh. "I don't know. Maybe next year."

* * *

Gretchen met me at the door with Scoop who seemed happy to see me. But he's a dog, so I didn't let it go to my head.

"My sister's home. She's asleep, but she's a light sleeper."

"No problem."

She reached into her pocket and withdrew the phone, dropping it into my purse. "Thank you, Robyn. For everything."

"It's okay," I said.

Back in my car I drove a few blocks to a grocery store where I pulled off into the lot and fished the phone out of my bag. It occurred to me that I should have been wearing gloves. Too late now. Mainly, I was curious as to how many calls Kendrick had missed. There were three voice mails. Two from Kat, one from a number without a name, where a man said, "Call me."

Curiosity runs deep in my family, and so I continued to snoop about the phone. He had no music downloaded and not all that many apps, most of which were the practical kind. No Angry Birds on Joe Kendrick's phone. On to his text message file, where I found one that he'd sent to Kat that simply said, "I'll be home late." Sad. I scrolled up and found one that I assumed was to Gretchen. "Be there at 8." But he'd sent one before that, to a number without a name, which was only two words: "Patchen knows."

Knows what?

I scribbled down the phone number and checked it with the voice mail. Same number as the "call me" guy. The easiest way to identify the number was to call it. But thanks to caller ID, my number would be out there to see. Not an option. I didn't know where this was leading, but I knew I didn't want any arrows pointing at me.

First things first. I used a tissue to wipe off Kendrick's phone, wrapped it in another and tucked into my purse. Then I pulled out my own.

As I punched in Kat Kendrick's phone number, I decided I'd see if I could pay Mr. Patchen a visit after I saw Kat. See if he could tell me what he knew.

Someone other than Kat answered her phone. Guess I should have expected that. When I asked to speak with Kat and said who was calling, the woman told me to wait a minute. I did, grateful for the time to put myself in a place where I could sound shocked. I also had to realize that there was a distinct possibility that Kat would not invite me over there. When I thought about it, why should she? Her husband being dead trumped my follow-up questions. But just showing up there, without being invited, seemed an awful thing to do to her. As if planting her dead husband's phone, not to mention her dead husband, wasn't enough.

"Hi, Robyn."

It was Kat. And she sounded broken.

"Kat? Are you okay?" This had been rehearsed.

"Yes. No. No, not at all."

"What's wrong?"

"It's Joe."

I waited.

"Did you hear on the news about that man they found in his car? Dead."

"That was—"

"Joe," she finished.

"Oh, God, Kat. I am so sorry."

She didn't say anything.

"Can I do anything? Is there anything you need?"

"No. Thanks."

"Do you need some company?"

"No, that's okay. I—"

I could hear her quiet sobs.

"You shouldn't be alone now."

"Beverly's here." She added, "My assistant."

I sat there trying to figure a way in and thinking, at the same time, that I should just toss Joe's phone in a dumpster.

But then Kat sniffed and said, "She's a great assistant but makes crappy coffee."

"Let me bring you some."

"No, I wasn't—"

"Really, I know a place that makes great coffee. I'll just drop it off. If you don't feel like talking I'll be on my way."

When she didn't object, I said, "How do you like your coffee?"

On my way to the Grenada Suites—Fowler's finest—I stopped at the Twisted Lizard for coffee and a couple of bagels and scones. I didn't know if Kat would be hungry; shock and grief can do weird things with your appetite. But I'd learned that criminal activity can also play havoc with the appetite and maybe that was why I was hungry.

I had to knock a couple of times before Kat answered. I wasn't sure what to expect when she opened the door. She looked pretty good, considering. No makeup and a pair of sweats worked better on her than they did on me. When she saw me, she forced an unsteady smile.

"Thanks, Robyn." She stepped back from the door. "Come on in."

As I entered, she took a step toward me, then stopped and retreated. I sensed I'd just dodged a hug. Maybe it was the hot coffee and the bag. Whatever, I had to admit I was relieved.

I walked into a spacious sitting room with a couple of couches and a wide-screen television that was turned off. A counter separated the sitting area from a kitchenette. This hotel suite was probably larger than my apartment. Magazines, makeup and a slouchy black purse were strewn over the surface of the coffee table and several articles of clothing—a red knit top, a blouse and a pair of jeans— were draped over the wide arm of a nubby green chair. Apparently Kat was not a neatnik. For some ignoble reason that heartened me.

Kat followed me and perched on one of the barstools lined up against the counter, resting her chin on a fist. She looked smaller than she had the other day, her shoulders slumped and brittle-looking under the thin T-shirt fabric.

I slid her coffee order toward her and dug for the food. "Bagels and scones with extra cream cheese."

When I lifted a bagel from the bag for her to see, she was watching me. But then she dropped her gaze as she pried the lid from her coffee. Still holding the lid, she blew on the tan liquid and took a sip. "Thanks." She set it down.

I nodded toward the sitting room. "Why don't we go where it's comfortable?"

She shrugged as though it made no difference. I situated her coffee in front of the chair and put myself in the middle of the couch, dropping my purse beside me.

Kat took another sip of the coffee and nodded. "That is good."

"Twisted Lizard."

"Weird name." She ran her thumb over the logo, which was a gecko-type lizard curled around itself.

"The owner is from New Mexico." I smiled. "She likes lizards."

Then, because we seemed to be the only two here, I asked about Beverly.

"She went out to pick up a prescription for me."

Neither of us spoke for a minute. Then I asked, "You doing okay?"

Instead of answering, she said, "I saw him yesterday. Just after lunch. He seemed fine."

"Can you tell me what happened?"

"They called me around two thirty this morning. Said they'd have to do an autopsy, but they thought it was a heart attack."

"Did he have problems?"

"He was on blood pressure medication."

Again, I recalled the unhealthy shade of red his face had turned when Kendrick had gotten upset.

"They needed me to . . . identify him."

"I'm so sorry."

She sighed and stared into the tall, paper cup. "This is uncomfortable, isn't it?"

I waited. This was uncomfortable on a number of levels.

"You and me sitting here."

"You shouldn't be alone now."

She looked up at me again, "What's strange is the other day at lunch I was feeling sorry for you."

Before I could react, she rushed ahead, "Not real sorry. It just seemed like your life hadn't turned out the way you'd planned it."

What I wanted to say was, *How would you know what I had planned?* What I said was, "Most lives don't."

She shook her head. "Mine did."

"Really?"

"I think so. I'm successful, I have a great kid and I married the love of my life." She broke down on that last part. Tears were leaking from her eyes. She sniffed. "Thought I had it all."

Maybe she was a little sparse in the friends category.

But she kept talking, so I figured all she wanted me here for were my ears. I was okay with that.

"He was so thoughtful. Funny. Smart. I don't know what I'm going to do without him."

I nodded, afraid if I responded something in my voice would give me away. So I just sat there, hoping she wouldn't be able to read any of last night in the stiff grip I had on my coffee or the way my other hand was clenched so tight I could feel my stubby nails digging into my palm.

"I don't know," she repeated.

It seemed strange for me—someone who is deft at avoiding emotional entanglements—to find myself for the second time in one week, no less, comforting a survivor. It had been easier with Clair's mother.

"You're a strong woman, Kat."

"Yeah. Right."

"You wouldn't be where you are if you weren't. Remember that."

"It's hard to . . . feel it now."

"You just need some time." I wondered if she was as aware of my platitude-spewing as I was.

I separated the two halves of a bagel, slathered cream cheese on one half and offered it to Kat. After a hesitation, she took it.

"What was that boy's name?" she asked.

I cocked my head.

"In high school."

"Oh. Brad Barth."

"That's right." She was nodding like it was all coming back to her. I had to wonder why she would think of that now.

But it must have been an aberration, because then she shook her head. "I don't know what I'm supposed to do."

"Is there anyone else you need to call?" I sipped the coffee, which was still pretty hot.

"I called my sister. She's in Arizona. She's calling some people."

"Is she coming here?"

"She's not sure she can. Not right now."

That seemed cold. "Okay, then . . . what about arrangements?"

"I don't know." She sighed and licked a speck of cream cheese off her thumb. "I still haven't been able to get hold of Russell. Can you believe that? Some places can't be reached by cell phone. I can't make any arrangements until I hear from him. I don't know how I'm going to tell him. He worshipped Joe."

"Have you been able to talk with the university?"

"Yes. They're trying to track him down." She shook her head. "Nothing to do but wait."

"I'd like to see a picture of him. Do you have one?"

She brightened. "I do. Just a minute."

And then, as I hoped, she got up and went into the bedroom. I dug into my purse for Kendrick's phone, which I'd stuck in a side pocket. As I removed it, still wrapped in the tissue, the room's phone rang. I froze. On the second ring, I heard Kat answer it in the bedroom. Before I allowed myself a sigh of relief, I checked to make sure Kendrick's phone was set to vibrate and leaned over to insert it between the cushion and the arm of the couch. Just then the door clicked and the handle began to turn. I jammed the phone down the crack toward the back of the couch, retrieved the tissue, and sat up again as the door swung open and a young woman walked in. Beverly, I assumed.

"You must be Robyn," she said.

"I am. Beverly?"

"Yes. Where's Kat?"

I nodded my head toward the bedroom. "Phone call."

She stepped over to the bedroom door and peered in. Apparently satisfied, she returned to the kitchenette where she set a bag on the counter. She was stocky and maybe five-foot-five in two-inch heels. Her features were drawn into a tight mask accentuated by a headband that pulled her blond hair off her round face.

Just as I was thinking that this looked like a humorless woman, Beverly turned toward me and said, "She shouldn't be bothered now, you know."

"I thought she could use . . . some sympathy." A little annoyed, I added, "I didn't think I was bothering her."

Beverly approached and, looking down her broad nose at me with rather lifeless blue eyes, she said, "Kat needs rest."

"I won't be here long."

I heard movement behind me and saw Kat leaning against the bedroom door jamb.

"I've got your pills, Kat," Beverly said, hustling to a cupboard in the kitchenette where she extracted a water glass. "The doctor said to take one now and one before you go to bed."

Kat walked into the sitting room. "That was the police."

She had our attention.

"He asked if Joe had a cell phone. I said of course, and he said they hadn't found one on him. Or in his car." She focused on Beverly. "Did you see his phone?"

"The only time I've seen Mr. Kendrick's phone is when he's using it."

"Huh." Kat sank into the chair. "That's odd."

I thought of suggesting that he left it somewhere, but Beverly mentioned it first.

"Maybe," Kat said, not at all convinced from the sound of her voice.

Out of the corner of my eye I checked out the place where I'd thrust the phone. It wasn't visible.

"Well, that's not your concern," Beverly said, handing Kat a pill and a glass of water.

"Thank you."

I supposed this was my cue to leave.

"Listen Kat, if you need anything, give me a call."

She gave me a hug. It was brief and relatively painless. "Thanks for coming by, Robyn."

As Beverly escorted me to the door, a fresh wave of guilt washed over me. If I hadn't needed to get rid of Kendrick's phone, I wouldn't have called her. I wouldn't be here.

Chapter 16

After I left Kat, I drove around for a while, not sure what to do with myself. I wondered how Kendrick's death would affect the Cedar Ridge project. And, speaking of Cedar Ridge, what was it that Glenn Patchen knew? Whatever it was seemed to bother Kendrick and whomever he was texting. I could try a reverse lookup, but if this were a private number, that wouldn't show me anything. I supposed if I gave Mick that phone number, he had some friend somewhere who could tell him who it belonged to. I pulled over in front of a ranch house with a For Sale sign in front of it. Averting my eyes, I called Mick. I drive stick shift, so it's virtually impossible for me to talk on the phone and drive at the same time. I imagine some people can pull it off, but I'm not one of them.

"Everything okay?" he asked.

"I think so."

"Good. I've got something for you."

He had to be talking about the guy in the photo with Lucky. "Already?"

"You pay for speed."

A giggle slipped out, and I was annoyed with myself for that. I never giggle.

"You ever heard of a Carl Wellen?"

"Nope." Then I remembered. "In Clair's notes, I found the initials CW. Must be him."

"He's a soil engineer."

"A soil engineer?"

"Yeah, that's someone—usually civil service type—who analyzes the soil for a proposed construction site."

"Really?"

"It's required for a building permit."

"Did he do the soil testing for Cedar Ridge?"

"That I don't know." He paused. "But you could find out."

"I will." I thought for a minute. "Maybe I'll ask Glenn Patchen."

"Who's he?"

"The architect I interviewed." Then I asked, "Do you know who would hire the soil engineer?"

"I don't know. Maybe the architect. Or the construction company."

"Okay, thanks."

"How's your friend?"

"Holding up. I guess. She's got a personal assistant."

"Maybe she needs one."

"I'd like one."

He chuckled. "What for?"

"I don't know. I'd just like to be able to say I have one. Not Beverly, though. A different one."

"Talk to you later."

"I didn't think you'd understand."

Next, I placed a call to Glenn Patchen, got his voicemail and left a message for him to call me. I wasn't sure how I'd explain how I knew that "he knew," but I'd figure something out.

No sooner had I disconnected and dropped the phone to the passenger seat, when it went off.

I saw on the screen it was my mother and hoped she'd gotten over her morning confusion. It usually didn't last long.

"Hi, Mom."

"Robyn?"

"Yeah, it's me."

"Oh, good."

"How are you feeling?"

"Well, I'm fine," she said as though it had been odd of me to inquire.

With barely time for a breath, she asked, "What did she say?"

I had no idea what or who she was talking about.

"What did who say?"

"Azalea's daughter," she told me, and from the way she stamped down on the words, she shouldn't have to be telling me this. "I have written on this napkin that you were going to see her at ten."

Uh-oh. "I wasn't able to talk to her, Mom." My mother had taken up this napkin-scribbling habit, and it proved to be effective in helping her remember. Except when she misplaced the napkin, which wasn't unusual. Why it hadn't happened with this one bolstered my suspicion that I had annoyed some minor deity.

"What do you mean? She wasn't there?"

At moments like these I questioned the severity of my mother's dementia. "No, Mom. Something came up. I couldn't keep the appointment."

"What was so important?"

She was taking that tone with me. The one she used on me when I'd been a thoughtless teenager, and the one she still trotted out when she needed to smack me down.

"It was an emergency, Mom."

Silence.

Okay, I'd go with the truth. More or less. "You remember Kat Kendrick? The woman we had lunch with yesterday?"

"The pretty one?"

"Yeah, that one." I sighed. "Her husband died last night. I went over to her hotel so . . . to keep her company."

"I didn't think you liked her."

"I didn't. I don't. I don't know. I was just trying to help out."

"What happened?"

"They're not sure yet." I didn't want to go into it here.

"Oh." After a moment she asked, "When are you going to see her?"

A normal person might have been unsure who my mother was referring to by "her." But I knew exactly who she meant. "See who?" I asked anyway, feeling a bit combative.

"Azalea's daughter," she snapped. I could picture her face, tight, and her eyes sparking.

"I'll call her as soon as I get home."

"You could call her now."

"I'm going home first, Mom."

Silence. Then a deep, deep sigh. "All right." Her voice got small, pleading. "You will let me know what she says, Robyn?"

"Of course I will." Even though I knew the pitiful voice was one of her tools, it always got to me. My mother, of course, understood that. "I'll see you this afternoon."

"I'm almost out of wine."

"Didn't I just bring you a bottle?"

"I shared it with a friend."

Right.

After I disconnected, I sat there for a few minutes thinking how many ways my life would change if she moved in with me. And, with the exception of the house, I didn't like the looks of any of them. Of course, with a house, there came problems. Upkeep. Something was always malfunctioning. I'd been the designated lawn mower and snow shoveler when I was in school. Hadn't done it since college. Didn't miss it a bit.

My route home took me past the real estate office where Sharon worked. I glanced at the dashboard clock and saw I was only about forty-five minutes late for our meeting. Still, I was half hoping she wouldn't be there. But she was, and she waved off my lame apology.

"I'm just glad you could make it in."

As she led me toward her desk, which occupied a corner of a large, open room filled with five desks, none of which were occupied at the time, she was telling me how she'd found several places she thought would be within our price range and well worth taking a look at.

After she'd gotten me seated, she went to get us some coffee. Sharon's desk had nothing on top that didn't belong there—computer, blotter, pen holder, tissue and a two-tiered file with a neat pile of papers in the top tray and a couple of folders in the lower. There were two photos in matching wooden frames. One I assumed was her family—she stood next to a pleasant-looking, middle-aged man with a receding hairline and a smile as wide as hers and two healthy-looking teenagers, a boy and a girl. Again that signature smile. The other photo was of Sharon and her mother, Azalea. Probably a recent photo, Azalea had a wide-eyed, slightly confused look, as though she wasn't sure why she was standing there being embraced by her daughter. Sharon must have gotten her smile from her father because Azalea's was almost a grimace.

"You said black, right?" Sharon set a plain white mug with steaming coffee in front of me.

"Yes. Thanks."

As she settled behind her desk and removed a thin file from the lower file tray, I was thinking now was the time to tell her that I was here only because I had promised my mother I would do this, and that the likelihood of the two of us living together was about the same as the Cubs winning the World Series in this century.

But she paused, with her hands spread out over the folder as though it contained some divine truth rather than home listings, and said, "I wish I could do this."

I snapped my mouth shut. "Really?"

"Oh, yes. I would love for my mother to live with us." She shook her head. "It's just not possible. We don't have the room."

If she did have the room would she be as enthusiastic? It's easy to say you would do something if possible when it's not. She continued, "I really admire you."

I was feeling guilty from all the accolades when she added, "Caring for our parents is the most loving thing we can do for them." She smiled. "You must be a good person."

"Um, actually, I'm not that good."

She had her elbow on the desk and her chin was resting on her fist, but now she cocked her head slightly, reminding me a little of Bix when he so wants to understand something.

I took a sip of the coffee, which surprised me by being strong and rather tasty. After another taste, I said, "Sharon, I have to level with you. I am here because I promised my mother I would talk to you. But I don't want to live with her. I really don't. We are like oil and water. Eminem and Michael Bublé. And if that makes me a bad person, then I guess I will have to be that bad person."

She stared at me for several moments, her brows pushing together. "Are you saying you don't want to live with your mother?"

"That is what I'm saying. Yes."

She nearly melted before my eyes. "Oh, thank God. Thank God." She dropped her forehead into her hands. She might have been praying. Then she looked up at me. "My mother has not stopped talking about you since Lizzie told her." She cranked up her voice a notch or two. "'Lizzie's daughter is moving so they can live together.' 'That daughter of Lizzie's is so considerate.' 'She's buying a house for them.'"

I started laughing so hard I had to set down my coffee. Sharon joined me. We both laughed until tears came. Sharon whipped out a couple of tissues for us. I wiped my eyes and blew my nose. After I had myself under control, I said, "You must have hated me."

Still smiling, she shook her head, "'Hate' is too strong. 'Resent' probably comes closer."

"I don't blame you." Then, to clarify, I said, "So you're not eager to have your mother move in with you."

"I'm not." She paused, as though considering her next words. "You know, I do love her. She's fairly easy to get along with. She loves the kids. But she never approved of Bob." She nodded at the photo of her family. "And the older she has gotten, the more freely she voices her opinions." She sighed and there seemed some honest regret there. "I can't inflict that on my family."

I nodded my understanding.

We sat in silence for several moments. Finally, Sharon said, "So, I guess this means you're not looking for a home."

"It's probably not a good time. As much as the idea of buying a home for myself appeals to me, I don't know how I'd spirit that one past my mother."

The edges of her mouth curled into a smile. She opened the folder, paged through a couple of listings, withdrew one, turned it around and slid it toward me on the desk. Before releasing it, she patted the sheet of paper. "I have to show you this one." Her words were hushed, almost as though there were others in the office who might overhear.

Against my better judgment, I picked up the paper and examined the listing. A ranch house. Three bedrooms. Big kitchen. Screened-in porch. Shockingly low sticker price.

"What's wrong with it?"

"Nothing. It's in wonderful shape. The family has to move. He's been transferred. Big promotion. They've already bought in the city they're moving to. They're highly motivated to sell."

"Why is it still available?"

"That school district is not the most . . ." she made air quotes ". . . 'desirable.'"

I sighed. Then I shook my head. "I'd never be able to pull this off."

"Just a look?"

* * *

The three-bedroom tan brick ranch house sat on a half acre that backed up to a wooded area, behind which was a middle school yard. The kitchen was large with a breakfast bar and new appliances. The bedrooms weren't spacious, but since there were three, I'd have my own office. The basement was partially finished. There was a fireplace in the living room. But what really sold it for me was the screened-in porch. While we stood on the porch looking out toward the tree line, three does edged out of the woods and nibbled at the grass.

The breeze gusted through the screen, and I gave myself a moment to enjoy the smells carried with it—grass, leaves, and traces of a wood fire.

One of the deer looked up from her grazing, her ears twitching like white flags.

I could imagine that scene with the changing seasons: winter white to green and then reds and oranges.

Then I added my mother to the picture, and, to my amazement, it didn't scare me quite as much as it had before. Yeah, I thought, this might be worth trying. If I could live in a place like this, it might be worth it.

* * *

Returning to the real estate office, Sharon asked me about my work. "Your mom said you're a writer."

"Yeah, freelance mostly. Right now I'm doing some work for the *News and Record.*"

"I heard about that reporter who died." Glancing my way, she added, "You knew her?"

"I did. Not real well. But she was a good person. Young. Smart. It's sad."

"Are you picking up some of her work?"

"I am." Then I decided to get a realtor's opinion of the new development. "I'm doing a piece on Cedar Ridge."

"I've heard about that. Drove out there once to see for myself. The trend is definitely going toward green housing. What do you think of it?"

I told her about my tour of one of the units and said that I'd been impressed with the environmental innovations and the family who was going to call it home.

"It's awful about Joe Kendrick. What a shock."

She had no idea. "Did you know the Kendricks?"

"I don't. I believe this is their first venture in Illinois."

"Yeah, I think it is."

"I wonder if this will change things." she said.

"I don't know. I hope not. For the sake of the homeowners."

"I know they've been selling slowly. It's the market."

I decided to see what else she might know. "Do you know Ed Leoni?"

She glanced at me before answering. I tried to keep my expression bland. Slowing for a red light, she said, "Sure I do. Everyone in real estate knows Lucky."

"What do you think of him?" I added, "Off the record."

"Why are you asking?"

"I'm not sure. I met him once and there was something about him that—I don't know—keeps nagging at me."

"'Nagging.' That's an interesting choice of words." I could hear the smile in her voice. "Did you by any chance meet Mercedes?"

"His daughter? Why, yes, I have had the pleasure. I've got a ruined pair of pants to show for it."

"That sounds like Mercedes." She chuckled. "Did you know he named his company after her?"

"Huh. Devil's Spawn Real Estate is an odd choice for a name." Sharon laughed. "Try Mercedes Properties."

"What's Lucky's reputation?"

"Well," Sharon said, "Let's just say he wouldn't be where he is without his father-in-law's money."

"Yeah, I've heard that."

"Did you meet Tabitha?"

"I did. She seemed like the best of the three." I wondered out loud, "What did she see in him?"

Instead of speculating, Sharon asked, "Why'd you ask about Leoni?"

"He sold the Cedar Ridge property to the Kendricks."

Nodding, she said, "That's right. I think he sold after he failed to get the commercial zoning he wanted. Probably killed him to split up that land."

"Split up the land?"

"He owns the property just east of there that borders the Crystal River. Word is that he's hoping to sell that riverfront land to

Stratford, International. Since Illinois expanded its casino policy, Stratford is considering this area for a casino site."

"And they're looking at Leoni's property?"

"Among others."

"I'd think with riverfront property he'd be in good shape."

"I suppose so, but I can't help but wonder why he didn't keep the land adjacent to it. You know, in case they want to do more."

"But he didn't know about the casino potential then, did he?"

She paused. "No. But I'd think you'd want to hold onto any property that could be used for expansion."

"Interesting. Now I'm also wondering why he sold." I added, "Ed Leoni doesn't strike me as either charitable or environmentally conscious."

"Oh, he's not. I'm guessing the Kendricks paid a lot of money for that land."

"How much would you guess?" She hesitated, and I prompted with, "Ballpark."

"In this area?" She wagged her head. "Several million. Give or take."

"That's a very large park, isn't it?"

"Do you know what they actually paid?"

When I told her I didn't, she said, "Now that you've got me thinking about it, my curiosity is aroused. Maybe I'll check it out."

"Thanks. I can ask Mrs. Kendrick," I said, adding, "But it might be interesting to double-check the number."

"No problem."

Chapter 17

Since I'd met Erika Starwise two months ago, our relationship had progressed from reporter versus subject to wary acquaintances to something closer to friends. We weren't ready to go shopping together or share a few drinks at Fingal's, but there was some kind of connection. Maybe it was my mother. I was pretty sure that we both loved her. I was her daughter so that went with the territory, but Erika saw Lizzie with all her oddities and still found her appealing. Other people's parents are sometimes easier to love than your own. Erika had almost left Fowler shortly after our paths crossed, but decided to stay. I'm still not sure why—she wouldn't talk about it— but I suspected that my mother was at least a small part of it. Maybe I was too. Erika and I had both done good things for each other. My story on her psychic business and what I'd experienced there had brought her a number of new clients. She wasn't outwardly appreciative, but she wouldn't take any money from my mother and had told me she'd be happy to read my cards for me any time I asked. So far, I'd resisted. Her odd predictions when we first met had been more accurate than I cared to examine closely.

Today she put on a CD of nature sounds—waves lapping against a shore.

"What did you want to ask Robbie today, Lizzie?" She clasped her hands together and looked from me to my mother. "I assume it has something to do with Robyn."

"We want to ask him if we should buy a house together."

Erika turned to me for confirmation.

"I'm here only because she'll ask him whether I'm here or not. And I want to know what he says."

"I see."

My mother leaned toward Erika. "You see what I have to deal with?"

"Well, let's get started." Erika lit three candles and switched off the overhead light.

We held hands and bowed toward a bowl in the table's center that contained two gardenias, floating in water. Robbie had loved the smell of gardenias and apparently it was something that nudged him out of his eternal slumber long enough to advise my mother.

Erika invoked his spirit, mentioning that I was here, and how we were honored to have him join us. I went along with this because it made my mother happy, but if he were to tell us that, indeed, we should immediately go out and purchase a home together, I just might have to pull the plug on this operation.

"Robbie, are you here?" Erika asked. And, sure enough, she was rewarded with a single rap.

This was the creepy part for me. I felt the hairs on the back of my neck standing up, and a familiar shivery feeling down my shoulders. I had the urge to turn around, see who was behind me. But I didn't. Mainly because Erika would have yelled at me, but also because I wasn't sure I wanted to know. In the few sessions I'd sat in on, there were times when Erika could see the person she was trying to communicate with; at other times, she had to talk to them via "yes" or "no" questions. But she had pretty good luck with my father, possibly because she had known him.

Erika squeezed my hand; I assumed my mother got the same treatment.

"He is here," she said, her voice hushed.

No one spoke for several moments. The room had gotten cool and the smell of gardenias was overpowering.

"Robbie is happy to see you here, Robyn."

I just nodded.

"He understands it's difficult for you."

I did not want to carry on a conversation with a ghost. I didn't care if he was my father.

"What about the house?" It was my mother.

"Let him get settled," Erika chided her.

We sat there for a minute or so. At first I could hear our distinct breathing patterns, but before long, we were breathing in unison.

Erika softly cleared her throat. "Robbie, Lizzie and Robyn have brought you a question today." She paused as though waiting for him to give her the go-ahead. "They are considering buying a home and living there together. What do you think?"

Through partially closed eyes, I could see Erika nodding, listening. As though there were really someone otherwordly in this room with us. My chills were returning.

"Yes," she said, "I will tell them."

To us, she said, "He would love to see this happen. You are the two people he holds most dear. It would please him greatly."

I started to pull my hand away, but Erika held tight.

"But he is sensing the unrest."

I snorted. "Well, he should be."

"Robyn," Erika warned me.

"I mean, why are we even asking him? He doesn't know me. He doesn't know if we get along."

"Robyn." Now my mother was admonishing me. It was like I'd let loose a string of profanity in front of a treasured guest.

"He understands this. He wants to know why you asked."

"Because she wanted to." I nodded my head toward my mother. "And no offense to you, Dad, but you don't get the deciding vote."

"Robyn—" It was my mother, launching a scold.

Again with the squeezed hand. "I think you should leave," Erika said.

"I am not leaving. I'm not some little kid who gets sent out of the room when her parents fight. I am staying—"

"I meant Lizzie."

"What?" asked my mother. I was too stunned to speak. Then, she said, "I'll do no such thing."

"Please, Lizzie," Erika leaned toward my mother, releasing her hand and giving her arm a pat. "It will only be a minute or two."

This was a no-win situation for me, so I held my tongue. I didn't want her to stay, so I wasn't about to ask Erika to change her mind. On the other hand, if I added my voice to her dismissal, she'd slip into a snit.

"All right," she finally said, breaking off the glare she had directed at Erika. It took her more effort than usual to get up, and as she moved toward the door she limped slightly, even with the assistance of her cane. After opening the door, she looked over her shoulder and into the room. "Good-bye Robbie." The door clicked shut behind her.

"He's not really here, is he?" I said to Erika.

She released my hand. "No. Not today. I think he senses your skepticism."

"So, if Robbie isn't here, you must be the one who needs to talk to me."

"I just need to know how you feel about this. I'm sensing you're not pleased with the prospect of living with your mother."

"You really are a psychic."

She gave me a dry look. "I'm trying to help, Robyn."

"How?"

"Tell me what you want."

I sank into the chair and released a sigh. "I saw this house I love. It's perfect. But I don't know how my mother and I can live together.

You know how anxious she can get. I couldn't leave her alone. She's up half the night. My life would be over." I paused. Erika waited. "But when I think of what she's done for me." I paused, reflecting. "To be honest, she hasn't always been there for me. But she's my mother." I shook my head. "I don't know."

As I focused on Erika, an idea came to me. "Could you tell her that Robbie thinks it's a bad idea?"

"I can't do that."

"Why not?"

"Because I would be abusing her trust in me."

"Erika, don't you do that whenever you make up things he says to her?"

"I don't always make things up, despite what you believe. But when I do, it's to make your mother happy. What you're asking me to do would be . . . manipulation."

I gave her a dubious look. "Your ethics line is kind of wobbly, you know."

"I would never hurt your mother."

I was about to point out that Erika gladly accepts money from her, but remembered she doesn't.

"So, what happens now?" I asked.

"I think you and your mother need to work this out without my—or Robbie's—help."

* * *

"How's the story going?" Nita was sorting the clutter covering her desk, attacking it one sheet of paper at a time, depositing each in one of three piles.

I'd dropped my mother off at Dryden and spent an hour at home trying to get hold of people. No one wanted to talk to me, so I'd decided to darken Nita's doorway. I felt stalled, and if she didn't have any suggestions for me, I could probably convince her to go out for a drink.

"Okay," I said, helping myself to the chair across from her. I watched her working, only vaguely wondering what each of those piles represented. "I can't get de Coriolis to return my calls."

"He's an ass."

"I know. But he's our ass. And you'd think he'd want to shed some good publicity on Cedar Ridge even though he didn't want it. I mean, now that it's a fact. You'd think he'd want to put a positive spin on the development and showcase himself as an environmentally astute politician."

Nita paused. "Yeah, you'd think."

I shifted in the chair. "I have a few questions for you. About Clair."

"Which I will try to answer."

"Just hear me out. Let me know if you think I'm nuts."

"I'd be happy to."

"A couple of things. First, there's the route Clair chose to walk Scoop that night." I had to explain this to Nita who, as a cat person, might not understand the big, dog-walking picture.

When I'd finished, she said, "So you think she was meeting someone on a dark road at eleven at night?" She shook her head. "Clair was too smart for that."

"What if it was someone she trusted?"

She regarded me for several moments, then said, "What do the cops think of this?"

"I imagine they've considered it. Not that they'd feel obliged to share anything they found with me. I will say that Hedges didn't seem crazy about my dog walking theory."

"Okay. So, whom do you think she trusted?"

"I don't know."

"Where are you headed with this?"

"I'm not sure. But you know that camera of hers?" When she nodded, I proceeded to tell her about the interesting photos I'd found. "It looked like a meeting of some kind. Unofficial. Between Ed Leoni and Carl Wellen. Leoni sold the Kendricks the property. And Wellen is a soil engineer."

"What, pray tell, does a soil engineer do?"

"Among other things, he tests the quality of soil. It's required in a sale. I called Mr. Wellen and asked if we could talk. He seemed reluctant, but when I mentioned Clair and Cedar Ridge, he said he'd call me back."

"Has he?"

"Of course not. But I'm going to pay him a visit."

Nita pondered this for a moment. "If Clair was following up on all this, why didn't she say anything to me?"

"Maybe she wanted to be certain." To be honest, I wondered that myself. "How long had Clair been working on his story?"

"Not long. Maybe a week before she died."

"Maybe she was waiting for some answers."

"So, what's next?"

I looked down at my own notes. Still lots of questions. "I left a message for Glenn Patchen. I have yet to hear from him. I think I need to pay him another visit."

"Sounds like a good move."

I flipped a page. "And I'm still curious about this Town and Country place. Why is it even in Clair's notes? Is there someone there she wanted to talk with?"

"Did you do a search on it?"

"Yeah, but maybe I need to do more."

She nodded. I thought she was being agreeable so she could get rid of me and return to paper sorting, but then she looked at her watch. "You got plans for dinner?"

"Probably something frozen. You have a better idea?"

"I was thinking of a burger. We could do some brainstorming."

"Let's find a place with WiFi."

"Sounds like a plan."

* * *

That place turned out to be The Tasty Morsel, a small restaurant tucked between a dry cleaners and nail salon. Nita and I puzzled over the reference in Clair's notes to Town and Country Residences in Camden Hills. An Internet search revealed it to be an upscale continuing care community. I wondered if perhaps Clair's grandparents might be candidates for this kind of facility, and I even called Clair's mother to see if that were a possibility. As it turned out, Clair's only remaining grandparent—Mara's mother—was living in Florida and doing quite well.

"It must be the who and not the what," I said to Nita.

She had looked up from her half-finished cheeseburger with chipotle sauce and asked, "As in one of the residents?"

"Yeah."

She keyed a few words into her computer. "You're probably right, but I don't know how we can access that information."

"Maybe if we start with a name."

"Whose name?"

I shook my head. "Not sure." I gave it some thought as I dipped a pita wedge into some red pepper hummus. "Okay, who's involved in this Cedar Ridge story?" I brought up the list of everyone referenced in Clair's notes. We did Google searches linking each name with Town and Country. It took some time, but we finally got a hit on David de Coriolis, whose father, Forrest, had moved into the facility a year and a half ago.

"You know," Nita said, her fingernail tapping the base of her wineglass, "I sort of remember something about this." She took the wine bottle and added another inch and a half of the zinfandel to her glass. "Forrest de Coriolis was this district's representative for years, back in the sixties and seventies. When he retired, he endorsed Derek Schmidt to replace him, but the belief was that Schmidt was just holding the place until Forrest's son, David, got a few years of lawyering under his belt. But when it was time for Schmidt to step down, he decided he liked the view from his D.C. office too much to give it up. Eventually he did, but there were some deals that had to be made."

"Threats?"

"Yeah," she said, nodding. "There may have been that too. There was also probably some money involved. Eventually he did retire and endorse David de Coriolis, who has been happily serving the district ever since."

I had to smile. "Your favorite politician."

She made a face. "He's gotten too comfortable. Just like his father. This district is solidly Republican and so long as he gets some earmark money and doesn't get caught *in flagrante delicto* with one of the pages, he's probably in for as long as he wants to be."

"And his father needs supervised care?"

"I think I read that he's got Alzheimer's." She stared past me for a moment, her chin propped up by her small fist. "Sad, really. He used to be quite the dealmaker. A powerful man."

"Why do you think Clair needed to see him?"

"Excellent question."

As I rolled this over in my mind, an idea came to me. I admit, I felt some shame at how quickly I wove my mother into this scheme.

Chapter 18

I started what turned out to be a busy day with a visit to Carl Wellen's office after he hadn't return my calls. I'd tracked him down to one of the government offices on the east side of Fowler. What was it about this story? For a nonthreatening, feel-good subject, people were surprisingly reluctant to share the goodness.

Wellen was in his fifties and balding with a softness to him that, for some reason, I imagined he'd had all his life. There was something about him—maybe the way he slumped with his head thrust forward like a turtle's—that made me think he'd had his share of bullying over the years. He also avoided making eye contact for more than a fraction of a second at a time.

"I don't have time to talk right now," he said, shoving some papers into a battered, brown leather briefcase.

Being a soil engineer apparently didn't give one secretarial privileges, and I'd found my way to his small office just by asking someone I ran into by the Coke machine. There was one other desk in the office, which wasn't occupied at the time.

"I just have a few questions."

He had small, droopy eyes and sparse brows, furthering the whole turtle look he had going on. "I don't know what I can possibly tell you."

"Why don't you let me ask you so you can find out?"

He lifted a gray windbreaker from a hook on the back of the office door. "I'm supposed to meet someone in ten minutes and it'll take me fifteen to get there."

"So you were late before I showed up."

"And now I'll be later."

As he started to walk out the door, I slipped a copy of the photo out of my bag and thrust it in front of him. "This is what I need to ask you about."

"What—" He stopped. His washed-out gray eyes flickered my way.

"That's your car, isn't it?"

"So?"

"Are you and Ed Leoni friends?"

"I—yes, we are." He made another attempt at holding my gaze and failed.

I nodded. "I found this photo on Clair Powell's camera. Do you know who she was?"

"Yes, I do." He glanced down the hall one way and then the other. Lowering his voice, he said, "I don't want to talk about this here."

"Call me. We can meet somewhere."

"Yes, I'll call you."

"If you don't, I know where you live." I didn't. Not yet anyway.

From the way he sort of caved into himself, I figured he believed me.

"I'll call you tomorrow," he said, then turned and shuffled down the hall.

* * *

On my way to Dryden, I called Patchen again and, again, got his voicemail. I tried to stress the urgency in the message I left, but wasn't optimistic. Lately, I'd been feeling like a pariah.

My mother was waiting for me in the lounge, wearing her coat, but she was uncharacteristically quiet as I helped her into the car. When I'd called her earlier and asked her if she wanted to go for a ride, she'd seemed eager, and why not? It was a bright, fall day and the leaves were reaching their color peak. When she asked where we were going, I told her I wanted to check on someone living at Town and Country. At the time she'd said that sounded nice, but now, as I maneuvered my Matrix up Route 37, toward the village of Camden Hills, she wasn't saying a thing.

"Everything okay, Mom?"

She inhaled deeply and released the breath in a sigh. "This is a cruel thing you're doing, Robyn."

"What is?"

My mother gave me a flat look. I honestly didn't know what she was talking about.

"Not wanting to buy a house with me is one thing. But sticking me in a place and forgetting about me . . . that's cruel." I could feel her glare. "You think I don't know what this place is. Well, I do. I asked around. It's one of those storage places for seniors."

So that explained it. I'd figured she was either confused or in a snit. Now that I had my answer, I could deal with it. I preferred her testiness to befuddlement. But now I wasn't sure how much I wanted to tell her.

"How could I forget about you?"

Failing at my attempt to lighten things, I went with the truth. "This isn't about you, Mom. I'm working on a story."

She sniffed.

"We're on a fact-finding mission."

"Oh. So, that's what you're calling it."

"Really, Mom." I paused. "I thought you'd enjoy a ride."

"Well, I usually do. But then I found out what this place is."

I decided it was time to tell her I wanted to use her. Although, I hoped she didn't see it that way. "I thought you might be able to help me."

After a few moments, she said, "Help you?"

I tried to think of a way to explain what I wanted her to do without making it sound like she was a prop. To be honest, I did feel a little shame, but I also knew my mother. And this kind of subterfuge might appeal to her.

"Okay, Mom. I need to talk to a resident at Town and Country. Forrest de Coriolis. I thought having you along would make it seem more authentic. Maybe lend credence to my claim that we know de Coriolis—if they have reason to question. You and he are about the same age; you could have a history together." The difficult-to-believe part had to do with our respective social statuses. In an attempt to compensate for our plebeian backstories, I'd worn a designer suit that I'd gotten at a resale shop and had suggested that my mother wear a nice pair of slacks and a blouse instead of one of her velour numbers.

"I see," my mother said when I'd finished. "So, you're using me."

"Sort of," I admitted, slowing down as I approached a red light. "But you wanted to get out. I guess I also figured you might think it was kind of fun to do a little role playing."

"'Role playing'?"

"Yeah, I'm an attorney married to an attorney." I was ad libbing. "We live in Barrington. We're very happy together and we've got two perfect children. Boy and a girl. One is attending UCLA and the other Harvard. You've been living with us, but since the kids left for college you're feeling a bit lonely. You're thinking you need some people your age to hang with."

"So, I'm living with you."

"Yeah, but you're not real happy."

Glancing her way, I saw that she was giving me her narrow-eyed look that suggested I'd best tread carefully. "This looks awfully nice for a senior storage place."

"Isn't that illegal? Pretending you're a lawyer?"

"Not unless I give someone legal advice."

When that didn't seem to mollify her, I added, "And I'm not the kind of lawyer who gives advice without being paid for it."

She looked me up and down. "You're a lawyer."

"Right."

"Is that why you bothered to wear an outfit that matches?"

"Exactly."

When I pulled off the road and onto the long drive that led to Town and Country, I got my first glimpse of the former Congressional representative's current home. It looked like a rambling mansion with heavily treed expanses of lawn and a couple of fountains, one of which occupied an area just west of the entrance. I knew it had been built less than ten years ago as an extended care nursing home, but it looked as though it had occupied these grounds forever. American nobility might have lived here. Along with their servants and horses. I hoped my mother didn't become too smitten with the place. Clearly, we were out of our league.

"Are you sure this is a senior storage place? It looks awfully nice."

"Of course it's nice. Wealthy people store their parents in lovely places. That's what Blanche told me. Her daughter wanted to move her to this place, but Blanche wouldn't hear of it."

I suspected Blanche had executed the sour-grapes defense, but I held my tongue.

I parked in the visitors' lot, which, except for one other car, was empty, and went around the car to help my mother out. I tried to talk her into wearing my coat—a serviceable, black three-quarter-length number—but she insisted on wearing her old royal blue coat with the frayed collar and ripped pocket. I'd never seen her wear the new one I'd gotten her a month ago. Said the color—camel—was all wrong for her.

Once I'd gotten her outfitted with the coat and her cane, she took a moment to look up at the edifice. Her mouth hung open for several seconds. But she snapped it shut and gave me one of her sweet smiles. "What a lovely place."

* * *

The foyer was huge, with slate flooring and chandeliers hanging from a vaulted ceiling. It looked more like a high-class hotel than a nursing home. When I told the receptionist that we were here to see Forrest de Coriolis, she asked, "What's your name?"

"I'm Robyn Guthrie and this is my mother, Lizzie."

My mother lifted her chin an inch, as though expecting a rebuttal.

The receptionist keyed something into a computer. She was about my age with short blond hair and way, way too much eye makeup. I wondered how long it took to get all that off at night. After studying the screen for a moment, she blinked heavily, looked up at me and said, "I'm sorry. Mr. de Coriolis only sees people who have been approved by his family. You're not on the list."

"Oh." I don't know why I thought it would be easy. I considered giving her one of the business cards I'd printed that morning. Technology is wonderful. With business card stock and a decent printer, anyone could be a lawyer. And I knew enough about web design to put together a website that made the firm of Abernathy, Guthrie and Harvey look like a reputable outfit. But I sensed that this woman had seen a lot more impressive ones over the years. So, I just put my arm around my mother, sighed, and looked down at her. "I'm sorry, Mom."

She looked up at me. The muscles around her mouth twitched, but she didn't say anything. I turned back to the receptionist. "Excuse us a minute."

I walked my mother over to a chair and helped her sit. "Will you go along with me on this?"

"What are you doing?"

"I'm just trying to get in to see this man. I think he might know something."

"What am I supposed to do?"

"Nothing, Mom. Just play along with me."

I was making this up as I went, and I had the feeling my mother knew it.

I returned to the receptionist. "My mother . . ." I nodded in her direction ". . . used to know Forrest. A long time ago. They went to the University of Chicago together."

The woman blinked again but didn't say anything. Just then her phone rang and she took the call. I had the feeling I'd been dismissed. But I get my persistence from my mother, and so I waited. It didn't take long to surmise it was a personal call. In my experience, one usually reserved the term "honey," along with scolding tones, for family members.

The call took several minutes, but I waited. And when she finally hung up, she seemed a bit surprised to find me still standing there.

I continued as though there hadn't been a four-minute interlude.

"My mom has been a little upset lately. I don't know, I think she's remembering the past with unusual clarity. She wants to see some of her old friends, but most of them are gone. You know? They're either not around here anymore or they're . . . gone."

A thin, vertical line appeared between her eyebrows.

"It's got her distressed. I thought if she could talk to someone she remembered, it might help her. Please."

"I'm sorry. I'm afraid I can't."

"Robyn?" It was my mother, who doesn't like being left alone for more than a few seconds in a place she doesn't know. Leaving her cane hooked to the arm of the chair, she started to stand. I rushed over to her, grabbing her arm as she teetered to one side. She latched onto my forearm. Once I got her standing, I reached for her cane, but she wouldn't let go of me. "Why do you do that?"

"I was six feet away, Mom."

Her mouth was open slightly and she blinked a few times as though trying to figure out where she was. From the confusion I guessed that she'd dozed off. Waking up in a strange place can be disconcerting for her. I needed to take her home. I'd try breaching Town and Country another day.

I got her to take her cane and we headed slowly toward the exit.

"Miss Guthrie?" It was the receptionist. We stopped. When she didn't continue, I figured she wanted to tell me good riddance but didn't want to have to shout it. Searching for a snappy retort, I steered my mother back toward the desk. When I got there, the woman glanced over her shoulder, looking toward a closed office door behind her, then leaned forward and, lowering her voice, she said, "Mr. de Coriolis eats lunch at the eleven-thirty seating."

I glanced at my watch. It was twenty after.

"He dines with Mr. Ralph Flannery." She patted the sign-in register. "He has severe Alzheimer's."

I nodded and signed us into the book as visitors for Flannery, wondering if I should tip the woman.

"Thank you." I nodded toward my mother. "Is it okay if we sit here until he comes down?"

"There's a lounge just outside the dining area." She indicated a hall off to the right.

I thanked her again and looked at my mother.

"You okay?" She nodded, and I thought she had returned to reality. Sometimes it didn't take long.

"Come on. He'll be coming down for dinner in a few minutes."

I escorted her into a large room decorated in shades of peach with green accents. We sat next to each other in matching Victorian chairs, which were more comfortable than they looked.

"You sure you're okay?"

"Of course I am!"

"Thanks." I patted her hand. "It'll just be a few more minutes."

This was an impressive place—tasteful and elegant—but it did have more the feel of a hotel than a home. I hadn't noticed any other visitors since we'd been here, which, admittedly, wasn't very long. And I reminded myself that this was during the day in the middle of the week. But I often visited my mother at Dryden, and was never the only visitor. In fact, my mother enjoyed critiquing guests and residents at the same time. "Louise's daughter—the one with the large derriere—never misses an open house with free food." I had the feeling that none of Town and Country's residents had large-butted visitors.

I retrieved the photo I'd found of Forrest de Coriolis from my purse. It was ten years old, but I couldn't find anything more recent. I'd memorized the bushy eyebrows and hawk-like nose. It was mainly the eyes that I noticed about this man. Shrewd and cold.

"What are you doing with that man's picture?"

"This is the man I need to talk with."

"Why?"

"I'm not sure."

I recognized him when he got off the elevator. He was bent over and shuffled along, pushing a walker ahead of him, but there was no mistaking that profile and the eyebrows that looked like fledgling wings sprouting out of his forehead. He was escorted by a nurse's aid who led him to a table for four already occupied by a man with thick, dark hair, horn-rimmed glasses and an empty look. He wasn't much older than me.

Although they were seated across from each other, neither made eye contact. The younger man—Ralph Flannery, I assumed—stared down at the white table cloth; de Coriolis was fidgety, lacing and unlacing his long fingers as he seemed to avoid looking at Flannery.

"Mom?"

"Hmm?"

I saw she was watching the residents accumulate in the dining room. Waitresses attended each table, snapping a folded napkin before settling it on a resident's lap. And while the room had the elegance of an exclusive restaurant—chandeliers and crystal water glasses—there was little interaction among the diners.

"I wonder how the food is here," my mother said.

Ignoring her, I said, "We're going to join those two men. Can you pretend you know the guy with the eyebrows?"

"Hmph. I doubt the other one would see me."

"It'll just be for a few minutes." I saw how she'd clasped her hands together. "If you don't want to, we'll leave. No problem."

She shook her head and I thought I saw some determination in the gesture.

"What's his name again?" she asked.

I told her. "You knew him at University of Chicago."

With a sigh, she said, "I don't know what you're doing, Robyn, but I don't think it's seemly."

"Probably not."

"Very well."

We walked over to the table. I held my mother's arm as we moved across the parquet flooring. When we came to stand beside Forrest de Coriolis and he gave no sign that he noticed us, I said, "Excuse me."

It took him so long to respond, I thought for a moment that he'd drifted off. But then he turned his head and tilted his chin up.

"Forrest?"

He looked from me to my mother and back again.

"Hello, Forrest," my mother said.

Now his eyes squinted as he studied my mother.

"May we sit?" I asked.

He lifted his shoulders in either a sigh or a shrug, so I maneuvered my mother into a chair and scooted around the table to grab the other.

"Could we talk for a minute?" I asked.

Again, he looked at each of us and then grumbled, "Anything's better than sitting across from that zombie."

"My name's Robyn."

He focused on me. "Do I know you?"

"No, but this is my mother, Lizzie." I swallowed. Lying to this man seemed wrong. But I had my script. "You were at the University of Chicago together."

He shifted in his chair so he was turned toward my mother. "Yeah?"

"I'm Lizzie," my mother said in way that made her sound like a young girl.

Forrest looked down at his palms. "I don't know. I don't know."

"How are you doing?" I asked, at the same time realizing it was a lame question.

Apparently Forrest thought so too, because he gave me suspicious look and said, "How do you think?" He turned toward my mother. "I know you?" He shook his head and looked down at this hands again, which he began rubbing together.

My mother reached out and touched his arm. "Don't you remember me?"

He shook his head and squeezed his eyes shut.

I was ready to call it off, but then my mother said, "It's all right."

Forrest sighed and nodded, opening his eyes. That was when I noticed how blue they were. Now they seemed more sad than shrewd.

My mother continued, "I quit school. Left early."

He studied her for a moment. "Why?"

She gave him a modest smile. "I went to Hollywood."

The eyebrows shot up so fast I thought he was going to rise out of the chair. "You an actress?"

"I did a few movies."

Careful there, Mother.

"What movies?"

"Did you see *Ben Hur*?"

Forrest leaned toward her. With his rolled shoulders, scrawny neck and beaky nose, he reminded me of a buzzard. "*Ben Hur*?"

"Moses!" It was Ralph Flannery, the man we were supposed to be visiting, who turned out to have a powerful voice. The occupants of nearby tables turned to see what was going on.

Forrest waved him off, but Flannery seemed to be engaged now. "Those tablets. Should've left 'em there."

With a sigh, Forrest shook his head. "Atheist," he muttered, and turned back to my mother. "What movie was that again?"

"*Ben Hur.*"

"Who'd you play?"

She hesitated for only a second. "A slave girl."

"Excuse me."

I looked up to see one of the waitresses. She was short and round and I could tell from her stern demeanor that she wasn't here to take our order. "Who are you?"

"Robyn Guthrie," I said. "We're visiting Ralph Flannery."

"Then why are you talking with this man?"

"Ralph won't talk to me," my mother said.

"I'll see about this." The waitress turned and headed in the direction of the offices.

I knew my time was limited so I pulled out a photo of Clair.

"Mr. de Coriolis, do you remember this woman?"

I laid the photo on the table in front of him. He took it in his hands and stared at it. I didn't want to rush him, but as the seconds turned into a minute, I feared he'd gone for a mind nap. But finally he nodded and smiled a little.

"She brought me candy. Chocolates. Not the kind that stick to your teeth. Milk chocolate. With cherries."

Why hadn't I thought of that?

"What did you talk about?"

He looked at me sharply. "Talk?"

I withdrew another photo from my purse. This one was of the Cedar Ridge property—pre-development. "Do you recognize this land?" Again, I pushed the photo toward him. But, this time, instead of taking it, he pushed it back toward me, rejecting it.

"Miss Guthrie?"

I looked up and there was the squealing waitress with reinforcements in the form of a tall, angular woman wearing a deep green suit with a dragonfly pin affixed to the lapel. She looked from me to my mother and then said to me, "May we have a word?"

"Of course." It's like being busted by the cops. It never hurts to be polite. I said to my mother, "I'll just be a minute."

"Of course, dear."

I didn't care for her tone. It might have been part of her act, but it also might have been a warning shot.

I followed the woman into the lounge, but she didn't offer me a chair. Instead, she turned, arms crossed over her thin chest and said, "You know Mr. Flannery?"

"I, ah, yes." I cocked my chin. "I'm sorry. What did you say your name was?"

She raised one eyebrow. "How do you know Mr. Flannery?"

"He's my husband's brother-in-law. I was just in the area."

"Why were you talking with Mr. de Coriolis?"

"Ralph wasn't saying anything."

Her expression remained grim. "May I see an ID?"

"Look, I don't want to cause any trouble. We were just in the area. I take my mother for drives, you know. She likes to ride in the car. And we were near here, so I thought—"

"Your ID."

"Why?"

"Because I'm going to check this with Mr. Flannery's wife."

"I see." I took a deep breath. "Well, my name is Robyn Guthrie and you can trust me on that." I wasn't giving up my drivers' license to this woman. I supposed I could give her a business card, but I didn't want her checking out my faux law firm.

Her jaw hardened. "Come with me."

I looked back at the table. My mother was talking to Forrest.

"This shouldn't take long," the woman said. "She'll be fine."

"Um, sure."

I followed her back to the reception area, where the mascaraed receptionist was giving me the nasty look that I deserved. The woman who wouldn't even introduce herself showed me into her office and went to her desk, picked up the phone and, after consulting a directory, punched in a number. She eyed me as she listened to it ring.

Mentally crossing my fingers, I hoped that Mrs. Flannery worked a job with normal hours. If so, she probably wouldn't be home and whoever this woman was would have to leave a message. I was already anticipating a hasty exit. Whether the woman was home or not.

"Yes," angular woman said, "Mrs. Flannery? . . . It's Marge Rayburn at Town and Country. . . . Yes, Ma'am. Ralph is fine. I just have a quick question for you." She gave me a triumphant smirk. Why I hadn't introduced myself as simply a friend of Ralph's, I'll never know. "Does your, um, brother . . ." she looked at me as though she needed prompting. I just smiled. "Or perhaps your brother-in-law . . . well, let me ask this. Do you know a woman named Robyn Guthrie?"

Busted. I could tell from the way she drew herself up, practically glowing with satisfaction. "Well, I don't want you to be concerned, but there's someone here claiming to be an acquaintance of Ralph's . . . Yes." They talked for another minute, Marge assuring the woman that her husband was fine. I considered bolting, but knew I couldn't collect my mother and make a hasty escape, so I decided it was best if I stayed here and dealt with the repercussions.

When Marge finally hung up, she looked me square on and, projecting her voice into the reception area, said, "Melinda, call the police."

"Before you do that, Miss Rayburn, maybe you should think about what you're doing." Although I drew myself up, I was still several inches shorter than Marge. "First, I don't think I've broken the law and second, how is it going to look if the police come in here and haul me off along with an eighty-four-year-old woman?"

Rayburn just stood there, staring at me. Melinda had come to the door and was, apparently, waiting for assurances that she was, indeed, to call the police.

Sighing, Rayburn sighed said, "Melinda, would you escort Miss Guthrie and her mother out of here?" She started to turn away but stopped. "What was it you wanted, Miss Guthrie?" Before I had to respond, she said, "Never mind. I'm sure you'd just continue with your lies."

Perceptive woman.

They had me wait in the reception area while a nurse's tech was sent for my mother. When the two of them emerged from the dining room hallway, the tech was laughing over something my mother had said. When my mother saw me, waiting there chastised, she shook her head. "I don't know why you're like this, Robyn." To Marge, she said, "She gets confused."

I bit my tongue.

"Let's go home, dear," she said.

Out in the car, I braced for a verbal assault from my mother, which I deserved. But, instead, she sat there looking out the window toward a copse of maple trees. "What a nice man."

"Mr. de Coriolis?" I asked.

"Well of course. That other gentleman—poor man—couldn't move past Moses and Charlton Heston." With a sigh she added, "I hope I never do that."

"You wouldn't, Mom. You never liked Charlton Heston." I looked over at her. "Were you really in *Ben Hur*?" She did have her Hollywood years, although they'd mostly been spent as a director's assistant. But most young women didn't go out to Hollywood to become director's assistants.

"Yes. Yes, I was."

I was brimming with follow-up questions, but my mother continued, "Do you want to know what Forrest had to say about those pictures?"

I felt my eyes widen. "Yes."

"I have them here." She dug into her purse and produced the two photos I'd shown him. Looking at the picture of Clair, she asked, "Who is she?"

"She's that reporter for the *Record* who was killed in a hit and run accident last week."

"Oh. She's lovely."

"Yes, she was."

"Forrest thought so too." She tucked Clair's photo behind the property photo. "She asked him about this land as well."

"He said that?"

She gave me a look. "Yes, dear. That's what he said."

"Did he say anything about the land?"

"It must have been quite valuable."

"Why?"

"He said it put his son through college." She squinted at the photo. "I can't remember where."

I waited.

"Started with an S."

I thought for a moment. "Stanford?"

She nodded slowly. "That may have been it."

"Really?" I stared past her toward the entrance. "Did he say anything else?"

"He said he thought I looked lovely in this shade of blue."

"Well, you do." Feeling so good about this nugget, I didn't think before blurting out, "On the way home, would you like to see that house Sharon showed me?"

She took a moment to consider my offer before saying, "Yes, I suppose that would be nice."

While I'd expected more enthusiasm, I figured she was still a bit peeved with me.

* * *

I pulled to the curb in front of the ranch house I'd fallen in love with and sat there while my mother took in the tan brick and the dark brown accents in the doors and trim. The porch was large with an overhang, and I could imagine sitting on a wrought iron bench as I wiped Bix's paws after a wet walk. Because if this were my house—or partly my house—there would be no muddy feet crossing the threshold. Ever since I'd seen this house, I'd been thinking more and more about living in it. But as I sat here now, with my mother beside me, I realized that I was envisioning living here alone. Not with my mother. And now I had to chide myself for showing it to her. That wasn't a nice thing to do. The last thing I wanted to do was get her hopes up.

"What do you think?" I asked. At the time I suppose I knew that showing her a house I had picked out would be no different than introducing her to a new boyfriend. There was always something. Always.

"Well," she said.

"What?"

"It's an odd color, isn't it?"

"It's tan brick."

She turned toward me. "I can see that. It's an odd shade of tan."

"Tan is tan, Mother."

She sighed and focused on the house again. "That's a large yard." I waited.

"It would be a lot for you to mow."

"It's a house, Mother. They come with yards. If you'd wanted a condo or a townhouse, you should have mentioned that."

She began kneading her black nylon purse. "You don't have to be short with me."

"I just want to know what you don't like about the house."

"I didn't say that."

"You didn't have to."

She sighed and looked at me again, blinking. "It reminds me of the home I shared with Wyman."

"The one I grew up in?" When she didn't protest, I continued. "I remember that house. It wasn't tan. It was brown."

"A *light* brown."

I gazed upwards, calling on any deity of any faith to come to my rescue. When none responded, I summoned my analytical abilities. There was something bothering her other than the color of the house. "What's wrong, Mom?"

"Did I say there was something wrong?"

"Not in so many words."

She didn't respond.

"You haven't even seen the inside." Now, why was I trying to sell her on it?

She clasped her hands tight as though holding onto a promise or a dream. "Can you show it to me now?"

"No," I said, sincerely sorry. "I'll need to talk to Sharon."

Eyes cast downward, she nodded.

"If she has time tomorrow."

She nodded again.

There was nothing more for me to say, and I supposed it didn't matter to her. I'd already given her what she wanted. At least that's what I thought at the time.

Chapter 19

I had two calls waiting for me when I got home. The first was from Sharon and the second from David de Coriolis's office, letting me know that the congressman had finally found fifteen minutes in his busy schedule to squeeze me in. Would I be available tomorrow at eleven thirty? Coincidence? Ha. I was sure it had more to do with my unauthorized visit to Town and Country then an opening in his schedule. Too bad. After what I'd learned, I wasn't ready to talk to him. Maybe, now that he was all primed, and maybe a little worried, I'd let him wait another day.

Since I'd just driven past the house I was thinking of buying, that was foremost in my mind when I returned Sharon's call. I was sure she would be happy to show it to my mother and maybe then my mother would tell us both what was wrong with it.

So I was a little surprised when she opened with, "You're not going to believe what Lucky sold that property for," she said.

"What?"

The number she gave me was half what her estimate had been. "That's low, isn't it?"

"Real low. And I did a little further digging. I wondered who Lucky bought the property from. Does the name Justin Adamo mean anything to you?"

"No. Should it?"

"I don't know. But he sold Lucky the property three years ago."

"For how much?"

She gave me a number that was closer to the amount Sharon believed it was worth. I wrote down the name Adamo and thanked Sharon. Profusely. "I suppose this means I'm going to have to buy that house."

She laughed. "Only if you want it."

"My mother wants to see the inside. I drove her past it today. I'm not sure, but I think she wasn't thrilled with it."

"You know," she said, after a pause, "it could be that you're not the only one having second thoughts."

This had not occurred to me and now that Sharon had mentioned it, I had a fleeting glimmer of hope. But I knew that my mother didn't often change her mind, so, shortly after thanking Sharon and hanging up, I let the hope sputter and die.

I got my mind off my housing crisis by doing an Internet search on Justin Adamo. The name wasn't all that uncommon, but the one that waved a little red flag at me when it came up was the Justin Adamo who was son of Salvatore Adamo, known as "Sweet Sal," a "reputed" mob boss. Hmm. I debated whether to run this by Mick or not. I had the feeling it would result in further dire warnings.

* * *

I'd been trying to get hold of Glenn Patchen for two days now. At first it had just been questions that I hadn't had the chance to ask the day at his office. But now that I'd managed to have at least a few words with Carl Wellen, I thought Patchen might have some idea as to why Wellen was involved. At the very least he should be able to tell me what it was that he knew. So, I headed out to Cedar Ridge.

I wasn't counting on him being there, but if he wasn't, I could use the opportunity to talk with the Sanduskys, Mary Alice's neighbors. I figured profiles of the Cedar Ridge families would help readers connect to the whole development better than anything a builder or an architect could say.

But when I drove past his mobile home office, I saw Patchen's Forester was parked there. I decided not to be offended by his inability to return a phone call. If he'd talk to me now, I'd pretend that never happened.

As I pulled my car onto the gravel next to his, I saw a car coming up behind me. When it drove by, I recognized Mary Alice. We waved.

When I knocked on the door to Patchen's trailer, no one answered. After another attempt and still no response, I figured he must be out on the site somewhere. I checked to see if the trailer was unlocked. It was, so I pushed the door open and stepped inside. I guess I was a little surprised to find Patchen there, at his desk, staring at the wall beside me. He didn't look my way, so I tapped my knuckles on the door jamb. He slowly turned his head in my direction and blinked once, slowly. He didn't focus and he looked like he'd just woken up. That was when I noticed the glass tumbler with a couple of inches of something Scotch-colored in it. I'm familiar enough with the effects of too many drinks to recognize that Patchen was on his way to drunk, if not already there.

He stared at me but gave no indication that he actually saw me. Not a word, not a nod, not an indifferent shrug. So, I closed the door behind me, walked into the room and sat in a chair facing him. His gaze followed me.

"You got another glass?" I asked. It was early and I didn't really want anything, but I thought he might be more inclined to talk if he wasn't drinking alone.

He continued to lock onto me with this lifeless gaze. I stared right back. After what was only about ten seconds, but seemed way, way longer, he pulled open the top left drawer to his desk and withdrew a white mug with the Green Haven logo on it. Then he leaned over and picked up something from the floor. It was a bottle of Scotch—not my brand, but Scotch—and poured a generous amount into the mug.

"No ice," he said.

"I'll pretend I'm British." I leaned forward and took the mug from him. After a sip I decided that ice would have done no favors for this brew. I took another drink to make sure I hadn't been too quick to judge. I hadn't.

We sat there in silence for a minute. I noticed he was drinking it like water. Since he didn't seem inclined to break the silence, I finally did. "Was Joe Kendrick a good friend?"

He shook his head. "I thought he was kind of a jerk."

I nodded. "He had his moments."

He smiled a little, lifting his glass in a silent toast.

I did likewise. There was something here, and although I had no idea what that was, I was determined to find out before I left. Or, more likely, before I drove him somewhere to sleep it off.

"There was a cryptic little text message that Joe Kendrick sent to someone. I thought you might be able to shed some light on it."

He waited.

"I don't know who the text was sent to, but all it said was, 'Patchen knows.'" I gave him a moment, and when he didn't respond, I asked, "Do you know what he was talking about?"

His gaze settled on me for a fraction of a second before he helped himself to another gulp of the Scotch.

"You must know," I said. "I mean, whatever it is, you know. That was the point of the message."

Patchen's human wall routine was starting to annoy me. I thought if he wouldn't talk about what it was he knew, maybe he'd succumb to small talk "I saw Mary Alice outside. Nice woman."

He pressed his mouth tight; it almost looked like he was going to cry. But he just nodded and swallowed. "She is," he said, then added, "and they deserve better than this."

"Better than what?"

Instead of answering me, he poured another half inch into his glass. Apparently if the level got below two inches something bad might happen.

"I was hoping we could talk some more about Cedar Ridge."

"I've got nothing else to say."

"How do you know? I haven't asked any questions yet."

"Go ahead and ask." His tipped back in his chair and picked up his drink.

"Okay, for starters, what's wrong?"

"Nothing." But he laughed, apparently amused by his own answer.

I jotted that in my notebook. "Okay, that's good to know. Now I've got a couple of questions regarding the acquisition of this property. Ed Leoni sold this property to the Kendricks, correct?"

He nodded.

"So is Leoni the person who would have had to make sure the property met certain standards, EPA standards for example, and all that?"

His chair landed on all fours with a loud thump. I waited.

Patchen ran a hand through his hair. "Either he would or the Kendricks. Depends."

"On what?"

"The arrangement."

"When would the soil have been tested?"

"Before the sale."

I nodded, punching the button on my ballpoint pen "I think there was something odd going on."

Now he leaned forward and rested his arms on the surface of the desk. "Like what?"

I produced a copy of one of the photos I'd found on Clair's camera and pushed it across the desk toward him. "This is Ed Leoni meeting with a man named Carl Wellen. He's a soil engineer."

Patchen looked down at the photo, but didn't touch it. "How do you know who's in the car?"

"License plate."

He nodded once. "Okay. So?"

I set my notebook and pen on his desk. "As I said, I think there was something going on."

He leaned back again without tipping his chair and looked up at the ceiling.

"Glenn, tell me about that message. What do you know?"

Finally, he focused on me again. "Off the record?"

I didn't answer.

"You won't hear it otherwise."

"Okay, let me see if I can guess."

He shook his head, but I continued. "It doesn't take a leap in critical thinking." To my own surprise, that was true. Once I started putting it together, I wondered what had taken me so long. "You knew something that Joe Kendrick and at least one other person didn't want you to know. I think there's a good chance that this other person was Ed Leoni. Ed Leoni was meeting someone in a parking lot—not your typical venue for a business meeting. That person turned out to be Carl Wellen, a soil engineer. Possibly the one who did the soil testing for Cedar Ridge." If any of this was either alarming or interesting to Patchen, his expression wasn't giving him away. "Is that correct?"

No answer. But he was still focused on me and hadn't had a drink since I'd begun speculating. I assumed my guess was correct. So I went a step further. "There's something wrong with the soil here, isn't there?" I knew I was right, and yet at the same time I prayed I wasn't.

But then Patchen pressed his thumbs into the corners of his eyes and lowered his head. He pulled in a deep breath and released it in a sob. "This land. This rich earth, these trees, these homes . . . this shining example of environmentalism. This metaphor . . ."

I didn't move.

". . . is sitting on top of a toxic waste dump."

I set the mug on Patchen's desk. "A toxic waste dump?" I repeated, not because I didn't believe him. In fact, I did.

"Are you sure, Glenn?"

"I had it tested."

I looked down at the photo.

"By someone I hired myself."

"Why?" His blank look prompted me to say, "You must have had your own suspicions about the land. Why?"

"A tip."

"Clair suspected, didn't she?"

When he didn't answer and instead turned his tortured gaze toward the wall, I knew I was right. "Why did Clair suspect?"

He shook his head. "That I don't know."

I pushed the photos closer to him. "She took these pictures. From her car. She was following one of these guys. Right?"

He kept shaking his head, and his cowering-drunk show made me angry. "So, that was why you came to her memorial. You were feeling guilty."

"No. I didn't . . . No." Even though he enunciated each word, his voice was thick from the Scotch and the emotion trapped in his throat. "I didn't have the soil tested until after she died. No, she was a good person. I just wanted to say goodbye."

My ass. "Clair's knowing may have gotten her killed."

"No. It was an accident," he said in the dead tone of someone who's been hearing that from himself a lot lately.

"No, I don't think it was. Why would Clair have been walking Scoop on a dark road at eleven P.M.? In the rain? I think she was meeting someone." When he didn't argue, I said, "Who?"

"It was an accident."

"Just keep telling yourself that, Glenn."

His eyes sort of glazed over.

I leaned forward and placed my forefinger on the photo. "So the original results were faked?"

"They must have been."

I sat back, taking the mug with me. Although Patchen was going through a major internal crisis, it all seemed pretty straightforward to me. I needed to report this. "Do you want to give me a quote?" I asked, snapping my pen again.

"You can't report this."

"Watch me."

"Don't you see? If this got her killed, who's next?"

Clearly, Glenn saw his own name on the list. "Not if the story gets out. Once the secret's out, there's no reason."

"There's more."

"Tell me."

He pressed his mouth tight again, but this time all I could see was anger. "Joe Kendrick knew."

"When he bought the property?"

Patchen nodded. "I'd bet on it."

"What makes you say that?"

"Because I told him about the results of the test I had done. And you know what he said? He asked me if I'd told anyone else. Not 'Oh, my God' or 'That can't be true.' He wanted to know who else knew." He shook his head. "That's when I knew I wasn't telling him anything he didn't already know."

"What did you say to him?"

"Said I hadn't told anyone and the guy who did the test didn't know where the sample had come from."

"So you're in on this with him."

"I'm not." He lurched forward in his chair. "No way. I'm just thinking of Green Haven. It's a good company. How do you think that's going to make them look? That Green Haven bought toxic property?"

He had a point. But if Joe Kendrick knowingly bought toxic land for a green community, then maybe Green Haven deserved what it got. Did Kat know about this?

"And it's not about me either. It's not about how I'm going to look," he said like he was talking to an idiot.

"It's not?" I was beginning to suspect that it mostly was about him.

"Think about it. What's going to happen if word gets out?"

"I don't know. A lawsuit. If they can prove that the samples were doctored, then I guess Leoni will have to do something."

"That's all well and fine. But what about the Tuckers? The Sanduskys? The Kellers?"

I saw where he was going. "Well, they'll be compensated." Even as I spoke, I knew that was naïve.

"This'll be in court for years. If they're lucky, they'll get something back. But it'll be years. Meanwhile, because they can't afford to go anywhere else, they'll be sitting on toxic land, drinking toxic water, their kids playing in toxic dirt."

I tried to figure a way to argue, but all I could see were families who had bought homes with all the available money they had, invested in a future. They didn't have money to pay lawyers.

Patchen interrupted my thoughts. "And there's more."

"What?"

"Leoni owned this property." He pounded his forefinger on his desktop. "His family is probably responsible for the waste here. And his family is . . ."

He was prompting me. "The mob."

He cocked his finger and put it to his head. "Bingo."

"But Leoni bought the land three years ago."

Patchen waited.

"From Justin Adamo."

He looked up at the ceiling. "Great."

I suspected that Patchen's main concern was winding up in some other landfill. I said as much.

He shook his head, and I couldn't tell whether he was disgusted with me or himself. "I'm an architect," he said "Not a whistle-blower."

"If you're not a whistle-blower, why did you have the soil analyzed?"

"I had to know."

"So, what? You ignore it? So when this place is filled with families, kids, dogs, they'll all be exposed to what's under the ground?"

"I don't know what to do."

"You blow your goddamned whistle."

He shook his head. "There's got to be some other way."

The Scotch had turned from mediocre to rancid. I set the mug on his desk. "So, what're you going to do?" I repeated.

"Get drunker."

"That's helpful."

He watched as I stood and slipped my notebook into my messenger bag.

"What're you going to do?" he asked. "You're not going to run this, are you? I'll be a dead man."

"There's a way out of this. I'm going to look for it."

He snorted. "Good luck."

"I'd like those test results."

He stared at me for several moments, then opened a desk drawer and pulled out a large envelope, which he tossed at me. I opened it and, although I'm no expert on toxins and soil, I know dioxins aren't a good thing. I'd have to find someone who could make sense of it for me. I tucked the envelope under my arm.

At this point, I wouldn't have minded seeing this guy crash and burn on his way home. But no one else deserved that fate, so I offered to give him a ride.

He shook his head. "I'm sleeping on the couch."

When I hesitated, he said, "Don't worry. I'm not driving anywhere."

As I turned to leave, he said, "You're not going to tell anyone about this are you?"

"Like I said, I'm going to do whatever I can for those families; if that turns out to be good for you, I guess you can just consider yourself lucky."

Chapter 20

When I left Patchen, it was just after five o'clock. I didn't know what to do with what I'd just learned. I needed to talk with someone about it, and the first—and only—person I could think of was Mick. But it was too early to find him home. So I stopped at the Twisted Lizard for some coffee and maybe a zucchini and cranberry mini muffin to feed my brain.

On one level, I knew I should drive straight to the newspaper and write up a story on the whole Cedar Ridge situation. Not only was it my job, but those families moving into Cedar Ridge needed to know. But, as Patchen pointed out, they stood to lose everything they'd invested, which, at least for the Tuckers, was all they had. So did Katherine. And I had the feeling, don't ask me why, that she hadn't known about the land.

So, was there another way? A way for these people to reclaim their money without it being dragged through courts for years? But they—and anyone else who moved to the development—could lose a lot more than money. Who knew what kind of toxins their green homes were sitting on top of? And if it came down to families losing money and families becoming ill, perhaps dying, well, the money didn't seem all that important. Easy enough for me to say. I would have to have someone explain these results to me, and perhaps we would need another soil test. My opinion of Patchen had taken a nosedive, but he hadn't been faking his distress.

I thought of Mary Alice and her boys. So thrilled to be in a place where they didn't have to worry about who was living under them. And now they were living on top of something a whole lot nastier than ill-tempered neighbors. Ideally, there'd be some way to sell the property in a deal where the buyer compensated the families. But who would buy the property once they knew what was buried there? And selling with its toxic secret intact was just wrong. . . . Unless, of course, the guy who sold them the property bought it back. I snorted at myself. Right. What would Lucky have to be smoking to do something like that?

I found a space right in front of the Lizard, next to a sable convertible Mercedes roadster. The shop was just starting to pick up the after-work crowd. I didn't usually drink coffee at this hour—caffeine could make for a sleepless night—but I truly hate the after-work bar scene when I'm alone. Besides, a decaf sounded okay, and the Lizard brewed a good pot.

I tucked myself into line behind a woman about my age with thick, shiny auburn hair who looked toned in a figure-hugging knit top.

Sighing, I focused again on Patchen's revelations, which were almost too big to wrap my head around. In the back of my mind, I'd suspected something like this, but to hear—and see—this awful truth and its implications, staggered me. True, I had the makings of a great story, but at what price?

As I was contemplating my options, I heard a familiar voice in the corner of the room. I couldn't place it, so I glanced in his direction at the same time he looked up and I locked eyes with Lucky himself, currently involved in an animated conversation on his cell phone. He must have been the owner of that Mercedes I'd parked next to. Of course he would name his daughter and his business after his favorite car. And then I remembered the car in Clair's photo had been a Mercedes. Seated next to him at the table was his wife, Tabitha, whose dark hair fell on either side of her face like curtains. She seemed to be focused on the electronic reading device in front of her on the table.

I looked away, hoping he wouldn't recognize me. I did want to talk with him, but I wasn't prepared. Also, Mick had been pretty adamant in his warning. Still, I was kind of pleased when, a few seconds later, someone beside me said, "You're that reporter, right?"

I took a deep breath and attempted to assume a casual air, turned toward Leoni and looked him up and down. He was taller than I'd recalled, probably around six feet, with eyes that crinkled up when he smiled but were also rather humorless.

I wasn't sure how to answer him, but I'd begun to learn that wasn't a problem with Leoni. He was quite capable of carrying on a conversation all by himself.

"Yeah," he said, "your name's . . ." he held up a hand ". . . don't tell me. It's Robyn. Right?"

"Yes."

"Shame about Kendrick." He shook his head. "Guess you never know when the old ticker's going to give out."

I was searching for something appropriate to say, but that wasn't necessary, as Leoni kept going. "But did you see how red he got at lunch? Wondered if it was the sun."

Was he serious? Kendrick's unease with Leoni's presence had been something the indoor pond's koi population must have sensed.

"You talk to Kat? I hear you two go back a ways."

"I did. She's doing okay," I told him, even though he hadn't asked.

"You still doing that story?"

I waited a few seconds, and when he didn't answer himself, I said, "Sure. Cedar Ridge is still there. Katherine Kendrick still owns it. So, yeah, there's still a story."

He wagged his head toward the table he'd come from. "Sit with us."

"I haven't ordered yet." The polished, fit woman in front of me had just stepped up to the counter to place her order.

"One sec," he said, pushing himself in front of the woman. "Gotta friend here, Amber."

"No." I stopped him. "I'll join you when I get my coffee."

Lucky gave me a "suit yourself" sort of shrug. "We're over here," he gestured with his hand, but moved only a few steps away.

The woman in front of me collected her coffee and as she turned, looked at me and, lowering her voice said, "I think there's a back door."

I grinned and thanked her, then placed my order—to go. No sooner had Amber set my cup on the counter, than Leoni jumped in and thrust a twenty dollar bill in front of the barista.

"Thank you, Ed, but I've got this." I pulled a five out of my bag.

"No, you don't," Lucky said. "Don't you take her money, Miss."

Amber looked to me, her eyes imploring, and I knew that winning wasn't worth a scene.

"Thanks, Ed," I told him, reminding myself not to call him Lucky. I didn't know how well one needed to know the guy to use the nickname. Whatever the requirement, I wasn't anywhere near it.

He got his change, tossed a quarter in the tip pot, and directed me toward his table.

Tabitha had been watching the scene, but from her bland expression I couldn't tell what she'd made of the exchange.

As I walked to their corner, I had a few seconds in which to wonder why this guy was interested in talking to me. And the only thing I could come up with was that he suspected I knew something about the property. But how? And would he risk bringing it up here? Or was he just going to poke me a bit, see how I reacted?

"You remember Robyn, Tab." He barely glanced at her.

It was a table with four chairs and I sat across from Leoni. I glanced at Tabitha's reading tablet and saw *Northanger Abbey* at the top of the screen. How long had the two been sitting next to each other without communicating with each other?

"Nice to see you again," Tabitha said with a smile that seemed genuine. Maybe she was relieved to have someone at the table who would talk to her rather than a cell phone. Not that he was going to let her talk.

"Robyn's writing a story on Cedar Ridge," Leoni said.

She closed her reader and folded her hands on top of it. "They're doing some innovative things out there, aren't they?"

"They are." I began to describe the solar panels, but Lucky interrupted.

"That's a rag you work for, isn't it?"

"Ed," Tabitha admonished him, but he continued to stare at me. He was smiling, as though this were all in good fun, but there was a hardness in his eyes that said he was assuming the alpha dog role here and anyone who messed with him did so at their own risk.

"I'm a freelance writer, so I work for a lot of places." I added, "But the *Record's* a good newspaper."

Lucky snorted a laugh and looked around to see if he had an audience. Fortunately for him, the tables were close together and Leoni had a voice that carried. It didn't seem to matter to him that these people had not come here to listen to this guy puff up his chest. "How many stories do you have to do on school board meetings and people who raise their own chickens?"

"Yeah," I said, "it's a shame we don't have a higher crime rate in Fowler. An armed robbery or a murder always perks up the front page."

Tabitha's eyebrows rose and she turned toward her husband so she must have seen the way his smile took a wicked twist. I thought—for a second—from the way he tensed, that he was going to hit me, and I almost drew back. But I took the charge, and then I wrapped my hands around my coffee cup, easing off slightly when the heat permeated my palms. "Seriously," I said, "what do you have against the *Record*? It's not required reading."

His gaze wandered briefly. "You've done a lot of writing. Just wondered why you're wasting your time there."

"I like it there."

Leoni picked his cup up by the rim and took a noisy sip. When he set it down, he crossed his forearms and leaned on the table.

He opened his mouth as though to speak, but I beat him to it. "I'm sure you didn't invite me over here to bitch about the *Record*."

Tabitha laughed and Leoni shot her a harsh look. She stopped laughing, but continued to smile. Leoni glared for a few more seconds, before slowly pulling his gaze from his wife and turning it on me.

"Okay," he said, shifting in his chair. "You're friends with Mick Hughes, aren't you?"

The question startled me, and warning bells went off. I wrapped my hands around the cup, feeling the heat sear my palms. He hadn't plucked that item out of thin air, so denying it was pointless.

"Yes, I am."

"Good friends, from what I hear." He grinned as he glanced at Tabitha, who was watching me.

"Good enough."

"That guy gets around." He grazed his wife with another look, then said to me, "You must be something special."

"I must be."

I was thinking that no amount of information I might glean from a talk with Leoni was worth it. I settled the lid back on my coffee, pressing it down to secure it.

Leoni said, "Me and Mick, we go way back."

"Do you?"

"Oh, yeah."

Tabitha turned toward her husband, her jaw hardening. Leoni ignored her.

"Be good to see him again."

This had to be going somewhere other than a reunion. What did he want?

"Think you could arrange for him and me to, you know, talk?"

I needed a moment to process that. Why would this guy want to talk to Mick? But there wasn't time for speculation, so I said, "Mick's a big boy. He decides who he wants to talk to. Why don't you call him?"

Tabitha looked down at the reader, tapping her nails against its cover.

Leoni wagged his head back and forth. "He might not be dying to talk to me." He tipped his head in his wife's direction. "Tab here and Hughes used to be an item. Then I came along." One side of his mouth curled into a grin. "Hughes didn't handle it very well."

Tabitha took a deep breath and turned toward husband. She looked as though she couldn't believe he'd bring this up. But she didn't say anything.

Now I had to know where this was going. "What do you want to talk to him about?"

"You his social secretary?"

"I must be. You're asking me to set up a meeting."

In response to Leoni's dull-eyed stare, I said, "If Mick doesn't like you, for whatever reason, it'll take some convincing." I drank my coffee through the sip hole. "If I give him a good reason, he might be more amenable."

"Okay," Leoni nodded as though that had been a reasonable argument. "Let's say there'll be a little something in it for him."

I shrugged. "I don't know. Mick's pretty comfortable."

"Okay." He sighed in resignation, lowering his voice. "Hughes knows some people at Stratford. I know that for a fact."

He was probably right. "So?"

"I'd like to see what kind of influence he has over these people."

"In relation to what?"

His mouth twisted in annoyance, and I knew I was pushing it.

"Some property they're interested in," he said.

He had to be talking about the river front property near Cedar Ridge. And that's when my half-assed idea began to take on some substance. But I didn't have time to examine it. Not then.

"No offense, but I can't think of a reason Mick would do this."

As he stared at me, a thin smile crept across his face. "Trust me. He will."

It took some effort, but I think I managed to sound rather indifferent when I said, "Okay. I can talk to him."

"Just like that?"

Of course it couldn't be "just like that." In Leoni's world everyone expected compensation. I was in real danger of appearing too eager. So I voiced the first thing that came to me.

"I'd like to do an interview with you."

He eyed me, wary. "Interview?"

"Yeah. A feature for the *Record*."

He scowled.

"You've had a huge impact on the revitalization of Fowler," I said, ashamed of myself for the blatant exaggeration. I was confident that Leoni wouldn't see it as flattery. "I'd like to focus on a couple of your projects, and see what else you've got in mind for this town." Actually, aside from an upscale restaurant that catered to the beef-eating crowd, I didn't know what he'd done. But I had the feeling that Leoni would be delighted to fill me in.

He snorted softly, but he was also smiling. But when I glanced Tabitha's way, I saw a woman who knew her husband had just been handed a steaming pile of shit and was deciding whether to smack me down or high five me. She must have noticed her husband's preening, because she backed down.

Leoni flicked his right hand. "Yeah, sure. Whatever."

"Good," I said, smiling.

"So, you're gonna set up this meeting?"

I nodded. "You'll want me there as well."

"How come?" This didn't make him happy, but in the back of my mind I was putting something together and I needed to be there. "You his consultant?"

"Let's just say that Mick values my opinion."

He grinned and glanced at his wife before saying to me, "So, you and Mick really are pretty tight."

I leaned toward him. "We respect each other's opinion. That's all."

"That's all, huh?"

I nodded.

With a sigh of resignation, he said, "Yeah, sure."

"Good," I said.

"Okay," he slapped his palms on the table as though finalizing the deal. "Give me a call." He dug a card out of his wallet and handed it to me, holding onto it for a couple of seconds before releasing it. Then he winked at me. I don't know how Tabitha could have missed it.

"Well," Leoni stood. "Gotta get a move on. Pick Mercedes up from her tennis lesson."

Tabitha regarded me with curiosity as she murmured some pleasantry and followed her husband toward the door. I watched as Tabitha got into the passenger seat of Mercedes. Lucky took his time, standing on the curb for a moment, openly admiring his car. He even removed a handkerchief from his back pocket and wiped a presumed smudge off the door. Auto-smitten.

I looked down at the card and the phone number in its corner. I thought I had a match but pulled out my notebook to be sure. It matched the number that left Kendrick's mysterious voicemail. Now, did that made me happy or did that make me scared?

Chapter 21

It was six thirty when I got to Mick's house and pulled into his driveway. When he didn't answer the door, I considered using my key. But now that we weren't officially dating, it seemed wrong somehow. I checked the garage and saw that he, indeed, wasn't home, so I pulled my Matrix out onto the street. Then I took up my vigil on his porch, which is a rather nice place to kill some time, with a couple of chairs and a small, wrought iron table painted forest green. Centered on the table was a pot filled with dusty miller and some small, purple flower. I tried calling Mick, but got his voice mail where I left a brief message. I wasn't alarmed that he hadn't come home yet, figuring something must have come up. And it did give me time to think. While I certainly planned to tell him about my conversation with Lucky, I decided I wouldn't bring it up until after I'd told him about Cedar Ridge. Once he understood the gravity of the situation, he might be more willing to take on Lucky.

I phoned Carl Wellen, figuring he'd ignore the call when he saw my name, and was almost startled when he picked up on the fourth ring.

"Mr. Wellen, it's Robyn Guthrie."

"I know." He sounded resigned.

"I'd still like to have that talk with you. Soon. Tomorrow?"

The silence lasted long enough for me to think he'd hung up.

"Mr. Wellen?"

"I'm here."

"I have a report I'd like you to take a look at."

After another long silence, he said, "I didn't know."

I waited.

"I thought it was going to be a racetrack." His voice sounded raspy.

"Can we talk? Please." When he didn't respond, I said, "Tomorrow morning."

"No, afternoon."

"At your office?"

"No." He gave me his address, which I scribbled on my notepad. "Five thirty."

"Sure. And thank you, Mr. Wellen."

He hung up.

If Wellen told me who was behind the deception, I'd have to run the story. I could tell Wellen I'd call him an anonymous source—maybe he'd be more inclined to talk—but I couldn't imagine he'd stay anonymous for long. Anyone could find out who had done the soil testing at Cedar Ridge.

I spent the next twenty minutes thinking this through from all angles and, at the same time, wondering where Mick was. It occurred to me that he might be out on a date. And did I want to be here if and when he brought her home? No. I rummaged through my purse for some paper and pen to write him a note. I'd just finished composing it when I saw his red Porsche approaching from the east. I stuffed the note back into my purse and waited. As he parked adjacent to the porch, I was relieved to find no one in the passenger seat. When he climbed out and shut the door, his shoulders were slumped and as he walked toward the porch, his limp was pronounced. I stood and when he saw me, he smiled. "What's with the welcoming committee?"

"I've got some news I need to share with someone. You're it."

He dropped into one of the chairs.

I waited. Mick wasn't one to prolong a moment.

I was sitting, facing him, with my hands around the base of the paper cup containing a half inch of cold coffee. He reached out and wrapped his hand around my wrist. "Good to see you."

"You too."

He eyed me. "How come you didn't let yourself in?"

"I wasn't sure if the rules had changed."

He gave me his slightly disgusted look. "As long as you've got the key, you can use it."

I was going to say "same for you" but stopped myself.

Inside, Mick turned on some lights and we headed into the kitchen where he began mixing us drinks.

"How'd it go with Kendrick's cell?"

"Okay. I stuck it in the couch while Kat was on the phone with the police talking to them about the absence of Joe's cell phone."

"Ironic."

"Yeah. Thought you'd like it."

"How's Kat?"

"Holding up."

He handed me my drink. "You hungry?"

"I could eat."

As I watched him remove a white butcher-wrapped bag from the fridge, I said, "I had a chat with Glenn Patchen this afternoon."

"The architect?"

"Right. He was drunk."

"I didn't know that was an occupational issue with architects."

"It probably isn't." Once Mick was out of the way, I dug lettuce, a red pepper and some green onions out of the crisper. While he put some dill seasoning on the salmon, I began to assemble a green salad.

Mick said, "Don't make me beg."

"He told me—" I paused. "This is between you and me for right now, okay?"

"And Patchen."

"Right."

"Okay."

"He told me that he'd recently learned something about the Cedar Ridge property. Something he'd told Joe Kendrick on the day he died."

"And are you going to tell me what that is, or are you going to force me to make profiteroles to get you to talk?"

"Are you grilling that salmon?"

"Yeah."

"Okay, you've got me." Then I said, "Glenn Patchen told Kendrick that he'd just had the soil retested. It's extremely toxic."

Mick stopped seasoning and looked up at me. "Cedar Ridge? Toxic?"

I nodded. "Either it's sitting on top of a toxic waste site or it's right next to one, and the waste is leaching into the ground." I sliced through a chunk of pepper. "The kind of toxic waste that can prove fatal—over time—to people and other living creatures."

"Did you see the results?"

I wiped off my hands and reached into my purse for the report I'd gotten from Patchen. "I'm not sure what to make of it. Don't know what a lot of it means. Although I know that 'dioxins' are a bad thing to be sitting on top of."

Mick spent a minute or two scanning the report, then emitted a low whistle. "Hello, Erin Brocovich." He nodded. "Those photos of the soil engineer with Lucky are making more sense now."

"Exactly. And I'll be talking with Wellen tomorrow. It sounds like he's feeling some guilt." Glancing up from my chopping, I said, "You don't seem at all shocked by any of this."

"Guess I'm not."

"Why not?"

He set the report on the counter and added a bit more dill to the salmon. "Before we started making everything overseas, Fowler was an industrial town. Industry creates waste. And before they started regulating what you do with the waste, it often wound up in land-fills, dumped in rivers, dumped anywhere."

214

"Who did the dumping?" I was pretty sure I knew the answer.

"Mostly the mob. Some families were making more money off waste than heroin."

"But it's regulated now."

"Sure. But it still happens. And those sites where they were dumping years ago, they're turning 'em into golf courses."

"Do you know about this firsthand?" Every so often I had to ask Mick a question like this. I knew his background was a bit suspect. For the most part, I didn't care, but this would bother me.

"No. Not firsthand."

Good.

He tapped the report. "Wouldn't hurt to have someone who knows what he's talking about take a look at this report."

"I was thinking that too. You know someone who won't go broadcasting it? At least not yet."

"No problem."

Figured.

I nibbled on a slice of red pepper. "I learned something else interesting."

He waited.

"I paid a visit to Forrest de Coriolis, David's father."

Mick frowned. "I thought he was dead."

"He's living at Town and Country. He's old and has dementia, possibly Alzheimer's, but he's alive."

"You oughta be good at dealing with that."

"Be nice." I paused. "He said something interesting after I showed him the 'before' photo of Cedar Ridge."

"What did he tell you?"

"Well, actually, he told my mother."

"Lizzie went with you?"

"Yeah, it was sort of a field trip for us."

He grinned. "Okay, what'd he tell her?"

"He looked at the photo and said the land helped him put his kid through college. Stanford, to be exact."

Mick set his beer on the counter. "You're sure he said that?"

"That's what my mom told me. And she wouldn't make it up."

"Interesting."

"Are you thinking what I'm thinking?"

"Bribes to look the other way while the mob dumped hazardous waste?"

"Yep."

"We're thinking alike."

"This is turning into quite a story." He took a swallow of beer.

"So now I have to figure out what to do."

"Okay, well, don't you just write the story?"

"That's not the point."

"What is the point?"

"Patchen thinks, and perhaps rightly, that Clair was killed because of this."

Mick nodded. "Sounds like he's also worried about himself."

"I'm sure he is."

"Well, better him than innocent families."

"Patchen's got family. Maybe he's thinking about them."

"Maybe," he said, not sounding at all convinced.

"But, you know, that's the other problem. The big one. These Cedar Ridge families stand to lose their entire investment if this comes out."

Mick was silent as he worked this through. Finally, he nodded. "Isn't it better that they lose some money now than their lives later? Let them decide."

"But what if there's another way?"

He waited.

"I mean, I met one of the families, the Tuckers. She and her boys are moving in this weekend. She's invested everything in this home. She'll lose it all."

"I take it you have an idea."

"I'm not sure."

"Okay. Let's hear it."

"It's still developing."

"I'm still waiting."

"Okay, first some background." I sprinkled chopped peppers over the two salads. "I ran into Lucky at the Twisted Lizard."

He gave me a sharp look. "I told you to stay away from him."

I ignored his authoritarian attitude and said, "He approached me. What was I supposed to do? Pretend I didn't know him?" Mick continued to scowl. "And he probably wouldn't have said 'boo' to me if it weren't for you."

His expression turned from snarly to confused.

"He wants to talk with you," I told him.

"Why?"

"How well do you know Mrs. Lucky?"

He considered that for a moment before saying, "I don't know Tabitha Leoni at all. I did know Tabitha Grecco. I dated her."

"You dated her."

"Right."

"Before Lucky did."

"Right."

That's one of the things I found interesting—not always in a good way—about Mick. Always something new to learn about his past. I knew that Mick had worked for Grecco and still had some loyalty to the man, although I doubted any of this spilled over onto the son-in-law. But dating the boss's daughter—that I did not know about.

"How did that end?" I asked. While I respected his privacy, I needed to know how this had played out between Mick, Tabitha and Leoni.

"We both moved on. She went to Lucky. I went somewhere else."

"So, that's not why you dislike him?"

"I dislike him because he's a slimy little pissant who preys on vulnerable people."

"Like Tabitha?"

"She was a nice person. Probably still is. And I wouldn't think he could prey on her too much with Chris Grecco as his father-in-law."

From personal experience I knew a lot could happen without anyone being the wiser, but I didn't need to tell Mick that. He was probably way ahead of me.

"So, what did Lucky want?" he asked.

"He wants me to set up a meeting between you two."

He snorted. "Right."

"Really. But it's not so much you he's interested in as your contacts."

"My contacts?"

"Of which you have many, I realize. In this case, he's interested in the people you know at Stratford International."

"How does he know—" He stopped. Must have figured it out for himself. "Okay, what about Stratford?"

"Lucky's got some property on the Crystal River that he thinks would make a great casino site."

Mick laughed. "Why would he think I'd even talk to him, let alone help him out?"

"He said you would. In fact, he said 'trust me.'"

I watched while that sank in.

He drained his beer and slammed the empty bottle down on the counter. "Then you can call him back and tell him to kiss my ass."

"I'd be happy to, but first don't you want to know what I was thinking?"

"I think this is where I get nervous."

I smiled. "You want to know. You know you do."

He locked eyes with me. "No, I don't. I really don't."

"Okay." I bisected a green onion.

Mick was silent for a few moments, and then he said, "I'll go start the fire."

"You want to split a potato?"

"Sounds good."

I let him alone. He'd be mulling this over while he was out there creating fire. Granted, he might come back with the same negative attitude, but I knew he'd want to know what I was thinking. Eventually.

I rinsed off an Idaho potato, poked it a few times with a fork, greased it up with some canola oil and set it on the middle rack in the oven. Next, I dug one of Mick's pale ales from the fridge and poured it into a stein and added a dribble to my Scotch. I found a hunk of Cotswold Cheddar in the fridge and cut off a number of chunks and added them, with some water crackers, to a small plate. I also cut up an apple into narrow wedges. After assembling all this on a tray, I took it out to the patio, where Mick was surveying his barbeque prowess.

"Nice fire," I said.

I got the eye roll.

"Really," I said. "It's a nice fire."

"Any idea involving Lucky is a bad idea."

"I know that now," I said, assembling our drinks and treats on the patio table. It was a cool night, but the three-season porch would provide enough shelter for our meal. "And I am chastened." I settled into one of the cushioned chairs.

Mick was watching me. "Yeah, right," he said. He likes that about me. I'm never chastened.

"Did I tell you that I checked out the recent calls and text messages on Joe Kendrick's phone?"

"You sneaky girl you."

"I know. One of those texts was to Ed Leoni. Leoni also called Kendrick. Lucky was kind enough to give me his business card so I was able to ID his number. Thoughtful of him."

Mick had his back to me, attending to the grill. But his grip on the tongs tightened.

"Hey, Fredo," I said to the ferret snuffling about his cage. It was almost sunset, an active time for the squirmy little guy. I offered him a piece of an apple wedge, which he accepted with gusto.

Mick sat with me at the table. We watched the fire, talking about inconsequential things until the coals were ready, then he put the salmon on. I inhaled the lovely scent of the grilling salmon, dry leaves and musty ferret.

When the salmon was ready, I got the potato out of the oven, cut it in half and put sour cream and butter on Mick's half and salsa on mine. After dressing the salads with olive oil and lemon, I brought everything out to the patio. Mick opened a bottle of zinfandel, which we drank as we enjoyed the cool fall breeze along with the meal.

Afterwards, we'd been sitting in silence for several minutes, when Mick said, "So, what's your plan?"

"If your Stratford friends were to convince Lucky that they'd be looking to make this casino thing a resort, if Lucky hadn't sold off the adjacent property—Cedar Ridge. If he still had the land, they'd be very interested." I hurried on before Mick could groan. "Lucky might be desperate enough to try to buy back that land, compensating not only Kat, but all those who have already invested."

Mick was watching me as though I'd misplaced a few marbles. "Um, sure. We'll do that in the morning. Save the afternoon for reversing the tides."

"I didn't say it would be easy, but I think we can figure a way to do this. We're good at this sort of thing—"

"No," he stopped me. "No, now don't go there, Robyn."

I looked up from feeding his ferret leftover scraps.

"You heard me," he said.

Instead of answering, I asked, "Do you know Justin Adamo, son of Salvatore?"

"What's he got to do with any of this?"

"He sold the Cedar Ridge property to Lucky to begin with."

"Keep clear of him. Never met him, but word is he's a sociopath, if not a psychopath. Gets it from his father." Mick shook his head. "In case you hadn't already guessed, the nickname 'Sweet Sal' is ironic."

"The Adamo family owned that land for years." I paused. "So they probably did the dumping. And Justin Adamo sold the property to Leoni. Do you think Lucky knew about the property when he bought it?"

He gave that some thought before saying, "My guess is yeah. Those two have a weird, symbiotic relationship. Went to college together. I think they each see themselves as family outsiders. Probably figured with the two of them working on it, they could turn the land for a decent profit without anyone being the wiser."

"Does Justin have a nickname?"

"Yeah. Justin."

"No sense of whimsy."

"None whatsoever," he said as though trying to drive home the point that this guy was bad news and best left alone. I chose to ignore this.

"You know," I took a sip of wine, "this plan would either work or it wouldn't. I mean, I don't see any big danger factor involved."

Mick looked at me as though I were simple-minded. "I'm not worried about what happens if it doesn't work. If it does work, and the

Stratford investors pull out after Lucky buys the land back, he'll figure he's been played—the guy isn't that stupid—he'll be madder than a . . . wet ferret." He fell silent, and I watched as he mulled it over.

Finally, he smiled a little and looked at me.

"Your friend Kat would have to go along with this," he said.

"Why wouldn't she? What's she got to lose?"

"What if she knew about the land?"

"Well, I'd have to figure that out first." I paused. "But I have this feeling she didn't know."

"You and your feelings."

He turned reflective again.

"It's all rather meaty, isn't it?" I said.

"You played that very smoothly, Miss Guthrie."

"Why, thank you."

"You know me pretty well, don't you?"

"I think we've gotten to know a lot about each other in a rather short time."

"So, you know what I'm thinking now?" he asked.

"I do."

He smiled and bobbed his eyebrows as he nodded toward the house.

I breathed once, twice. "Have you . . . come to any decisions yet?"

"Decisions?" He canted his head. "Let's not worry about that now, okay?"

"I'm looking out for myself here, Mick. If I stay with you tonight, I'll be telling myself we're back on. And then tomorrow when you get iffy on me again where will I be? Well, I don't know how much on again off again I can take without starting to resent the whole thing."

It was dark now, but I could hear him sigh. "You ever get tired of being right?"

"You know, I do. I really do."

Chapter 22

The next morning, and for the second day in a row, I had a caller. This time I was sleeping, but the banging woke me. I'm a light sleeper and as soon as the noise registered, I bolted up in bed, wide-awake, my heart pounding. Seven fifteen. Beside me, Bix squirmed, trying to bury his head under the pillow. The knocking stopped, and moments later my phone went off. Couldn't have been coincidence. Caller ID said Katherine Kendrick.

Uh oh.

No use pretending I wasn't home. "Yeah?"

"Robyn. You and I have got to talk."

"What is it?"

"I'm standing right outside your door. Let me in or I am going straight to the police department and tell them you were fucking my husband the night he died." Her breath was coming in angry gasps. "If you try to deny it, you will see just how much of a bitch I can be."

"I'm coming."

I pulled on a pair of jeans and a sweatshirt. I grabbed my phone and on my way to the door called Mick, figuring I might need backup. I cursed when I got his voicemail. "It's me. Kat is at my door accusing me of being with Joe the night he died. If you're not too busy I could probably use your help. If my body turns up in some dumpster, you might suggest the police talk to this woman." I hit End Call and slipped the phone into my pocket.

When I got to the door, I pushed back the cheery little white lace curtain and saw Kat glaring in at me. Judging from her appearance, she hadn't bothered with make up or even a hair brush. We had a light rain going and that didn't help.

"Let me in, Robyn."

I unlatched the chain and flipped the deadbolt, then pulled open the door. Kat stood there, arms crossed tightly over her chest and her jaw set. She was as clenched as a person can get without imploding.

"Come on in," I said, stepping back, trying to remain calm. While I'd done nothing wrong (with the exception of moving her dead husband's body) it took little imagination for me figure out how she'd interpreted things. I'd just have to hear her out, let her calm down a bit and then explain myself. If I lived that long. I began to regret the lovely oak knife block I'd invested in along with the requisite cutlery, which was within easy reach on the counter. I was a fanatic about keeping my knives sharp. I regretted that as well.

Fortunately, Kat was fully focused on me. "You bitch," she said. "You had to get back at me, didn't you? You've always been jealous of me. I know your life is pathetic, but I thought you had some decency."

"Kat—"

"Shut up." She took a long stride into my kitchen and now had the advantage of looking down on me. Water dripped off her nose and cheeks, which were flushed red. "You're a sorry little bitch. Have fun telling the police how my Joe wound up in some parking lot." She moved closer. "Or is that where he was fucking you?"

I fought my reflexes, which told me to back up. Not only do I not like someone getting in my face, but her breath smelled sour. "I was not with your husband."

"Don't you lie to me." She unwrapped her arms and extended her right hand, which held Joe Kendrick's phone. The one I had so cleverly buried behind the couch cushion. She shoved it under my nose. "I'm sure you recognize this. I found it this morning in the couch. The last time I saw him, we were in the car and he had it with him. He didn't come back to the room after that. Aside from me and Beverly, the only person to sit on that couch was you, Robyn."

Outside, thunder rumbled, and I heard the rain spattering the tile floor. It was my excuse to move. "It's raining in," I said and stepped around her to shut the door. As it clicked shut, a gust of wind and rain slashed the window.

When I turned back to Kat, I said, "I wasn't with your husband—"

"Don't you lie to me." With one hand she shoved me up against the door with such force and abruptness I lost my breath for a few seconds. "How did it feel? Was it sweet? Waiting all these years to get back at me. So, how did it feel?"

She was the image of rage—crazed eyes, wild hair, bared teeth. But there was also a touch of smugness that comes with knowing how to wield this kind of anger, how to make other people scared. Mean girl Kitty was back. It was at that point where my sympathy eased up enough to let a little anger creep in. I wasn't the one who had cheated on my spouse and had a heart attack.

"I wasn't the woman with your husband. He was with someone that night, but it wasn't me."

She still had me pinned to the door, although I could have broken away at any time—she wasn't that much stronger than me—but I was still considering my next move. Kat narrowed her eyes and breathed twice before saying, "You're lying."

"No. I'm not."

Again, she shoved the phone under my nose. "You're saying you didn't plant this in the couch?"

"Actually, yes, that I did."

Her chin lifted slightly. "Why?"

"It's a long story." She didn't ease up.

"Who was he with?"

I stared right back into those crazy eyes. "Back off."

After another few seconds, she released me.

"Joe was with a call girl."

She hesitated. "Quit lying to me."

I shook my head. "No, I'm not. I'm sorry."

Now she studied me, and I had the feeling that my revelation did not shock her. That made some sense. Kendrick was one of Gretchen's regulars. If he ever got careless, Kat would be smart enough to figure it out.

All she said was, "How do you know?"

"Let's sit down."

I pushed past her and walked into the living room. After a few seconds she followed.

"How do you know?"

"If you want to know what happened, sit."

Again, she hesitated, but then she lowered herself down on the edge of my purple chair, with her back to the kitchen.

Relieved that the knives were out of her sight, I sat on the couch.

Clasping my hands together, I chose my words carefully. "I was with my friend, Mick, that night. He got a call from a woman he knows who is a call girl."

"A prostitute."

I nodded. "She was upset because her . . . client . . . had died. And she didn't know what to do."

"You call an ambulance, not your pimp."

"He's not her pimp." While that clarification wasn't essential to the story, it was to me. I continued, "And, well, yes, an ambulance would have been a good option. But she hadn't been in the room at the time he died. She was taking a shower." That wasn't much of an excuse. Still, by the time Mick and I had gotten there, he seemed quite dead. "Once she found him, she didn't think she could do anything for him."

"Is this slut a doctor?"

"She knows CPR. And she did try to revive him." I swallowed.

"So, she was qualified to pronounce him dead?"

"She was not." Kat knew that, of course. What she didn't know was that she was fast approaching the limits of my self-restraint. There was only so much meat in her "I'll report you to the police" threat. She'd have to prove our complicity.

At this point, I was having a hard time reading Kat. I knew she still angry, but she also seemed to be taking time to think this through. And the one thing I had not seen was grief. Still, perhaps anger trumps grief. Finally, she said, "So, you moved his body."

"Yes. We did."

"Why?" She leaned toward me. "You expect me to believe that you were worried about my feelings?"

"Believe it or not, that was part of it. Also, this, uh, call girl is trying to get out of that line of work. She lives with a relative who doesn't know about it. And I thought about Cedar Ridge. Green Haven. And, yes, I thought about you. Losing a spouse is hard. Losing one that way—"

"How the hell would you know?"

"Well, I do know. Sort of. My mother's husband. My stepfather."

As she watched me, I saw recognition seep into her eyes. "That's right," she said quietly.

A memory popped to the surface. One of those repressed ones that come back when you least expect them and send you into therapy. I'd gotten teased at school. That I remembered. But now I had a clear image of a gang of girls on the bus, jeering at me and calling my whole family—dead stepfather and all—ugly names. Kitty had been leading the pack.

I wanted to ask her what it was about me that brought out the bitch in her, but that would have changed the subject, and we weren't through with this one yet, although I wasn't sure how much more I wanted to tell her.

"Who was she?" Kat asked.

"It doesn't matter."

"It does." She clenched her fists. "Don't you tell me it doesn't matter."

I shook my head. "I can't tell you."

Nodding, she leaned back into the chair, crossing one knee over the other, and was actually smiling a little when she said, "Is that what you're going to tell the police?"

This was what I was afraid it would come to, and I didn't know how I was going to talk her out of it. They might not believe her—all she had was a story about the no-longer-missing cell phone—but then again, she was a founder of Green Haven, an altruistic company bringing a community of solar homes to our town, and I was, well, Robyn Guthrie.

Kat must have read the situation the same way because her smile deepened as she said, "So, you were being thoughtful." I didn't think I imagined the sarcasm. Smug *and* sarcastic.

I drew in a deep breath and slowly released it. "Maybe it wasn't well thought out, but we were trying to do what was best. For everyone."

"Well," she cocked her jaw and gave me this arch look, "I'm sure the police are going to appreciate that."

Just as it occurred to me that Kat Kendrick was going to enjoy telling the police about me, I saw movement in the kitchen and then a male voice said, "You might want to think about that."

Kat jumped up and spun around as Mick entered the room. I wondered how long he'd been standing there, listening.

"Who the hell are you?" Kat looked at me, then back at Mick. "I warn you, Beverly knows where I am. If anything—"

"Relax, Kat," I said.

Mick walked towards the couch. At that point Bix came mincing out of my bedroom. Mick bent to pat him.

"Who is this?" Kat demanded.

I assumed she was talking about the human. "My friend. Mick."

She nodded in recognition. "The pimp."

Mick didn't rise to the bait. "I was there."

"You're a part of this cover up."

"Kat—" I started.

Abruptly, Kat came around the chair and headed toward the door. Before she got there, she shot back at me, "You'd better tell that little whore friend of yours that she'll be getting a call."

"There's something you need to know first."

"I doubt it."

She kept walking.

"It's about Cedar Ridge."

She stopped but didn't turn around. "What about Cedar Ridge?"

Mick and I exchanged a look.

"There's something wrong with the land."

Now she turned and, crossing her arms over her chest, said, "There's nothing wrong with that land. I've been there. I've seen it."

"It's what's in the land. Toxins."

She snorted. "That's ridiculous. We had the soil tested before we bought it."

"When's the last time you talked to Glenn Patchen?"

"I haven't—not for a couple of weeks."

"He had the soil re-tested."

She stared at me, as though debating the validity of what I'd just told her. "Why?"

"He had suspicions."

She shook her head. "I'm supposed to believe you?"

"Talk to Glenn."

"You are pathetic. Both of you." And with that she spun around, yanked open the door and, without hesitation, stormed out into the pouring rain.

I followed and stood at the door looking over the balcony. Kat had already gotten into her BMW and, as the rain pelted my face and chest, she swung out of the parking space and gunned the little car out of the lot. I shut the door and grabbed a dishtowel to wipe the water from my face. I leaned against the door, dripping, then clicked on the coffeemaker, which I'd primed the night before.

When I returned to the living room, Mick was on the couch with Bix.

"That went well, didn't it?" I said.

Mick smiled and patted the cushion beside him. After a brief hesitation, I joined my ex-boyfriend and my current dog on the couch. Mick put his arm around me, and I rested my head on his shoulder.

"What do you think she'll do?" he asked.

"I have no idea. I am a long way from understanding how Kat Kendrick's mind works."

"She's smart, isn't she?"

"Yes," I admitted.

"She'll talk to Patchen before she does anything else."

"With any luck, he'll be sober."

"So, did you two talk about your plan for Lucky to get stuck with the land?"

I laughed. Hysterically. I buried my face in his shoulder.

He kissed my head and I tilted my face up so my mouth wouldn't feel left out. After that, it was a matter of moments before my defenses crumbled. By the time the coffeemaker dinged, we'd found our way to my bedroom.

I suck at breaking up.

* * *

I spent the rest of the morning working on a story for a rat terrier website. You specialize where you can. After sending it off, I put on a pair of jeans, a white sweater and a raincoat and headed out to pick up my mother. We'd missed our usual coffee yesterday when we'd gone to Town and Country. I thought that outing was at least the equivalent of coffee, but my mother disagreed.

As I dashed down the steps to my car, hood pulled over my head, I thought of that house with the attached garage. Winter might not wear me down as fast as it usually does if I didn't have to scrape the car's windows and shovel it out every time it snowed. And it would be nice to be dry when I got in the car.

Coffee was uneventful. The only odd thing was that my mother didn't ask me about the house. Not once. As we left the Twisted Lizard, she did ask if she could have a cigarette. I didn't have anything on my schedule until my meeting with Carl Weller later that afternoon—unless, of course, the police stopped by to arrest me—so, I agreed. She'd never quite gotten over the craving, although at times she did forget about it. It would surface again when she was around anyone whom she used to smoke in front of, which, actually, was limited to me. I guess I reminded her of the habit she often forgot about, but had no desire to kick.

I'd gotten her settled into her place on the end of my couch with an ash tray and a glass of wine. Bix, in one of his cheeky moods, had snuggled up next to her. My mom was so happy with her smoke she didn't bother to shove him away.

As she smoked and drank, I was sorting through my laptop bag, which doubles as a catch-all for papers, notes and what-all. I heard faint footsteps and a knock at the kitchen door.

My heart started pumping like crazy. *Please don't let this be the cops. Not when my mother is here.* I was actually relieved when I saw Kat Kendrick standing on the porch. This time she wasn't wet and had combed her hair and applied some makeup, but she didn't look much happier than first thing this morning. Although she didn't look angry either. Grim, defeated maybe, but not angry. I felt a pang of sympathy. I fought it.

All she said was, "We need to talk."

"My mom is here," I told her, but opened the door for her. As she stepped past me, she glanced into the living room where my mother watched and smoked.

"Hi, Lizzie," Kat called from the kitchen.

"You remember Kat," I said.

"Of course I do." The sight of my high school nemesis seemed to brighten her day. She blew a stream of smoke up toward the ceiling. "How lovely to see you again. Do come in."

Like it was her place.

Kat walked right past me and into the living room.

"We've been out for coffee," my mother told her. "And my daughter is allowing me my last cigarette."

"Keep it up, Mom."

I asked Kat if she wanted anything. "I've got coffee, beer, wine. Something harder."

"Actually, I'd like one of those cigarettes."

I thought my mother was going to leap out of her chair and embrace the woman. But she just handed her the pack with the lighter embedded beneath the cellophane.

"Thank you," Kat smiled at her and lit up one of Mom's Virginia Slims. She glanced at me, as though prepared to fend off my disapproval. When none came—who was I to judge—all she said was, "I'm not much of a smoker. But every now and then one can really hit the spot." She glanced lovingly at the narrow, white cylinder, then said to me, "Have you got any soft drinks?"

"Water."

She made a face but accepted my offer.

As I filled a glass from the filtered carafe in the refrigerator, I watched Kat settle into my purple chair and begin chatting with my mother. The two of them actually had quite a bit in common.

Smoking and husbands who died while cheating on them. But I bit my tongue and served up Kat's water. Then I plopped myself down on the opposite end of the couch from my mother.

"So, what brings you here?"

"Robyn," my mother scolded, "that's no way to talk to a guest."

What was I supposed to say? Lovely to see you, my dear friend. Have you reported me to the police yet?

"That's all right," Kat said. "Robyn and I have a couple of things to talk over."

And I didn't want to have this discussion in front of my mother. Not that she was going to go blabbing what we said all over Dryden. But something might slip. Also, my mother insisted on details, and she'd keep interrupting us. But I wasn't going to tell Kat we'd have to talk later.

Kat must have had the same idea, because she said, "Can we go for a walk?"

My mother's head shot up. "You can talk in front of me." She stubbed out her cigarette.

"I know, Mom."

I couldn't leave my mother alone. Not for long anyway. So, I improvised.

"Kat, I can take only so much smoke in my apartment. What say we go out on the porch while you finish that?"

"It's chilly out there," my mother piped in.

"You stay here, Mom. We'll just be a couple of minutes. When we get back you can talk to Kat." I pocketed her cigarettes. "And you can have another one of these." That seemed to mollify her.

I grabbed a sweatshirt and a dishtowel and Kat followed me out the door and onto the porch, where I pulled back the curtains so I could keep an eye on my mother.

The rain had left its chill behind. Kat had on a heavy sweater and my sweatshirt would do for a short time. After wiping most of the moisture from the chairs, I leaned my butt against the railing and, still smarting from her last visit, said, "Okay, what's up?"

She tapped an ash off her cigarette and looked down at the slatted wooden porch. "I talked to Glenn."

"Was he sober?"

"Actually," she said, tilting her chin as though examining a thought, "he appeared to be hung over. He was also in need of a bath." Her brows drew together and she looked at me. "How does a man schedule his drinking so his hangover occurs in mid-afternoon?"

"You're asking me?" I didn't have time to get huffy, but I regarded her with a cool gaze for a moment before steering us back on course. "Did he tell you about the land?"

"Only after I pressed him."

"And he told you . . . ?"

"You were right." With a sigh, she sat in one of my lawn chairs and pulled the edges of her cardigan sweater tight across her chest.

"What else did he say?"

"Not a lot." She dragged on her cigarette and tilted her chin back as she released the smoke. "He cried," she said, squinting. "Did he do that when you talked to him?"

"No." Although his emotions seemed close to the surface.

"Are we sure he's right?" she asked, and it was almost a plea.

"You should get the soil tested again. Hire someone you trust to do it." I added, "But I did see the report."

"Aren't these people supposed to be reliable?" She waved off my response. "No, don't. I know. I'm being naive. Doing a lot of that lately."

"I talked to the guy who we think faked the samples. I'm meeting with him in a couple hours. Maybe I'll know more then. Like, did Leoni know?"

"Leoni? As in the guy we bought the property from?"

"Right."

She canted her head and eyed me for a moment. "You think he knew?"

"Maybe."

"If that's the case, we'll sue his ass off. Get our money back so we can give the homeowners their money back."

She squeezed her eyes shut, pulled in a deep breath and released it. Then she blinked her eyes open to look at me and continued, "The problem is, it takes money to sue, and we don't have a lot of disposable income." She regarded the cigarette between her fingers as though it were a strange appendage.

"Who does?" With the exception of my mother, that is.

"I got a briefing from our accountant this morning."

I watched as she took one last hit off the cigarette and dropped it onto my porch, grinding it out with the heel of her black leather boot. "I knew we took a hit when the stock market plunged, but I didn't know it was this bad." She pressed her lips together and squeezed her eyes shut. "I guess I didn't want to know. Joe kept saying we were okay, and I guess I wanted to believe him."

"How bad is it?"

She shook her head and didn't respond.

"There's insurance, right?"

"It's not going to go very far."

I gathered she didn't want to share any more. That was fine with me, but I wondered how much of her personal finances affected Cedar Ridge. "What about Cedar Ridge?"

"Cedar Ridge is okay." She glanced at me. "Financially, at least. For now. We need to sell more homes." She stopped. "But with this . . ."

She didn't have to finish.

"If you need some financial advise, Mick might be able to help you."

"I thought he was a jockey."

"He's also my accountant. And financial advisor."

She snorted a laugh, then finger combed her thick, lightened hair off her face. "I told you I have an accountant."

"A second opinion never hurts."

When she didn't argue, I persisted. "He's good."

"I'll bet he is."

I didn't need her attitude, so I just said, "Talk to him." *And ask me if I care.*

I took a moment to peer into the apartment and saw my mother had nodded off. "How long has Beverly worked for you?"

Her eyes narrowed. "Couple of years. Why?"

"Is she friendly with Leoni?"

"No. Why?"

"Just wondered. I ran into him yesterday." I added, "I want to get more access to him. Find out what he's about." Kat was watching me. "He knows that you and I went to high school together." I let that sink in. "I don't know who else he would have learned that from."

She gave it some thought. "Joe?"

"That day at lunch we'd talked about it before Leoni showed up."

"Maybe they talked later."

"Maybe," I conceded, although I've never considered myself the kind of woman men chatted about.

"What are you saying?" she asked, so she must have had the same epiphany.

"I'm not sure." I was fishing here, and I suspected she knew it. "Who recommended that piece of property?"

"Beverly did. Along with several other locations." Sounding a bit defensive, she added, "That was part of her job."

"Did she push that property any harder than the other locations?"

Kat gave that some thought before saying, "She didn't have to. Joe was on board with her. He liked the deal Leoni was offering."

"What did you pay for it?" Rude question, I realize, but I wondered if Kat knew the real price.

After a hesitation, she said, "Two and a half million."

While that probably sounded like a good deal to Kat, it was also about a million more than the purchase price Sharon's search had uncovered. But before I could point that out, she continued.

"But, it was also a good choice," Kat said, as though interpreting my silence as sticker shock. "We were looking for something in the Midwest. Beverly's good at research. She found ten possibilities— from Iowa to Ohio and as far south as Kentucky. We narrowed it down to five and then chose Fowler."

"Why?"

"Location. Close enough to an urban area, but still out in the country. Again, great location. Near the river. There's talk of new industry coming out here. Joe was pushing for it."

I debated whether to mention that I thought Joe knew about the property's "issues," but decided that since it didn't make much difference and she was already feeling lower than a worm, to not say anything right now. What I did tell her was, "I'd be careful what you say in front of Beverly."

She shook her head. "What difference does it make?"

I studied her as she stared off into the parking lot, wondering whether now was a good time to share some of my semi-larcenous thoughts with her. I opted to wait until after she talked to Mick. Maybe he could help her with her financial woes—whatever they were—and if he couldn't, well, welcome to the world the rest of us live in, Kat. Maybe she'd have to sell that home in Vail. Move from her two-story Minneapolis condo with the wine cellar and the roof garden. But then I scolded myself. Envy was such a negative emotion. Not to mention my favorite mortal sin.

I shifted my stance and folded my arms across my chest, "I may have an idea."

I heard the door open and looked up to see my mother, afghan wrapped around her narrow, rounded shoulders, totter out onto the porch. "You said you were just going to be a minute."

"We're almost done," I said.

"We're done," Kat added.

"I'd like that cigarette. But I want to smoke it indoors."

Kat stood. "I'd better get going."

"Why don't you talk to Mick?"

She hesitated. "When?"

I nodded toward the kitchen. "Take my mom back in and you both have a smoke. I'll call him now."

"I don't know why you talk like I'm not here," my mother whined.

I handed Kat the pack of cigarettes, and my mother followed her into the apartment like Mary's little lamb.

Mick answered on the first ring. "Hey."

"You busy?"

"Nope." And before I could tell him why I'd called, he said, "I had someone look at that report."

"And?"

"You name it, they were dumping it. Wastewater, paint, mercury, pesticides. Oil. Want me to go on?"

"I get the picture. Thanks for doing that."

"What're you going to do with this?"

"Well, that's kind of why I called. I'm here with Kat. She needs to talk to you."

"What about?"

"Her finances," I said. "And then I think maybe we can help those people at Cedar Ridge."

"I was hoping you'd forgotten about that weird idea of yours."

"Helping is a good thing."

"No offense, Robyn, but your ideas aren't always, um, fully formed."

"I have to start somewhere." Switching gears, I said, "Besides, it's not as though you've never encouraged one of my amorphous plans."

He sighed. Deeply. I pushed on. "We'll be there in a half hour," and added, "Um, might be a good idea to give Gretchen some time off?"

"Done."

Hmph. Like all my ideas were half-assed.

I slipped the phone back into my pocket and returned to the living room where my mother, cigarette waving in the air, was describing her Hollywood years to Kat.

I let her finish—after all, we had a few minutes to kill—and then told Kat that Mick was expecting us.

"Why don't I take you home, Mom?"

She straightened. "Why? Am I in the way?"

"Well, Kat and I need to go over to Mick's."

She lowered her voice as though passing on a national secret to Kat. "He's her boyfriend. He's nice, but short."

"I can hear you, Mom."

My mother just smiled. "Now you know what it's like to be talked around."

Kat intervened. "It's just boring stuff, Lizzie."

My mother affected a pout. "Well, all right. I suppose you might as well get rid of me."

"It's not forever, Mother."

But she was already attempting to stash the cigarettes in her purse. I intervened and earned a haughty sniff.

Chapter 23

Kat rode with us to Dryden, and after we dropped my mother off, I swung by Grenada Suites so she could pick up some financial papers.

As I slowed for a red light, I glanced Kat's way and saw she was just staring down at the brown folder in her lap. I wondered if she was crying.

"You want to talk about this?" I asked.

After a few seconds, she lifted her head. "I should have known." With a manicured nail, she scratched at a spot on the folder.

"What?"

"That Joe wasn't sleeping with you. You're not his type."

Of course I wasn't.

"So," she continued to focus on that spot, "I'm sorry I accused you. Like I said, I should have known."

I didn't respond until she looked over at me. "Yeah, you mentioned that."

Was it that hard to believe? I didn't think I imagined that little flirtation in the car as I drove Kendrick to Schaumburg. But, of course, I would keep that to myself.

Her sigh and the way her gaze darted up toward the sky, suggested she really didn't want to do any more talking right now. Especially with me. So I was surprised when she said, "I don't know how I could have been so stupid."

I didn't know if she was talking about the money situation or the hooker, so I waited.

"How long would he have kept this from me?"

Again, I wasn't sure of the subject.

"He was the one with the investment background."

Oh.

Her shoulders slumped and she shook her head. "Stupid, isn't it? It's not like I never saw the numbers. But I only saw the ones he showed me."

"You trusted him."

She snorted and shook her head again. "Dumb, huh?"

"He was your husband."

"Dumb," she repeated.

While I didn't know the extent of her money troubles, I did realize that, at least to Kat, they were serious. I knew I should have been more sympathetic. I understood money problems. But I had to wonder what Mary Alice Tucker would think of Kat Kendrick's money problems.

"Do you think he knew about the property being . . . ?"

I hadn't been planning to share this. Not now. But she'd asked.

"I think he did."

I could feel Kat watching me.

"You said you paid two and a half million."

"Right."

"Did you actually see that amount? See it recorded?"

"No. Why?"

"Because you actually paid one and a half million."

"That's ridiculous."

"It's on record."

After a minute, she said, "So you're saying he did know."

"I think it's likely."

"Well, aren't you an intrepid little reporter."

I didn't rise to her sarcasm. Just kept driving.

We rode in silence for a few blocks. I started to hear little sniffling sounds and I realized she was crying.

"I'm sorry, Kat."

She shook her head and wiped tears from her cheek with the back of her hand. "What am I going to tell Russell?" After digging through her purse for tissue, she blew her nose. "We raised him to care about the environment, and that's how he's living. How am I going to tell him his father knowingly had green homes built on a toxic dump? How am I going to tell him?"

I didn't have an answer for her. "Have you heard from him yet?"

"No. That's another thing. I can't bury him until Russell gets home."

She dabbed at her eyes and the tissue came away with a black smudge. "But that's not your problem, is it? I'll bet you can't wait to run this story. It'll make your career," she added with a bitterness I didn't think I deserved.

"Actually, I'm more interested in seeing if those people who have invested in Cedar Ridge have some options."

Several moments passed before she said, "Like what?"

"Let's wait until you talk to Mick." Suddenly, I saw the lameness of it all and was afraid she'd scoff or do something else aimed at putting me in my place. I looked for another direction to take our conversation.

"So, Joe handles—handled—the money. What about you? How do you fit into Cedar Ridge?"

"The building. I hired Glenn to design Cedar Ridge. I've got some experience with green building."

Staring straight ahead, her features seemed to relax, as though she were reliving a pleasant moment.

"From where?" I asked, curious to see where her thoughts had wandered.

She folded her hands together and rested them in her lap. "I got interested when I volunteered with Habitat for Humanity after college, which isn't necessarily green building . . . at least it wasn't when I started there . . . but I learned a lot about building from those projects. Got into the green building in California. Late eighties, early nineties. That was when timber supplies were starting to dwindle. Indoor air quality became an issue. Earth Day. Then I worked with a couple of builders in Oregon."

As she continued, talking about projects, some of them volunteer, up and down the west coast, I realized there was more to Kat Kendrick than I'd given her credit for. After college I'd grabbed the highest paying job I could find, which, as an English major, wasn't terribly impressive. "Where did you go to college?"

"U of I." She pulled down the visor to get the mirror so she could apply lipstick. "It changed me."

"How?" I really wanted to know.

She took a few moments before answering. "It made me more thoughtful."

When she didn't continue, I decided I'd done enough digging into Kat's history for the time being. I was a little ashamed of myself for being more comfortable with Kat as the mean girl bitch than Kat the green crusader. I'm not always proud of myself.

"But you don't actually build. Or do you?"

Frowning, she shook her head. "Not much. Although I can swing a hammer and hit a nail. I'm the procurer. I find sources for builders. Work deals. Talk to people out there who are coming up with green products. I've got lots of connections."

We rode in silence for a while. Then I had to say it, "You've changed a lot since high school."

She glanced at me. "Haven't we all?"

"No. Actually, many of us haven't."

Fortunately, she let that one lie. We turned into the lot for Mick's office.

* * *

When we got to this office I saw that, true to his word, Mick had given Gretchen the afternoon off.

Mick's door was open and Kat followed me through.

He stood as we walked in. She was quite a bit taller than Mick. Most people were, but Kat was quite tall—probably five-nine. He muttered something about it being nice to see her again and waited for us to get comfortable before sitting. Really, Kat was not only tall, but she held herself with a confidence I could only have faked. Then I reminded myself of why we were here and the past couple of days in Kat's life. Clearly it was not all a bed of roses, which never seemed like an apt analogy to me. I mean, a bed of roses would be lovely, but, given the thorns, rather painful.

Mick was casual today in a striped shirt with its sleeves rolled up. He sat back in his chair and bounced his fingertips together. "So, Robyn says you need some help."

"Yes." She looked down at him. "I know I don't have to tell you about my husband's death."

"Uh, no."

"I spoke with our accountant this morning, and . . ." she glanced my way, but it was Mick who said, "Robyn, maybe you'd better—" He nodded toward the door.

I couldn't believe he was tossing me out. But Kat wouldn't look at me, so I figured I'd been voted off the island.

"Uh, sure." I got up. Slowly, in case she changed her mind. But she didn't, and I retreated to the waiting room where I tried to find escape in the latest *People* magazine. Mick once told me he used to provide copies of *Architectural Digest* and *Conde Nast*, but perusing them before talking with Mick only seemed to heighten his clients' expectations.

I was in the middle of an article on blond, overweight starlets when I was allowed back into the inner sanctum.

I noticed Kat was blotting her eyes with tissue again. There was a glass of red wine on the edge of Mick's desk and another beside Mick's computer keyboard.

Kat blew her nose. "I don't know how we can reimburse those people who have invested in Cedar Ridge homes."

Mick put his arm around my shoulder and gave it a squeeze. "That's where Robyn comes in. She's our idea woman." He pulled back a chair for me. "Care for some wine?"

"Sure."

Kat continued to sniff and wipe, and I had to wonder about the horrors those papers described. But, that wasn't for me to know. At least not now. Mick poured me a glass from a bottle of Meritage, one of his personal favorites, pushed the glass toward me and, with a sardonic smile, said, "You're on."

"You're with me on this, aren't you?"

"I am. But I want to see if it sounds as insane when you explain it to Kat."

"Okay." I perched on the credenza so I could face both Kat and Mick, the latter of whom could probably use a bit more convincing. "If we break a story about solar homes being built on toxic land, there's going to be all kinds of courtroom drama involving Ed Leoni and Kat and god knows who else. Leoni's going to say he knew nothing about the contamination; Kat, you are probably going to say he knowingly sold you toxic property. There are going to be subpoenas and witnesses for both sides and, even if you do win, the families who already own land there, are living there, have invested their savings in this property, are going to be the losers. It'll get held up in court for years and they're not going to be able to afford to move and every day they live there the odds of them or their children dying of cancer or some other disease is increased. I've done some research and this is what happens."

"I thought you had an idea," Kat said, glancing at Mick.

Mick's eyes jinked from me to Kat and back again.

Ignoring my less-than-dazzled audience, I began, "Ed Leoni owns the property just east of Cedar Ridge. Right on the Crystal River. He'd like nothing better than to sell it to Stratford International, a hotel group, which is considering building a casino in this area. They've been scouting locations for a few months now." I went on to explain the plan I'd laid out with Mick, finishing with, "The beauty is that Leoni would buy back the land from you, compensating the investors, and then get stuck with it."

Kat looked at Mick. "Someone from Stratford would go along with that?"

"No," Mick was quick to point out. "That's where the role-playing comes in."

"Oh." Now she looked at me. "Who would play this Stratford person?"

"We've got a couple possibilities," I said.

"This is kind of insane." But she sounded thoughtful when she spoke.

"Maybe." I leaned toward her, lowering my voice as I said, "But what do we have to lose except a little time?"

The three of us fell into another silence. I imagined Mick and Kat were thinking that I was quite close to being declared legally insane. Maybe they were right. This was nuts. But, what was there to lose by trying? I thought of the Tuckers and the Sanduskys who had already moved into their new homes, and were, as we discussed my idiotic plan, sitting on top of toxic waste.

I stood and collected my purse, slipping it over my shoulder. "I know what I need to do right now."

Mick smiled. "See if you can bring peace to the Middle East?"

I ignored him. "I need to talk to Mary Alice Tucker. If she wants the story out now, that's exactly what I'll do. But if she wants to go for it, then I'm going to do it. With or without you."

After a moment, Kat stood. "I'm going with you."

I hadn't expected this, figuring that Kat Kendrick wasn't the hands-on type. But then she added, "Someone has to apologize to her."

Although I had to admire her temerity, I doubted that would be enough for Mary Alice. But I supposed Kat knew that.

Chapter 24

When we pulled into Mary Alice's driveway, I saw that curtains now framed the windows and a wreath filled with dried flowers in the colors of fall—red, gold and green—hung on the front door. There was also a small wrought iron table on the stoop with a concrete Buddha greeting visitors with his calming smile.

Mary Alice, wearing jeans and a Bears jersey that swamped her small frame, opened the door.

"Hey," she said, smiling when she saw us, "visitors. And I've actually got chairs now. And a table. Come on in."

I introduced her to Kat, saying she was the person behind Green Haven.

"Wow. Is it ever great to meet you." When they shook hands, Mary Alice took Kat's hand between both of hers and held on for a few seconds. "I can thank you in person."

Kat gave her a tight grin and a nod.

"We're a ways from being settled, but at least everything's here." She held her arms out to her side and pulled in a deep breath as though drinking it in.

It really was looking like a home. In addition to the table and chairs in the dining area, she had a couch, a couple of chairs and a small-screen TV perched on a low table. Above the couch was a grouping of paintings—watercolors of birds and trees. An empty bookshelf was stationed next to the TV, several boxes labeled "books" nestled up against it.

"Are the boys around?" I asked, hoping they weren't.

"No, they're visiting with a couple of friends from town." She folded her arms over her chest. "I do love it here, but until we get some neighbors, we're in the middle of nowhere."

I nodded toward the common wall. "Aren't the Sanduskys here yet?"

"Not 'til next weekend. Problem with the mover."

While Mary Alice and I talked, Kat was looking around, craning her neck to see into the kitchen, but apparently waiting for an invitation from Mary Alice before she wandered.

"I just made some coffee. Can I offer you a cup?"

I found myself hesitating. I knew that I would and that one cup of water from this toxic land wasn't going to kill me, but it did give me pause.

It was Kat who said, "Yes, thank you." I followed with a nod and another word of thanks.

We watched as Mary Alice moved around the kitchen, taking mugs from a cupboard filled with plates and glasses, pouring coffee from the carafe. She placed the three mugs on a teak tray and added a sugar bowl and a carton of half and half. "We're very formal here," she said with a grin, leading us to the small dining room table.

I wanted to ask her what decorating plans she had and what she was going to do with the small yard, but those were the kind of questions one asked a new homeowner with a big, bright future ahead of her in that home. In light of the news we had for her, that seemed almost cruel. But once we got to talking, the conversation naturally headed that way. Mary Alice started telling us about ideas she had for some accent painting and items of furniture she wanted to buy. I couldn't speak for Kat, but while I was listening, all I could think about was how would I introduce the elephant in the room.

Then Mary Alice stopped abruptly, looking from Kat to me and, with a little shake of her head said, "Wow, I'm going on aren't I? Sorry."

"No, don't be," I said, rubbing at a water spot on edge of the blue mug. "It's just . . ."

"I suppose you had a reason for coming here."

"Well, I did want to see what the place looked like with you in it." I managed a smile, but it did take some effort.

"But . . . ?"

"Yeah, there is something else." It was up to me. On the way over, I had agreed to break the news, seeing as Kat was a stranger to Mary Alice. I wasn't much more than that, but I thought we'd hit it off pretty well. "Something we need to tell you."

A line formed between her brows as I saw the first traces of concern. "About what?"

"This property."

She shook her head, and there was nothing for me to do but go ahead.

I released the coffee mug and folded my hands together. "There's a possibility . . . I mean this isn't a for sure thing. Further tests will need to be done. But two preliminary tests have shown significant levels of dioxin and some other elements in the soil here at Cedar Ridge." I paused, watching Mary Alice whose eyes darted from me to Kat and back again.

"Dioxin?" Before I could answer, she said, "That's poison, isn't it?"

"It can be."

"'Can be'?"

I wasn't handling this well. I glanced Kat's way, thinking the least she could do was help me out.

"In the ground? Under my house? In the water?"

"Possibly."

She sat there for a minute, looking from me to Kat and back again as though waiting for one of us to say this was a joke in very bad taste. With a quick shake of her head, said, "No. These homes are

green. They're the way everyone should be living. There can't be—"
She uttered a nervous laugh. "That's crazy. There must be a mistake."

"I'm afraid there isn't."

She'd been holding her mug between her palms. Now she looked
down at it as though she could see the poison curdling the coffee. "If
it's in the ground . . ." She dropped the mug. It had only a couple
of inches to fall, and when it hit the table it bounced, splashing
coffee onto Mary Alice's hands. She looked at the brown liquid as
though it were blood dripping from her fingers, jumped up from
the table and went into the kitchen where she ran her hands under
water, soaped them up and rinsed. Then she stared at her hands as
though disembodied, dried them off and applied sanitizer. Her jaw
was rigid as she returned to the table. Placing one hand on the back
of her chair, she said, "So, we . . . my boys . . . Bobby . . . Alex . . .
and I have been drinking this stuff.

"It's been only a few days, I don't think—"

"You don't think what?"

I'd started, so I had to finish. "I, um, think it takes more than a
few days to have an effect."

Mary Alice shook her head as though to clear it.

"Did you know this?" She stared at Kat, disbelieving.

"No. No, I didn't." Kat swallowed. "Not until today." She hesitated. "But it's possible that my husband did know."

"Possible?"

"I don't—can't know. He died . . . two days ago."

Mary Alice shrank back slightly, focusing on Kat. "Oh. I'm—sorry."

"No," Kat interrupted. "Please don't. This isn't about feeling
sorry for me."

She seemed to refocus. "I guess not."

Kat just shook her head. "I'm sorry. I never would have bought
the land if I had known. Of course. I guess I'll never know exactly

what Joe's reasoning was. How he justified this. But it's mine to deal with now and I'm going to do everything I can to make sure you're compensated."

Mary Alice's gaze flickered my way and back to Kat. Her jaw firmed and she studied Kat for a minute before saying, "That's all well and good. I suppose I've got no reason not to believe you. But, tell me, just what exactly are you going to do to 'compensate' me? Are you going to buy back this property?"

"I—"

"Because I don't see any way else that compensation is going to happen." She leaned toward her. "Do you?"

Kat shook her head. "No, I understand. Really. It's just that . . ."

"Just that what?"

Kat looked up at her. "Financially, that isn't possible right now."

"Of course not." Mary Alice gave her a grim smile. "Of course there's no money. There never is. What the hell did you do with the money?"

The color had risen from Kat's throat. She wet her lips and swallowed once. "I'm not sure, Mary Alice. My husband . . . I don't . . ." She squeezed her eyes shut and shook her head. "I don't know yet."

When Mary Alice looked at me, I realized that I had to believe Kat when she said she didn't know what Joe had done with the money. Because if she was complicit—and I had only her word that she wasn't—then I was also being played.

"It's not her fault, Mary Alice."

"Okay," Mary Alice said. Her eyes glistened, but I had the feeling she was too angry to let them spill over. "So what am I supposed to do now?"

"I have an idea," I said. "I don't know if it'll work, but if it doesn't we'll run this as a story in the *Record*. It'll be picked up everywhere."

I could see her working that out in her head. "And if you run the story, then what happens?"

"I don't know. It's possible there will be litigation. I imagine the man who sold Kat the property will put up a fight."

"It could go on for years. Couldn't it?"

I hesitated, but only for a second. "Yes."

"I don't have that kind of time." She got a panicky look. "There's no time. My boys. One day is too much. But we're prisoners here. Aren't we? Who would buy this place?"

I shook my head.

"We've got to get out of here now."

Kat said, "The effects of these toxins take years to accumulate."

"Okay, then let's trade places."

"I think if you use bottled water for the time being, you should be okay," I said.

"You 'think'? How do I know it's not being circulated in the air? How do I know I'm not breathing it?"

I was ashamed with myself for not knowing more about these toxins. "I don't know. I'm not an expert."

"We've got a case of water in the car," Kat said and must have realized how lame that sounded.

"So that's your plan? Bottled water?"

"There is more," I said.

"What is it?"

"I think the less you know, the better."

She narrowed her eyes as she studied me. "You don't actually have a plan, do you?"

"I do. But it needs a little work."

With a sigh she lowered her face into her hands and breathed deeply a few times before looking up at me. "How long do you need?"

"We'll know in a week." When Mary Alice didn't respond, I added, "Just a week."

"I don't suppose I have anything to lose, do I?"

Mary Alice closed her eyes and sighed. I took that as reluctant agreement. So, I pressed on with a question.

"Did Clair ever indicate she thought there was some kind of problem? You know, looking back? Did she say anything?"

She gave it a moment, then shook her head. "No. Not that I can remember."

"Would you let me know if you think of something?"

"Yeah. Sure."

Mary Alice turned toward Kat. "You do know that I have everything invested in this home." Kat nodded and Mary Alice kept going. "You say you've got money troubles and I say you have no idea what money troubles are. I don't know how you wealthy people do it, but you can be broke and still hire the best attorneys money can buy to defend you. And that's exactly what you're going to do if Robyn's plan doesn't work. You'll do whatever you can to save yourself."

"Green Haven. It's Green Haven I want to save."

"The hell with Green Haven. It's Alex and Bobby—my boys' lives we're talking about."

Kat nodded.

"Okay," Mary Alice said. "Maybe you don't have enough to compensate us, but maybe you have enough to buy this house."

Kat met her gaze and held on longer than I think I could have. Finally she said, "Here's what I can do. I'll pay for you and your boys to stay in a motel until this is over."

"What do I tell people?"

"You're having some painting done."

She gazed out the window at the barren back yard. "That would look weird. And what about the Sanduskys?" Turning to Kat and me, she said, "A week is a long time to keep my kids inside. But I'll do it."

We left then, after we'd given Mary Alice the case of water.

Driving out of Cedar Ridge, neither of us spoke until I'd pulled my car out onto Route 28. That was when Kat said, "I deserved that."

I wasn't going to argue.

With a resigned sigh, she said, "How do we start this?"

"With a call to Lucky."

Chapter 25

After dropping Kat off at her car, I turned around and headed to Carl Wellen's house in east Fowler. A confession from him could go a long way in getting Lucky.

Wellen lived in a small, white two-story Cape Cod with a detached garage. I rang the bell and waited a few minutes. Rang again and decided either he wasn't home or he was hiding. There was no car parked in the driveway, but when I noticed the garage window, I decided to see if there was an Acura parked in there. If there wasn't, then maybe I'd just park myself on his front porch and wait until he got home. Better yet, I'd hide in the bushes. This guy was really starting to piss me off.

As I walked up the drive, I realized that checking out the garage window wouldn't be all that easy. I had to go into his gated yard, so I was probably trespassing, and I also had to step carefully so as not to damage any of the hostas that lined one side of the garage. They weren't blooming, of course, but I wanted to give them a chance for next year. There was a door on the side, but I thought I'd check out the window first. After all, I only wanted to know if there was a car in there.

Turning away from such a sunny day caused momentary blindness. But when my eyes adjusted I saw no car. However, it was a rather cluttered space, so I wondered if he might be hiding in here. I stepped over to the side door and opened it wide enough to peer inside.

"Mr. Wellen?"

It certainly felt empty. At the same time I realized how silly this was—if he wanted to hide from me, surely he'd do it in his house, and breaking into a house was not something I was willing to do.

"What do you think you're doing?"

I spun around, my heart pounding, and found myself on the business end of a rifle. The woman holding it had gray-streaked dark hair and a pair of reading glasses hanging from a chain around her neck. This wouldn't have been odd except there were also a pair of glasses perched on her nose.

I raised my hands. "I'm looking for Carl Wellen," I said. "I've, ah, got a five-thirty appointment with him."

On closer inspection, the weapon aimed at me appeared to be an air rifle. Still, a well-aimed BB could, well, shoot my eye out.

"Do you now?" the woman said. "Well, you're not going to find him in there."

"Yes. I can see that."

She watched me over the top of her reading glasses. "You don't look like one of them others."

"What others?"

"You're not the only one looking for Carl these days." She shook her head. "I swear, you live next to a man for five years and he never makes so much as a peep. Then all of a sudden there's people poking around, sitting in their cars in front of the house. Knocking on my door. You know what that's about?"

"I don't." A lie. "I'm working for the *News and Record*. I had some questions to ask him."

She shifted the gun so it was cradled in the crook of her right arm. I took that as a sign that she wasn't planning to shoot me just yet, so I cautiously lowered my arms.

"You work for the *Record*?"

I nodded.

"We watch out for our neighbors here."

"That's good."

With a little frown, she added, "Can't say Carl's done much for the neighborhood watch, but we don't hold that against him."

"You said someone's been to your house?"

"Yeah. Just this morning."

"Do you know who it was?"

As she gave that some thought, I had a chance to appreciate the fact that she was wearing a red sweatshirt with appliquéd Christmas ornaments on it, the center one featuring Rudolph. "Didn't tell me," she finally said.

I nodded my understanding. "Just thought I might know him. There was supposed to be a photographer out here earlier."

She brightened. "Yeah? What'd Carl do?"

"Did you know he's the cousin of . . . Dustin Hoffman?" Where I pulled Dustin from, I have no idea.

"No." But she was grinning a little. "Doesn't look a thing like him."

"We wanted to do a feature on him."

"Well, that Carl is a pistol, isn't he?"

"Apparently that's what Dustin says."

Now she lowered the rifle so its snout pointed at the ground. "Well, I wonder where Carl was going today."

"He left?"

"Yeah. This morning. With a suitcase. And a cat carrier."

Okay. Carl had fled. No doubt.

"Well," I said, "I guess I'm going to have to find something to fill that column at the paper."

With a sympathetic nod, she said, "Our neighbor on the other side tells me she's a distant cousin of Hillary Clinton." She made a face. "But I don't know if I believe her."

"I'll mention it to our editor. Maybe we'll send someone out."

She stepped back as I navigated my way through the foliage. Before I passed her I stopped and asked again about the man who had been there earlier

"Didn't say his name. I didn't ask. Unpleasant sort. Short. Stocky. Had a high voice for a man."

That fit no one I could think of, but I thanked her.

"Oh," she said, "speaking of people lurking around here. Check out that car across the street. He's been sitting there the whole time we've been talking."

This woman was more observant than I was. Sitting there in his little black car, with his arm resting on the door, was none other than Kurt Vrana. Talk about lurkers.

I thanked her and slung my bag over my shoulder. Then I marched straight toward Vrana's car. Enough was enough. He pushed his aviator sunglasses down on his nose and peered at me over them as I approached. As I stared into those gray eyes I couldn't read his expression for the life of me. With the middle finger of his left hand, he pushed his glasses up again, so now I had no chance of reading anything in his face.

"Why have you been following me?" I asked.

"You seem to know what you're doing."

That was news to me.

He nodded toward Wellen's house. "He split?"

"With the cat." At first I wasn't sure why I was telling him this, but then I realized that it made no difference. "But you know that."

"Actually, I didn't know about the cat." He nodded to himself. "Probably a smart thing that he did. But he's got a long way to run if he expects to stay out of this."

I glared at his dark glasses. "Do you want to talk?"

He drew up one side of his mouth in what I suppose was a smile. "Thought you'd never ask."

"You're the one doing the stalking."

He removed the glasses. "You hungry?"

"Not really."

"Well, it's dinner time. And I'm hungry." He nodded toward the passenger seat. "Hop in."

"I'll follow you."

He gave me a "suit yourself" shrug and waited for me to return to my Matrix. As I pulled behind him heading west it occurred to me that I had no idea where we were going. Well, I was in my own car and could bail if necessary. If the place looked too bad, I'd just keep driving.

We wound up on the western edge of Fowler at an Indian restaurant called Raj's Diner. On the way there, I was thinking about my next move. After thoroughly interrogating Vrana, of course. If Wellen had fled town, maybe it was time to quit being coy with Congressman de Coriolis. I pulled into the lot behind Vrana, and as soon as I got my Matrix parked I called his office. It was late—almost six thirty—but I figured I could leave a message asking if I could talk with him tomorrow. So I was a little surprised when a young-sounding man identifying himself as Mark answered the phone and asked if he could help me. I told him who I was and said I wanted to arrange to speak with the congressman.

"Hold on," the man said.

As I waited, I jotted a few questions in my notebook. I really hoped he didn't put his boss on the phone right now. Vrana had climbed out of his car and was leaning against it, hands sunk into his pockets, watching me. I gave him a little wave.

A minute later, Mark was back on the line. "Congressman de Coriolis wants to see you now."

"You mean right now?"

"Yes." He hesitated. "That is if you have time."

260

Interesting. And I thought *he* was the public servant. Apparently the congressman really wanted to meet this woman who breached security at Town and Country Residences. "Actually, now isn't good for me. Would tomorrow work?"

"Uh, yes. Early. Say, eight thirty."

"Perfect. Thanks."

When I got out of the car and headed toward the diner's entrance, Vrana fell in step beside me.

"Calling for backup?" he asked.

The place was small, holding about ten or twelve tables. We sat in a booth by a window. There was a small tear in the blue vinyl seat that tugged on my jeans as I slid across it. The waitress, a young woman with thick dark hair and almond-shaped eyes, handed us menus and filled our water glasses. Vrana ordered one of the beers advertised on a small, tent-folded placard on our table next to the window. I ordered a different beer.

Neither of us spoke as we studied the menu. I wasn't hungry, but I supposed I needed something. I also wasn't familiar with Indian food, but I didn't want to admit that to Vrana. He immediately ordered something called palak paneer.

I fumbled with the choices and wound up going with an appetizer called choella, which involved chicken. I perused the beer's label.

"I make you nervous, don't I?" Vrana said.

I looked up at him as I set the bottle on the table. He'd removed his sunglasses and the way he was watching me seemed more curious than hostile.

So I decided to put it all out there. "You remember the first time we met?"

"At the newspaper?"

"No, that wasn't the first time." I waited.

"Oh. You mean that thing at the bar."

"Yeah. That 'thing' where you threatened my friend."

He snorted and shook his head. "Wrong. And wrong." He ignored the glass, picked up the bottle and took a couple of swallows. When he lowered the bottle, he said, "First, I didn't 'threaten' her. And I doubt she was much of a friend."

"How would you know?"

"She's not your type."

"What's that supposed to mean?"

He was looking at me as though he expected me to answer my own question.

"I didn't say we were close."

"Yeah, I know." He settled into the seat and rested his arms on the table. "If you had been, maybe you'd have known what her husband was up to."

"Ex. He was her ex."

"He wasn't her ex when he ran a dog-fighting ring."

I flinched and tried to cover by taking a drink. "She knew?"

"He was using their garage."

I remembered the time she came over to my apartment and seemed so comfortable around Bix.

"Makes you look back, doesn't it?"

"Who are you?" I asked.

"A concerned citizen."

"What do you know?"

He got some time to think that over when the waitress delivered our food.

After forking a bite of what looked like tofu, he looked up and said, "Probably some of the same things you know."

"For instance?"

He took the bite in his mouth and took his time chewing. "I think you know the Cedar Ridge property is toxic."

"What else?"

"Your turn."

"Did you know Carl Wellen's involvement?"

"I'm just guessing, but he's a soil engineer. He wrote a false report. That's why I think he has probably disappeared permanently." He fished something out of the corner of his cheek with his tongue. "Hope the cat's okay."

"Cats are survivors," I said without thinking and, more charitably, added, "Wellen seemed to have regrets."

Vrana snorted his disgust. "Good for him."

"Did you know Clair?"

"Sure."

"How?"

"I guess you could call me a source." He washed down a bite with some beer. "Where's Scoop?"

I'd been shuffling my food around with a fork, but when he said that my head shot up, and before he looked away I saw a stab of pain in his eyes that I didn't think was about the dog. "You met Scoop?"

He nodded. "You didn't really know Clair until you met Scoop."

"Yeah," I agreed. "Scoop's with a young woman who needs a dog as much as Scoop needs a person."

He studied me for a moment before nodding. "Good."

"How'd Clair find you?"

"She was good at her job."

Then he asked, "Why do you think it wasn't an accident?"

"Where she was walking Scoop. I've got a dog and we stick to sidewalks and parks. Not highway shoulders in the dark. Especially on a rainy, moonless night."

"You tell the cops that?"

"Yeah. Don't know if they thought much of it."

I watched as he alternated between bites of little white tofu squares and spinach. I had many questions for this guy but went with the one that covered all of them: "Who are you?"

He gestured toward my plate. "Aren't you going to eat?"

"I'm really not very hungry."

He pushed a wire basket filled with teardrop-shaped breads. "Try one of these."

"Why won't you answer my question?"

He stopped chewing as he seemed to give that some thought. "I know a few things about the environment."

"Do you work for someone? Or are you one of those caped crusader types?"

His mouth twitched. I think he was trying not to smile. All he said was, "Right."

"Which is it?"

When he didn't answer, I asked, "Is Kurt Vrana your real name?"

"What do you think?"

"I think it's a cool name—I'm a crow fancier—but I also think it's manufactured."

"Why?"

"Because when I do an Internet search on you, nothing—and I mean nothing—comes up."

He smiled, nodded as though that pleased him and said, "What else do you know?"

"Nothing for sure, but I've got my suspicions."

"Such as?"

"Mostly conjecture. You're infuriated by dog fighting. You asked about Scoop. Care more about Wellen's cat than Wellen. So, you may be an animal rights activist."

"Or just a decent human being."

"Maybe." I glanced at his plate. "There's not a speck of meat there, so you could be a vegetarian. Not vegan because it looks like you've got some yoghurt in that." I glanced out the window toward the parking lot where his Mini Cooper was parked. "You drive a car that gets very good mileage, but it's not electric so you don't have that much money to spend." I took a peek under the table. "You're wearing non-leather trainers, and a canvas jacket. You may be opposed to wearing any clothing made from animals." I stopped and waited to gauge his response.

He stared at me for a minute and then nodded, "Good guesses."

"Am I right?"

He just shrugged.

"Is Vrana your real name?" I pressed.

He nodded. "It's real enough."

"Are you off the grid?"

"Pretty much."

Annoyed at how little I was getting from this guy, I ate the piece of chicken, which turned out to be pleasantly spicy. He hadn't told me anything I couldn't have figured out for myself.

When one of us spoke again, it was Vrana with his own question. "Who do you think killed Clair?"

"I'm not sure yet." I paused. "You have any ideas?"

"I think Ed Leoni looks good for it."

"Maybe."

"What do you know about de Coriolis?"

I had to think for a minute why he'd even ask that. Then it hit me. "You followed me to Town and Country?"

"You talked to his old man?"

"You followed me."

"Sure," he said. "How'd you get to talk to him?"

"You couldn't get in?" He shook his head, and I smiled. "You didn't have an old lady."

"Gotta get one of those," he said, and I wasn't sure if he'd just made a joke.

Then he asked, "What about the Kendricks?"

"Kat didn't know about the land."

"You sure?"

"As sure as I can be."

"Joe?"

"He knew. And judging from the price he paid for it, I'd guess he knew when he bought it."

He nodded as though working it out in his head. "So maybe Clair knew that."

"Maybe."

Frowning, he shoved a cube of tofu back and forth with his fork. Finally, he said, "Are you going to run the story?"

"Eventually."

"What's that mean?"

"There's a lot at stake here. For starters, I don't want the people living in Cedar Ridge to lose everything."

"Why do you care?"

"Because they don't deserve it."

"Shit like that happens all the time."

From the way he said that, I wondered if he was testing me. He wouldn't be pursuing this if he didn't care. I ate another bite of the choella and chased it with some beer.

As he watched me, nodding to himself, he pointed a finger in my direction. "You're up to something."

"No. I'm not."

My cell phone rang. I'd have let it go, but I saw it was Mick.

"Excuse me," I said to Vrana and answered the call.

"We're on," Mick said. "Tomorrow at Leoni's office. Eleven."

This wasn't the time to go into the details. "Okay, so listen. I'll call you back in a few minutes."

"Where are you?"

"Talk to you later."

I slipped the phone back into my bag and looked up at Vrana. He raised his eyebrows and cocked his chin. "Anything wrong?"

He nodded as though confirming a suspicion. "You can tell me."

No way was I going to share our plan with this guy. Not only was it rather far-fetched, but I had no reason to trust him. However, I still wanted to know a few more things.

When I didn't answer, he said, "So, you're not going to tell me."

"There's nothing to tell."

"I think there is." He reached into a pocket inside his jacket and extracted a photograph, which he examined for a moment before placing it on the table and pushing it toward me. "And I'm a good listener."

At first I wasn't sure what I was looking at. The photo was taken at night and the images were grainy. It was two cars parked together and . . . I peered closer . . . and three people were lifting something out of one of the cars. I could make out the license plates and . . . *oh, shit.* I looked up at Vrana. "You *are* following me."

"I thought we'd already established that."

"What is this?" I waved the photo. "Extortion?"

He watched me without answering.

My first instinct was to tear up the photo of Mick, Gretchen and me transferring Joe Kendrick's body to the driver's seat of his own car, which, in this age of digital everything was just plain stupid.

"Why do you care?" I asked.

"I have my reasons."

"Try sharing one. Just one."

As he studied me with his narrow eyes, I saw something in them soften. He swallowed and said, "Clair."

"She—"

"Was special. Let's leave it there."

I leaned toward him, my voice lowered. "Kurt, this probably has nothing to do with who killed Clair."

"What is the plan?"

I hesitated.

"Please," he said.

I tapped the photo. "If I let you in on this, how do I know you won't use this again?"

"I'm a man of simple needs." Seeing that that didn't mollify me, he added, "I'll delete the image."

"Is that even possible? To permanently delete an image?"

"It is if I do it."

I didn't see where he'd given me a choice. "It's all about greed with these people."

He nodded as though that were a no-brainer. "You talking lawsuit?"

I shook my head. "Takes too long."

"Then what?"

"Give them a reason—a really good one—to want that property back."

"And what would that reason be?"

"A casino.

"A casino?"

"Cedar Ridge isn't far from the Crystal River. Leoni owns the land on the river. What if Leoni were convinced that Stratford International was interested in building a casino there? And not just any casino. A casino complex. A hotel, maybe. Or a racetrack. They'd need the Cedar Ridge land."

He leaned back. "That's it?"

"I didn't say it was spectacular."

"So, who's going to convince him?"

"A representative of Stratford."

"Just like that."

"Actually, someone who is posing as that representative."

"Who's your actor?"

"We've got a couple of possibilities."

He studied me for a few moments. "Okay."

"Okay what?"

"I'll do it."

I was about to tell him that wasn't necessary, but then he tapped a finger on the photo. "I will do it."

He made a persuasive case.

"I'll have to talk to Mick."

"Who's Mick?"

I cocked my chin. "I thought you've been following me."

"The short guy."

"You'll have to convince him."

He nodded as though that wasn't a problem.

"I'll give him a call."

I took my purse with me to the women's room, which was unoccupied, and punched in Mick's number.

Mick answered with: "What did Wellen have to say?"

"Nothing. He's gone."

"Permanently?"

"A neighbor saw him leave with a suitcase and his cat."

"Someone was nervous."

"Yeah. And I don't think it was the cat." I leaned against the cool tiles. "Have you got someone to be your Stratford friend?"

"I'm working on it."

"I think I've found him."

When that met with silence, I said, "I've just been talking to a guy who wants in. I think he'd make a good Stratford representative. I—"

"Wait. Who've you been talking to?"

"Kurt Vrana. You know, that guy I told you was following me."

"There's been someone following you?"

Guess I'd neglected to mention my shadow.

Mick sighed. "You really are crazy. You know that, don't you?"

"Um, well, he made a rather convincing case for joining. He's got a photo of us that night we moved Joe Kendrick's body."

Deadly silence. Then he said, "You're joking."

"I wish I were."

"Why didn't you tell me there was someone following you?"

"Well, I didn't know how good he was at his job until today." I decided I'd best tell him everything. "Can you meet us? We're at Raj's Diner. West side of town."

"You're having dinner with the guy who's been following you?"

"What was I supposed to do, Mick? How else am I going to find out what he knows, which is about as much as we know. He was one of Clair's sources." I hesitated. "And I think he loved her."

"That's the last thing we need—an avenging lover."

"What else could I do? He's got that photo."

"You don't trust him, do you?"

"Of course not. But I think we've got the same objectives. What's the line? 'The enemy of my enemy is my friend' or something like that."

He breathed a deep sigh. "I'll be there in fifteen minutes."

Vrana and I spent most of that time eating. Apparently neither of us were any good at small talk, and at this point, prolonged silence was a respite from the verbal jousting.

When Mick walked up to the table, Vrana stood. I suppose it was the polite thing to do, but it immediately established his vertical superiority. But that was one of the things I loved about Mick Hughes. He never let the taller guy think he had an advantage.

They shook hands and Mick, looking up at Vrana, said, "I hear you've got a photo that's supposed to make us nervous."

"Depends on you," Vrana said.

I scootched over so Mick could sit next to me and when he did, Vrana placed the photo on the table and sat across from us.

Mick picked it up, glanced at it, and flipped it back at Vrana. It skidded off the table and landed on his lap. Without taking his eyes off of Mick, Vrana returned the photo to his pocket.

By then the waitress had arrived and Mick ordered a beer, shaking off her offer of a menu.

After she left, Mick said, "I'm not impressed."

"So why are you here?"

Mick studied Vrana for a few moments before saying, "I want to know why you care about this so much."

Vrana didn't answer.

"Robyn told you the plan. If it works, and that's a big 'if,' it's not going to make you rich."

"I don't want to be rich."

The waitress delivered Mick's beer and he waited until she'd walked away before saying, "Then what's this about? Clair?"

"Partly."

"Because this isn't about finding her killer. So, what's the other part?"

Vrana nodded in my direction. "Because Robyn's right. Those people living at Cedar Ridge shouldn't get screwed. And Leoni should." Focusing on Mick again, he added, "Clair's death fits in somewhere."

"Who are you?"

I hoped he had better luck getting an answer out of him than I did.

Before Vrana could do one of his evasive maneuvers, Mick said, "Because if you don't tell us something, this isn't going to happen. None of it."

After a moment, Vrana nodded. "Okay. I used to work for the EPA. Criminal investigation division. I didn't like all the bureaucracy. Decided I was more effective on my own."

Mick and I exchanged a look. "You're a rogue EPA agent?" I asked.

He smiled. "Guess that's what you could call it."

If this was true, and I had a feeling it was closer to the truth than not, then Vrana had little to gain by fouling the plan.

"There's one thing," Vrana said. "Actually, two things. First, how are you going to convince Leoni that this Stratford ringer is the real thing? And, second, have you thought about what's going to happen when Leoni finds out he's been screwed?" Beside me, Mick shifted and Vrana kept going. "I can leave when I'm through here. What are you two going to do?"

"Ed Leoni doesn't scare me," Mick said. I wished I had his confidence and hoped he wasn't faking it. "He's a greedy guy. Not all that smart. There'll be some fallout, but I can handle it."

Vrana didn't look convinced, but seeing as he'd be gone—probably living happily off the grid somewhere—when this was over, I supposed this issue didn't matter much to him.

To the other point he'd made, I said, "I may be able to help with the credibility issue." I didn't want to talk about how—and the plan was just forming—in front of Vrana. In an attempt to appease him, I said, "What's the worst that can happen? Leoni tells us to get lost, and we're back where we started." I smiled. "The *Record* runs the story. You get your wish. Leoni gets screwed."

We all sat there for several moments exchanging looks. Finally, Mick nodded and raised his beer. Vrana did the same and so did I.

"Game on," Mick said, without much enthusiasm.

Chapter 26

When I arrived at de Coriolis' office the next morning, there were three staff people—two women and one man, all college-aged. They were laughing about something as I walked in, but immediately sobered and the young man put on a business smile as he walked over to me. He was a lanky kid with blond hair and pale eyebrows.

"Can I help you?"

I assumed this was Mark. "Robyn Guthrie. I'm here to talk with Congressman de Coriolis."

"Yeah, sure. With the *Record*, right?"

I said I was, and he asked me to wait while he let his boss know I was here.

He ducked into an office, tapping on the door first before opening it and entering. I was left with the two coeds. One went back to keying something into her computer and the other grabbed a couple of DVDs and scurried toward some shelves on the back wall. Apparently Mark was the personable one.

A moment later, the young man exited the office and told me I could go in. The way he was watching me as I walked past him, I could have been a sacrificial goat. That wasn't all bad. I know a few things about goats. The door clicked shut behind me.

The first thing I noticed about David de Coriolis was his size. Even though he was sitting behind his desk, I could tell that he was huge. I'd seen him on television, but never in person. He stood. TV didn't do him justice. He'd played football at Stanford; I didn't remember what position but assumed it was one where size mattered. He was six-three or four and had the square jaw that went with his block-like build. I guessed that he'd been out of college for more than twenty years, but there wasn't a sign that any of that football muscle had gone to fat. On television, he used his size to convey his role as protector of his district—his people. He liked to pose for photos where he had his arms around a couple of constituents or was shaking the hand of a little kid—the kid's hand engulfed by de Coriolis' bear paw. But I suspected there was another, equally convincing side to him.

I felt his gaze do a sweep of me, then he waved toward the chairs facing his desk.

I selected one and sat down, telling myself I was in no physical danger. At least not right here; de Coriolis would have a difficult time explaining how an interview had landed a reporter in traction.

"You know," he finally said, "I've known some reporters in my time. Some good, some not so good. And then there are the ones who will do anything to get a story."

I waited.

He moved around to the front of his desk where he sat on its edge so he could look down at me in close proximity. I felt as though I were in the shadow of Mount McKinley. "But . . . Ms. . . . . Guthrie, is it?"

Like he didn't know everything he needed to know about me. I nodded.

"I have never . . . never heard of one stooping low enough to harass an old man with Alzheimer's." He folded his arms over his chest. "My father honorably served this district for thirty-two years. Congratulations. You've shown me a new low." He kept his tone low and even, but it had a depth that carried.

Sensing he wasn't finished yet, I forced myself not to look away.

"You may not have broken any laws when you misrepresented yourself yesterday, but you sure stretched the bounds of decency."

"Is that what this is about? Decency?"

He bent toward me. "I'll bet you're recording this."

I wasn't, but I have been known to secretly record a conversation, and I didn't feel I should attempt to occupy the higher ground now. So, all I said was, "I'm not."

He rubbed his large hands together. "Why should I believe you?"

"You probably shouldn't. Just to be safe."

He narrowed his eyes as though adjusting his image of me and said, "I'm going to tell you this one time, and one time only. And then I want you to leave." He gave me a little nod. "You got that?"

I had no intention of leaving—he may be almost finished, but I hadn't even started—I gave him no response. Although it was getting difficult not to flinch under the force of his anger. This guy really disliked me, but I couldn't tell if that was because I'd breached Town and Country or because he was afraid I'd learned something from his father that could destroy both the father and the son. The distinction, I realized, was important. If he was being protective of his father, that I could understand. If he was covering up his father's misdeeds, I had little sympathy for him. Either way, I thought I could use him.

He must have interpreted my silence as submission, because he said, "You are never to set foot in Town and Country again."

"I won't. Not only is the place too expensive for my mother, but she didn't care for it. Also, I believe I got what I came there for."

After a brief hesitation, he shook his head, "I'm not biting." He stood and walked around his desk and returned to his seat. Apparently he believed the message had been delivered. He snatched a folded sheet of paper from his desk and focused on the words it contained, effectively dismissing me.

I wasn't going anywhere.

"Look, I don't 'harass' old men with Alzheimer's without a damned good reason. And, by the way, your father was quite taken with my mother."

"Mark!" he hollered.

"It's about Cedar Ridge," I persisted.

Judging from Mark's response time—maybe three seconds—he'd been waiting on the other side of the door for his master's voice.

"Miss Guthrie is leaving," de Coriolis told him.

I stood. "Did you bring in Clair Powell for a dressing-down when she talked with your father?"

When he didn't look up, I said, "You know who Clair was. The reporter who was hit by a car and left to die on Keffling? She visited your father."

His eyebrows pulled together slightly. That, plus the fact that he didn't have an immediate response, suggested that this may have been news to him.

I pressed it. "She brought him chocolate-covered cherries."

Mark had his hand around my arm and was attempting to pull me toward the door. He was stronger than his lankiness implied, but I resisted.

"Good-bye, Ms. Guthrie."

I shook off Mark's grip and reached into my messenger bag, extracting a copy of the soil evaluation report I'd gotten from Patchen. I slapped it down on de Coriolis's desk. "You should look at this."

"What is it?"

"It's a soil report."

As de Coriolis looked down the paper, I dug my heels in.

Still, Mark was stronger than he looked, and I'd been hauled halfway out the door before de Coriolis said, "Wait."

We stopped.

"Give us a minute."

Mark, looking both confused and curious nodded, left me in his boss's office and shut the door. When I turned toward de Coriolis, he was reading the soil report. And as I watched his features darken, I began to wonder if there wasn't a third possibility. Maybe he hadn't known about any of this at all. I guess I'd assumed from the way he kept his father sequestered that he was afraid of what he might say. But what if he didn't know?

He looked up from the paper. "Where did you get this? And what's it supposed to mean?"

"I got this from someone who had another soil sample taken at Cedar Ridge. It's—"

"There's nothing wrong with that land." He shook the paper in his hand. "What is this?"

"It's a second report."

"Why should I believe it?"

"Do you know Carl Wellen, the engineer who did the first report?"

"No."

"Well, then you may not get the chance." I paused. "He left town yesterday."

"What's that got to do with this?" he asked, but he wasn't sounding as forceful now.

"After he agreed to talk to me about that." I pointed at the paper he held. "The second report."

"What are you saying?"

"The last time I talked to Wellen he said, and I quote 'I didn't know. . . . I thought it was going to be a race track.'" I realized those weren't exactly damning quotes, but I pressed on, "Either someone got to him, or he figured out for himself that he was a liability."

"Well, when he decides to talk to you, maybe you'll be worth listening to."

"When I was at Town and Country I showed your father a photo of the Cedar Ridge area—before the development was started—and do you know what he told my mother?"

"I'm sure you're going to tell me."

"He said that land put his son through Stanford."

He hesitated. "He says a lot of things. And most of it doesn't make much sense. He's old."

"Don't be telling me about aging parents. The whole way up to Town and Country my mother was begging me not to put her there. She said it's a place to store old people. And, you know what? She was right."

"Now wait a minute."

"When's the last time you saw your father?"

He didn't answer.

"A week? Two weeks? A month."

"Now it really is time for you to leave." But he didn't call for Mark.

"I think that a long time ago, your father covered up some very bad business practices."

"Don't bring my father into this."

"I think he accepted bribe money, and I think it paid for your Stanford education."

He came around the desk fast and I braced for a collision, but he stopped just short of me.

"You can't prove any of that."

"I think your father was paid off by the Adamo family to look the other way while they dumped all the stuff no one else would touch into that land."

God, he was big. But he wasn't throttling me yet, so I pressed on.

"This story is going to come out. But when it does, it doesn't have to mention your father."

"What are you waiting for?"

"I'm interested in seeing that the Cedar Ridge homeowners aren't stuck living on land that's killing them."

His smile conveyed all the distain he was feeling. "How much?"

"I don't want money."

"Too easy to trace?"

"I wouldn't know."

He crossed his arms over his chest. "So, what do you want?"

"I want you to do something for me. Something that might end up helping the Cedar Ridge people." I paused. "All you have to do is lie."

He stepped back and sat on the edge of his desk. I took that as a sign that he'd listen.

"I'm assuming that Ed Leoni has been a generous campaign contributor. Especially when the zoning battle was going on over the Cedar Ridge property. I don't suppose he's too happy that didn't go his way."

"I wasn't either. An outlet mall would have been a godsend for this town."

"I want Leoni to think he's still got a shot at this casino. A Stratford rep is going to meet with him today. He's going to tell Leoni that if he had more property to sell, Stratford would be very interested."

He studied me for a minute. "So, what am I supposed to do?"

"Leoni is going to want some assurances that this Stratford rep, who for obvious reasons needs to be discrete, is who he says he is." I showed him the photo of Vrana I'd taken with my cell phone last night. "If Leoni asks you about this guy—we're calling him Mr. Smith—you tell him he works for Stratford and is one of the decision makers."

He took my cell phone for a closer look, then shook his head. "I've never seen this guy."

"That's because he's *posing* as a Stratford representative." Did I have to explain everything? "We just need to convince Leoni to make an offer so that Green Haven and the people living at Cedar Ridge will be compensated now and not in fifteen or twenty years."

Nodding, de Coriolis handed my phone back to me. "And when the deal doesn't happen?"

"Mr. Smith will be nowhere to be found."

Bracing his hands again the edge of his desk, de Coriolis looked down at the floor. "What else?"

"If Leoni asks about rezoning the area, it would be nice if you told him there'd be no problem. If there actually were a casino complex being built, there probably wouldn't be. So, that part would not be a lie. If that sort of thing bothers you."

He continued to stare at the floor.

"That's all we want," I said.

When he looked up at me, he said, "My father was a good man. He did a lot for this area."

"Maybe you could help do something good for Fowler. That toxic mess isn't going away."

He nodded.

I waited.

"I'll do it."

* * *

At eleven, Mick, Vrana and I all put on our various personas and drove to Leoni's office. The meeting the night before with Mick and Vrana had not been what I'd call pleasant, but they seemed to come to a mutual understanding. Neither trusted the other, but Mick was used to working that way, and I had the feeling that Vrana was as well. And neither could figure a reason the other would try to screw him. Still, it was, at best, an uneasy alliance. We'd gone back to Mick's place and he spent some time coaching Vrana on how to play Mr. Smith.

Mick had agreed to meet Lucky at his office, which was in a building nested among four others—Fowler's version of an office park. In Fowler's better days, the land had been a small shopping mall. The bland landscaping was dominated by young trees and a few bushes. Mercedes Enterprises split the fourth floor with a photography studio that specialized in pets and children. In that order.

As Mick, Vrana and I were shown to Leoni's corner office, I couldn't help but be impressed with how well Vrana had cleaned up. Although he did manage to retain that rustic quality he seemed to favor, wearing a gray sport coat over a striped shirt and jeans. Mick had told Leoni that his Stratford friend could not reveal his identity. What he'd be doing could get him fired, if not thrown in jail. We were all counting on Leoni's greed getting in the way of his judgment.

Mick actually did have a friend at Stratford who was aware of what was going on. He'd given Mick the names of several properties Stratford was considering. If Leoni asked, Mick could tell him. Just to lend some veracity to the venture. Either Mick's friend owed him big time or they were friends who did that kind of thing for each other. I wouldn't have doubted either. The understanding was that if this turned into a terrible mess—a distinct possibility—his friend would disavow any knowledge of our actions. So to speak. I just hoped we all weren't going to self-destruct in five seconds.

Standing at Leoni's door, Mick gave me one last sideways glance that said, basically "this is nuts." I smiled. But when we passed the threshold, those tinny alarm bells in the back of my head went off. Leoni was not alone. Another man sat in an upholstered chair against the wall. He wore a black leather jacket and was slumped in the chair, his right ankle resting on his left knee. He looked up at us as though we were intruding. And when Leoni got up from behind his desk to greet us, this other man didn't budge.

Beside me, Mick had stopped and was looking at this new guy. I guessed from the way he seemed to tighten—I could practically feel it—that those alarm bells were also chiming in his head.

"Hey, Mick." Leoni came around his desk with his hand extended. After a hesitation, Mick pulled his gaze from the man in the chair and shook Leoni's hand.

But after dropping Leoni's hand he said, "What's he doing here?"

Leoni took a step back. "That any way to talk to a friend of mine?"

"You didn't say anything about anyone else involved in this."

"We're talking a lot of money, Mick." Leoni shook his head as though regretting this fact. "Justin here is interested in partnering with me on this." He turned his attention on Vrana.

Justin gave Mick a thin smile that bordered on smug.

Mick did his best to ignore it, and introduced Smith/Vrana. Leoni shook his hand with such enthusiasm, it was like he was meeting a rock star rather than a guy who worked for a hotel conglomerate. "Pleasure to meet you Mr. Smith. A pleasure." He stepped back to include his seated friend. "Justin Adamo." He ran through our names for his friend, who nodded from the chair.

"Sit down, sit down." He gestured toward several chairs facing his desk, none of which were upholstered like Adamo's. "Anyone like a drink?"

"No," said Mick. "This isn't social, Ed."

Leoni produced a bottle of Laphroaig from a bar cabinet and, holding it up by the neck, said to Vrana, "Thirty years old."

Vrana glanced Mick's way, then nodded to Leoni. "Thank you. I will."

Leoni poured a small amount into a single malt tumbler, taking a whiff of it before handing the glass to Vrana.

I could smell the peaty aroma, and I wondered what I'd do if Leoni offered me a glass. Mick wouldn't be happy if I were to accept. Still, it was a thirty-year-old smoky single-malt from Islay and perhaps worth the repercussions.

But I needn't have worried. Once Leoni had poured himself a glass, he put the bottle away. Then he lifted the glass. "To good business," he said.

Vrana drank without acknowledging the toast, but after swallowing, he nodded his approval.

We finally sat. Mick was in the middle, and I was on the side nearest Adamo. I'd worn a flared skirt and heels and I could feel the silent one's eyes on my legs. I resisted the urge to tuck them under the chair.

After settling onto the edge of his desk and enjoying another sip of his Scotch, Leoni cleared his throat and said to Vrana, "I want to thank you for coming, Mr. Smith."

Vrana just nodded.

"I believe our mutual friend," he nodded in Mick's direction, "told you what this is about."

"Why don't you tell me again?"

"I have a piece of property that Stratford should be looking at. Perfect spot for a casino."

"So Mr. Hughes tells me," Vrana said. "It's that riverfront property three miles west of here, right?"

"That's it." Leoni removed some color photos from a folder, stood, and handed them to Vrana. I had to look over Mick to see them, but was able to get a pretty good look. The five photos showed a heavily treed strip of property along the river at one of its widest points. It was a pretty scene, and one I'd hate to see spoiled by a casino. But that's just me.

"What could be better than a great-looking casino right there on the river?" Leoni said. "I know you folks are looking at it. I'm just hoping you'll seriously consider it."

Nodding as he looked through the photos, Vrana said, "I agree. It's a beautiful space. And I know that some Stratford people were impressed."

Leoni looked from Adamo to Mick and then back to Vrana. "But? Is there a 'but' coming?"

Vrana handed the photos back to Leoni. "It was in the running, high on the list, in fact." He flicked his hand as though shooing a thought away. "Until we decided to go with a resort—hotel, golf course—and there's not quite enough land for that."

Leoni returned to his chair, tossing the photos onto his desk. Leaning on his elbows, hands clasped on the desk's surface, he opened his mouth as though to speak, but nothing came out.

"It's all about big these days, Mr. . . . Leoni," Vrana said as though struggling to come up with Lucky's name. "'Bigger is better' may sound like a cliché, but it's true more often than not." He nodded toward the photos. "Riverfront is nice. Real nice. But not if it forces us to scale back. Stratford isn't looking for just a casino. We're looking for a place to take the kids for the weekend. A place to throw a wedding. A bar mitzvah."

I could only imagine what was going on in Lucky's mind at that moment. I hoped, along with kicking himself in the butt, he was also figuring a way to make this work.

Vrana gave Leoni a regretful smile. "Sorry." He started to push himself up from the chair.

"What if there was enough land?" Everyone turned toward Adamo, who had finally spoken. It was a rather high voice, and not one that went with this dark, ominous-looking guy.

"But there isn't," Vrana corrected him. "And from here on, you're wasting my time." He was standing now.

I kept watching Adamo. A high voice. Since he was sitting it was hard to judge how tall he was, but he was definitely stocky. And that voice. He sounded a lot like the man that Wellen's neighbor had described.

Adamo noticed he had my attention and winked; then said to Vrana, "Don't be in such a hurry to leave."

Drumming his nails on the desk, Leoni asked, "Would forty more acres be enough?"

Frowning, Vrana canted his chin as though working out a math problem in his head. "Yeah," he finally said. But then he smiled and shrugged. "But it's not there," he said as though he thought he'd made the point already.

"We've heard . . ." it was Adamo again, who waited for everyone's attention before continuing, "that Cedar Ridge might be willing to sell that land back to us."

Liar. But I liked how he was thinking.

Leoni did the math for everyone. "That's my eighty acres—lots of that riverfront—and forty more."

Mick caught my eye and I thought I saw a trace of a smile. He said to Leoni, "What about the people who live there?"

"They'd be compensated," Leoni said, waving it off as though it were no issue.

"They like it there," I said, and Adamo regarded me as though he liked me better when it was just my legs talking.

"Nicely compensated," Leoni clarified.

Vrana had taken a seat again, but he held his silence. I appreciated how he wasn't rushing this, and that probably wasn't easy. I wanted to get out of here as fast as we could. Being in a room with Leoni and this Adamo guy made me nervous. But Vrana studied both of the men, and it was as though he had dozens of mental calculations going on in his head. After what seemed like a very long minute, he said, "All I can say is that that would be a very desirable piece of land. Very. But I can't promise anything. I can't even bring it up until you own that land. We don't want to be associated with running some people out of their homes."

"Not like they won't get paid." Leoni glanced at me. "Well paid."

Vrana shook his head. "We don't want any—and I mean any—bad publicity. A lot of people don't like casinos. We don't want to give them another reason."

"So," Adamo uncrossed his leg and leaned toward us, "what kind of assurances will we have you'll buy the place if we buy this property up?" In a mocking tone, he added, "After we do it nicely."

"None. None at all. But as I said, your riverfront property," Vrana looked directly at Leoni, "was desirable until we decided to go bigger. So, I'd say you've got a real good shot." He lifted one hand. "But that's all I can say."

Adamo snorted his disgust.

Leoni said, "If you help make this happen, I would be happy to make a donation to a charity of your choice, Mr. Smith."

Vrana nodded. "That would be most appreciated." But he frowned and gave his head a little shake. "I'm afraid that the timing of this project will be a problem. We're making a decision in a matter of days. I don't see you making this proposed transaction of yours happen that fast." Clucking his regret, he nodded at Leoni. "Your property could be perfect. But I'm not going to halt the process unless it becomes available. That would be . . . suspect. And transactions such as this often take thirty days or more. I'll tell you right now, we don't have that kind of time." With another nod, he added, "You've got your work cut out for you."

Leoni smiled with the confidence of a man who had anticipated this. "Not to worry. You'd be surprised how fast things move when there's cash involved."

I glanced at Adamo and saw he was also smiling. Perhaps that explained his presence. The cash man.

Vrana took several moments, then bowed his head. "I hope you're right." He pushed himself up from the chair. "Please let me know. After it's . . . a fact."

Mick and I stood, and as I hooked my purse strap over my shoulder, Leoni said, "Hey, Robyn, Wait here for a second."

I caught Mick's eye and nodded toward the door, willing him to leave without going all macho-protector on me.

He glanced back at the two men, then said to me, "Holler if you need anything."

After they left, Leoni took his place behind his desk. He waved toward the chair I'd vacated, but I remained standing. After an indifferent shrug, Leoni said, "You're friends with Katherine Kendrick, right?"

"We're acquaintances."

Narrowing his eyes as he watched me, he seemed to be considering that. After a few moments he said, "What will convince her to sell?"

I could feel Adamo's eyes on me.

"I don't think she will. Not if it means those families will have to leave."

He smiled. "What if they agree to sell?"

I gave that a pause. "If they do, I think she might sell. But the price would have to be right. She has more than money invested—she has heart. It's the green thing."

"Green, my ass," he muttered. "The only green anyone gives a crap about is the shade printed on money."

He paced back and forth a few times. Adamo watched him with a bland expression. Finally, Leoni stopped and said to me, "I want to talk to these people."

"You?"

He leaned closer. "What's wrong with that?"

I didn't want to come right out and mention his mob connections, although I'm sure it was obvious to us both.

"Aren't I the up-and-comer who's done so much for Fowler and who you were dying to write an article about?"

"You were—are—indeed."

"So, what's the problem? Set it up."

"They don't know you. You want them to make a difficult decision fast, and they've just met you."

He returned to the bar and poured himself another shot of the Scotch, which he drank in one gulp—what a waste—before turning back to me. "You come with me."

I adjusted my purse strap and crossed my arms over my chest. "Why should I?"

"You'll get a consultant's fee. A nice one."

I pretended to give that some thought before I said, "I'll try to set something up."

Leoni nodded. "Do that."

As I left the room, I heard him snort and repeat his mantra, "Green, my ass."

*　*　*

Once outside again with Mick and Vrana, I allowed myself a deep sigh, then said, "I'm setting up a meeting with Leoni and the homeowners."

"This is far, far from over," Mick warned me.

"I know. I'm just glad to get out of that room. Leoni's bad enough, but that Adamo guy gave me the creeps."

"He should."

"You think he's a large contributor?"

"Right. My guess is he's fronting the money. No way Leoni has enough to pay cash for this. And he's not going to his father-in-law for a handout, that's for damned sure."

"Adamo has that kind of money?" Vrana asked.

Mick shook his head. "No, but his old man does."

Chapter 27

Things moved quickly.

I was able to arrange a meeting with Cedar Ridge's homeowners for the next morning, and it went pretty well. Mary Alice, who had assumed the alpha-homeowner role, was appropriately reluctant at first. But, with the advice of a "consultant" (i.e., another friend of Mick's), she was convinced that Leoni was offering her a good price. It helped that the other lots were selling slowly. After Mary Alice gave in, the Sanduskys and Kellers soon followed suit.

I'd actually begun to feel a little optimistic about pulling this off.

* * *

Later that afternoon we all gathered in Kat's room at Grenada Suites. As planned, Mick and I were to get there ahead of Lucky, and when I walked into the room, I saw that Mick had beaten me there and was in a discussion with Kat. I was about to see if I could figure out if something was going on when I was distracted by the sight of Mary Alice Tucker sitting there on the couch. Why was she here? She seemed reserved and avoided looking at me. Maybe it was the conservative brown suit. But I didn't get a chance to ask about her presence because Beverly was the next to arrive, carrying a cloth bag filled with food. Apparently she'd been sent on a refreshment run, because she immediately began setting out a platter of cheese and crackers along with plain white plates and napkins.

This struck me as an odd thing to do; it was as though she wanted to put a social spin on a rather unfortunate event. Afraid my throat would seize on me if I tried to swallow something other than saliva, I passed on her offer.

Leoni and his silent but deadly friend Justin Adamo arrived only minutes later. Leoni seemed at ease until he saw Mary Alice. "No offense, but what're you doing here?"

Mary Alice glanced Kat's way, and I saw how Kat tensed up. If the two of them had come to odds over this, I was going to explode at one of them. And her name started with a K.

Mary Alice managed a weak smile and, although she looked up at Leoni as she spoke, maintaining eye contact with him seemed to come with an effort. "It's just that I'm going to be more comfortable about this if I can believe that Mrs. Kendrick is going to proceed with everyone's best interest at heart." Her hands were folded in her lap and her knuckles white. She must have sensed the glare she was getting from Kat.

"She doesn't trust me," Kat said, still assessing Mary Alice.

"Huh," Leoni said, seeming amused as he made himself comfortable on the opposite end of the couch from Mary Alice. He helped himself to a cracker with a slab of gouda. "I guess I can't blame you," he said around the bite.

Mary Alice's presence made me even edgier than I already was. It added a wild-card feel to the proceedings that I didn't like. It also implied that I didn't know Mary Alice as well as I thought I did. Of course, why should I know her? We'd met twice. Maybe she and Lucky had some master plan in the works, and I was about to be crowned the queen of stupidity. Adamo stationed himself in the kitchenette. He'd rejected Beverly's offer of a drink, but helped himself—without asking—to a bottle of water from the fridge. I was too jittery to sit and had propped myself up against a wall where I could view the proceedings without, I hoped, having to participate. Mick helped me hold up the wall. He seemed to be taking it all in stride, but he was more practiced at this sort of thing than I was. I suspected he recognized that, and had positioned himself next to me to keep my hysteria at bay.

"We'll dispense with the small talk," Leoni said to Kat, brushing cracker crumbs from his hands.

"Please do," she said dryly. She seemed composed, but the strain of the last week showed in her eyes.

He glanced my way. "Your friend told you why I'm here."

Kat regarded me briefly, and then she nodded. "Yes, Robyn told me." She turned toward Leoni. "You want to buy Cedar Ridge. I can't imagine why you think I'd sell it to you."

When she set her glass on an end table, I noticed a smudge of lipstick on its rim. She looked polished today, and I worried for a moment that she might have overdone it. After all, she was a grieving widow in financial crisis. But then I realized that this was how she wanted to play it—vanquished, but proud. And she needed meticulously applied makeup to pull that off. Fair enough.

Apparently Leoni didn't think a response was necessary, because he grabbed another chunk of cheese off the plate, popped it into his mouth and chewed.

Kat crossed one leg over the other and drew herself up straight. "Why do you want the property?"

"My family doesn't like that I let it go," Lucky told her. "You know how family is."

"Not really." She smiled a little. I just hoped she didn't overplay it. Perhaps I should have reminded her that she was not the one who landed the role in *Glass Menagerie*.

"Well, let's just say you don't know my family." Leoni seemed a bit annoyed with her prodding.

He leaned forward, placing his elbows on his knees. "I gave you and your husband—your late husband, and I am very sorry to hear that—I gave you a very nice price on that property. And I am prepared to pay you exactly what you paid me."

Kat leaned forward. "So, what? I sell you Cedar Ridge and all I get is the price we paid for it?" She shook her head as though she couldn't believe what she was hearing.

"This is just a guess, but I'm betting that money would come in handy right about now."

She drew back. "What—what about the improvements we've made? Water. Roads. The whole infrastructure." All of this was spoken like a woman who had no idea what was beneath that soil.

"I'm talking cash," Leoni said and Kat fell back against the chair. Smiling, Leoni nodded. "Cash." Then he added, "We'll compensate you for half the improvements."

Recovering, Kat shook her head as though to clear it. "It's still a ridiculous price."

"I've already had my people speak with Mrs. Tucker, the Sanduskys and the Kellers." He gave Mary Alice a nod. "I made them all very generous offers and they're willing to sell." He smiled. "How are you going to sell a bunch of empty houses in the middle of nowhere?"

Kat looked at Mary Alice, who bowed her head and focused on the glass she held.

"Is this true?"

Mary Alice nodded. "Yes," she said, without looking up.

Kat's jaw hardened and she looked like she wanted to spit at both of them. Instead, she just said, "You're a bastard, Mr. Leoni."

He chuckled. "Tell me something I don't know."

At this point, Mary Alice scooted up to the edge of the couch, set her drink on the coffee table and placed her folded hands in her lap.

"Um, Mr. Leoni? Can we talk about that price again? What you're offering for my home? Just briefly."

The first traces of concern skittered across his face. "What? We had an agreement."

"We did," she conceded. "But then I told Alex and Bobby. My boys. And they were upset."

Leoni shook his head in disbelief. "Do they own the house? Or do you?"

"It's their house as much as it is mine." On hearing the indignation in her voice, Leoni drew back an inch. But Mary Alice raised one hand as though to calm everyone. "I don't mean to get emotional . . ."

"None of us do, Mrs. . . . ."

"Tucker," Mary Alice reminded him. "You know, Mr. Leoni, my boys love Cedar Ridge."

He snorted. "How much are they going to love it when you're the only ones living there?"

Mary Alice nodded as though that were a reasonable question. "Well, we've talked about that very thing. And, you know," she smiled a little, "my boys find it kind of exciting. They feel like pioneers. Of course, they will get lonely after a while, but more people will come. We've no doubt." She glanced at Kat and nodded. "Once the economy gets a little better there'll be more people coming to Cedar Ridge. I believe that." She leaned toward Leoni. "I don't know if you have children, Mr. Leoni, but what would you do if your child cried when you told him you were selling the place because you got such a good price? It's not all about money. There is no price for my children's happiness."

I was beginning to think it was Mary Alice who deserved the acting honor today.

"No, huh?" Leoni glanced Adamo's way and then named a new, highly impressive figure. "You think that'll help dry the tears?"

Mary Alice's eyes widened when she heard the amount, but she quickly tempered her response. "That is a kind offer."

"Okay," Lucky stood, clapping his hands. "I guess we're good—"

Mary Alice continued in her quiet way. "Please wait. I'm not trying to be an obstructionist. It's just that moving is a chore—"

"We'll pay for movers." Leoni's exasperation was starting to show.

"Oh. Why thank you." And before Leoni could close the deal, she said, "And we'll need to find a place to live until we find a home that's as special to my boys as Cedar Ridge."

Leoni gazed heavenward as he shook his head. "Okay, I'll kick in for three months rental. How's that?"

She gave him a timid smile. "Six months would be better."

"Six months."

Mary Alice gave that some thought. Finally, she said, "All right. That's fair." She smiled at me. "I can't wait to tell the Sanduskys and the Kellers."

Lucky jumped in. "Wait a minute. Don't be telling those people."

Her eyes widened again and she tilted her chin. "They're going to find out."

Lucky gave her a disgusted look. "Not if you don't tell them."

"It is public record, Ed," Kat interjected.

"No way."

The room fell silent. I could hear a clock ticking somewhere and the sound of Adamo gulping his water.

Finally, Kat said, "All right. Here's what I'll do." Leoni waited. "I'll let you have the property for what we paid for it, if you give all the residents the same deal you're giving Mary Alice."

I saw the greed flicker in his eyes, but he assumed a deadpan, added a resigned sigh, and glanced at Adamo. When he nodded, Leoni said, "Okay, it's a deal." Before anyone could intercede, he rubbed his hands together and said, "We leave it to the lawyers now."

* * *

Lucky and Adamo left a few minutes later. The rest would be settled by the lawyers, and we'd all see how quickly they could move when motivated.

Once the door clicked shut behind them, it was all I could do not to let out a "Whoopee!" but I waited, fearing I'd be heard echoing down the halls of Grenada Suites. And then I felt Mick's hand on my arm and got a warning look from him. Confused, but compliant, I waited to follow someone's lead, seeing as I seemed to be clueless at this point.

Kat leaned back in her chair, tilting her head against the cushion. "My life is over," she said.

Mary Alice reached out and put her hand on Kat's arm. "Thank you. Thank you so much."

I found I'd regained my swallowing function and helped myself—Adamo-style—to some water. Beverly gave me a dirty look, which I ignored.

"You'll be okay, Kat," Mick was telling her. "You're going to have to watch your finances for a while, but you'll be okay."

"What about Green Haven?"

I settled into the desk chair and watched Mick console Kat, still not sure what in the hell was going on. This had been my idea—one no one else wanted to own—so why was I feeling like the outsider?

Beverly was going through her purse, as though looking for something. "Kat?"

Kat had her forehead braced against her hand as though dealing with a migraine. "What?" she said without looking up.

"I thought I'd gotten that prescription refilled. Don't know what I was thinking when I went to the store. Maybe I should run out now."

Kat squeezed her eyes shut. "Please, Beverly. I'm going to need something very soon."

"Right away." She tucked her purse under her arm, grabbed a tan jacket and left.

We all sat there in silence for almost a minute. Then I noticed that Mary Alice was doing one of those silent giggle collapses. Kat was smiling. Mick was looking at me with one of his apologetic grins.

"Okay," I said. "What just happened?"

"I'm sorry, Robyn," Kat said, sounding almost sincere. "I just really needed to keep up the poor house appearance and the more people who believed I was in serious trouble, the easier that would be."

Okay, she was still a bitch.

Mick said, "Kat really just needed a creative accountant. She's taken a hit, but she'll be okay."

"You're not broke?"

"No."

"Well, thank God," I said without a trace of sincerity.

"But I needed Leoni to think I was," Kat said as if that explained everything.

Mick added, "Otherwise he'd never have believed she'd settle for that amount. And he had to believe he was getting a deal."

I sat there with my water trying to put this all together. Kat wasn't broke, but Leoni was more likely to take advantage of her if he thought she was. While this made perfect sense, I still didn't understand why I was the last to know. But before I could ask that, Kat spoke up again.

"But, if it weren't for you, Robyn, I wouldn't have done a really thorough check into Beverly's background." She paused. "Justin Adamo is her second cousin."

"Really?" Hooray for me. I'd gotten something right. Beverly had always smelled a bit off to me.

"A lot of things made sense after I learned that."

Mary Alice said to me, "Kat came up with the 'deal' we negotiated just before you got here. We didn't have time to tell you."

I doubted that; Kat was pretty deft with her cell phone.

"Well, it worked out," I said, not feeling as happy as I thought I would. "And that's good."

Kat grinned at me. "Now are you going to give me some credit for being able to act?"

I took a drink of the water. "You still didn't get that part in high school."

Shrugging it off, she said, "I was too pretty." She winked at me, but I wasn't sure how to interpret it.

Everyone laughed. Some of us laughed harder than others.

Chapter 28

Things started to unravel the day after the papers were all signed—
the morning after we'd all quietly celebrated. Mick and I had taken
Kat to dinner; she was excited because Russell had been found and
was on his way to Chicago, due to arrive in a day or two. Kat was
considering closing down Green Haven, maybe starting over with
another company, but at least she had some options now.

Mary Alice and her boys had a six-month lease on an apartment,
covered by Lucky. They could all take their time finding a new place,
and they had all the money they'd invested in Cedar Ridge.

In keeping with tradition, I took my mother to the Lizard for
our weekly coffee and sweets outing.

We settled at a table by the window, and I opened my laptop. My
first article on Cedar Ridge had turned into a reporting of its sale,
which had actually made it a pretty hot topic right now. And Vrana
was about to sic some of his EPA contacts on the land, which was a
story I was looking forward to breaking.

I grabbed my wallet. "What're you in the mood for, Mom?"

Instead of answering me, she'd cast a disapproving gaze on the
computer. "You're not going to be working, are you?"

"I told you I had a few things to do. We'll still be able to talk."
Before she could start whining, I plunged ahead, "What shall I get
you? You in the mood for chocolate?"

She looked up from the computer. "Why, yes," she said,
brightening.

"Chocolate chip muffin?"

"That sounds lovely."

After delivering two coffees, a muffin and a scone I tapped open my story.

"We can talk while I'm working," I told her.

"Good," she said. "Did I tell you about the sketching class I'm taking at Dryden?"

"No, you didn't." This seemed odd; she'd never exhibited any interest in art, whether she was drawing it or hanging it on the walls. "What are you drawing?"

"Well, first it was round things." She continued, telling me about the ornaments and the apples.

I'd been listening to my mother for long enough to be able to read and ask questions at the same time. While she talked, I read over my follow-up Cedar Ridge story. I had mixed feelings about the whole thing. Although I believed we'd managed to pull off the Cedar Ridge deception, I was no closer to knowing who killed Clair. Leoni was still a possibility, and his friend, Justin Adamo, probably wouldn't have hesitated. But without proof, which I didn't have, my conjectures were useless.

"Who else is in the class?" I asked when my mother seemed to run out of steam.

"Oh, some of the usual mopes."

"Azalea?"

"No. She's learning how to crochet." My mother snorted softly and added, under her breath, "At her age."

She launched into a critique of a few of Dryden's residents. Most were either bossy or submissive. I wondered if there was a "bitchy" category. As she talked, I scrolled down to an unfinished paragraph. I still needed a quote from Glenn Patchen. I'd tried him a couple of times, but hadn't spoken with him since the sale. He hadn't been in

on the charade, but he'd kept mum about the property long enough
to allow it to happen. Although, I tended to think his silence had
more to do with self preservation than anything else. I wondered
what he was looking to do next. Seemed a shame to waste his talent.
Even if he was a sniveling coward.

I waited until my mother stopped talking and turned her attention on her muffin. "I've gotta make a quick phone call, Mom."

"Don't let me disturb you, Dear."

She gave me a pleasant smile as I punched in his number, and
she murmured something about the traffic being rather heavy today.

When I didn't get an answer on Patchen's cell phone, I wondered
if he'd gone back to Chicago to be with his wife. I did a search for
him on the Internet and found a number. When a woman answered,
I told her who I was and asked to speak with Glenn. She said, "He's
not here."

"Is this Joanna West?"

She hesitated, then said that she was.

"Glenn talked about you. Said you're a photographer." Not sure
why I mentioned that. I guess I was feeling a bit of a chill on the
other end and wanted to know why. Then, for some reason, I added,
"Clair Powell was a student of yours, wasn't she?"

She emitted a humorless chuckle. "I don't mean to be unpleasant, Miss . . ."

I repeated my name.

". . . Guthrie. Glenn doesn't live here anymore. I believe he
moved into that trailer. You might find him there."

She disconnected. Interesting. I hit End on my phone and set it
beside my computer.

"What is it, Robyn?"

"Probably nothing. But this guy I need to talk to isn't living with
his wife anymore."

"Who is he?"

"Glenn Patchen. An architect."

She broke off a chunk of muffin and nibbled at it. "So, he's available?"

I chose to ignore that and attempted to digest the news. I supposed this wasn't a shock. I knew he'd spent at least one drunken night at his trailer. And then there was that tendency to get emotional when talking about Clair.

"Robyn."

"Just a second, Mom." I needed to think this through.

"Robyn."

It wasn't until I looked up to ask my mother for a little patience that I saw her attention had wandered elsewhere. Standing next to our table were Lucky Leoni and his lovely daughter.

"Hey, Robyn," he said.

Without waiting for an invitation or even an acknowledgment, he pulled out the chair next to my mom's and waved his daughter into it. Mercedes looked at her dad as if he were joking, apparently saw he wasn't, then sat in the chair as though it was covered in wet paint. She regarded me with a mixture of scorn and boredom before turning to look out the window.

Leoni smiled down at my mother and said, "Who's this lovely young lady?"

"Don't make me blush," my mother said with an edge that I didn't think Leoni caught.

"That's my mother, Lizzie Guthrie. Mom, Ed Leoni."

He turned his smile on me and, as usual, I found the coldness behind it unsettling. "I see who you get your looks from," he said.

I forced down my mouthful of pastry with some coffee, swallowing with an audible gulp. When I first saw him standing there, I was afraid that he'd learned that Stratford had chosen another location for the casino. While I knew that was going to happen—and probably soon—I'd hoped to be nowhere in Lucky's vicinity when he learned of it. But now that I'd gotten over my initial panic, I realized he wasn't being any creepier than usual. I allowed myself to relax a little.

"I keep running into you here," he persisted. "Must be fate."

"Or something." I tapped open an email from "Tea of the Month Club" and pretended to read. I really didn't want them to stay, and yet I'd come to know Lucky well enough to realize that my discomfort would not send him away. On the contrary, Lucky Leoni was a guy who liked making people squirm. So I tried my best to appear preoccupied rather than uncomfortable.

"Mrs. Guthrie, this is my daughter, Mercedes."

My mother nodded as Leoni said to his daughter. "And you remember Robyn."

"No," Mercedes said, her gaze skimming past me before focusing out the window again. Leoni placed a hand on her shoulder, but he didn't get her attention until he asked her what she wanted to drink.

"Decaf skim latte with one and a half shots of caramel and chocolate bits," she told him. Leoni went to the counter, and Mercedes returned her attention to the street scene. I could hear her deep sigh from across the table. When I looked up, I saw that my mother was watching her with that little, tentative smile that appears innocent, but means she's up to something.

Without looking away from the street, Mercedes said, "Why are you staring at me?"

Instead of answering, my mother reached toward Mercedes and touched the sleeve of her khaki jacket. This caused the young girl to start and draw away, regarding my mother as though she'd just spat at her.

My mother said, "Aren't you a bit young to be drinking coffee?"

"No." Mercedes' lip began to curl.

"It will stunt your growth, you know."

"No it won't." Mercedes looked toward the counter where her dad, waiting for their order, winked at her.

My mother settled back in her chair, smiling at Mercedes. "It's bad for your bones."

"That's stupid," she said, tossing her hair.

"It will make your hair thin." My mother touched her own short, still thick, white hair. "And you'll gray sooner."

I pressed my lips together and watched Mercedes struggle to hold it together.

"Mercedes plays tennis," I said to my mother.

"Really?" She turned to Mercedes. "Why?"

It was as though my mother had spoken in Latin or some other dead language.

"She's a number three seed," I offered.

"Oh." My mother worked her jaw a couple of times. "What's a seed?"

"It means two other people play better than she does."

"Oh," my mother said, giving Mercedes a tender smile. "I'm sorry."

Mercedes' nostrils flared and her eyes sparked. Finally, she burst out with, "You're old!"

"Hey, what's going on?" Leoni sat so his back was to the window, set his daughter's frothy drink in front of her and blew some of the steam off his black coffee.

"My mom and Mercedes were getting acquainted." From the body language displayed, it looked as though my mother had been talking to the back of Mercedes's head.

Leoni, unfazed by his daughter's rudeness, asked me, "What do you hear from Mr. Smith?"

"Nothing yet."

"Yeah, I suppose I'll know before you do."

"I wouldn't be surprised."

"Who's Mr. Smith?" my mother piped in.

"A businessman," I told her

"I'm kind of busy here," I said to Leoni, opening a browser in search of a subject to sidetrack him.

"We'll just be a couple of minutes. Mercedes has her tennis lesson in a half hour."

As the page loaded I looked up and saw my mother's eyes widening. "She shouldn't drink coffee before tennis."

Just as I felt a laugh trying to escape, my gaze fell on the "Chicago Today" feature, and I sobered real fast as I read the headline: Stratford Chooses Wildwood for Casino Site. *Shit.*

Of course, this didn't stun me, but I did have to marvel at the timing. I skimmed the article, which had been posted less than an hour ago. The spokesperson for Stratford, Amanda Troy, spent a lot of time praising the northwest location.

I must have made some odd noise, because when I looked up from the article, both my mother and Leoni were watching me.

"Nothing," I said. "Just my horoscope."

Now both my mother and Leoni looked confused.

"Dad?" It was Mercedes.

"Pisces is rising. That's, um, usually good. Except when Mercury is—"

"Dad!" This time we all looked to see what was going on and, at the same time, I heard a crash.

My mother gasped. I jumped. It wasn't inside the Lizard. Not that close. I saw Mercedes with her mouth hanging open and followed her gaze out the window just as I heard the noise again, Only this time there was a sort of *thunk* to it.

"What the—" Leoni was now standing, staring out the window onto Main Street at Justin Adamo, in his soft leather jacket, with a baseball bat raised over his head. As I watched, he brought it crashing down onto the windshield of a sable-colored Mercedes convertible. Its left fender had already taken a hit and one of the headlights had been taken out. The little car looked like it was winking at us. In the time it took all this to sink in, Leoni was out the door, hollering obscenities.

"Dad! That's . . . " Mercedes watched as her father bore down on Adamo. ". . . our car." Her voice trailed off.

She hesitated, apparently saw her other choice was to stay with us, and she followed her father.

My mother took a sip of her coffee. "Is that that young man's car?"

"Yes, it is, Mom. And we need to get out of here."

"I haven't finished my muffin."

I hastily wrapped it in a napkin and shoved it into her handbag. "We have to leave." I tried to sound urgent, but not panicked.

I closed my laptop and slipped it into my messenger bag, which I slung over my shoulder. I took my mother's arm and led her to the small phalanx just outside the Lizard's door, stopping short of Mercedes, who stood at the front of the crowd but didn't seem inclined to interject herself into the scene.

"What the fuck are you doing?" Leoni lunged for Adamo's arm and tried to grab the bat from him. Adamo twisted out of his grip and smacked the bat against the passenger side door, leaving a ball-sized dent. Leoni came at him, but now Adamo backed off a couple feet, waving the bat in front of him, almost taunting Leoni. Leoni stopped. "You wanna tell me what the fuck you're doing?"

"You want to tell me you didn't know about Stratford's new casino site?"

Leoni stopped, almost rearing back. "What're you talking about?"

I slipped my mother and me behind one of the Lizard's taller patrons, at the same time looking for an escape route.

"What is he talking about, Robyn?"

I shushed her and didn't check to see if I'd gotten a withering look in return. Probably.

"It's Wildwood, asshole. Don't tell me you didn't hear."

Peering around my human wall, I saw Leoni stop, raising his hands in an almost prayerful gesture. "Why are you trashing my car?"

Adamo spat on the car's roof. "You set this up."

That suburb was a ways north of us, and also a river town.

"No. No, man. Don't do that." Leoni was begging now. "I'll fix this."

"Then I'll owe you for a window," Adamo said just before he took out the passenger-side window.

Now I could hear police sirens. Coming this way. We needed to get out of here.

Just then Adamo backed up another step as though to do some damage to the trunk, and Leoni lunged at him again, knocking him off balance at the moment he had the bat raised over his head. The bat went flying as Adamo's arms pinwheeled, and as he stumbled back another step I heard brakes screaming. I think there was a moment of recognition on Adamo's face just before the car bore down on him. I held my mother to me. The impact sent Adamo flying like some kind of stunt dummy into the other lane. A loud honk, more screaming brakes was followed by a moment of shock-filled silence. It was as though everyone had gasped for a breath at the same second. Then there were a couple of moans, one woman screamed and the sirens got louder.

"Oh, my goodness," my mother breathed. As I watched, Lucky turned away from the accident with his hand covering his eyes. He staggered a couple of steps, groping for something to hold onto and found his car. But when he brought his hand down on the shattered window, he recoiled, stepped back and took in the wreck that had been his beloved car. In a matter of seconds, his expression changed from shock to rage. He spun around, looking into the small crowd around the Lizard's door.

I felt like we were standing on the tracks with a train speeding toward us, but I was powerless to turn away. But then Lucky saw his daughter—maybe she was who he'd been looking for—and he buried his face in his hands. Someone had pulled Mercedes into the Lizard and away from the scene. Her eyes were wide and she seemed in shock. I never thought I'd feel sorry for Mercedes Leoni, but I did. I really did.

But I didn't have time to dwell on that because the cavalry, in the form of the police, pulled up to the corner. Lucky stepped back, apparently reassessing his priorities. That was when I felt someone's hand on my arm and a voice in my ear. "Let's get out of here."

I looked up and saw Vrana, but I was still in frozen mode so he had to drag my mother and me a few steps before I got the hang of walking again, and I let him lead us to his little black car.

Sometimes being followed wasn't such a bad thing.

He'd taken each of us by an arm, and my mother was the first to shake him off. "What are you doing?"

"It's okay, Mom," I told her. "This is Kurt Vrana. He's a . . ." What was he? Stalker? Fellow collaborator? I settled for the easiest, ". . . friend."

He gave her a gracious nod and a slight bow. She was pleased.

I leaned against his car, afraid my knees would give out.

"Did you see what happened?" my mother was asking, and before she got an answer, she continued, "There was this tall woman in front of me. I did see a man in the air." She looked at me. "Are you all right?"

"I'll be fine," I told her, relieved she hadn't seen much.

I was thinking I needed to call Mick, but this wasn't the place to do it.

"Did you see what hit him?" Vrana asked as he observed the activity.

"Other than a car? No."

He turned to me. "A Prius." With a bob of his eyebrows he added, deadpan, "The silent, green death."

I tried to keep a straight face, but I couldn't.

When Vrana opened the passenger door for us, I declined and gestured across the street. "Got my car."

My mother was studying him with keen interest. "How good a friend are you?" she asked.

Grinning, he said, "Good enough, I guess."

He closed the door and leaned against the car. "You've got a different end for your story now." He glanced toward Main Street where a police officer was signaling traffic to go either north or south. The street had been swiftly closed.

"Yeah, I guess."

"You think Adamo killed Clair?"

"He's got—he had—the personality for it."

"I don't like not knowing."

I thought of Clair's parents. "Nobody does."

"Why are you still following me?" I asked.

"Force of habit, I guess."

"Well, just to save you the effort, I'm taking my mother home now." But I stood there, trying to think of something that had escaped me.

"What?" Vrana asked.

"There was something else I was going to do." I shook my head. "I was just thinking about it in the Lizard. I hate that when I can't remember something."

"Was it about that architect?" my mother asked.

I sighed. "Yes, it was," I said, a little distressed to find my mother's memory exceeding my own.

"You talking about Patchen?" Vrana asked.

"Yeah. I just learned he and his wife have separated. He's living at Cedar Ridge. In that trailer."

"I thought you needed to see him," my mother said.

"Later."

Vrana stared off for a minute, then shook his head. "Tough break."

I adjusted my bag's strap on my shoulder and put my hand on my mother's shoulder. "Time to be getting to back to Dryden."

"Wait until Lionel hears about this."

"Who's Lionel?" I asked.

My mother started. "Oh. Just one of the residents."

Indeed.

I said goodbye to Vrana and steered my mother toward my car. By the time I got her situated and executed a three-point turn to avoid Main Street, Vrana was off to his next destination. Wherever that was, I figured he wouldn't be right behind me.

As I navigated the side streets to avoid the accident scene, my mother content watching the homes of Fowler pass by, I realized that something was nagging at me. I reran the meeting with Vrana, and when I got to the part where he said, "You talking about Patchen," I stopped. Had I ever mentioned Patchen to him? I didn't think I had. Of course, if he'd been following me, it would have been easy enough to find out who Patchen was. And then there was the timing of his separation from his wife. The sadness he'd exuded when we talked about Clair. And Vrana's interest in him. I knew that Vrana had loved Clair. Had Patchen gotten carried away in his own affection for her? I couldn't imagine him killing her, but my imagination can be surprised at times.

I turned at the next corner, planning to head back west toward Cedar Ridge. I pulled over and dug my cell phone from my bag and called Mick.

"You heard?" he said when he answered.

"Yeah. You won't believe what just happened, and I can't go into it right now. Adamo's dead. I think. I'm on my way to Cedar Ridge. I have a bad feeling about Patchen and I have another, equally bad feeling that Vrana is on his way there."

"What's Patchen doing at Cedar Ridge?"

"I think he lives in the trailer. He and his wife separated."

"On my way," he said.

As I pulled away from the curb, I said, "You mind going for a little ride, Mom?"

I heard her sigh. "Do I have a choice?"

Chapter 29

Construction equipment and vehicles were gone when I pulled into Cedar Ridge. It had the feel of a ghost town. Then I saw Patchen's Jeep and, beside it, Kurt Vrana's Mini Cooper.

I pulled next to the Jeep, putting as much distance as I could between my car and the trailer door. I turned to my mother, "Promise me you'll stay here, Mom."

"What's going on?"

"Probably nothing," I lied. "Just stay here, okay."

"I heard you the first time."

"Thank you, Mom."

I had nothing to use as a weapon, not that I was sure I'd need one. I knew I wasn't one to talk about vigilante justice, but I did have my limits, which, I suspected, Vrana wouldn't hesitate to exceed if it involved Clair.

I couldn't decide whether to try to sneak in or knock on the door. I opted for a compromise. I climbed the steps without tiptoeing and opened the door as though I wasn't expecting to find anything unusual on the other side.

Boy, was I wrong.

Patchen was in his chair, pushed back a foot from the desk, his hands raised in front of his chest. Vrana faced the pasty-looking architect with a gun aimed at his head.

A sheen of sweat covered Patchen's face. His hair was unkempt and his shirt wrinkled. The trailer had a stale, dead smell to it. Without moving his head, he shifted his gaze in my direction. "Robyn," he croaked. "This guy is crazy."

"Shut up," Vrana told him.

I approached Vrana from his left side, stopping when I got within a few feet. "Kurt, you don't want to do that."

He glanced at me. "He killed her, Robyn. He's the one who killed Clair."

"Wait a minute, Kurt. Please."

He wagged the gun at Patchen. "Tell her. Tell her what you told me."

Patchen shook his head. "I . . . I . . ."

"Tell her!"

"It was an accident." He was crying.

"Keep talking," Vrana said. "And tell Robyn."

Patchen shifted his head slightly. "It was an accident. I don't know how . . ."

"What happened, Glenn?" I asked.

"I had a couple drinks. Was thinking about her. Drove by her place."

He swallowed. "I saw her with her dog." He stopped.

I felt myself shivering, even though it wasn't cold, and wrapped my arms over my chest. "Tell me, Glenn."

"I don't know. I pulled over and we talked a little, and I asked if she wanted a ride home. It was starting to rain." He swallowed again and when he continued, I could hear the strain in his words, as though his throat was fighting them. "They got in. We got to talking. I thought . . . I thought she was interested. I drove around."

"What did she say?" Vrana interrupted.

"Let him finish, Kurt."

Patchen shook his head as though still confused. "I didn't mean . . . I just thought . . ."

"What happened next?" I prompted.

"She told me to stop the car. I said I'd take her home. She wouldn't let me. I stopped there on Keffling. In the middle of nowhere. And I let her out." He bowed his head as though finished.

Vrana took a step closer. "Then what did you do?"

Patchen was looking into his hands, which were now laced together in an approximation of prayer. He sobbed once. "I lost it. Just for a second. I lost it. Or, I don't know. Maybe my foot slipped. But she was walking away from me. And I couldn't let her go. And then she was lying there . . ." The sobs were coming on strong now. "And it was too late."

I couldn't speak. I'd never felt so sorry for a person and so mad at them at the same time. But the more I thought, the more the anger took over. How dare this sniveling coward take the life of someone like Clair?

"You've got a choice to make," Vrana said. He swapped his gun into his right hand and used his left to pull another out of a shoulder holster hidden beneath his jacket. He set this gun on the desk. "Either I kill you." He pushed the gun toward Patchen. "Or you use the one bullet in here to do it yourself." He paused. "One way or the other, you're not going to be alive when I leave here."

"Kurt?" Did he know what he was doing? It only took one bullet to take out either of us.

"This is wrong, Kurt," I said. "Let the law handle this."

"No. Let him decide. Which is more than he did for Clair."

Patchen dropped his face into his hands, and I could hear him suck in a deep breath, which he released in a rush. Then he lifted his head, looked from Vrana to me and back again, and reached across the desk for the gun.

"Don't do this, Glenn." I said.

Patchen held the weapon in his two hands, touching it with a caress. He pressed his lips together into a tight line and took the gun in his right hand. With his left, he reached under his glasses to wipe away some moisture. Then he nodded, put the gun to his right temple, and pulled the trigger.

It clicked.

He pulled the trigger again.

Again, it clicked.

He dropped the gun on his desk and sat there shaking his head, staring at something unseen.

I backed up and slumped against a shelf, telling myself to breathe.

Vrana let his hand fall to the side, the gun pointing toward the floor. "I wanted to know how sorry you are."

Tears streamed down Patchen's face. He slipped his fingers under his glasses and pressed his eyes. His entire body shook. When, after a minute, he lowered his hands, he blinked a few times and looked up at me.

"It was raining, you son of a bitch," I said. "You left her in the rain."

He opened his mouth as though to respond, but the only sound that emanated was a low moan.

"So, this is how it ends?"

We all turned toward the voice at the door. It was Mick, of course, sneaking up on people again. Bless him.

Vrana took the gun from the desk and returned it to the holster. "This is it for me."

"You should get out of here," Mick said, giving Vrana a guarded look. He pulled out his cell phone. "Better do it now if you don't want to be around when the cops get here."

With a parting bow to Mick, Vrana stepped over to me. I was still leaning against the shelf, not confident my knees would support me.

"You did some good work," he said.

"Thanks. You too." I guess.

He leaned over and kissed me on the cheek then delivered a bit of a smirk to Mick as he walked out the door, passing my mother on her way up the stairs.

She followed her cane up the trailer's steps, gingerly placed her foot onto the floor, then lifted her other foot over the threshold where she steadied herself. She smiled at Mick and said to me, "Are you all right, Dear?"

"Yeah, Mom. Everything's fine."

She regarded Patchen, staring at the far wall, turned to me and said, "Is this the architect?"

Chapter 30

Happy hour was a recent phenomenon at Dryden Manor. I'm not certain, but I think my mother had something to do with it. On the afternoons when I'd bring her bottle of Chablis, I'd often find her in the lounge where she would introduce me to her "good friends." Then, as if I were her personal sommelier, she'd ask me to open the bottle. I learned to carry a corkscrew in my purse. While I scared up some plastic cups, she'd regale these pseudo friends with stories of her past, which had become a lot more interesting since she'd owned up to that youthful affair with the movie producer. Her attendants got to share the bottle with her, which they paid for by sitting there and listening to her go on about the Hollywood scene in the sixties.

I think Dryden's other residents came to resent the little clique my mother had initiated and, in an effort to include everyone in the merriment, the staff declared Friday afternoons from four to five as Happy Hour. This pleased my mother because now she didn't have to share her wine with others, although I believe her audience had dwindled.

I usually timed my arrival near the end of Happy Hour, since she liked to use me as an excuse to make her exit and would have me escort her up to her room. There, after we shared a glass, I would slip the bottle into her mini-fridge next to the bag of apple slices.

Today, I delivered her wine with a side of disappointing news. Sharon had called me less than an hour ago to tell me that house I'd fallen in love with had been sold to someone else who not only fell in love with it, but had done something about it. I had mixed feelings. This would put off any move, which was good. And there were other houses. Fortunately, I didn't have to think about them today. I was still jittery about the entire Cedar Ridge affair. Lucky was doing the proverbial canary-song to the authorities regarding his involvement with the property and the Adamo family. Wellen's disappearance was discussed. There was talk of Lucky becoming a state's witness, which meant he was desperate. I doubted he was feeling very lucky these days. Still, we didn't know how much Lucky was saying about Mick's and my involvement, nor how the Adamo and the Grecco families would react. So far, so good, but I didn't know how long that would last. Times were tense.

Although, I reasoned, if there were a hit on me, I'd be dead already. I'm not a difficult target. Somehow, that didn't do much to cheer me up.

The story had run a week ago in the *Record* and had created quite a stir. An anonymous tip—thank you, Kurt Vrana—had alerted the EPA about Cedar Ridge and cleanup was already underway. No one knew how long it would take.

I walked into Dryden with the bottle stuffed into my messenger bag. As large as the liter was, it still fit as long as I left my computer at home. Mom had been drinking the same Chablis for years. We Guthrie women were nothing if not consistent. It was a jug wine with little distinction and totally bereft of character. A year ago I tried to surprise her with a good bottle of the stuff. She took one sip, wrinkled her nose and declared it undrinkable. It tasted fine to me later that night in my apartment. So I continued to buy her the jug, which was carried by only one liquor store (probably because it was the one I patronized) and cost seven dollars and change.

I headed toward the lounge area, where floor-to-ceiling windows looked out on a bed of rust-colored asters still thriving and found her sitting in a group of four. There were three women, including my mother, and one man. I recognized the women, pudgy little Effie with the perpetually arched eyebrows and Annabeth, Effie's "stooge," as my mother called her. But I did not recognize the man. Age had been kind to this fellow. He had a thick head of unruly white hair and angular features that made me think of an egret with a white tuft. A wizened but nice-looking egret. When my mother introduced us, he looked at me with the calm scrutiny of a man who has summed up many women in his lifetime.

"This is Lionel Harkness. Lionel, I'd like you to meet my daughter Robyn."

Lionel leaned forward and set his glass of red wine on the coffee table. Then he stood and extended his hand to me. I wasn't sure whether he wanted to kiss it or shake it so I preemptively grabbed his hand and gave it a shake.

After we exchanged pleasantries, he remained standing. As I'd suspected, he was tall, well over six feet. Effie beamed up at him. Annabeth beamed at Effie. My mother's smile looked like it hurt.

"Why don't you join us for a glass of wine, Robyn?" Lionel said, gesturing toward an empty chair across from him.

My mother's smile trembled with the effort and before I could respond, she said, "That's all right, Lionel. Robyn's just dropping something off. She's got plans for the night."

"I can spare a minute," I said, only partly to annoy my mother. I was curious about this guy. Men at Dryden are outnumbered by women at least four to one, and some of these men were there with their wives. An attractive, ambulatory man could send shivers through the female denizens.

"Let me get you some wine," Lionel said. "Red or white?"

"I'll have—"

"She's driving," my mother informed him.

"—red," I finished. Turning to my mother, I added, "I can handle a glass of wine."

Lionel winked at my mother as he strode toward a table holding two bottles of wine and a stack of plastic glasses. Her smile softened. Effie glared. "That wine is for the residents," she muttered under her breath.

"Is Lionel new here?" I asked.

"He just moved in," Effie said. "He's from Florida. He's an artist. Moved up here to be closer to his family."

Annabeth added, "He has a son in Fowler."

My mother sipped her wine. "Lionel and I were just talking about our families."

"You mean *you* were talking about your family," Effie said, giving me the stink eye.

At that point Lionel returned, handing me a full glass of wine. "I understand you're a writer, Robyn." He settled back into the chair beside my mother's and crossed one long leg over the other.

"Mostly freelance." The chilled red wine had a sharp taste.

"She's dating a man who used to be a jockey," my mother told him. "What's his name again?"

"Mick." As if she didn't know.

Effie had perked up. "Is he short?"

"He's on the short side," I said.

"He limps," my mother added.

"Why is that?" Annabeth asked in seeming innocence.

"An accident."

"Whatever does a former jockey do?" Effie asked, her eyebrows looking like they were about to leap off her forehead.

The pack had turned on me. I had invaded their territory and they were prepared to either chase me off or take me down. The company had turned more acidic than the wine. I didn't need this.

"You know," I said, setting the wine on the table. "I just remembered there is something I need to do." I stood. "Thank you for the wine, Lionel. It was nice meeting you."

"Likewise," he said, standing as he nodded and smiled.

My mother touched my hand. "Don't forget to drop off my wine."

I looked down at her. "You want to give me your key?"

She removed the green curly elastic band that held the key from her wrist and handed it to me. As I walked toward the elevators, I thought I heard the "snick" of claws retracting.

I glanced back at my mother before I stepped onto the elevator and saw her beaming at Lionel. I had the feeling the Guthrie women wouldn't be in search of a house any time soon.

Chapter 31

A few days later, Mick called just after eleven in the morning. I'd been working on an article on foods to eat before a Pilates workout and thinking if I wanted to branch out into travel writing, I would have to get used to leaving the apartment. I'd been living with the shades drawn for the last week, taking Bix on short walks and limiting my visits with my mother to Dryden. Of course, she was complaining, but I was used to that.

"I'm worried about you," Mick said.

"That makes two of us." I shifted the phone to my other ear and tucked my legs beneath me in my chair.

"I'll be by in an hour."

"What for?"

"We're going somewhere."

"Where?"

"You'll find out."

"That's annoying, Mick."

"Trust me. I've got my reasons for not telling you yet."

I did trust him. "All right. Should I dress for a night on the town or something a bit more subtle?"

"The latter." Then he added, "But, you know, don't wear that stuff you write in."

"Got it."

"See you in an hour."

We drove north around Chicago and into the North Shore sub-
urbs. Despite my prodding, Mick wouldn't tell me where we were
going.

Mick had approved of my outfit—black pants and a turquoise
jacket and a scarf which included all my favorite jewel stones. I'd
worn a pair of boots with two-inch heels. They were leather, and I
had a brief moment of Vrana-induced guilt about that. By "brief," I
mean a nano-second.

Mick drove us into a subdivision filled with large, impressive
homes on half-acre-size lots with curving roads that were lined with
maple trees and flowerbeds. He pulled into the driveway of a large
Georgian home, red brick surrounding double doors that looked
like solid oak.

He shifted into neutral and switched off the ignition.

"Okay," I said. "Who lives here?"

"Christopher Grecco."

"Oh, shit. What are you doing?"

"We're going to talk with him."

"Why didn't you tell me this?"

"Because I didn't want you jumping out of the car when we were
on the tollway."

Good point.

"Either that or you'd have gotten yourself all stressed out."

Also a good point.

"This is a scary guy, Mick. Why do I need to talk to him?"

"So you'll leave that apartment again."

"I like my apartment."

"Bix looks like he's put on a few pounds." I interpreted that as
code for "You've put on a few pounds."

Trust is a powerful incentive. I'd never have gotten out of the car
and followed Mick up to the door had I not trusted him completely.

I expected to be shown in by a maid or someone whose job description included "answering the door." So I was stunned when we were greeted by none other than Christopher Grecco. I was beyond stunned when he cried, "Mickey!" and engulfed my friend in a ferocious hug and began pounding him on the back. "How long has it been?"

While Grecco was recognizable from photos and news clips, he was also larger than I'd imagined and projected an energy that hadn't been caught by the camera.

After releasing Mick just before he suffocated, Grecco turned to me. I almost jumped back. Prolonged hugging makes me tense up.

But instead of hugging or even approaching, he stopped, turned to Mick and said, "So, this is the one you were telling me about?"

"This is Robyn Guthrie."

Grecco tilted his head back as though trying to view me through bifocals. I attempted to smile, but it was probably a bit sickly.

I started to reach my hand out, but saw that he was keeping his to himself so I aborted the attempt, lamely using the movement to shove a lock of hair behind my ear.

He gave me a nod and turned back to Mick. "What took you so long?"

Without waiting for an answer, Grecco led us into his home and we followed him past the entrance, through a wide-open area with vaulted ceilings and wooden floors polished so highly it felt like I was walking on ice.

Mick and Grecco made small talk as we moved. I half listened to the banter about Grecco's wife, who was off at some charity event. Mainly I was fascinated by the fact that every area we passed through had a view of a large back yard with a pool and gazebo.

We ended up in a room with a floor to ceiling fireplace and a wet bar.

"What would you like to drink, Robyn?"

I was deciding whether to be safe and stick with iced tea or go for wine when Mick said, "You and Robyn have something in common."

Grecco arched one bushy eyebrow and glanced at me from the corner of his eye, then directed his dubious gaze on Mick.

Mick said, "Famous Grouse."

That eyebrow rose a fraction of an inch as he turned toward me. I nodded. He didn't smile, but there was a slight crinkle around his eyes that gave me hope.

It was the silliest thing for success to hinge on, but if that's what it took to impress Christopher Grecco, I would take it.

After he served Mick a beer and poured generous amounts of Grouse over the rocks for us, we settled into soft beige chairs angled toward both the fireplace and the yard. Within arms' reach was a low, round oak table that held dishes filled with assorted munchies: cheese, nuts, celery, sunflower seeds and pork rinds. Mick must have called ahead.

"So, we gonna talk about the elephant in the room, Mickey?"

"That's why we're here," Mick said.

Grecco shifted in his chair so he faced me. "Mickey here tells me you're worried someone's going to take a bite out of you for what you did."

"Um, yes, I guess so."

"You 'guess so'?"

"Yes," I said. "Yes, I am concerned."

"You should be."

"Chris—"Mick started.

"I'm not finished." Without taking his eyes from me, he managed to cut Mick off.

My grip on the glass tightened. I knew I trusted Mick. But could Mick trust Grecco?

"This thing was your idea?"

"Basically."

"What do you mean 'basically'?"

"Yes, it was my idea."

"Why?"

"I thought those families needed someone on their side. They could have sued, but that would have taken years."

"So you decided to stick it to my son-in-law."

"He was the one who sold them the land."

"Not without Kendrick knowing it."

"The people living there didn't know it. That's what mattered."

He took a drink and sucked up an ice cube, which he tossed around in his mouth for a few moments before biting down on it.

I plunged ahead. "I was also trying to find out who killed Clair Powell."

"Coulda' told you Ed didn't do her." Grecco shook his head.

"I know that now."

Glancing Mick's way, Grecco said in an off-handed way, "Ed didn't have the stomach for that kind of thing. Didn't do that dirt guy either."

"Is Wellen dead?" I asked.

Grecco just smiled at my naiveté.

"You know what Ed's doing right now?" Grecco asked me.

"No."

"Exactly what I tell him to do."

I glanced at Mick but couldn't read his expression. "I suppose that's wise."

"Damned right it is."

Mick took a drink of his beer and licked a bit of foam off his upper lip. He seemed to realize that Grecco didn't want him involved in this exchange.

Grecco picked up a pork rind and popped it into his mouth. He chewed thoughtfully, swallowed, and washed it down with some Scotch. "Who knows you did this?"

"Mick. Kat. Katherine Kendrick. Mary Alice Tucker—one of the homeowners. And a . . ." I hesitated. Not because I was trying to cover for Vrana, but I didn't quite know how to describe him. "I guess you'd call him an environmental vigilante."

"Where's he now?"

"I have no idea."

Grecco nodded to himself, smiling a little. "Nobody else?"

I was going to say "I don't think so" because I wasn't certain, but I was picking up on what Grecco wanted to hear, so I said, "No one else."

He prompted with, "Did Justin Adamo know you set this vigilante up as the hotel guy?"

My breathing had become quite shallow. I needed to take a couple deep breaths or risk swooning. "I don't know. I don't think so. I think Mr. Adamo may have died before he was aware of that whole, um . . ."

"Lie?"

"I was going to say 'deception,' but I suppose it's the same."

"Yeah. It is."

He reached for the bottle of Grouse and poured himself another half inch. He tipped the bottle toward me.

"No, thank you. Not right now."

Glancing Mick's way, he nodded his approval.

He leaned back into the couch, bringing a pork rind with him and sat there—drink on one hand, pork in the other—and was silent for more than a minute. His brows were pulled together and he appeared to be in deep concentration. I looked at Mick who gave me the briefest of nods.

Finally, Grecco popped the rind in his mouth and as he chewed it, he seemed to be smiling. After swallowing a gulp of Scotch, he said, "I think we're covered."

Mick just nodded, but I could see the tension draining from his shoulders as he relaxed.

"So, what happens to Ed?" Mick asked.

"We're going to . . . suggest . . . that he make a deal with the state's attorney. A deal that should make the Adamos very uncomfortable." He smiled at the thought. "That Cedar Ridge place isn't the only land they used for dumping." He shook his head. "Shameful business."

Now I had to ask. "Won't that make him . . . um, vulnerable?"

"Not if he goes into the witness protection program." He sighed. "Lucky may be a worthless piece of flesh, but he's my Tabby's husband." He gave Mick a look he couldn't have missed. He sighed again. "Mercedes's father." He looked at me. "Have you met Mercedes? She's a firecracker."

"I have. And, yes she is."

"Chris." Mick seemed confused, as though he hadn't heard correctly. "You're letting Tab and Mercedes go?"

Grecco's brows shot up. "Are you kidding? Tabby just needs an excuse to dump the baggage." He paused, thoughtful for a moment. "Mercedes will miss her old man, but she'll come around."

Given a choice between her father and her tennis lessons, I had no doubt where Lucky's daughter's affections lay.

We all sat there in an oddly comfortable silence until, after a minute, Grecco said, "You know . . ." He waited until he was sure he had our attention. "There is one thing I'd like."

* * *

On the way out, Grecco gave Mick another one of his hugs, turned toward me, seemed to back down then shrugged and wrapped his arms around me. I, wisely I believe, didn't resist. When he released me, he turned to Mick and said, "This one's all right. She's no Tabby, but she's all right."

I would settle for that.

Once in the car, Mick told me to wave as he backed out of the driveway. "He likes that."

Whatever Grecco liked.

"Mick, what did you think of Grecco's idea?" I asked once we were clear of the house.

"All depends if Kat's on board with it."

"I don't know." But I had to laugh. "Green Haven being financed by the mob to build another environmental development. Wow. Do you think he actually cares that much about green building?"

"Probably not as much as he likes the idea of this shining example of futuristic technology being called Grecco Landing."

"Gotta admire the moxie."

"That's how he got where he is."

As we pulled out of the subdivision, I said, "Grecco never forgave you for not marrying Tabitha, did he?"

"He's used to getting what he wants."

"What about Tabitha?"

"She takes after her dad. Only nicer."

"You know," I said, "you never did tell me what Ed Leoni had on you. Why he knew you'd help him."

He pulled up to a stoplight that had just turned red. "He knows something. It's more about Tab than me."

"You want to tell me?"

It wasn't until the light changed and we surged forward with the traffic that he continued. "Toward the end of our relationship, Tab got pregnant. She wasn't the kind of person to strong-arm someone. I told her it was up to her. I'd support her and the kid, but I wasn't ready to marry her." He glanced at me. "Makes you proud to know me, doesn't it?"

"At least you were honest."

"Yeah," he said with a dry laugh.

Then a thought hit me like missile. "Mick, Mercedes . . . she isn't your daughter, is she?"

He glanced at me again and then laughed. "No. No, Mercedes is Ed's daughter. All Ed's."

I sighed.

"No. Tab had an abortion. If Chris knew . . ." he tapped the gear shift knob, "well, he wouldn't be happy. And Tab would catch most of that. Chris considers himself very pro-life."

Ironic, I thought. Then I asked, "How did Lucky know?"

"Tab told him. She didn't want any secrets." He shrugged. "Full disclosure is overrated."

"Yeah. Some mystery is good."

How scary to have a parent like that. "Are you worried about Lucky spilling to Grecco now?" I asked.

"Hell no. The last thing Lucky wants to do is put his father-in-law in a worse frame of mind than he already is."

"That makes sense."

This all took a while to digest. We were on the expressway heading south before I could talk about what I'd been mulling over. "I can understand your not being sure about having kids."

"That's part of it, I guess." He shrugged. "And then, like I was saying the other night, I just don't know."

I looked over at him, studying his profile backlit against the afternoon sun. "So, we're right where we started. The other night."

"It seems we are."

And wasn't that a long, long time ago?

He glanced my way, "You're still sure about that kid thing?"

"Yes. I am."

Nodding, he said, "So what happens now?"

"I don't know about you, but I don't feel like backing off."

"Me neither."

I watched as a blue van zipped past us in the left lane. "Let's see what happens if we don't."

I could hear the smile in his voice when he said, "I like the way you think."

"Yeah. Me too."